NIGHT OF THE RAVEN, DAWN OF THE DOVE

NIGHT OF THE RAVEN, DAWN OF THE DOVE

RATI MEHROTRA

WEDNESDAY BOOKS
NEW YORK

First published in the United States by Wednesday Books,
an imprint of St. Martin's Publishing Group

NIGHT OF THE RAVEN, DAWN OF THE DOVE. Copyright © 2022 by Rati Mehrotra.
All rights reserved. Printed in the United States of America.
For information, address St. Martin's Publishing Group,
120 Broadway, New York, NY 10271.

www.wednesdaybooks.com

Designed by Devan Norman
Map illustration by Rhys Davies
Case stamp bird illustration © Shutterstock.com

The Library of Congress Cataloging-in-Publication Data is available upon request.

ISBN 978-1-250-82368-7 (hardcover)
ISBN 978-1-250-82369-4 (ebook)

Our books may be purchased in bulk for promotional, educational, or business
use. Please contact your local bookseller or the Macmillan Corporate and Premium
Sales Department at 1-800-221-7945, extension 5442,
or by email at MacmillanSpecialMarkets@macmillan.com.

First Edition: 2022

10 9 8 7 6 5 4 3 2 1

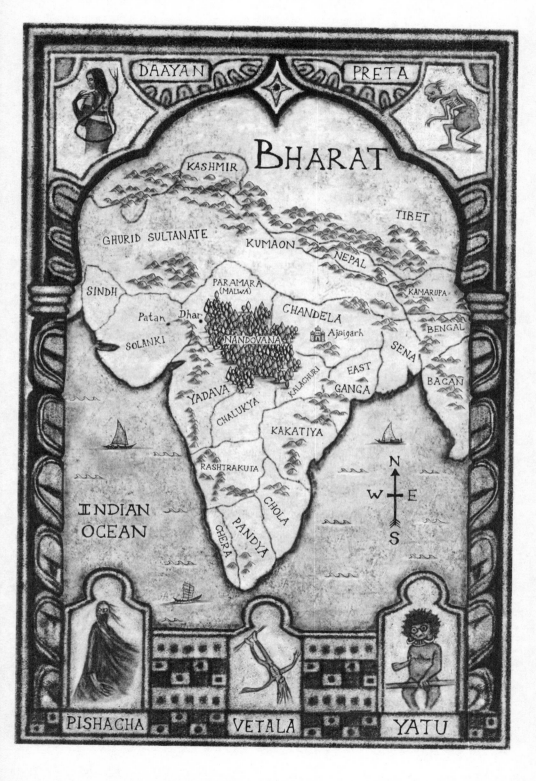

NIGHT OF THE RAVEN, DAWN OF THE DOVE

CHAPTER 1

A LIGHT BREEZE WAFTED THROUGH THE LATTICED WINDOWS of the royal bedchamber, carrying with it the scent of night-blooming jasmine and drying the sweat on Katyani's brow. The night was warm—too warm for spring. She'd been waiting for the assassin for over an hour, hidden behind the half-drawn drapes, inhaling their musty odor and trying not to sneeze. Her right foot had gone to sleep, and the windowpane dug into her back, but she dared not move. A nightjar called, its trilling coo startling her before devolving into a series of clicks. She clutched the wooden pipe in her hand, her nerves thrumming with anticipation.

Moonlight filtered into the room, hiding more than it revealed. But she knew every inch of the space, from the ornate wardrobe in one corner to the gilded mirror opposite, from the rich tapestries that covered the wall to the massive four-poster bed in the middle—the bed on which the king and queen of Chandela would have slept tonight had Katyani not made them switch rooms. The blue butterfly tattooed on her neck gave a single reassuring beat of its wings. The queen was safe—for now.

The door edged open, and her heart jumped. She strained her eyes, peering through a crack between the drapes. A dark figure crept into the room, moonlight glinting on the blade in his hand. Black-masked, cat-footed, silent as death, he approached the bed and raised his blade.

Now. Katyani stepped out and blew the sleep dart from her wooden pipe. It flew straight and true toward the intruder's chest. At the last moment, alerted by the minute *whoosh* of air, he tried to twist out of reach. But the dart buried itself in his shoulder. He clutched it and staggered back to the door, which had been left unguarded for him.

He had great vitality; she had to give him that. The dart would have paralyzed an ordinary person instantly. But he managed to make it out the door before collapsing.

She went into the corridor and rang a brass bell embedded in the wall to summon Garuda, the elite royal bodyguards. Then she bent over the unconscious assailant to examine him. Torchlight flickered from sconces further down the corridor, revealing a bald, skinny man clad in a black cotton tunic and pants, his face covered with a mask that appeared to be melded to his skin. His hand was still curled around the hilt of his weapon: a double-edged dagger with an ivory handle. There was no insignia on his clothing or his blade, but interrogation would soon reveal who he was working for. Triumph welled up in her. They'd finally caught one of the bastards alive.

Five burly guards dressed in the Garuda uniform—dark gray knee-length tunic, leather sword belt, baggy pants, and white turban—came running up as she patted his body down for weapons. At their head was Tanoj, the chief of Garuda, a heavyset, gray-haired, middle-aged man with piercing eyes and an unmistakable air of command. He frowned as he took in the scene.

"One of the men can do that, Katyani," he said, a note of reproof in his deep voice. He'd known her for years, taught her what she knew of sword fighting, and he still never got used to seeing her manhandle male offenders. His attitude irked her, but she wasn't going to argue with him in front of the others.

"Yes, sir." She withdrew a kukri knife from one boot and a push knife from the other and handed them to Falgun, a junior guard. "Have these examined. Be careful. The edges might be poisoned." As they'd learned to their detriment from the *first* assassination attempt, six months ago. The guard who'd handled those weapons had been sick for weeks.

Falgun bowed and took the knives with a gloved hand.

Tanoj squatted beside the comatose man. "Have you identified him?"

"We'll soon see." She began to peel the mask away from his face. A smell of burning flesh seeped into her nostrils, and she snatched away her fingers. "Damn!"

His face was melting before her eyes. She tried to smooth the mask back into place using the hilt of her dagger, but it was too late. She coughed and scooted back, her gut clenching.

Tanoj backed away as well, his lips pinched, his eyes hard. The third time in six months an assassin had died before he could be questioned. The king and queen would *not* be happy.

"What happened?" sputtered a guard from a safe distance behind her, holding his nose.

She sighed and got to her feet, tasting the bitterness of defeat in her mouth. "He's dead."

"But we haven't interrogated him yet," said Falgun, sounding outraged.

Tanoj rose, rubbing his chin as he contemplated the body on the floor, the face a ruin of melted flesh and bits of burned cloth. "The mask was poisoned," he grated. "Only his handler could have removed it safely. A clever way of ensuring his silence."

"What are we to do now?" asked another guard, his hand on his sword, as if a sword would solve this mess.

"Try to find out who he is," said Tanoj. "Take all precautions when removing his clothes and examining his weapons. Wash your hands afterward. I don't want anyone dying of carelessness." He leveled a finger at Katyani. "You. Report to the king and queen."

Her shoulders slumped. "Yes, sir." That was her job as his second-in-command, especially when there was nothing good to report. It was not a task she was looking forward to. The queen would be disappointed in her failure, and she hated disappointing the queen.

She turned away as the guards rolled the corpse onto a sheet. The royal couple were sleeping in the west wing of the palace tonight. She'd made them and Crown Prince Ayan change rooms every night since her network of spies had gotten wind of yet another assassination attempt. And she'd made sure the room they actually slept in was different from the one ostensibly planned by the palace staff. The assassin might get wind of the room switching, but he couldn't read her mind. That strategy had paid off tonight.

Partially paid off. As she walked down the marble corridor, she replayed the events of the last hour in her head, wishing she had not been so eager to pull off the assailant's mask.

She'd been promoted over the heads of older, more experienced men in Garuda. No one grudged her this; they all knew the special relationship she had with the queen. Still, *Prove yourself,* said their eyes. *Prove you're worthy of your post.* Every moment of every day since her promotion, she'd been judged on her abilities, her successes, her failures.

Her record so far? Six months, three assassination attempts, and zero leads. Queen Hemlata would not be pleased with her latest blunder. She would certainly not consider Katyani's request to get out of accompanying the princes as their bodyguard to that remote school run by—what was his name?—Acharya Mahavir.

Katyani didn't want to leave the palace. She wanted to stay right here and protect the queen. What would happen to the bond she shared with Hemlata if she was away from her for so long? But the queen had dismissed all her pleas and concerns with implacable calm.

She slipped through a narrow door into another corridor, curving around the inner walls of the north tower. The flickering light of torches fell on the Kurukshetra battle scenes painted on the wall: war chariots clashed, horses charged, elephants trumpeted, and soldiers bled, while above them, Krishna watched with beatific, blue-faced serenity.

At the end of the curving corridor was what looked like a dead end with a floor-to-ceiling painting of the palace itself. But place a palm on the dome, and the whole section of wall swung open to the whispering gallery that ran the circumference of the central hall. She could have taken a more obvious route to the king and queen by going through the entrance hall and up a different staircase to the west wing, but where was the fun in that?

The palace was a labyrinth, but it was a labyrinth that was dearly familiar to her. Not even King Jaideep knew it better than she did. She'd always won the games of hide-and-seek she'd played with Ayan and his cousins, Bhairav and Revaa, when they were children. Even now, there were secret passages in and around the palace that she hadn't fully explored.

And the queen wanted to send her away from here. Katyani understood *why* but she hated the thought of leaving her home, leaving Hemlata.

She had almost reached the secret door hidden by the painting when a soft footfall sounded behind her. She stilled.

There it was again. Someone was tailing her, and by the sound of the footsteps, she thought she knew who it was. She backtracked so she was hidden by a curve of wall and strained her ears, waiting for the right moment to surprise her follower.

Someone exhaled inches away.

Katyani stepped around the corner and said, "Boo."

"Ahhh!" Revaa clutched her chest. "Katya, you nearly gave me a heart attack."

"You're terrible at this," said Katyani in a stern voice, trying not to smile. "I could hear your footsteps a mile away. I could hear you *breathe*. You shouldn't be out tonight at all."

"If I don't practice, how will I get better?" protested the younger girl, scowling. She'd made an effort; her waist-length hair was gathered in a simple plait, and her round face was devoid of makeup or rings. She'd dressed in plain black robes without a speck of jewelry on her plump royal person and worn soft cloth slippers on her feet. But it would take more than that to sneak up on a member of Garuda.

Katyani gave Revaa's plait an affectionate tug. "My sweet sister, the nieces of kings may not be spies. Sadly, they may only be the cossetted and coddled wives of handsome princes."

"You call me sister, but you don't really feel that way about me," Revaa grumbled. "Or you'd teach me, despite what Auntie says."

"I dare not disobey the queen, and you know it well." Katyani leaned down and planted a kiss on her forehead. Without her heels, Revaa only came up to her chin, and without makeup and jewelry, she looked twelve instead of fifteen. "Go back to your room, love. I must report to your aunt and uncle."

Revaa pouted. "Do you promise to come by later?"

"I promise." Katyani blew her another kiss as she walked reluctantly back the way she'd come.

It was too bad the youngest member of King Jaideep's family was also the most ambitious. She was quick and clever and would have made an excellent spy with the right training. Instead, she was stuck being the pretty little princess of Chandela. Katyani did what she could, giving her lessons on spy craft, self-defense, and poisons and their antidotes. But she had to be discreet about it.

She went to the end of the passageway and placed her palm on the painted dome. A soft click and a whirr, and the wall swung open. She stepped past it and entered the whispering gallery. Here were no torches, no paintings, and no sculptures. Above curved the dome of the palace, vanishing into darkness. A waist-high railing ran the length of the narrow walkway. In the distant hall below, two guards stood at attention, unaware of her presence.

She exited the gallery at the opposite end, went down a short flight of stairs, and arrived at the royal couple's temporary bedroom. The two men who stood guard at the brass-studded double door saluted and stepped out of her way, and she knocked in the code she shared with the queen. The door creaked open, and a slim, beringed hand pulled her into a lamplit room.

The blue butterfly tattoo on Katyani's neck fluttered, and she bowed. "Your Majesty."

The queen shut the door and turned to Katyani, her face alive with anticipation. "Tell me everything."

Hemlata was surely one of the most beautiful queens in all of Bharat, with her high cheekbones, lustrous eyes, and an aquiline nose set in an oval face. Tall and statuesque, she wore an embroidered silk gown and an ivory comb set in her perfectly coiffed ebony hair. In contrast, Katyani was clad in the Garuda uniform and had barely combed her unruly hair that morning. Why bother when it would do whatever it wanted anyway?

The queen wasn't just a pretty face, though. Anyone who made the mistake of thinking that soon paid for it when she directed one of her incisive remarks at them, delivered in a velvet voice, which made it worse.

Katyani glanced at the four-poster bed set against the opposite wall. The translucent white drapes were drawn, so she couldn't make out whether it was occupied. "The king?"

Hemlata gave a dismissive wave. "Let him sleep. I'll fill him in later. Come, sit."

She led Katyani to a rosewood divan. As succinctly as possible, Katyani told her all that had transpired. As she described how the mask had dissolved the assassin's face, Hemlata grew still, and her eyes narrowed. Katyani sensed her displeasure and frustration through their bond.

"I'm sorry," she said, her voice faltering as sick green waves of the queen's disappointment rolled through her, rocking her core. "I botched it." She'd known how Hemlata would feel, and she'd known how those feelings would affect her. But the reality was worse than her imaginings. This, the third time they'd failed to catch the assassin alive, had hit the queen the hardest.

Hemlata took a deep breath and another. Slowly, the waves of negativity retreated. "Our murderous mastermind has been one step ahead of us all the way."

Katyani swallowed, relieved the queen had controlled her adverse emotions. Hemlata might not blame her, but the depth of her displeasure sharpened Katyani's sense of guilt. "You think it's one person behind all these attempts?"

"One person, or a group of persons." Hemlata frowned and plucked at the threads in an embroidered silk cushion. "The methods are all diverse, yet they fall into a pattern."

"I should stay here in the palace." Katyani leaned forward, knowing she was taking a risk by bringing this up again. "Protect you and the king."

The queen sat up and squeezed the cushion as if she would throttle it. "We've discussed this, Katya," she said sharply. "There are enough people here to protect myself and the king. *You* need to safeguard the princes. You're the only one I trust to go with them."

"Tanoj has thirty years' experience in combat and spying," she pointed out.

Hemlata snorted. "Tanoj will never be more than what he is. But you are like my daughter. Acharya Mahavir's gurukul is the most famous ethics and military arts school in Bharat. He is renowned in all the kingdoms for his spiritual power and monster-banishing skills—skills that would be valuable for you and the princes to develop. This is a tremendous learning opportunity. In three days, you will accompany Ayan and Bhairav to the gurukul. I'm not about to change my mind."

Of course she wasn't. If Katyani had managed to capture the assassin alive, if they had interrogated him and found out who he was working for, she could have argued that *none* of them needed to go anywhere.

Hemlata gripped her shoulder. "Don't be sad. It's only for five months."

Five months sounded like forever, and Katyani's stomach shrank at the prospect. "I've never been away from you for more than a few days," she muttered, twisting her hands in her lap.

Hemlata's face relaxed into a smile. She ruffled Katyani's hair, sending a sweet wave of affection to her. "Are you worried about the bond? Don't be. Nothing can break it before it's time. And when it's time, you and I will both know."

When your blood debt is paid, she did not say, but it was what Katyani knew to be true. It was something she both looked forward to and dreaded.

"Any news from the peace envoy sent to Malwa?" she asked.

The queen's lips tightened. She clasped her hands, gazing into the distance with large, anxious eyes, as if she could see the unfolding conflict. "He has returned with ill tidings. Talks have broken down. We hope to avoid another all-out war, but it might come to that."

Katyani grimaced. They'd had fifteen years of tenuous peace with their warlike neighbor. Certainly, it could not last forever. Malwa was ruled by the Paramara dynasty, ancient foes of Chandela. They disputed Chandela's rightful claims to many of its border towns and territories. If King Jaideep, his father, and his grandfather had not fought them to a stalemate in previous wars, the Paramaras would have swallowed half the Chandela kingdom by now. Shamsher Singh, the current regent of Malwa, was reputed to be a cold and heartless man. *Not* someone she wanted to meet in her lifetime.

"At the same time, there have been three assassination attempts, and we've been unable to discover who is behind them," the queen continued. "I fear these two things are related, that Malwa is trying to break us from both within and without. I want the crown prince out of harm's way, and there is no safer place in all of Bharat than Acharya Mahavir's gurukul."

"I thought you didn't like that weirdo," said Katyani, making a face.

"Katya!" Hemlata put a finger on Katyani's lips. "He's not a weirdo, no matter what you may have heard. Never say so again; it will bring bad luck. He is a man of great spiritual and magical powers. And it's not that *I* don't like *him*. It's that *he* doesn't approve of *me*."

"Because of the bond," said Katyani. "Right?"

Hemlata sighed. "Men prefer to keep power to themselves. They make rules that dictate who gets to use it, and how, and why. I broke those rules when I saved you with my magic, and I'll never regret it." She opened her right palm and planted a kiss on the blue butterfly tattooed there—a mirror of the one on Katyani's neck.

A warm glow suffused Katyani. She had no memory of how she'd come to have the tattoo, but Hemlata had told her the story many times. When Katyani was three, her parents—vassals of King Jaideep—had died, and she'd fallen mortally ill. None of the queen's physicians could do anything for her. As her life ebbed away, Hemlata had turned in desperation to forbidden magical arts. She'd created a soul bond between herself and Katyani and *commanded* her to recover. Baby Katyani had obeyed. The blue butterfly was the only physical reminder of that spell.

But the bond the queen had created to save her life had persisted. Katyani had grown up knowing, at every moment, where the queen was in the palace and how she was feeling. Hemlata had been able to admonish her or lavish affection on her at will, all without speaking a single word. Petitioners used to seek Katyani out to ask her whether the queen was in a good mood before approaching the throne. She hadn't realized there was anything unusual about this situation until she was older and understood how rare a true magical bond was.

"Acharya Mahavir is not a patient man or a forgiving one," warned the queen. "You must not anger him. If he says anything about the bond, stay silent. Make sure Ayan and Bhairav don't get into trouble."

"Revaa won't be happy to be the only one left behind," said Katyani.

Hemlata rolled her eyes. "Revaa is promised in marriage to the crown prince of the Kalachuris. It's an excellent match and ensures we have one less neighbor to worry about. What will they think if they hear she's traipsing about in a gurukul full of strange men? The sooner my niece accepts her fate, the better. It's a fate most girls would kill for."

But it's not what Revaa wants, Katyani could have said. Except they'd had this conversation before, and it never went well. She might be "like a daughter" to the queen, but the rules for real princesses were obviously different than they were for adopted ones. Katyani thanked her lucky stars for that.

Hemlata grasped her hand. "One day, Ayan will be the king," she said in a serious tone, "and you will be his most trusted advisor. Take this as an opportunity to learn statecraft and cultivate royal friendships." Her hand tightened on Katyani's, rings digging painfully into her flesh. "Please. For my sake."

She really knew how to manipulate people. A mixture of annoyance and affection rose within Katyani. She bowed her head, giving in. "I'll try my best, Your Majesty."

But it was with a deep sense of foreboding that she left the queen's bedchamber. Of course she would do as Hemlata wished. But what would it cost them both?

CHAPTER 2

THE NEXT DAY, KATYANI WOKE EARLY SO SHE'D HAVE THE training ground to herself. Two days left to enjoy training in peace and quiet. After that, who knew? A school in the middle of a forest rumored to be infested with monsters—no, she could not picture it. A workout would take her mind off the unknown, make her less anxious about the future. She'd already made her preparations: all four of her spies would now be reporting directly to Tanoj, as would all of Garuda. Falgun had been given a temporary promotion to take her place.

The training ground was a large enclosure west of the palace, surrounded by a seven-foot-high brick wall and open to the sky. She arrived soon after sunrise but, to her surprise, the ground was occupied. As she pushed open the creaky wooden door to the yard, she heard grunts and the clash of swords. Tanoj said in a long-suffering voice, "Not like *that*, Prince. You'll end up stabbing yourself."

"Maybe I should," said Bhairav in an aggrieved tone, panting as he leaned on his sword. "Then they won't send me anywhere."

Katyani shut the door behind her, lips twitching. The two were standing in the fencing arena: a grassy, circular patch ahead of her. Tanoj often gave Bhairav extra lessons in an effort to improve his skills and bring him up to Ayan's level. Pity classes, Ayan called them, because swordsmanship did not come naturally to Bhairav. None of the fighting arts did.

"You'd better not stab yourself," she said, strolling up to the arena. "I'll have to carry your wounded, bleeding body to the gurukul. And you know how blood attracts monsters."

Bhairav turned to face her, scowling. "Why do *I* have to go? Ayan is the one who enjoys that sort of thing."

"What does Ayan enjoy?" came a familiar voice from behind her. Ayan pushed open the door and entered, a cocky smile on his face.

"Monsters," she told him.

"Fighting," Bhairav corrected her. "And I simply do not. I would much rather be in a library. Surely I am more use in a library!"

"Sadly, you are no use anywhere," Ayan informed him. "Leave you in a library and you'll forget to eat and drink, and in a few weeks, we'll be prizing your lifeless hands from some dusty old tome on magic no one's read in a million years."

Tanoj cleared his throat. "If you are here to practice, do not waste time, Crown Prince."

Chastened, Ayan walked up to them. Tanoj threw him a wooden sword. Bhairav was obviously tired, but Tanoj tried to persuade him to spar with his cousin.

Katyani did stretches to loosen her body, content to watch the drama for the time being. Early-morning sunlight bathed the yard, and the grass glistened with dewdrops. Her pulse slowed as her mind relaxed. The training ground had been one of her favorite places ever since she was a child. She'd wielded the wooden swords, shot arrows at the painted targets, hurled spears at the straw dummies, and even punched the grain sacks, making the men laugh, until she grew older and better at it than them. No one had laughed at Katyani in a long time.

Bhairav finally agreed to spar with Ayan, probably to make Tanoj shut up. The results were predictable. Ayan beat Bhairav back to the wall of the storage shed and had his sword at Bhairav's throat in less than a minute. Bhairav threw his sword down in disgust. Tanoj made him pick it up and put it away in a rack with the others.

Katyani fell into a series of squats, struck, as always, by the similarities and dissimilarities between the two royal cousins. Tall, bronze skinned, well built, and fine featured, both of them drew adoring glances wherever they went. There was just a year's gap between them; Bhairav was eighteen—same as Katyani—and Ayan was seventeen.

The differences lay in their skills and temperament. Ayan excelled in swordsmanship, archery, wrestling, horse riding, and stick-fighting. He was the one opponent Katyani enjoyed sparring with. Bhairav, in contrast, was better at statecraft and science. He would make a great advisor or ambassador for the kingdom one day—if he didn't expire in a library, as Ayan had predicted.

Bhairav stamped over to her. "Do me a favor, Katya, and beat my cousin. Look at that insufferable grin on his face."

She rose from her squat and swung a friendly punch at him, which he deflected. "With pleasure. But what will I get out of it?"

"The satisfaction of beating him," Bhairav said, raising his eyebrows. "What can be better than that? Besides, us orphans ought to stand up for each other."

Katyani laughed and gave him a fist bump. The "orphans" thing was a running joke between them. It was, of course, true that they were orphans. Bhairav and Revaa's father, Prince Karandeep, had been killed in the same battle with Malwa that took the life of Katyani's own parents. Their mother had died some months later of "a broken heart." Katyani didn't remember her own parents, and she wondered sometimes if that wasn't a blessing. Bhairav had been nearly four when his mother passed, and he still talked about her, still missed her. Revaa envied him his memories—she'd been a baby at the time—but she was more interested in molding the present to her advantage than dwelling on the past.

Katyani went up to Ayan. "I am here to take revenge on behalf of all the orphans of Chandela. Also to wipe the silly grin off your face."

"I am your crown prince," said Ayan with a lordly air that made her want to smack him. "I order you to be beaten by me."

Tanoj snorted. "The day she yields to you because of your title is the day you both stop being my pupils."

"I was only joking," said Ayan, his eyes widening.

"Then fight like you both mean it," grated Tanoj, throwing Katyani a wooden sword, which she caught.

"Go, Katya!" called Bhairav from behind them.

"Not fair," protested Ayan. "The crowd is rooting for her, sir. The crowd favorite always wins."

Tanoj pressed a hand to his temple. "Go, Ayan," he said in a flat, I-can't-believe-I'm-doing-this voice.

Ayan leaped at her, and she barely stepped back in time. He pressed forward, pushing the advantage of his initial surprise. She danced sideways and thwacked his forearm, making him wince.

"Minus points, Crown Prince," shouted Tanoj, circling them.

Ayan bore down on her, but she kept her distance from him, not letting him close in. He had the advantage of size and weight, but she was nimbler on her feet and way more patient. She kept it up for several minutes until she sensed his frustration, then gave him an obvious opening, raising her sword for an overhead strike. If he had been thinking, he would have realized it was a feint—they'd sparred nearly every day of their lives, and he knew all her little tricks—but he was too intent on winning. He thrust his sword at her chest. She threw herself low, swept up from underneath him, and knocked the sword out of his hand.

Bhairav clapped his hands and crowed, "Once again, Katya displays her superior swordswomanship against the unworthy crown prince of Chandela."

Ayan grabbed her wooden sword. "I'm not done yet!"

"You would be dead if that was a real sword," Tanoj noted. "Accept that you have lost this round."

Katyani hooked her foot around Ayan's leg and jerked, toppling him to the ground. But he was still hanging on to her sword, which meant she tumbled to the grass along with him. Ayan tried to wrestle her hands back, but she kneed him in the stomach, making him groan in pain. Bhairav joined in and ended up landing on them both, nearly squashing her. She extricated herself from the princes, breathless with laughter, covered in grass and mud.

"A win for Katyani in the sword fight, a draw in the tomfoolery," said Tanoj in a dry voice. "Don't behave like this in the gurukul. Remember, you will be representing the kingdom of Chandela. Have some dignity."

"Yes, sir," said Katyani, wishing more strongly than ever she could get out of going.

Tanoj checked the sun, which had risen further. "Time for breakfast."

He glanced at Bhairav. "If you wish, Prince, I am available in the evening for another practice session."

"Okay, sir, although I don't see why you waste your time with me," said Bhairav.

"I also do not see it," began Ayan, but Katyani dug an elbow into his side, making him shut up.

Soldiers had entered the training ground by now, although, as per protocol, they ignored the princes and focused on their own warm-up exercises. Ayan, Bhairav, and Katyani bowed to Tanoj before leaving.

"Smell those roses?" Bhairav sniffed deeply as they strolled past the rose gardens on the way to the palace. Gardeners were already at work, pruning the bushes, watering the plants, removing weeds and dead leaves. Large, luscious pink and red roses bloomed on the bushes, bending the stems with their weight. "It's the last we'll get of their fragrance till next year."

"Maybe there are roses in Nandovana," said Ayan. Nandovana—the forest in which the gurukul was located—covered a large swath of central Bharat, crossing the boundaries of five kingdoms: Chandela, Paramara, Yadava, Kalachuri, and Chalukya.

"Such roses don't grow wild in jungles," scoffed Bhairav. "They have to be cultivated. You don't know much botany, do you?"

Ayan grinned. "A flower is just a flower, but I know a hundred ways to kill an enemy soldier."

Bhairav rolled his eyes, but Ayan had made a fair point. It wasn't necessary for the crown prince of Chandela to know about plants. He had gardeners for that and advisors for everything else.

"Two days left," said Katyani. "Enjoy the baths and the food. After that—who knows?"

Bhairav clutched her sleeve, looking appalled. "Surely they will have baths."

Katyani hoped so. But she took extra time with her bath that day, soaking in the jasmine-scented water until her maid Chaya inquired if she wanted her skin to prune permanently.

After breakfast, they were summoned to the palace library by Shukla, the chief royal priest.

The palace library was Bhairav's favorite haunt. Located in the top section of the western tower, it occupied three levels, connected by a winding staircase. The lowest level was the most frequented, containing books on history, science, mathematics, and philosophy. The middle level had older manuscripts, maps, and documents in various languages from around the world. Visiting scribes and scholars could request access to this level. The top level was locked and barred to outsiders; it housed ancient books of magic, inherited from the founders of the Chandela dynasty. Only the queen had the key, although most of the books were indecipherable even to her. She had brought Ayan, Bhairav, Revaa, and Katyani there a few times and explained about the magical wards on Ajaigarh Fort, although only Bhairav had been keen enough to ask intelligent questions and request permission to return.

One of King Jaideep's ancestors had created magical wards to protect the fort from the monsters in Bharat. A yatu or vetala approaching the walls of the fort would combust. Such advanced magic was beyond Queen Hemlata—beyond anyone in the family. With each succeeding generation, it seemed, the powers of the Chandelas had faded until now even the simplest of spells was difficult to summon. The queen went over the basics with them, but magical theory bored Ayan and Revaa to tears, and Katyani had no gift for it, much as she wanted to please Hemlata. Bhairav enjoyed the *reading* more than the actual *doing,* and at last the queen gave up, contenting herself with teaching them how to maintain the ancestral wards with a daily ritual that involved fire, sandalwood oil, and a chant.

Shukla met them in the middle level of the library. Bookshelves lined the curving wall, as high as the ceiling, so the occupants of the room were encased in a cocoon of books. Some people might have enjoyed the dust and the old-book smell, but it made Katyani's nose itch. And sure enough, as soon as she entered, she gave an enormous sneeze.

Shukla narrowed his eyes at her as the princes joined their hands and bowed to him. A thin, cadaverous man with sunken eyes and a crooked nose, he reminded Katyani of a bird of prey that had gone hungry for far too long. "So inauspicious," he muttered.

Katyani wiped her nose with a sleeve and glared at him, and he averted his gaze from her with a contemptuous sniff. *Stuffy old hypocrite.*

The mere fact of her existence, with the forbidden mark of the queen's spiritual sacrifice, was enough to make her suspect in priestly eyes. But she had also been the worst student the Ajaigarh priests had ever endured. She questioned instructions, refused to take part in rituals, played pranks on the priests, and ran away from punishment. It was difficult to say who was more relieved when the king released her from formal education: the teachers or the pupil.

"Sit, Princes," he said, indicating the mats around him, pointedly not including her in his address. She sat anyway, right opposite him so he would be forced to look at her. Bhairav and Ayan sat on either side, suppressing grins. They knew her long-standing enmity with the priest.

"Acharya Mahavir is a renowned teacher," he began. "You are lucky to be able to study with him."

"What's he renowned for?" asked Ayan. "Apart from being a crank."

"Monster-banishing skills," said Katyani, remembering what the queen had told her.

Shukla threw her a disdainful look. "Also *ethics,*" he said cuttingly. "An important part of your education."

"I don't see why we have to go to the middle of a monster-infested forest and learn ethics from a crank," said Bhairav. "Ajaigarh already has the best teachers in Bharat. Like you, Panditji." Unlike Katyani, Bhairav had been a model student. All the priests loved him.

The compliment obviously pleased Shukla, but he summoned a stern look. "He is not a crank. He is a great sage, one of the most formidable persons in all of Bharat. He has the kind of spiritual power that can stop an army in its tracks. Be diligent in your studies, and you will be able to enhance your own spiritual strength under his guidance."

"I thought spiritual power is innate," said Katyani. She wasn't much into the theoretical aspect of it, but she knew that just as every living thing was made of the five basic elements, so also every living thing had spiritual power. Tanoj had taught them meditation and yoga techniques to harness that power. Magic—what the queen had done to bond her and save her life—was the use of power that didn't rightly belong to you.

Shukla's lips thinned. "If you had ever paid attention in *my* classes instead of playing the disruptive fool, you would know that with the right training, a true warrior can access ever greater pools of power within himself."

Katyani could have sworn he'd never said that, but she held her tongue.

"Acharya Mahavir is also famous for his curses," Shukla continued. "If someone angers him, he has the ability to curse them such that whatever he says comes to pass. You'd better be respectful to him. Don't make him angry, or you will regret it." He glared at Katyani. She resisted the urge to stick her tongue out at him.

"The forest is not a safe place," he went on. "It's full of yatu, vetalas, and pretas. Acharya Mahavir will teach you how to deal with them."

Ayan perked up, looking interested. They'd had a few, distant encounters with yatu, away from Ajaigarh, but none at all with vetalas or pretas. Of course, pretas were invisible, so they were hard to spot, let alone exorcise. Vetalas—evil spirits that occupied corpses and preyed on humans for their blood—preferred to dwell in forests. They were rumored to be able to tell the future, but humans in their vicinity generally didn't last long enough to have much of a future.

Even yatu were few and far between these days. The kingdom of Chandela had been overrun by them in bygone years, but Jaideep's father, Vishwadeep, had driven them back into the jungle.

"We're pretty safe from monsters here," said Katyani. "They can't enter the fort, and yatu were removed from the kingdom years ago."

"That doesn't mean they can't come back," said Shukla. "They probably *want* to come back. Remember, humans are their natural prey. The queen wants you to learn how to subdue them."

"I thought my mother was sending us there to keep us safe?" said Ayan.

Shukla smiled. It was not a nice smile. "Crown Prince, do you know how a mother bird teaches her baby to fly? She pushes it off the nest. This is the next phase of your education. Learn to fly, if you do not wish to fall."

He dismissed them, and they filed out, a little wiser than when they had filed in.

CHAPTER 3

TWO DAYS LATER, THEY SAID THEIR FAREWELLS IN THE PALACE entrance hall: a spacious, light-filled room with a marble fountain, stained-glass windows, and murals of elephants and tigers on the walls.

Ayan and Bhairav had dressed as commoners, in simple beige cotton tunics and pants. Katyani had discarded her Garuda uniform for a red-and-yellow salwar kameez, such as many women in the fort wore. She'd retained her sword, of course; they all had.

King Jaideep stood before the marble fountain, a genial giant of a man with a thick mane of gray hair, a handlebar moustache, and shrewd eyes. He cut an imposing figure in his richly brocaded tunic and garland of milk-white pearls. Beside him, Queen Hemlata was her usual flawless self in a red silk sari and elegant gold diadem.

Ayan and Bhairav touched the feet of the royal couple and the priest.

"Yashasvi Bhava," Shukla intoned, flicking drops of holy water on their bowed heads. *May you attain eternal success and fame.*

"Keep your swords close and your wits sharp," said the queen. "Once you enter Nandovana, you will be in the Acharya's jurisdiction."

"Why can't a few soldiers accompany us?" asked Bhairav, looking worried.

Ayan elbowed him. "Scared, cousin?"

"Better one of us scared than both of us dead," retorted Bhairav.

"Don't worry, Katya will protect us both." Ayan flashed a grin at Katyani.

"*Katya* will protect herself," said Katyani. "You have a sword; use it for something other than admiring your reflection."

Bhairav smirked. Ayan's fondness for polishing his sword until it gleamed was well known.

"You cannot have soldiers because the rules of the gurukul state only prospective pupils may enter Nandovana," said King Jaideep.

"As you *should* already know," said the queen with asperity. "Do not make me doubt your level of preparation."

Bhairav wiped the smirk off his face and gave her a hurried bow. "We remember everything our teachers have told us, Your Majesty."

"I hope we're not breaking the rules by taking a coachman," said Katyani, only half joking. What kind of place had such strict rules?

"If the Acharya is rigid enough to send us back for that, it's not our fault," said Ayan.

"It most definitely will be your fault," said the queen. "Obey the Acharya and pass all his tests. I expect nothing less from you two. Fail me, and you will get a taste of Chentu."

The princes quailed. Chentu was the queen's ancestral weapon, a black horsewhip rumored to be sentient. She always carried it wrapped around her wrist. It could flay not just the skin, but the memory and spiritual power of the person being beaten. It was a weapon she reserved for only the most hardened criminals.

"We will not fail you," promised Ayan.

"Remember what I said about the gurudakshina," said the queen. "You must agree to give him whatever he asks for. It is a matter of honor."

Ayan bowed. "Yes, Your Majesty."

The first rays of the sun filtered through the stained-glass windows, throwing crimson shadows on the marble floor. "We should leave," said Katyani reluctantly.

"Go in safety, return in glory," said the queen, conferring her favorite blessing. She locked eyes with Katyani, sending a wave of reassurance toward her. *Everything will be okay. Trust me.*

Katyani bowed to the queen, her heart too full to speak. They filed out of the massive wooden doors and down the marble steps to the carriageway that led to the palace gates. On each side of the steps, palace servants had formed a line to say good-bye and throw rose petals on them. "Return soon, Your Majesties!" they called.

Katyani smiled as a few errant petals found their way into her hair. How they all loved the princes—especially Ayan. He was the sun around which everything revolved.

At the bottom of the steps, a small carriage was waiting to take them to the gates of the fort. It was a lovely morning; the sky was a pale, cloudless blue, and the gardens were a riot of color. White and yellow blooms crowded the lily pond, and water splashed into fountains, sparkling in the sunlight. Already, at this early hour, the air was suffused with warmth, promising heat later in the day.

They climbed into the carriage, waving good-bye to everyone. As the carriage rolled down the drive, a peacock fluttered indignantly out of their way and leaped onto one of the amaltas trees that lined the path. Katyani turned her head for a last glimpse of her home, her heart clenching in anticipatory homesickness.

The yellow sandstone palace of the Ajaigarh Fort loomed above them, its circular dome guarded on each corner by an octagonal tower. At the top of the marble steps, the king and queen stood surrounded by courtiers. As if she sensed Katyani's regard, the queen smiled and blew a kiss toward the carriage just before it turned around a bend and they lost sight of each other.

"The month of Chaitra," said Bhairav with a huge sigh. "The most enjoyable time in Ajaigarh and the worst time to roam around in a forest."

"Why is it the worst time in a forest?" asked Ayan.

"Monsters are at their most active," said Bhairav.

"That's not true." Katyani turned back to the princes. "There's nothing *seasonal* about monsters. They're not like your plants, Bhav."

They continued to argue as the carriage exited the palace gates and clattered past temples, water tanks, and orchards, finally entering the fort's outer courtyard: a massive stone-paved square lined with stables, barracks, and storehouses. Cleaners swept the courtyard, and delivery carts lined up outside the storehouses, but the square was not yet crowded this early in the day, and they made it across without the coachman having to yell at anyone to get out of their way.

Guards pulled open the iron doors of the gatehouse, and they dismounted from the carriage. The curved gateway would not allow even a small carriage to squeeze through, let alone an elephant. This, along with the six hundred steps you needed to climb to access it, was one of the defense features of the Ajaigarh Fort.

On a hill twenty kilometers distant, Ajaigarh's twin fortress, Kalinjar, jutted into the sky like a black tooth. It was administered by King Jaideep's maternal cousin, Prince Okendra. Unlike Ajaigarh, Kalinjar had no magical wards, but it was ably defended by over five hundred superbly trained archers. Kalinjar, too, could only be accessed by a series of steep steps up the hill. Jaideep visited from time to time, ostensibly to keep up morale, but also to keep his cousin's power in check.

Legend held that the two forts were connected by a secret passage, but no one knew where it was. Katyani and the princes had spent many days looking for it when they were children before coming to the reluctant conclusion that it didn't exist.

"We'll miss Holi," said Bhairav as they descended the steps. Holi was the spring festival of colors, enthusiastically celebrated throughout the Chandela kingdom. "I was looking forward to strolling the streets of the city, girls running after me to pat my cheeks with colored powder."

"Girls don't run after you," said Ayan. "They run *from* you."

"They just like to be chased," said Bhairav. "The king probably orders them not to run from you because you're slower on the uptake than a snail."

They continued to banter as they made their way down. Katyani tuned them out, savoring the familiar sights and smells of the early-morning walk, all the more precious because it would be months before she returned. The hillside was covered with teak and tendu trees, but she caught occasional glimpses of the white roofs and pagodas of the city that sprawled at the foot of the hill—also called Ajaigarh, after the fort—and the distant Ken River, shimmering in the sunlight. The steps wound down the hillside, dizzying to contemplate. At the halfway mark was a checkpoint. Guards saluted and scrambled to get out of their way.

"Get used to people not bowing and scraping before you," Bhairav told Ayan once they were out of earshot of the guards. "Being a crown prince doesn't mean much in the gurukul."

"Being a prince means even less," retorted Ayan.

"Stop it, you two," said Katyani. "You're spoiling my walk."

"I'm hungry," said Ayan. "When are we eating?"

Katyani rolled her eyes. "I will buy samosas in the city, okay?"

The carriage that would take them to Nandovana was waiting at the foot of the hill, loaded with their luggage and gifts for the gurukul. It was a roomy, enclosed vehicle with two benches, facing each other, and four horses, impatient to be off. They climbed in, Ayan and Bhairav taking a window seat each and Katyani sitting opposite them in the middle. The coachman clicked his tongue, and the carriage rolled away down the road into the city of Ajaigarh, capital of the Chandela kingdom. As promised, she made the carriage stop near the market and bought them samosas, crisp and hot from the vendor's wok. They ate the fritters dipped in tamarind chutney while the coachman bullied his way down the crowded streets.

The next two days passed in increasing discomfort as the novelty of their westward journey wore off. Traveling incognito meant they couldn't stop at guesthouses for fear of being recognized. The princes slept on the floor of the carriage or curled up on the benches while Katyani kept watch for would-be assailants. The further they went from Ajaigarh, the weaker the bond grew, until she could no longer sense Hemlata at all. She'd known this would happen; she'd been apart from the queen before, after all. She tried not to dwell on the emptiness of the space inside her that the queen usually occupied. Hemlata had said it would be all right; she had to trust that.

They changed horses and coachmen at Tikamgarh, the last major town before Nandovana. Finally, they left the settlements behind, and the road was reduced to an unpaved dirt path winding through wheat fields. The forest of Nandovana loomed in the distance, a forbidding wall of green that seemed to touch the sky. Never had Katyani seen such enormous specimens. The trees of the forest behind the Ken River would have looked like saplings next to them.

Bhairav peered out of the window and recoiled. "Of all the places in Bharat, why *here*?"

"He's famous for his eccentricity," said Ayan.

"He's famous for other things too," said Katyani. She'd spent the last couple of evenings in the palace at the library, gleaning what she could about the man and his gurukul to supplement the information Shukla had given them. "People troubled by vetalas, yatu, and pretas beg him for help. He visits hotspots with his magic staff and some select disciples and makes short work of any demonic creatures."

"It'll be fun learning how to deal with different monsters," said Ayan.

"It's part of the curriculum," she assured him. "The forest is full of them."

"You two can kill monsters, cover for me while I hide," said Bhairav.

Katyani frowned, leaning out of the window to check their progress. The forest was still some distance away, but they were headed for a path that cut into the gigantic trees. "You will not miss a single class, Prince."

"Or what?" challenged Bhairav. "You'll complain to the queen?"

"Or else you will fail," she said flatly. "A shame the king and queen will not allow you to forget." She shuddered at the thought of Hemlata's reaction if either of the princes got sent home in disgrace.

Bhairav scowled. Ayan nudged him with his elbow. "Hey, it won't all be terrible. There might be pretty girls in our class to flirt with."

"Don't count on it," said Katyani. "Even if there are, you'll probably be forbidden to speak about anything unrelated to the curriculum."

"You're no fun," said Ayan. "You're supposed to be on our side. You ought to be helping us flirt with girls."

"I *am* on your side," she said. "One of those girls could be an assassin. Have you considered that?"

"Assassins in the gurukul?" Ayan shook his head. "You see danger everywhere."

"It's my job," she said. "I take it seriously. I hope you, too, will take your job seriously. Which, for the next few months, is to be the best possible students at the gurukul. Win glory for yourselves and for Chandela."

"You're better than both of us in swordplay and martial arts," Bhairav pointed out. "You can win the glory, take the heat off us."

"Not happening," she said firmly. "I will do what is required, but I don't have to excel like you do. I just have to pass." For once, she didn't want to do better than them; she wanted *them* to shine. That would make the queen happy, too.

As evening came on, they entered the path into the forest. The carriage bumped over uneven ground, fallen twigs crunching under the wheels. The thick, rich smell of growth and decay invaded their nostrils. Katyani poked her head out of one window and Ayan the other.

Huge sal trees towered above them, light green leaves whispering in the breeze. *Good.* Sal was one of the most important hardwood tree species in central Bharat. More to the point, it was not much favored by monsters. The coachman hummed loudly, either to give himself courage or to buck up the horses. Somewhere, an owl hooted, as if to counter the humming.

"You think there's a vetala hiding in one of these trees?" whispered Ayan.

"Not unless it's a banyan or a mango tree," said Bhairav.

Ayan, who wouldn't know a mango tree if the fruit fell from a branch onto his head, peered at the trees as if words would magically appear on their trunks, telling him which was which.

Katyani took pity on him. "These are sal trees, generally considered safe. Monsters don't like the medicinal smell of their leaves."

"See? Botany *does* come in useful," crowed Bhairav.

Ayan rubbed his chin. "Katya, please point out the different kinds of trees to me."

This was the first time the crown prince of Chandela had shown any interest in green things that were inedible. "Oh well, since you ask nicely."

At first, they only saw sal, the occasional silver-gray laurel, and the stately kadam tree. After a while, though, the quality of the forest changed. Sal gave way to sheesham, peepal, neem, and mango. When the first enormous banyan made its gnarly, ropy appearance, Katyani grabbed Ayan's arm and pulled him away from the window. "Best to stay inside until the forest looks friendlier."

"All forests look equally unfriendly to me," said Ayan. "Where are you going?" he asked as she got up from the bench and reached for the carriage door.

"To keep the coachman company," she replied.

But before she could open the door and hop down to the carriage step, the carriage itself came to a sudden halt. One of the horses whinnied in distress. The coachman gave a short scream, abruptly cut off. There was a blood-curdling growl, and the awful, wet sound of rending flesh.

Katyani froze, her hand on the door. Ayan and Bhairav clutched their seats in alarm. Had assassins followed them from Ajaigarh? Was it a wild animal? Or something worse? Multiple scenarios flooded her mind; she sifted through them at lightning speed, picking and discarding options to keep the princes safe.

"What's going on?" Ayan leaned out of the window.

"Fool!" Katyani jerked him back, heart thudding.

Just in time.

A thick, red-skinned arm adorned with a bracelet of human teeth thrust itself inside and made a grab for them with a hideously clawed hand.

Bhairav shouted and scrambled backward. Ayan reached for his sword, but Katyani pushed him behind her. There was no space in the carriage to wield a sword. She unsheathed her obsidian knife, grabbed the black-clawed hand at the wrist, and sliced it off, hacking through flesh and bone and sinew. It fell to the floor of the carriage, leaking a grayish fluid. The bracelet broke, scattering teeth everywhere. The arm was snatched back from the window, and there came a thin, inhuman shriek of pain and rage. *Yatudhani.*

Katyani slammed the window shut and turned to the two princes, panting. "Stay inside until I tell you it's safe to come out," she snapped. She gripped the hilt of her sword, preparing to jump out. "Understood?"

Bhairav nodded, but Ayan said, "I'm coming with you."

"You are *not,* Prince—"

To her dismay, he pushed open the door and leaped out of the carriage. She followed at his heels, furious both at him for disobeying her and at herself for letting him slip past.

A gory scene met their eyes. All four horses stood unnaturally still while a yatu drained the blood from the neck of the lead horse into a huge wooden bucket.

The coachman was dead. He was also mostly eaten. What was left of him was scattered on the forest floor, a few meters from the carriage. Half a dozen hulking yatu crouched over his remains, chewing limbs and spitting out bones, wicked-looking maces and clubs balanced on their shoulders. Over six feet tall, wild-haired and red-skinned, they would have looked like a massive and ugly species of human but for the tusks curving out of their gaping mouths. The stench was enough to make Katyani vomit. She'd seen yatu before, but never so close. And never *eating*.

Ayan unsheathed his sword. The yatu stopped eating and glared at them with bloodshot eyes. One of them rose and uttered a menacing growl that made Katyani's hair stand on end.

She grabbed Ayan's arm, keeping the yatu in her sights, her mind spinning. "Go inside. There are too many of them!"

"Exactly why you need me," he grated. "Stop talking and fight."

He was right. She hated to admit it, but there were too many for her to tackle by herself. And he wouldn't be any safer inside the carriage. Once they'd killed her, they'd surely attack anyone else left alive. Their best chance was to confront the yatu together. She took a deep breath and withdrew her blade from its leather scabbard. It came out with a sound like silk on steel. *Be true to me today.*

"Two Swords, One Soul," she commanded. They had practiced this last-ditch defensive maneuver many times in the training ground. But she'd never thought they'd actually have to use it one day.

He gave a sharp nod and stood back-to-back with her, sword gripped in both hands, ready to deflect or strike. She kept the carriage to her right; it wasn't an insurmountable obstacle, but it would reduce the chance of attack from that side.

With a ferocious roar, the yatu dropped the remains of their meal and lumbered toward them. The yatu bleeding out the horses just watched, as if enjoying the show.

"For the goddess!" Katyani summoned her spiritual power; it surged into her veins, giving her strength and speed. She leaped into the air and brought her sword down on the head of the lead yatu, cleaving his skull. He gave a wet, gurgling scream and fell to the ground. The force of the blow numbed Katyani's shoulder. She staggered back, sickened by the ruin she'd made of the monster's head.

"For Chandela," shouted Ayan, lopping off a yatu's arm.

But even a hacked limb did not stop the yatu. The injured monster turned around, shrieking in pain and anger. Before Katyani's horrified eyes, he lurched forward, smashing his mace down on Ayan's sword, even as gray lifeblood fountained out of his severed arm.

Katyani plunged her sword into the monster's chest and twisted, her arm nearly wrenching out of its socket. "Aim for the head and neck," she instructed, dodging a blow from a nail-studded club. That was the theory she remembered from one of the books she'd read, but there was a wide gulf between theory and practice. Fighting yatu was nothing like fighting humans. Wounds that would have felled a man merely made them angry. They got up each time, howling for revenge.

Katyani and Ayan fought on grimly, hacking and stabbing and parrying the hulking monsters with the wicked tusks and curving talons. The only thing in their favor was that they were faster than their attackers. But there were so *many* of them. Katyani had to not only defend herself, she also had to protect Ayan and keep an eye on the carriage to make sure Bhairav was safe and no yatu sneaked up on them from that direction. She stabbed a yatu in the stomach, and the monster lunged for her face, uncaring of the blade in his belly. One of his talons connected with her cheek, scratching it all the way down to her neck. She stumbled back before it cut open her veins.

She managed to decapitate another yatu, but that still left four, plus the bystander with the horses. She was tiring fast. So was Ayan. Her spiritual power had drained away to almost nothing. Without it, she had no hope of beating back the monsters.

Bhairav screamed.

She spun around, heart leaping in alarm. She'd forgotten the yatudhani whose hand she'd cut off. The monstress was pulling Bhairav out of the carriage by his hair. His body thumped down the steps, and the yatudhani dragged him away, kicking and struggling. Katyani's chest tightened in fear. Bhairav didn't have the capacity to fight off a determined human, let alone a yatudhani.

"Go help him," she shouted to Ayan.

"If I break our formation, both of us will die." He stayed at her back, grunting as he blocked yet another mace blow. Amazement crept into his voice. "Bhav is doing fine."

Katyani couldn't help herself; she took her eyes off the yatu for a split second to glance behind. Bhairav had freed himself and was holding the yatudhani off with his sword, fighting with a speed and ferocity she'd never have believed if she hadn't seen it. Relief and pride coursed through her.

But it was short-lived. She turned her attention back to the yatu to see them converging on her in a concerted effort to finish her off. Two clubs swung in the direction of her head. She danced aside, slashed one of the arms holding a club, and brought up her sword to block the other. But something hard hit the side of her head. For a moment, she couldn't fathom what had happened. She couldn't *think*. She stumbled and fell. Dazed and in pain, she lay on the ground, her breath coming in short gasps.

"Katyani!" Ayan was blocking two maces at once. "Get up!"

For the first time in her life, control of the situation ebbed away from her. Black spots danced before her eyes. A horrible scream came from behind her, but whether it was Bhairav or the yatudhani, she could not make out.

A yatu raised his club to finish her off. She stared at his fearsome face, petrified.

The blow never came. Instead, an arrow struck the yatu's forehead, and the club dropped from his hand. His eyes lost their bloodshot focus, and he toppled to the ground.

Where had the arrow come from? Bhairav wasn't carrying a bow— not that he was capable of such a shot.

Move, you fool. She grabbed her sword and scrambled to her feet, ignoring the throbbing in her head and cheek. She ran forward and stabbed the neck of the nearest yatu, retching as a foul-smelling gray fluid poured out of his torn throat. He staggered back with a roar of pain.

Another arrow pierced the forehead of a yatu who had been grappling with Ayan, trying to take his sword. Katyani cast a quick glance back. Bhairav was no longer in sight, but the yatudhani lay dead on the ground, her head some distance away from her body. Had *Bhairav* done that? She prayed he was all right.

Now only two yatu were left. The horse-bleeder had vanished into the forest, taking his bucket with him. Katyani raised her sword to deflect the mace of the injured yatu, but before she could parry and strike, the flash of a golden blade cut through the evening air. A young man in flowing sky-blue robes landed lightly beside her and decapitated the yatu in one smooth stroke.

The last one tried to run away. But, in an incredible display of strength and speed, the man flung his sword into the fleeing monster's back, felling him instantly. A powerful weapon, to be able to take out a yatu like that. And a powerful man, to do it in such a calm, relaxed manner. He wasn't even out of breath. The sword flew back into his grip, and there was a moment of silence. Six yatu and one yatudhani lay dead before them, their rotten odor filling the air.

Bhairav—where was he? Katyani spun around. "Bhairav?"

He poked his head out from behind a tree, disheveled and wild-eyed. "Here. I'm here."

Relief so sharp it was almost painful flooded her. She gave a shaky laugh. "Goddess, Bhav, were you hiding?"

"Of course I was," he said. "Are they all dead?"

"Yes, thanks to the skillful archery and swordsmanship of this gentleman." Ayan sheathed his sword and bowed to the stranger. "Thank you for saving our lives, Airya. We are in your debt. My name is Ayan, and that boy hiding behind the tree is my cowardly cousin Bhairav, although he's shown talents today we never dreamed he possessed. And this lady is our sister, Katyani."

The stranger gave a curt nod. He was tall and well-built—taller even than the princes—and had a stern, handsome face with high cheekbones and long, lustrous lashes. His robes were those of a monk or a mendicant, but he appeared not much older than them. His wavy black hair was pushed back from his face, except for a single lock that fell on his forehead. With the bow on his back and the sword in his hand, he could have been a warrior monk from one of the folktales Katyani had grown up reading.

He looked at Katyani, taking in her gore-spattered appearance, the gash on the side of her head, the tattoo on her neck. She stared back at him, unsettled by his regard, though she could not have said why. Perhaps because of what he might think of her tattoo. Anyone with enough spiritual power could recognize it: the mark of a magical bond.

Or perhaps because his gaze was so intense. *I see you,* it said. *I know you.*

Which was absurd, because she'd never met this man in her life. She would have remembered it if she had.

It was he who looked away from her first. "You must kill the horses," he said, his voice deep and mellow.

"What? Why?" she sputtered. "Surely we can save them."

"We meant them as a gift to Acharya Mahavir's gurukul," said Ayan.

Bhairav joined them, his hair mangled, his face bruised, his clothes torn. "They look fine," he chimed in. "They're of excellent stock."

"The horses have been turned," said the man slowly, as if explaining to a child. "The yatu drain their blood to drink and replace it with their own body fluids, binding them." Such terrible words, uttered in such a matter-of-fact tone. Katyani couldn't stop looking at him.

"What?" Bhairav pointed a trembling finger at the preternaturally calm animals. "You mean they are now yatu horses?"

"Yes."

"But if we kill the horses, how will we get to the gurukul?" asked Ayan.

The man gave a pointed glance at Ayan's feet. His meaning was clear.

"We'll never make it in time," said Ayan. "And we were warned not to be late. We'll surely be punished."

"Better to arrive alive in one piece than not at all," said Katyani, finally remembering to speak. She made herself turn away from the handsome stranger and studied the horses instead. They were as still as statues, and their eyes had taken on a cloudy, reddish hue. She recollected how they'd stood quietly while the yatu drained their blood. Normal horses would have broken the traces and escaped. *Normal* horses would be cropping the grass right now.

A sour taste entered her mouth. "Well, if there's no help for it, I'll put them out of their misery." She half hoped one of the princes would offer to share the burden of this ghastly task, but they hung their heads, looking unhappy. Both Ayan and Bhairav loved horses, so she didn't blame them. Hell, she loved horses too.

But these were no longer horses. They were things in the shapes of horses that would become more dangerous the longer they were allowed to live.

She gripped her sword and walked up to the animals with leaden feet, hating what she was about to do. She unbuckled the traces and told the princes to push the carriage back, her voice sounding hollow to her own ears.

When the carriage was out of the way, and she was sure there was enough space between the dead-eyed creatures, she began to euthanize them one by one. She tried not to think about what she was doing as she slashed the carotid arteries and jugular veins on both sides of their necks. Blood gushed from their open veins, but not as much as she had expected. The yatu had already bled them half out. None of them moved or showed any sign of fear, even when the first one crashed to the ground. It sickened her, both what had been done to them and what she was being forced to do herself. She'd never wanted to go to the gurukul; she'd *begged* to be let out of it, and look at the terrible mess she had to clean up now. If she'd still been connected to Hemlata, she'd have railed against the queen, made her feel a little of what she was going through.

When the last horse was done, she walked away from their twitching bodies and leaned against a tree trunk, dizzy and disoriented. Putting down the innocent animals had been harder than fighting the yatu. Her head was throbbing worse than ever, and they were in the middle of a deadly forest with several miles still to go before they reached the safety of the gurukul. How would they manage it?

Leaves crunched behind her. "Here," said a calm voice. "Breathe."

The stranger stood beside her, holding up a small cloth bag filled with fragrant herbs. She gazed at him in mingled astonishment and suspicion. But he wouldn't have saved them from the yatu just to poison them with sweet-smelling herbs. She bent forward and inhaled deeply, and clarity returned to her thoughts.

"Keep it. You'll need it again." He thrust the bag into her hand and turned away.

"Where are you going? Who are you?" she blurted out, afraid she'd never see him again. Which made no sense; why should she care whether she saw him again or not?

But he did not answer. She watched him walk away, heading southwest, and her chest tightened with an odd mixture of regret and annoyance. In a minute, he was lost in the darkness of the oncoming night.

The forest closed around, thick and watchful and far unfriendlier than it had been in his magnetic presence. A chorus of crickets started from behind them. The undergrowth rustled, and she remembered, her stomach twisting, all the *other* things she must protect the princes from: wild animals, vetalas, snakes, scorpions.

"Well, that was weird," remarked Ayan. "He didn't even tell us his name."

"Can we get away from here?" begged Bhairav. "These rotten carcasses make me want to puke."

"What about the carriage and all our stuff?" asked Ayan.

"We must leave the carriage," said Katyani, her mind working fast. The dead bodies would attract scavengers; it was best to leave as soon as possible. "We'll carry what we can, and we'll borrow horses from the gurukul and retrieve the rest later."

It was hard choosing what to carry. In the end, they took sufficient food and water for the next two days, a lamp, the silver amphora of gold coins and the purse of precious stones Queen Hemlata had chosen as gifts from the treasury, and a box of laddus made of gram flour. Sweets were auspicious, and it wouldn't be right to arrive empty-handed at the gurukul, no matter how dire their circumstances.

The next few days were awful. Katyani knew they had to go southwest, and there was a path of sorts. She was able to keep them going in the right direction, but she had no idea how far they were from the gurukul. The princes suffered dreadfully. Despite her pain and fatigue, she maintained an outward calm, chivvying them along whenever they flagged. At first, they tried to take it as an adventure. But the fear of being attacked by yatu kept them alert and unable to rest at all. Hordes of mosquitoes hounded them in the night and tiny black flies in the day. They came across mango trees but were afraid to climb them and pluck the fruit because such trees were often occupied by vetalas.

Their food ran out by the second day, although they found a stream of clear water to replenish their empty gourds and wash their wounds. At last, only the box of laddus was left. Katyani had to threaten to beat the princes if they tried to eat those.

Anytime she felt dizzy or her wounds hurt too much, she opened the cloth bag the stranger had given her and inhaled the fragrance of its herbs.

It never failed to work, even as the scent grew fainter. Once, while they were resting during the heat of the midday sun, insects buzzing in irritating clouds above their heads, Ayan asked her what was in the bag and why she kept sniffing it. She didn't answer. Perhaps she should have shared it with the princes, but she couldn't bring herself to. He'd given it to *her*. And she'd been the one to euthanize the horses, so she deserved it.

On the evening of the third day, the forest thinned and gave way to neat squares of cultivated plots. Starving and footsore, the trio stopped in front of rows of beans, sweet peas, eggplant, bottle gourd, and okra, scarcely believing their eyes. A ten-foot-high stone wall covered with money plant and bougainvillea ran the length of the plots; a pagoda-topped building rose in the distance behind it. The wall had a solid wooden gate reinforced with wrought iron; it stood partly open, beckoning them in.

Katyani wanted to weep with relief. It was like returning to the lap of civilization after endless days in the dark. She couldn't wait to have a bath, apply salve to her wounds, wear clean clothes, and eat a normal meal again.

"Can we eat raw eggplant?" asked Bhairav, eyeing the vegetable plots. "It is considered a delicacy in some parts of Bharat."

"It is *not*. Raw eggplant will give you indigestion." Katyani dragged them both toward the gate. "There will be time to eat later. First, we must present ourselves."

"Like this?" Ayan pointed at their grubby, torn clothes.

The three of them looked as dirty and disreputable as it was possible to get. But it could not be helped. Hopefully, Acharya Mahavir did not lay too much store by appearances.

"We'll explain what happened," said Katyani. "It's not our fault."

As soon as they arrived, however, the gate swung closed and the bolt clanged shut. She glared at the gate in frustration. After all they had been through, was the gurukul going to turn them away?

"Tell them we'll eat all their vegetables if they don't let us in," whispered Ayan.

"Quiet," she hissed, although she was hungry enough to raid their sweet peas. "You want a bath and clean clothes, don't you?" She raised her sword and knocked sharply on the gate with the hilt.

"Identify yourselves," came a cold voice from within. It was vaguely familiar, but she couldn't place it.

She jabbed Ayan with her elbow. He stepped forward and bowed low. "Greetings. I am Crown Prince Ayan of Chandela. This is my cousin, Prince Bhairav, and this is our adopted sister, Katyani. We humbly request Acharya Mahavir to accept us as his pupils."

"What do you bring with you?" the voice asked.

"We brought grains, blankets, and clothes, but unfortunately we were attacked by yatu on the way," explained Ayan. "Most of our stuff is still in the carriage. We can fetch it later."

"What do you bring with you?" the voice repeated.

"We have one box of laddus," said Bhairav.

"And precious items from our kingdom's treasury, which we beg you to accept," added Katyani, holding out the amphora and purse.

"For the third and last time, what do you bring with you?" said the voice. It had acquired an edge.

Oh no. It was a riddle. Couldn't the speaker have warned them first? She put a finger to her lips, shushing the princes. "We bring our minds, thirsty for learning, our hands, eager for work, and our hearts, open to knowledge," she said, hoping that would satisfy the gatekeeper.

The gate creaked open. On the other side was a vast courtyard adorned with a single peepal tree in the middle. All around were low, white buildings covered with thatched roofs. Flowerbeds lined the edges of the courtyard, and potted plants graced porches and windows. At the far end was the biggest building, three levels high, topped by a pagoda that glinted gold in the setting sun.

But it was the young man who stood at the gateway, surrounded by a group of blue-robed disciples, who snagged Katyani's gaze and robbed her of breath. It was the stranger who had rescued them from the yatu, regarding them with an expression of stony indifference on his beautiful face, as if he'd never laid eyes on them before.

CHAPTER 4

"YOU'RE *HIM*," AYAN BURST OUT. "ACHARYA MAHAVIR!"

A disciple coughed and stepped forward from the group. He was a few years older than them, rake-thin, with an earnest face and prominent jug ears. "You are mistaken, Prince," he said. "This is Airya Daksh, the son of Acharya Mahavir. I am Varun, and I'm responsible for welcoming newcomers."

Daksh. Would it have killed him to introduce himself when they first met? Was he mad for some reason? His features looked as if they were carved from granite. Maybe that was his normal expression. Even when he was killing yatu, his face barely twitched.

Katyani tore her gaze away from him and proffered the amphora, purse, and laddus to Varun. "Please accept these humble tokens of our regard," she recited, as Hemlata had instructed her to.

Varun accepted the offerings and passed them to another disciple. "If you come with me, I will show you to your hut," he told Ayan and Bhairav.

Katyani made to follow the princes, but Varun held up a hand. "Not you, lady. Please wait, and I will have one of the women disciples take you to their quarters."

"I'm staying with the princes," said Katyani flatly. "I'm a royal body-guard of Chandela."

The disciples gasped and murmured. Daksh quelled them with a glance.

"She is also our adopted sister," said Ayan hastily. "We request you to allow her to stay with us."

"Most irregular," said Varun. He looked at Daksh, and Daksh gave a slight nod, which Katyani would have missed if she hadn't been watching him. "Very well. You may stay with your brothers."

Daksh hadn't spoken a word. He hadn't even looked at her—not obviously, anyway. And he still had that same expression of cold indifference on his face. *You saved us from yatu,* she wanted to shout. *You gave me those sweet-smelling herbs! At least say hello?* She knew she should follow the princes and Varun inside, but she couldn't help herself.

She joined her hands together and bowed. "Thank you for your help against the yatu, Airya Daksh. It would have been extremely helpful if you'd stayed a minute longer and given us directions to the gurukul. We'd have been able to arrive hours earlier."

Still, he said nothing, just gazed at her expressionlessly out of those deep, dark eyes of his. At least she'd made him look in her direction. She had a sudden desire to stick her tongue out at him to get a reaction. She bit her lips to stifle a giggle and was gratified to see a minute crease appear on his forehead.

"Lady, we only interfere if the lives of our guests are in peril," said Varun. "For the rest, you are supposed to be able to make your own way here. Many turn back at the first hint of danger. Our gurukul is not for cowards or fools. Think of your journey here as a test of your resilience and spiritual power."

"What? The yatu were some kind of entrance test?" Bhairav looked aghast, no doubt thinking of how the yatudhani had dragged him out by his hair and nearly chomped him alive.

"The forest is populated by a variety of monsters and nature spirits," said Varun. "All travelers face some problem or the other. The Solanki prince was attacked by a vetala, and only the intervention of Airya Uttam, the Acharya's elder son, saved his life. If by some miracle a pupil arrives without mishap, we make them camp out in the forest for a week without food or fresh water before we let them enter."

"Well, we are fortunate only our coachman was eaten," said Bhairav sarcastically.

Quiet; let me do the talking, Katyani finger-spelled, and Bhairav subsided. "The coachman was an innocent victim of your test," she said. "We will compensate his family, but nothing can bring him back. You should have warned us in advance; we'd have been better prepared, and a life would not have been lost."

Varun exchanged a glance with Daksh. "We are sorry we did not arrive in time to prevent this tragedy. But it was a complete surprise to us. The yatu in Nandovana usually do not interfere with humans. We keep out of their way and they keep out of ours. They appear to have targeted you for some reason." His words struck Katyani cold. She hadn't thought of that.

"What do you mean?" demanded Ayan.

"Prince, you ought to be able to answer that question better than I can," said Varun.

Ayan opened his mouth to argue, but Katyani caught his eye and shook her head. Varun had a point. The Chandela kings had driven the yatu out from their kingdom. Perhaps some of them had ended up in Nandovana. If so, they and their descendants might harbor hatred and resentment against the royal family of Chandela. But there was no point discussing this in front of outsiders.

"How many new pupils do you expect this year?" she asked instead.

"Fifteen, including the three of you," said Varun. "The Solanki prince is accompanied by his cousin sister, so you will not be the only lady."

"Lucky me," muttered Katyani. "Have there always been so few girls?"

Varun hesitated. "I do not know. Please come with me now. I have other duties to attend to."

The three of them bowed to Daksh, getting barely a nod in response, as if he were a king and they his lowly subjects. Katyani straightened, irritated. *So it's like that, is it? I'm going to make you regret that attitude, see if I don't!*

She threw him a cold glance—not that he noticed—and they followed Varun into the vast stone-paved courtyard of the gurukul. As they entered, Katyani's neck tingled with the proximity of a strong magic. She looked at the princes, and they both finger-spelled *wards,* confirming what she had sensed: powerful wards on the walls of the gurukul that would keep intruders out—both human and monster, she suspected. It would make the gurukul safer for the princes.

The ancient peepal tree in the center of the courtyard sheltered a stone well beneath its spreading branches. All around were multiple white-walled huts, set against the walls, leaving plenty of open space in the middle.

Varun waved his hand at the pagoda-topped building at the opposite end. A plant-filled porch wrapped around it, and a small citrus tree grew to its right. "That's where Acharya Mahavir holds his classes on ethics, governance, and statecraft. The second level is a library you can visit accompanied by an elder disciple like myself. The top floor comprises the Acharya's private quarters."

"Where's the kitchen?" asked Ayan. "Where does everyone eat?" Katyani perked up. She was famished. Although a bath was even more necessary than food right now. She probably stank of yatu gore and dead horse. The grueling trek through the forest had not helped. Chaya would have wept at the state of her hair, which was a tangled mess of mud, leaves, and dead insects.

Varun pointed to a long, low building to the right of the main one. "That's the dining hall. The kitchen is behind it. Meals are twice a day: midday at noon and evening at seven. It's six thirty right now. You have half an hour to wash up and get ready. I'm sure you're hungry."

Understatement of the year, thought Katyani, her stomach rumbling.

He indicated a windowless building opposite the dining hall. "That's the armory. All weapons in the gurukul owe their allegiance to the Acharya, including the ones you've brought."

"What does that mean?" asked Bhairav.

"No one here can take up arms against him," said Varun smugly.

That was incredible. The Acharya was even more powerful than Katyani had thought.

"The smaller hut to the left of the armory is the women's dormitory," Varun continued.

The women's dormitory was set apart from the other huts, not just by distance but by a three-foot-high brick wall with a wooden gate. The wall was covered with pots of daffodils, sunflowers, and aromatic herbs. The hut looked pleasant but out of place, hemmed in by the wall.

"Why is there a wall around it?" asked Katyani. "And why is the wall so low? It won't keep anyone out."

Varun gave a superior smile. "The wall is symbolic. It represents the divide between man and woman. No one dare cross it."

Katyani snorted. The princes didn't say anything, but she knew they were trying not to laugh. Men and women mixed freely in the Chandela kingdom, and gender roles were more fluid than they appeared to be elsewhere. Except for princesses. Poor Revaa. Katyani wondered how she was getting on. Was Hemlata going easier on her in their absence? And the queen—was she missing Katyani the way Katyani was missing her? She rubbed the tattoo on her neck, as if that could conjure Hemlata. But the butterfly remained dormant, the space within her silent, and she dropped her hand, stifling a sigh.

They stopped before a small hut, identical to the ones on either side: two windows, a narrow porch draped in vines, and an entrance hung with a grass mat.

"Here is the room reserved for you, Princes," said Varun. "Only two pallets, but I will have someone bring extra bedding for your bodyguard-sister."

"Where can we bathe?" asked Bhairav.

"There's a stream behind the gurukul," said Varun. "Bathing hours for men are between five and six in the morning. You'll find washcloths and an antiseptic neem salve for your wounds inside the hut."

He bowed and left before they could respond.

Bhairav gave a bitter laugh. "I better resign myself to not bathing until we're back home."

"You will go tomorrow morning and clean up before class," said Katyani. She would have to find out where the women bathed. She was dirty and tired and hot, and her feet ached like she'd walked on live coals. "We must make do with what we have."

Bhairav and Ayan looked at the hut with a marked lack of enthusiasm. The palace servants had bigger quarters than this. Even Katyani's room could easily have fit three such huts inside it. But she wasn't going to fret over their living space, and she wasn't going to let the princes fret either.

She climbed the three steps up to the porch and flicked aside the grass curtain. There was an unlit lamp in one corner, two pallets, one on each side of the room, and a low table with a pitcher of water and a small jar of greenish-brown paste—the neem salve, most likely. On each pallet was a sky-blue robe. A few washcloths hung on a hook in the wall.

"Come on, you two," she called. The princes entered and gazed in dispirited silence at their austere surroundings.

"Let's clean up and use that neem paste," she said briskly before either could start complaining. She wet one of the washcloths in the pitcher and scrubbed her face and hands, wincing as it passed over her cuts. The princes followed suit. She made them sit still while she dabbed the salve over their wounds, and then Bhairav did the same for her, his face puckered in concentration as he applied it to the gash on the side of her head. The salve stung a bit, but it was cooling, and the pain lessened almost at once. Afterward, she sat on the porch outside, trying to disentangle her hair with her fingers while the princes changed into their gurukul robes.

A young disciple with a shy smile and a snub nose arrived a little later, bearing a grass mat, a cotton sheet, and a set of robes for her. She accepted with gratitude. "Where do the women of the gurukul bathe?" she asked.

"Same place as the men," he told her. "There's a waterfall and stream behind the gurukul. Turn left from the gate and walk until you reach a grove of mango trees. The stream is behind the grove. You can't miss it."

She put aside the clean robe and made up her mind. She would wear it only after taking a dip in the stream, and she would take a dip that very night. This close to the gurukul, there wouldn't be any monsters about. Surely it would be safe. And since the men could only bathe between the ridiculous hours of five and six in the morning, she would have the stream to herself.

The princes emerged, clad in their new gurukul robes, and they hurried to the dining hall, anxious not to miss the food. Other pupils were making their way to the hall, and some of them did quick introductions. People stared at Katyani's tattoo, although they were too polite to ask her about it. They'd probably never seen a bondswoman before; her presence in the gurukul as a quasi-student/bodyguard was bound to stir curiosity.

The attention discomfited her; for the first time in her life, she wished she had wrapped a dupatta around her neck. Not that she was ashamed of the mark in any way. It was part of her, just like it was part of the queen.

She wondered what Hemlata would say to all the inquisitive starers. *Jealous of our bond,* she would whisper, and she would kiss the tattoo on her palm, giving Katyani that special smile that excluded everyone else.

Thinking of Hemlata lightened her heart, and she stepped into the dining hall, head held high.

The dining hall was a pleasant space lit by oil lamps and filled with the fragrance of herbs. A series of windows let in fresh air, and netting kept mosquitoes out. Coriander, mint, and sacred basil plants crowded the windowsills, and a long, low table with cushions on either side occupied the center of the hall. The table had been laid with copper brass plates and bowls, which gleamed in the lamplight. It could easily have seated a hundred people, but less than half that number were present. All but a handful were men, dressed in identical blue robes. Nobody had sat down yet; they stood against the walls, talking in low voices, so Katyani and the princes remained standing as well. Servers carried dishes of steaming vegetable soup, platters heaped with fruit, baskets of flatbreads, and pitchers of lassi to the table. Katyani's mouth watered at the aroma.

At last, a tall, bony man with a shock of white hair, piercing black eyes, a long beard, and a crooked wooden staff entered the hall, followed by a group of half a dozen older disciples. Unlike everyone else, he was dressed in white robes. There was a power and presence about him that made her guess who he was, even before everyone bowed to him and Varun ushered him to the head of the table.

So this was the famous Acharya Mahavir. Katyani stared. His robe was rumpled, his hair uncombed, his beard straggly, and his staff resembled a crude black branch instead of the polished stick she had imagined.

His gaze landed on her, and he frowned. Hastily she lowered her eyes.

"Sit," he said in a stern voice, and everyone rushed to obey. Katyani sat on a cushion between the princes near the end of the table. The seniormost disciples sat close to the Acharya. The few women were clustered together in the middle.

On the Acharya's right was a handsome man who resembled him the way a young tree resembled a gnarly old member of its own species. That must be Uttam, his elder son. He had a similar height and build to Daksh, but he was more like his father than Daksh, with the same piercing eyes and the same shock of unruly hair, except his was black. The biggest difference between the two brothers, though, was in their expressions. Uttam had a kind face, calm and serious but also welcoming—the sort of person you would go running to in any emergency. Daksh might be as adept as his elder brother, but his cold demeanor ensured you'd let your house burn half down before asking him for help.

She scanned the dining hall for the Acharya's younger son, but he was nowhere in sight. Too high and mighty to eat with the rank and file, she supposed, even though the rank and file included many princes of Bharat.

The Acharya led them in a simple prayer of thanks for the food. After the prayer, Varun stood and cleared his throat. "I will repeat a few rules for the benefit of new pupils who arrived today. Always wait for Acharya Mahavir to sit before you do. Sprinkle a few drops of water around your plate before you start. There must be no talking while eating. Fill your stomach, but do not be greedy. Wear your gurukul robe at all times." He paused to direct a meaningful glance at Katyani, which she pretended not to notice. "Wash your hands both before and after eating. After the meal, retire to your rooms. There must be no nonessential activity in the gurukul at night."

Hurry up, you pompous fool, thought Katyani. *I'm dying of hunger.*

"Once a week, every Monday, we fast," continued Varun. "No food is prepared or eaten on Mondays. Anyone caught eating will be severely punished."

Ayan's mouth fell open in horror. *I'll die,* Bhairav finger-spelled. *Not if I can help it,* Katyani retorted. Monday was two days away. That left today and tomorrow to stuff themselves in preparation.

At last, they were allowed to eat. Katyani sprinkled a few drops of water around her plate as the others did and fell to. For a while, she was too busy feeding her starved stomach to pay attention to anyone else. The food was okay, though bland compared to what she was used to. The gurukul did not approve of spices, onions, or garlic, apparently. After her third helping of flatbread and mixed vegetables, she slowed down enough to take a look around.

The disciples were of all ages. She guessed the young ones were mostly new pupils like herself. The older ones must come back year after year. And some probably lived here permanently—a ghastly thought.

Acharya Mahavir finished eating and rose along with Uttam. "Tomorrow morning at seven we will have our first class," he announced in his gruff voice. "Latecomers will be forbidden entry."

He stalked out, followed by his retinue of senior disciples. Everyone else rose to leave as well, chattering as they pushed the cushions against the walls and stacked the used plates on the table to help the servers clean up. Mealtime was over, and so was the rule of silence. Bhairav grabbed a flatbread and slipped it inside his pocket.

"I'm pretty sure a server saw you," Katyani whispered to him, stacking their plates in a neat pile. "Don't do that again."

"This is for Monday," he told her. "You know I cannot fast."

"You can and you will," she said as they filed out. "Remember, the queen has instructed you to perform well. Think of it as a once-in-a-lifetime training."

"Training, my ass," muttered Bhairav under his breath.

Both the princes were too tired to linger and talk with the others. In any case, most people appeared to be heading to their rooms. The trio went back to their hut.

"I'm not going to survive this place," announced Bhairav, throwing himself onto his pallet. He twisted and turned, groaning. "This feels like a bed of nails."

"Don't be silly," mumbled Ayan, his eyes already closing. "Nails are more comfortable than this."

"Your mother hates us, doesn't she?" said Bhairav. "She hates us and wants us to suffer."

"She wants us to stay strong under misfortune." Ayan yawned. "Go to sleep. We have to wake up at five if we want to wash off all the yatu guck."

That reminded Katyani of Bhairav's incredible feat separating the yatudhani's head from her body. He'd always been the weakest of the three, but when it mattered most, he'd delivered. Tanoj would be proud of him. All those extra classes had paid off. "I can't believe you killed a yatudhani," she said. "You've been holding out on us all these years. Hasn't he, Ayan?"

But Ayan was already asleep, his face slack, his mouth open.

Katyani giggled. "Remember we used to put grasshoppers in his mouth?"

"Don't tempt me. What kind of sister are you?" Bhairav twisted and turned some more, grumbling under his breath.

Katyani blew out the lamp and settled on her grass mat near the entrance. In a few minutes, Bhairav's quiet breathing told her he was asleep too, despite his complaints about the bed.

It was too early for her to sneak out. Some pupils might still be lurking in the courtyard. Katyani tried to rest and meditate, emptying her mind. Going for a bath in the stream counted as an essential activity, as far as she was concerned. If she got into trouble for it, she would claim ignorance. She'd been told the hours of bathing for the men, not the women. Still, it would be best to avoid bumping into anyone.

When the half-moon rose in the sky and she judged it was close to ten o'clock, she grabbed her clean blue robe and a washcloth and flicked aside the mat at the entrance. She poked her head out, ready to retreat if anyone was about.

But the moonlit courtyard was empty. A breeze sighed through the peepal tree, and crickets chirped. She stole to the back of the hut and followed the gurukul wall until she arrived at the main gate. There were no guards; perhaps the Acharya thought none were required. If it was *her* in charge, she'd have set up a night patrol with all the disciples taking turns, despite the magical wards.

She slipped out, shutting the gate behind her. Moonlight fell on the cultivated plots, transforming the humble vegetable garden into something strange and otherworldly. She walked along the front wall and turned left, heading for the rear of the gurukul.

Here were no tame plants. Sal, peepal, and sheesham trees gathered thick and close, their branches blocking the sky. She stayed near the wall until she reached the end and the forest gave way to a grove of mango trees. The half-sweet, half-musky odor made her sneeze. Moonlight dappled the leaves and she thought, for a moment, of vetalas. Mango and banyan trees were their favorite haunts.

She followed the sound of water until she arrived at her destination. It was only a small waterfall, barely twice her height, but it glittered in the moonlight like a living thing. Water gushed into a little pool and tumbled over rocks into a sparkling stream. A large night-blooming jasmine shrub bent over the pool, its white, star-shaped flowers filling the air with fragrance. *Perfect.* Monsters hated jasmine.

She placed the gurukul robe on a rock, undid her cotton hair tie, and stripped off her dirty salwar kameez and underwear. She wished she could throw them out, but given that all her clothes were stuck in a carriage several miles away, surrounded by corpses, she was better off washing them. First, though, she would remove every last vestige of yatu gore from her skin.

Naked, she stepped into the stream and shivered in delight. The water was cool and fresh and scented with herbs. She went deeper into the pool and immersed herself. The dirt sloughed off her skin, the dust washed off her tangled hair. A feeling of peace came over her. If she could do this even once a week, she'd manage to survive this place.

Katyani held her breath for a minute, and raised her head, gasping.

She gave a yelp of surprise, swallowing a mouthful of water.

On the bank of the stream, stripped down to his waist, was Daksh. Bare-chested, he was even more impressive than when robed, with broad shoulders, rippling muscles, and a taut, flat stomach.

He looked at her, eyes wide, mouth open in shock, frozen in the act of untying his inner robe.

At last, an expression from that block of ice, she thought through her befuddlement and horror, and that made her laugh—a big hiccupping laugh that made her lose her balance and almost slide underwater. She righted herself and clamped a hand on her mouth to stop the snorts. *Oh no.* The worst person who could have caught her in such a state, and now he would think she was laughing at him. Not that she cared what he thought of her.

He grabbed his outer robe and slipped it on, hiding his well-muscled body from her interested eyes. "You aren't supposed to be here," he said in a flat voice, trying to assume his mask of cold indifference. But she could see he was still rattled.

"Bathing is an essential activity," she protested, ready with her excuse. "And a disciple told me the women of the gurukul bathed here."

"Between four and five in the morning," he snapped, jerking his sleeves down with unnecessary force. "Not at night."

Between four and five in the morning? Unbelievable!

"Nobody told me that," she said. "Anyway, aren't the men supposed to bathe between five and six? Or are the rules different for you?"

His lip curled. "I don't bathe with the others."

"Neither do I." Her bare shoulders peeked out of the water, and he averted his gaze from her. She bit back a giggle. They were just *shoulders*. "Look, I'm sorry. This is my first day, and I didn't know about the timings. I didn't realize I was breaking any rules. But four in the morning is a ridiculous hour to be up; it's not fair to the women. I'm not hurting anyone, am I? I'll finish my bath and go back to our hut."

"Go back now," he ordered.

"Airya Daksh, we were attacked by yatu on the way," she said. "You should remember, since you were there. I was covered in gore. I smell of rotten yatu and dead horse. Do you blame me for wanting to clean up before I wear that nice gurukul robe?"

"I said, return now." His voice was as unyielding as stone.

She made a face. "The first time we met, I was impressed by your swordsmanship and archery. You are an excellent fighter and yatu-killer. But you are also a very unreasonable person."

"Did I ask for your opinion?" He glared at her.

"No, but I like to give it anyway." She raised her arms out of the water and gave an unhurried stretch, smirking at how that made him look away again. "Where I come from, women are allowed to speak their minds. My queen holds as much power as my king."

"Are you not her bondswoman?" he said, cutting his gaze back at her.

That stopped her cold. No one had ever called her that to her face. Rude man! "I am bonded to her, yes," she said, forcing evenness in her voice.

"That kind of magic is forbidden for good reason," he said.

"She did it to save my life! And she has raised me with care since I was a child." The queen hadn't just saved her life; she'd *adopted* her. It was because of her that Katyani had Ayan, Bhairav, and Revaa to call brothers and sister. She'd grown up with them, studied with them, played with them. They were her family, no matter what anyone else thought.

"If she truly cared about you, she would give you your freedom," he said.

"It's not that simple." She stumbled over the words, her chest tightening in mingled confusion and anger. "A bond cannot be released at will. The debt must be paid in full before it will work."

He frowned. "You are a royal bodyguard. You must have saved their lives more than once. Have you not repaid the debt many times over?"

She was unable to answer. She wanted to defend the queen, to tell him he was wrong, that the debt she owed Hemlata could not possibly be paid.

She had not sensed the queen, not once, since she left Chandela. Her hand flew to the tattoo on her neck. "I would not expect you to understand the relationship I have with the royal family of Chandela," she said coldly. "It is founded on mutual respect and love. Do you know what that means, Airya?"

His eyes narrowed. "This discussion is meaningless. Please go back to your hut."

"How can I come out of the water while you're staring at me?" she inquired, wanting to discomfit him the way he'd discomfited her. "Unless you wish to see me naked?"

He swallowed visibly, then turned and strode away, not looking back.

"Good night," she called.

He didn't deign to respond. She emerged from the pool and made a beeline for her clothes. She was sure he wasn't around; he wasn't the peeking type. Still, she felt dreadfully exposed. She wiped herself down hurriedly with the washcloth, squeezed the water out of her hair, and donned the clean robe. It was in two parts: a short inner robe you tied around your waist like a petticoat, and a long outer one you slipped your arms into like a loose kurta.

But she didn't have any clean underwear. She'd have to wash her bodice and panties and hope they were dry enough to wear in the morning. Then she would go to the women disciples and beg them for supplies.

She immersed her dirty clothes in the stream one by one, squeezed them, and repeated the exercise. She was wringing out her bodice one final time when someone spoke behind her back:

"You've still not gone?"

She leaped around, nearly falling into the stream. Daksh loomed behind her, scowling.

She took a deep breath and counted to ten. When her heart rate had reduced, she said, enunciating each word carefully, "I am washing my underwear. You realize people need underwear? I don't have any. All our stuff is in the carriage."

"You should have asked the women disciples for some," he said, radiating disapproval.

She rolled her eyes. He was stating the obvious. "Yes, I know. I will tomorrow. Now be a good boy and leave me alone." She turned her attention back to her clothes, squeezing the last drops of water out of them. At least they didn't smell anymore.

A hand grasped her upper arm and hauled her up.

Years of training kicked in and her body responded before she could think. She swung around and punched him on his chest with the heel of her palm. Not hard enough to damage him, but hard enough to make him stumble back, clutching his chest.

Her hand flew to her mouth. She'd hit the Acharya's younger son. "You took me by surprise," she said, which was as much of an apology as she would give him, consequences be damned.

He straightened, breathing hard. "Leave. *Now.*" His eyes sparked with anger. He looked so upset, she thought he might throw her back into the water. If it came to fisticuffs, she'd give as good as she got, but then she'd have to return in ignominy to Ajaigarh, and the queen would not be happy with her at all.

"I'm going, I'm going." She pointedly dusted her upper arm where he had grabbed it. "Was that just an excuse to touch me?" She knew she shouldn't tease him, but it was his fault for laying hands on her without her permission. He *deserved* to be teased.

His lips quivered and clamped together. She mentally revised her estimate of his age. She'd thought he was a few years older than her. But he couldn't be more than nineteen.

"Why did you come back?" she asked, picking up her damp clothes. "Just to chase me away?"

He looked away from her. "I want to bathe."

"Well, I'm not stopping you. Stream's big enough for both of us *and* my clothes," she remarked.

"How can you be so shameless," he muttered, fixing his gaze on the jasmine shrub.

"The people of my kingdom aren't hung up on these things. Have you heard of the temples in Khajuraho? They have very *explicit* carvings. Oh, I forgot." She peered at him. "The gurukul teaches brahmacharya until the age of twenty-five, right? Virtue, restraint, celibacy, etcetera. You're not even supposed to think of naked women, let alone look at them."

His lips tightened. "Just go."

She tossed her hair back with a self-satisfied smile. She should leave now. She'd won this round, hands down. But she couldn't resist one last zinger.

"But back when I was in the water, and you were talking to me . . . you were thinking of how I looked naked, weren't you?"

He finally turned his head and raked her with his eyes. A frisson ran through her at the touch of his gaze; had the night turned warmer? "You should not be here. You do not belong."

"Why? Because I am a woman?" she challenged. "Or because I am a *bondswoman*? In either case, you betray your own prejudice."

"You do not belong because you do not have the temperament," he stated. "Good night, lady."

She stalked away, muttering under her breath. Who did he think he was with that divinely muscled body, those perfect, bow-shaped lips, those eyelashes you could trip over? Arrogant, standoffish creature! She'd have liked to take him down a notch or two further. The worst part? She would have to give up the idea of bathing here at night again.

CHAPTER 5

THE NEXT MORNING FOUND THEM IN THE LECTURE HALL, a large, airy room in the main building with windows that looked out into the courtyard. The windowsills were covered with gardenia, lemon balm, and miniature jasmine plants. A soft, warm breeze blew into the room, carrying with it the fragrance of flowers and the scent of the small citrus tree that grew outside.

Katyani fought back a yawn as the Acharya's voice drifted into her ears like a lullaby. She'd been careful to sit behind the other students, but to her dismay the Acharya had risen and was circling the hall like a hawk, keeping them all in his sights.

"Spiritual energy is everywhere, in everything, because it comes from the five basic elements of nature: agni, vayu, jal, akash, and prithvi. Control yourself, and you control the elements. The two are related. Once you gain mastery over your thoughts, emotions, speech, and actions, even a blade of grass can become a weapon." The Acharya paused to cast a disparaging glance at them. "Not that any of you will achieve such a feat in a single lifetime."

How encouraging, thought Katyani, curbing her desire to ask him why. The Acharya reminded her of Shukla at his worst. Around her, pupils took notes, scribbling on parchments. Bhairav, she was pleased to see, was writing assiduously. Ayan was staring out of the window with a glazed expression on his face. She'd have to talk to him about paying attention in class.

"There are five restraints for proper conduct for a spiritual warrior," the Acharya droned on, pacing the lecture hall. "Ahimsa, the principle of nonviolence, should govern your lives. Satya, or truthfulness, must shape your words, thoughts, and deeds. You must practice asteya, and refrain from stealing. Take the vow of brahmacharya and remain chaste. Lastly, observe daya, compassion for all mortal beings."

Was he talking about normal people or those who lived in gurukuls? Did he have any idea what life was like outside these walls? Katyani raised her hand, unable to stop herself. She'd tried her best to stay awake and stay silent all through his monotonous monologue, but if she didn't speak now, she'd burst.

"Yes?" Acharya Mahavir frowned at her. Ayan and Bhairav perked up, as did the twelve other pupils. In one corner, seated in the lotus pose, Daksh opened his eyes. But he kept his gaze averted from her, looking instead at his father with polite interest.

"How do these principles apply in practice to a warrior?" she asked the Acharya. "Many of the pupils here are from royal families that wage war with neighboring kingdoms. I myself am a royal bodyguard. I have killed in the line of duty. How can we practice nonviolence and stay alive?"

Acharya Mahavir stroked his beard. "A question that displays your ignorance and lack of formal education. Would anyone like to answer?"

Katyani bristled. Calling her ignorant because she'd questioned him!

The other pupils looked down at their parchments, unwilling to risk saying the wrong thing.

The Acharya gave a contemptuous snort. "No one? Daksh, please answer."

Daksh stood and gave a respectful bow to the Acharya. What must it be like to have Acharya Mahavir for a father? To sit in one ethics class after another, year after year? It couldn't be easy. Uttam seemed comfortable in his role as the Acharya's heir, but Daksh was still a youngster. What did he dream of? What did he aspire to? Besides hanging on to his celibacy.

"The principle of ahimsa applies to everyone," he said, facing the students and speaking in a soft, modulated voice that carried through the lecture hall. "Do no harm to other creatures, and let no action of yours cause injury. However, you are allowed to defend yourself from harm. If, through your actions to protect yourself, harm comes to your attacker, the principle is not violated."

"What about war?" she challenged. "That's not the same as self-defense, is it? Not if you're the one who's the attacker."

He stiffened at the sound of her voice and looked at his father. *Look at me,* she wanted to say. *I won't bite.*

"You may answer," said Acharya Mahavir, waving his hand.

"War should be avoided, if possible," said Daksh, gazing at the floor. "Force is a last resort. If war is necessary, it must be a lawful and just war. The objective must be to defeat the wicked and obtain peace. Secondly, conduct during war must be moral. Weapons used must be appropriate and not cause excessive destruction and pain. Wounded and unarmed warriors should not be attacked. All noncombatants must be spared."

In what storybook world did these people live? "Anyone can persuade themselves their cause is just," she said. "Who decides which side is right? As for moral conduct during war, that disintegrates pretty quickly once your soldiers start dying around you. Have you ever been on an actual battlefield?"

His eyes flashed. "Have you?"

"Yes." Triumph filled her at having bested him in this argument. "Last year, I fought in a battle against invading Mongol horsemen. I was in Crown Prince Ayan's contingent."

Ayan gave her a conspiratorial smile. Queen Hemlata had not wanted either of them on the battlefield. But Ayan had persuaded King Jaideep to allow them to fight. It had only lasted a couple of days; they routed the Mongols on the borders of their kingdom and sent them packing.

But it had been more than enough. Sometimes, she could still smell the blood and hear the death cries of soldiers as they fell to enemy lances. War was not nice or glorious or *ethical.* It was heads being chopped, blood fountaining from severed limbs, piles of dead bodies littering the stained ground. And afterward, the funeral pyres, the stench of burning flesh. The only sentence Daksh had uttered that made any sense was that war should be avoided, if possible. The Mongols had not given them that choice.

"Any fool with a sword can fight," said Acharya Mahavir. "A true warrior never forgets the rules of moral conduct."

"But——" she began.

"Quiet!" he barked. "Let us continue the lesson."

She had a dozen more questions, but she sensed the Acharya was not used to being interrupted by his pupils. Having talked about the restraints, he launched into a lengthy explanation of the five virtues for proper conduct. Daksh returned to his post in the corner of the room, settling in the lotus pose once more. The perfect son, the perfect student. Was he anything more?

She stopped listening to the Acharya and wrote in her parchment instead, a coded message for the queen, giving her an update on the situation. She would beg the use of a messenger pigeon. Hemlata had asked her to write, and it was a way for Katyani to feel connected to her. She pictured Hemlata unfurling the parchment, lips moving as she decoded the message, smiling at the funny bits.

As she wrote, the sensation of being watched came over her. She raised her head and caught Daksh looking at her. Nor did he turn his gaze away even after being caught. His lips were pursed, his eyes flinty. Perhaps he was remembering their encounter last night. She gave him a sweet smile, and he turned his face away, reddening.

He was no match for her. She suppressed the laugh bubbling up inside her and turned her attention back to the letter. She wondered how her spies were getting on. She had personally trained two maids, a junior courtier, and a palace guard in covert operations. No point asking the queen about them, though. No one knew their identities apart from her and now Tanoj. But she would ask if there had been any more assassination attempts and if Garuda had found any leads. If only she was back in the palace where she belonged, keeping an eye on security, instead of wasting her time here on useless lectures.

The ethics lesson was followed by an introductory swords practice in the courtyard, which would have been fine except Katyani's stomach was growling by then. They'd already had yoga and meditation in the morning. And *nothing* to eat.

By this time, she knew the names of most of the other pupils. Not all of them were from royal families. The Acharya's gurukul was open to anyone who had the talent and desire to learn military and diplomatic arts. One pupil was from the nomadic sheep-herding community of Ku-maon, and another was the son of a leather worker from the Yadava king-dom. Two were from tribal forest villages to the north of Nandovana; they were reputed to be the best bowmen in the gurukul.

The heir of the Solanki kingdom was called Irfan; he was a slender, attractive young man with a cleft chin, hazel eyes, a thatch of curly black hair, and a permanent grin on his face. He kept staring at Katyani during swords practice. She knew of him through reports from her spies. He had a decent reputation, unlike his good-for-nothing younger brother.

Katyani had never had any suitors. She was bonded to the queen, after all, and was a member of Garuda to boot. No one dared look at her in the palace. Not in *that* way. But Irfan's eyes lingered on her in appraisal when they were sparring, making her a bit uncomfortable, until the teacher—a senior disciple called Jayesh—made him go spar with Ayan instead. She was paired with Irfan's cousin Nimaya, a tall, willowy girl with large, doe-like eyes and surprisingly good swordswomanship. Few royal fami-lies taught their daughters as well as they taught their sons, and Katyani's opinion of the western kingdom went up several notches.

When they finally broke for the noon meal, Katyani, Ayan, and Bhairav cheered along with some of the other pupils. Jayesh told them coldly that if they could not curb their enthusiasm for food, they might need to fast two days a week instead of one. They hung their heads and went to the dining hall, chastened.

Katyani decided to sit with the women disciples to see if she could glean more information about the gurukul—and also obtain some clean underwear. There were only four of them apart from herself and Nimaya. Two appeared to be in their fifties or sixties, but the other two were just a few years older than Katyani.

She bowed and introduced herself to the oldest, Atreyi, a short, plump woman with iron-gray hair coiled in a tight bun, deep-set eyes, a gener-ous mouth, and an air of utter calm.

Atreyi smiled and blessed her, right palm out. "It is always good to see talented young women here. Come to me if there are any problems, child."

"Ah, about that." Katyani explained her clothes predicament, leaving out any obvious references to underwear, not wanting to scandalize the senior-most lady of the gurukul.

Atreyi gave a nod of understanding, her lips twitching. "Go to the women's quarters after the meal, and Shalu will give you what you need."

Shalu was one of the younger women, small and slender in build, with hair that made up for it by being inordinately thick and long; she wore it in twin plaits that reached down to her lower back. She gave Katyani a quick smile and bowed, her eyes dancing, and Katyani smiled back, liking her at once. In fact, she liked the looks of all the women disciples—even Vinita, the other older woman, who had a stern, unsmiling mouth, and only gave a stiff nod in response to her bow.

"Have there always been so few women here?" she asked Atreyi as they stood against the wall, waiting for the Acharya to arrive. Around them, other disciples were clustered together, chattering among themselves. Bhairav and Ayan were standing with Irfan. They glanced at her and laughed at something he'd said. She ignored them.

Atreyi's face clouded. "There used to be far more women at one time. Nearly as many as the men. Then something tragic happened, and Acharya Mahavir stopped accepting women disciples."

Katyani's ears pricked up. Had there been some sort of scandal in this pristine place?

"Vinita and I were allowed to stay, as we were married to two of the male disciples at the time," Atreyi continued. "Sadly, they have now passed. Still, we are part of the gurukul, and the Acharya would not ask us to leave. As for Shalu and Barkha, they are orphans who were left at our gate as babies."

"I feel privileged to be here," remarked Nimaya, rolling her eyes at Katyani.

Atreyi smiled, oblivious to the sarcasm. "It is indeed a privilege, child. The Acharya never accepts more than one or two promising girls in any year. Nor can you return, unfortunately. The boys have the option of staying or returning year after year. The girls must be content with their single term."

Katyani suppressed a snort. She would never want to come back here. This place had too many rules and too few women. She missed the comforts of the palace, the maze of rooms and corridors, the gossip of the courtiers, and the hubbub of the audience hall. Most of all, she missed the queen: being able to talk with her whenever she wanted, sense her moods and emotions, answer unspoken little questions no one else could guess at. There was a constant undercurrent of anxiety in her now, not being able to sense Hemlata any longer.

Acharya Mahavir entered the dining hall, followed by his retinue, and she was unable to ask Atreyi about the tragic thing that had happened to make him close his gurukul to women.

The meal was far more austere than last night's—just yogurt, flatbread, and fruit. She ate quietly, sitting between Nimaya and Shalu, not wanting to draw attention to herself.

But she drew it anyway. She looked up to see Prince Irfan devouring her with his eyes from his place further up the table. He gave her a mischievous smile and raised his glass of water in a mock salute. What a fool. She wanted to box his ears.

"Clown," murmured Nimaya. "He can never resist a pretty girl. Ignore him, Katyani."

Katyani showed him her teeth. "I will beat him senseless if we're ever matched in martial arts."

"I would like to see that," said Nimaya.

Vinita, who was sitting on the other side of Nimaya, cleared her throat in warning, and they fell silent. That didn't stop Irfan from staring at her like she was a particularly delectable dessert. She wanted to throw something at him. She would have to await her opportunity in the training ground.

To her annoyance, Irfan wasn't the only one looking at her. Ayan and Bhairav kept trying to finger-talk with her from across the table. *The food's no good today. Did you see how I beat the Yadava prince in swords? Irfan's sister is stunning. Why are you sitting with the women?*

Shut up, she finally finger-spelled, and they subsided. She didn't want anyone else to notice their chatter. She was sure the rule of silence at mealtimes extended to nonverbal communication. Besides, the finger-talk was *their* secret; she didn't want Irfan observing it with his curious eyes.

That left Daksh. She'd avoided looking in his direction since the meal started, but a quick sideways check confirmed her suspicion. He was sitting beside the Acharya, eating. But his gaze alternated between her and Irfan, and a disapproving frown creased his forehead. He must have noticed Irfan trying to get her attention. She bent over her plate, struggling to focus on the food. If this was how meals were going to be, she'd get permanent indigestion. Why was Daksh interested in who was looking at her anyway? Did he think bondswomen didn't belong here, that she was a bad influence? That her mere presence was corrupting her fellow pupils?

This was what came of putting a pack of men together and telling them to practice celibacy. She wondered how many of them were actually celibate and how many were secretly in love with each other. Did the Acharya think men could not desire each other? Or did he think that only the desire between unwed men and women was unchaste? She pictured him coming upon two boys kissing in the library and suppressed a laugh.

At least they were allowed to get married after the age of twenty-five. Then they entered the next phase of life: grihastha, which implied marriage, family, and children. Of course, some disciples would skip this step and go straight to sannyasa, the renunciation of all worldly things. Daksh, for instance, was a born sannyasi.

After the meal, there was a two-hour break when pupils were free to rest or stroll around the courtyard. At three, they would have a class on warfare and at four, a martial arts lesson. After some weeks, the afternoons and evenings would be devoted to practical monster-banishing.

Katyani took advantage of the break to accompany Shalu to the women's dormitory to borrow some clothes. Nimaya tagged along. The Solanki princess was staying with the women. Irfan had a hut all to himself.

The women's building was small but better appointed than she had expected. There was a separate room for sleeping, with grass mats and sheets neatly arranged along the walls, and a separate room for studying, lined with bookshelves and decorated with lamps and cushions. In one corner was an old sitar, the polished wood gleaming in the sunlight that filtered in through the window.

"This is a nice space." Katyani gazed around in appreciation.

"You should stay with us," said Shalu, opening a cupboard full of linen. "We could easily make a bed for you here."

"I'm supposed to guard the princes," she said. "Sorry, I can't leave them." She didn't think they would be in any serious danger in the guru-kul; assassins were unlikely to have followed them to Nandovana, but it was best not to take any chances.

"You can come here in the evenings," said Nimaya, sitting on one of the cushions. "I play the sitar, and Atreyi tells us stories from the olden days of the gurukul."

"I'll do that," she promised. "Did she tell you about the tragedy that turned the Acharya against women?"

Nimaya and Shalu exchanged a glance. "It's really sad, so it's not some-thing we like to talk about, but I'll fill you in. Wait a minute." Shalu rooted about in the cupboard and emerged with a pile of underclothes and a spare robe. "Here, take these. Oh, this too." She held out a round sponge.

Katyani eyed it dubiously. "Is that for . . . ?"

"Periods," said Shalu. "It works well; you just have to make sure you clean it. Be careful when you take it out. They tend to spatter during heavy flow days. Better do it by the stream so you can clean yourself."

Ew. Katyani had originally packed some thick rags, but of course, she had none here, and it would be difficult washing them anyway. Perhaps the sponge *was* a better idea. "You were telling me about the tragedy," she reminded Shalu.

Shalu shut the cupboard and sat on a cushion next to Nimaya, waving at Katyani to join them. "It happened nearly eighteen years ago when I was a child," she said. "I pieced it together later. The Acharya's wife was a brilliant and beautiful woman. You've seen her sons; aren't they gorgeous? They got her looks—especially Daksh. But she passed away when we were all quite young. Uttam was five, like me, and Daksh was just one."

She'd been right about Daksh's age. "How did that turn the Acharya off women?" asked Katyani. "Broken heart?"

"Oh no, nothing like that," said Shalu. "I mean, of course he was sad. Everyone was. But things went on as usual. The gurukul women helped take care of his sons. Then rumors started that the Acharya was going to marry one of them, a woman called Devyani. Actually, Devyani herself started the rumors. She claimed she was the Acharya's mistress."

"What did he do?" asked Katyani, fascinated. She hadn't dreamed such sordid affairs were possible in this uptight, rigidly controlled environment. But people were people, even when you stuck them in a gurukul in the middle of a forest. They still had feelings and desires. They could fall in love, make terrible decisions, have their hearts broken.

"He threw her out," said Shalu. "Told her to leave and never show her face again."

"Oh, *harsh*."

Shalu shrugged. "He said she was lying, that he had no intention of remarrying, and she had tainted the memory of his dear wife. Everyone turned against Devyani. She had no option but to leave. But she cursed the Acharya before she left that she would be the end of him, no matter how many years it took. Unfortunately, she was killed in the forest that very night. Her body was found three days later, drained of blood."

"A vetala?" Katyani winced. It was a painful way to die. All the stories she'd read and heard about vetalas were unanimous on that score.

Shalu nodded. "They cremated her with the full rites, hoping to grant her spirit peace. But her spirit decided otherwise."

"She came back as a daayan to haunt the forest," burst out Nimaya. "She's been waiting all these years to suck the life force out of Acharya Mahavir. Isn't that awful?"

It was jaw-droppingly awful. Katyani's gut clenched in sympathy, both for the Acharya and his sons. Daayans were the restless spirits of wronged women who were unable to reincarnate until they had taken revenge. They were the most powerful monsters of all, with superhuman strength coiled in their long black hair and able to shapeshift at will. They served Goddess Kali and were impossible to kill. Even other monsters avoided them.

"How is he still alive?" asked Katyani.

"The Acharya has great spiritual power and control over the elements," said Shalu. "Maybe she's met her match in him. Or she's biding her time."

"Well, she died because of him," said Katyani. "He shouldn't have made her leave the gurukul alone."

"He acted without thinking," said Shalu. "That's why he makes self-control the basis of his curriculum today. I know that Barkha and I are alive only because of him. I also know that anytime anyone has a problem with yatu, vetalas, and pretas, they ask him for help. He never refuses, and he never charges fees. He has done a lot of good in this world."

Katyani didn't say anything, but it gave her chills to think how one mistake could determine your fate. No matter how much good the Acharya did, it would not lift the daayan's curse from his shoulders. No wonder Daksh was so repressed and weird. She would be, too, if she grew up hearing a story like that about her father.

The only stories she'd heard of her own parents were about their valor and loyalty. Hemlata had told her they'd both been excellent fighters in service to King Jaideep's father, Vishwadeep. They'd died beside their king and Prince Karandeep—Jaideep's half brother and the father of Bhairav and Revaa—in the war against the Paramara kingdom fifteen years ago. Jaideep had ascended the throne, and three-year-old Katyani had passed into the guardianship of the queen.

She wished she could remember her parents' faces. But the illness that nearly killed her had also robbed her of whatever memories she had. The first three years of her life were a blank; she had only Hemlata's words to fill those empty pages. She was lucky the queen had taken a personal interest in her. How many war orphans were adopted by the royal family? She would always be deeply grateful to the king and queen for taking her in.

At least Daksh still had a father. She hoped, for his sake, that Acharya Mahavir managed to stay out of the daayan's clutches.

She left the women's quarters a little later, meaning to find Ayan and Bhairav. But they weren't in the hut. She stashed her new clothes on the bed—they would make a decent pillow—and went out to look for them.

Several pupils were walking or sparring or sitting under the shade of the peepal tree. But the Chandela princes were nowhere in sight. Her chest tightened in anxiety as she scanned the courtyard. Where had they vanished?

"Lady, may I have the honor of a round? I hear you are excellent at sword fighting, and we didn't get much time to spar today."

Prince Irfan stood behind her, a hopeful smile on his face, his sword in his hand.

"I'm looking for Ayan and Bhairav," said Katyani.

"The princes have gone for a walk in the forest with Varun," said Irfan.

"What?" She pressed her lips together, annoyed. "I'm going after them."

"Wait!" Irfan made to reach out for her, but thought better of it when she gave him a warning frown. "Please don't venture into the forest without a senior disciple. They'll be back before the next class. Meanwhile, why not test your skills against mine?"

She was about to say no when she spied Daksh leaning against the trunk of the peepal tree, watching them with hooded eyes. Why not indeed. She'd show him this bondswoman could fight better than any prince. She withdrew her sword and fell into stance. "On guard." Without waiting for Irfan, she swung her blade in an overhead strike. His eyes widened, and he brought his sword up to block hers. But it was a feint; at the last moment, she danced away and swung her blade sideways to his neck. It stopped an inch from his throat. "Yield," she snapped.

He froze. "Um, I wasn't ready. Can we try again?"

"All right." She backed away a step, her body taut, her sword gripped in both hands. "Make your move."

He darted forward, striking his sword down on her shoulder. She leaned back and brought her own sword down on his with all her force. Before he could react, she slid the tip of her blade over his, all the way to his throat. "Yield," she repeated.

"Once more?" he pleaded with a winning smile. "I'd like to try a different move, Katya."

How dare he address her with such familiarity? She sheathed her blade, seething. "No. And I did not give you leave to address me by that name."

"What must I do to earn the privilege?" he asked.

He was persistent; she had to give him that. And he didn't appear to mind that she had bested him. This was a point in his favor. Some men hated to be bested by a woman. In the palace training ground, they'd learned to avoid her. Still, she was uninterested in letting him "earn" any sort of privilege with her.

She turned away, not deigning to answer, and stared right into Daksh's face. Her pulse quickened.

"I must pair you with a more skillful fighter in tomorrow's class," he said, giving her an appraising look.

"I *am* a skillful fighter," protested Irfan. "Katyani is just having a better day than me."

Daksh frowned. "Only those who have better days survive an actual fight, Prince. Those were very basic moves. Pay attention in tomorrow's session—*both* of you."

"Tomorrow is fast day," said Katyani, recovering her voice. "My stomach will be growling too loudly for me to pay attention to anything."

Irfan gave a snort of laughter, quickly suppressed.

"You may have to fight hungry at some point," said Daksh. "Think of it as training for that day." He walked away before she could think of a clever retort. She made a face at his retreating back.

Ayan and Bhairav sauntered through the gate with Varun. Relief flooded her. She marched up to the princes and scolded them until they squirmed and apologized, promising not to venture into the forest again without her.

"Katya has been sparring with me," piped up Irfan from behind her. "She's just as good as you said, Ayan."

Ayan gave her a sly wink. "Is it *Katya* already?"

Katyani gave Irfan a sweet smile. "If you address me with such familiarity again, Prince Irfan, I will break your royal nose. Ask the princes of Chandela if you doubt me for one second."

Irfan's hand flew to his face. "Not my nose! It's my best feature. She's trying to scare me, isn't she?" he appealed to the princes.

"She can beat us both," assured Bhairav. "And she's quite heartless. You're better off trying to flirt with a stone, Irfan. At least it won't jump up and brain you."

A gong sounded for the next lesson. Katyani hurried to where the rest of the disciples were gathered under the peepal tree, thankful the silly conversation had been cut short. She didn't want Irfan getting any ideas about her. The only reason she'd sparred with him had been because Daksh was watching and she wanted to impress him with her sword fighting skills. And then she was annoyed with herself for wanting to impress Daksh in the first place. It didn't matter how skilled and accomplished she was. In his eyes, she was a bondswoman, tainted by forbidden magic. She'd best get over it and put him out of her mind.

CHAPTER 6

DAYS TURNED INTO WEEKS, AND THE WARMTH OF SPRING into the heat of summer. The pupils settled into a routine of meditation, ethics, sparring, and weapons training. The mangoes in the grove ripened, and the youngest disciples were given the task of harvesting them. For days afterward, the delicious yellow fruit was served as a dessert after the noon meal.

A trio of senior disciples accompanied Katyani and the princes on horseback to their abandoned carriage so they could retrieve their belongings. First, though, they had the grim task of giving the last rites to the remains of the poor coachman. The yatu corpses had vanished, presumably retrieved by their clan members. There wasn't much of the coachman left either; wild animals and natural decay had taken what the yatu had left uneaten. They found a hand, a rib cage with some bits of torn cloth, and a gray shank bone. They built a pyre and spoke the words to give peace to the departed. Afterward, they burned what was left of the horses too.

Katyani still chafed at the rigid rules that dictated how they spent nearly every waking moment, but, to her surprise, she gradually got used to them. Even more surprising, she got used to being disconnected from Hemlata. The silence within her, so strange and upsetting at first, became natural. She still worried about the queen, but Hemlata's reply to her letter assuaged the worst of her fears. Everything at the palace was fine, there had been no more assassination attempts, and no more leads either. *Do well and take care of the princes,* her letter concluded, so Katyani tried to do just that. She'd pick up the investigation when she returned home.

She enjoyed the sparring and weapons training, even though she continued to have a hard time staying awake during lectures. Sometimes she fell asleep even during the meditation hour.

Fast days were the worst. She trained herself to expect only two simple meals a day, but her stomach rebelled at the prospect of no food at all. Ayan and Bhairav took to stealing mangoes from the grove, but unfortunately they were caught by Uttam and punished by having to endure an extra fast day. Ayan bore it stoically, but she had to smuggle a flatbread to Bhairav to keep him from falling apart. At least Bhairav was loving all the classes. He even took permission to visit the library to pore over all their old manuscripts. Ayan, like Katyani, preferred the physical training.

She hated having to get up at four in the morning if she wanted a dip in the pool, but she didn't want Daksh to catch her breaking the rules again. He'd report her for sure, and she wouldn't even have the excuse of not knowing what the bathing hours were.

Fifteen pupils in the class, and he seemed to have marked her for special attention. He always sat in one corner of the lecture hall, keeping her in his sights in an indirect I'm-not-really-looking-at-you way.

Or perhaps that was just her overactive imagination. The memory of his direct gaze heated her insides, and she tried not to dwell on it. He taught a few of the sword classes, and they turned out to be some of the most interesting ones, because he made sure she was paired with the best sword fighters in his class.

In kalari, or empty-handed sparring, she was often matched with Nimaya, who wasn't anywhere near as competent as she was. The men were reluctant to spar with her, especially after she'd beaten them a few times. Spearplay and stick-fighting were harder, but she gradually improved her skills.

Archery was fun, even though it wasn't her favorite sport, because it was highly competitive. Everyone tried—and failed—to match the skills of the two bowmen from the tribal forest villages. The Acharya asked them to demonstrate before every class so the rest knew what they were up against. They had nerves of steel; each time, their arrows hit the mark, no matter how far away and tiny the target was. Ayan was pretty good—although nowhere near as good as them—but Bhairav was among the worst; his arrows were likelier to end up embedded in trees than the targets painted in the courtyard wall.

It became clear there was more to archery than any one of them had dreamed when the Acharya demonstrated his arrows of fire and rain. His lips shaped the words of a mantra, and he shot an arrow into the sky, releasing an explosion of fire midair. As the pupils scurried to take shelter, he shot another arrow, quenching the fire and soaking them all in a deluge of water.

"Every ordinary arrow can be transformed into a weapon of mass destruction," he proclaimed as they stood before him, drenched and dazed. "Your aim must be true and your intent pure. Never use these arrows against someone who is of a lower skill level than you. Nor must you share the mantras to summon them with anyone outside the gurukul. If you misuse this power, you will be cursed."

That was assuming they would be able to use it in the first place. Only those with great spiritual control could work such transformations. They spent every archery class after that trying their utmost, but not one of them managed so much as a spark of fire or a drop of water. That didn't stop the Acharya from making them practice for hours on end every week. "The mantra is embedded in your mind already," he told them after a particularly frustrating afternoon spent shooting and retrieving hundreds of arrows. "You must summon the weapon with your soul."

Which didn't help at all. Katyani suspected that out of all his pupils, only Daksh and Uttam had the ability to summon such weapons. Good thing, too. Such power was dangerous, curse or no curse.

One afternoon, when they were resting after an exhausting kalari session, a disciple popped into their hut to tell Katyani the Acharya required her presence in the library.

"Oh no," said Bhairav, propping himself up on his pallet. "Should we prepare for your last rites?"

"What have you done this time?" chimed in Ayan, fanning himself from his corner.

"Nothing!" She went to the library, butterflies in her stomach, wondering if Daksh had finally told his father how she'd hit him that first night. The gurukul had a tiered system of punishment. Extra fast days were imposed for most minor offenses, but more serious transgressions could result in a whipping. Katyani hadn't seen anyone whipped, but the threat was enough to make the most arrogant disciple toe the line.

The library was on the second floor of the main building, accessed by narrow wooden steps that spiraled up the exterior, next to the citrus tree. She inhaled the sweet, lemony scent of the tree as she climbed, and it calmed her a little.

Midway up the winding staircase was a large, airy room with multiple windows, which covered the entire second story of the building. Floor-to-ceiling shelves stuffed with books and scrolls ran the length of the walls. In one corner was an ancient teak desk, laden with parchment, quills, and ink. The middle of the room was bare apart from grass mats and cushions. The Acharya was seated on one of the mats, Atreyi on his right.

"Sit," said the Acharya brusquely, waving Katyani to a cushion opposite. She sat cross-legged, trying to quell her nervousness. Atreyi gave her an encouraging smile, which heartened her.

"You are the first person with a magical bond I have accepted in my gurukul," said the Acharya. "I wish to observe your tattoo. From a *distance*," he added, as her hand flew to her neck in mingled suspicion and alarm. No one had ever dared ask her this before. Hemlata would have punished such intrusive curiosity back in the palace.

But Katyani was not in the palace, and the queen had told her to do nothing to anger the Acharya.

Reluctantly, she let her hand fall from her neck. Ten minutes of concentrated glaring followed. Katyani bore their combined scrutiny in silence. A warm breeze blew into the room from the open windows, and the scent of citrus mingled with the smell of old books and faded ink. No wonder Bhairav enjoyed spending time here.

At last, the Acharya withdrew his gaze. He pressed a hand to his forehead, as if it hurt. "Tell me about your family."

Katyani was floored. Of all the questions he could have asked her, this was the most unexpected. "My parents were subjects of the old king of Chandela. They were killed in the war with Malwa fifteen years ago."

"What were their names?"

"Mala and Dinesh," she said, her bewilderment increasing.

"Surname, please," said the Acharya.

Her face grew warm. "I never asked." Why was he so interested in them?

He raised his eyebrows. "And the queen never told? Very well. What about your extended family? Uncles, aunts, cousins?"

She shook her head, shifting awkwardly on her cushion. "I don't have anyone. Acharya, why are you asking me about my family?"

"The more pertinent question is, why have *you* not asked her more about them?" said the Acharya.

She stared at him, unable to answer. Why had she not asked the queen for more details? She didn't understand it. Nor did she understand the purpose of his prodding, unless it was to make her feel bad about her lack of curiosity. "They were vassals," she said at last. "I'm lucky to have been adopted by the queen."

He tugged his beard, making it even more untidy. "Luck has little to do with it. Do you remember anything of your life before you were bonded by the queen of Chandela?"

"No," she said. "I was so ill I nearly died. The illness took away my memory."

"A very neat coincidence, no?" His eyes bored into hers. "Your parents die and you lose your memory, just when she binds you?"

She shot to her feet, trying not to shake as anger coursed through her. What was he implying? "Acharya, I know you don't like the queen, that you disapprove of what she did. But she did it to save my life."

"I have made you uncomfortable," said the Acharya. "*Good.* Sometimes, we must be shaken out of our comfort to question the things we've been told. Go, Katyani. But one day, when you have the courage, ask your queen who you really are."

She didn't need to ask anyone who she was. And she wouldn't let the Acharya fill her with any doubt on the matter. "I am Katyani," she bit out. "Royal bodyguard of Chandela, protector of the king and queen. That's all I need to know."

The Acharya opened his mouth, but Atreyi laid a hand on his arm. "Enough." Her voice was soft but authoritative. To Katyani's surprise, the Acharya subsided.

"You may go," he said, sounding tired.

Katyani left, her thoughts in a whirl. How dare he talk to her like that! It was none of his business. But . . . what *was* her family name? Did she truly not have any living relatives? Why had no one talked to her of her parents apart from the queen?

When she returned to the hut, Ayan pounced on her. "Are you in trouble? Did he kick you out?"

"Stop it," said Bhairav, watching her. "She'll tell us if she wants to."

She threw him a grateful look. "Everything is fine. I just need some time to myself."

Bhairav dragged Ayan out for an extra round of archery practice, which was pretty heroic of him considering how little he enjoyed it.

Katyani collapsed on her mat and stared at the roof. Questions roiled within her. She missed Hemlata more than ever. If only the queen were in front of her, she could vent to her about the Acharya.

If she couldn't vent in person, she could at least vent on paper. She got up, grabbed a quill and a blank parchment from Bhairav's stash, and wrote the queen a coded letter, describing what had happened. Then she rolled it up tightly, sealed it with hot wax, and dropped it off at the gurukul dovecote to be sent by the next available messenger pigeon.

In the month of Jyeshtha, when the heat was at its peak, the Acharya announced that his sons would lead a vetala-banishing expedition, choosing a few pupils each. Apparently, the vetalas had become a menace, threatening forest villages on the outskirts of Nandovana. The only way to get rid of them was to perform the proper funerary rites, releasing the evil spirits from the dead bodies they were occupying.

Uttam chose Ayan, Nimaya, and three older disciples. Ayan beamed as his name came up, and pumped a fist into the air.

"I will accompany Crown Prince Ayan," said Katyani, frowning at him.

"Why, do you not trust me to protect him?" asked Uttam, his voice gentle.

Well, of course she did, but——

"I don't need you hovering around me all the time, Katya," said Ayan.

"Besides, you're coming with me," said Daksh.

Katyani's jaw dropped. "I am?" She hadn't expected him to choose her.

He knitted his brows. "Unless you do not wish to learn how to banish vetalas?"

"Of course I wish to learn," she said hastily.

Daksh chose Irfan as well as Varun and two other disciples called Sagar and Lavraj. Bhairav, to his relief, was not chosen at all.

They set off on their expedition the following evening, since vetalas were only active at night. At the gate, the two groups diverged, Uttam's to the east and Daksh's to the west.

It was the first time they had ventured into the forest at dusk. The evening light filtered through the trees as they walked, and a koel called, its voice sweet and piercing. The air was thick and warm, heavy with the smell of damp earth, crushed leaves, sap, and ripe fruit. Katyani's heart lifted. It was good to be out of the gurukul, even if it was to hunt the bloodsucking evil dead.

Irfan walked beside her, chattering like a monkey. She'd beaten him several times in both kalari and swordplay, and yet he remained by her side like a cheerful, oblivious pest. Why had Daksh chosen them both for this expedition? It was certainly not because he liked her or respected Irfan's skills.

She trotted ahead, past Varun and the others, and caught up with Daksh. "Why did you pick me?" she asked. "It can't be because you like my company."

He did not look at her or respond, but kept striding at the same even pace, staring at the trees ahead.

"Vetala-hunting requires stamina and skill," came Varun's smooth voice behind her. "Liking or not liking a person does not factor in such a choice."

She sighed. "Are you his mouthpiece, Varun? Do you always speak for him? Why can he not speak for himself?"

"Airya Daksh has taken a vow of silence today," said the insufferable

Varun. "He will not speak, except for the last rites to subdue the vetalas. This will make the last rites more effective."

"What?" She peered at Daksh's immovable face. "How did I not know this? Oh, right. He hardly talks anyway. But how is he going to teach us vetala-hunting without speaking a word?"

"By *doing*," said Varun. "I will do any talking necessary. Please follow our example closely and try not to make any noise. Vetalas have excellent hearing."

"I bet I can make you break your vow," she murmured to Daksh, and was pleased to see his lips tighten. Really, it was *his* fault for picking her.

She stepped back to join Irfan, but Varun stopped her. "You will walk between us, lady, being the weakest member of the group."

What ridiculously patriarchal thinking! And that too after months of seeing her outperform the men. "I'm *not* the weakest member of the group," she snapped. "That's Prince Irfan."

"She's definitely stronger than me," admitted Irfan. "Maybe we can both walk in the middle."

"You were attacked by a vetala on your way here, weren't you?" she asked.

Irfan nodded, his face darkening. "It dropped down from a tree and latched on to my throat." He lowered the collar of his robe and raised his neck. "See?"

There was a red, puckered scar at the base of his throat, right where his artery was. He'd nearly died from that encounter. And yet, Daksh had chosen him. Why?

As if he sensed her unspoken question, Irfan said, "I asked to join any vetala-hunting expeditions as soon as I recovered. I need to learn how to deal with them. The Solanki kingdom is plagued by monsters of all kinds. The people expect their prince to lead by example."

Varun gave an approving grunt, and Katyani was impressed. Irfan was no coward.

An hour passed, and the darkness deepened. An owl hooted from the branches of a sal tree. The moon peeked out, bathing the forest in silver light. Irfan hummed tunelessly until Varun told him to be quiet. Katyani was beginning to feel bored when Daksh held up a hand. They all stopped. A huge banyan tree loomed before them, its thick branches dropping aerial roots to the ground.

"Why have we stopped here?" whispered Katyani to Varun, who was standing behind her and Irfan.

"Banyan trees almost always have a vetala," said Varun.

"Only one?" said Katyani. "How do you know there aren't any more?"

"Vetalas are solitary creatures as a rule," murmured Varun. "Quiet now."

Katyani fell silent, watching Daksh as he advanced closer to the tree. This should be interesting. There weren't many vetalas in the vicinity of Ajaigarh. Forests were their habitat of choice. But it would be useful to know how to neutralize one. Vetalas could suck a man dry in fifteen agonizing minutes. As for children, they practically inhaled those.

Irfan gripped the hilt of his sword, his face set. She wanted to tell him it would be fine, that one vetala was no match for five swords, when a slight whooshing sound alerted her. She took a step back, bumping into Varun, breath trapped in her chest. Everyone's hands went to their swords.

A vetala descended from the tree and crouched among the roots at its base. It was a thin creature with long, spindly limbs, wild gray hair, and fish-white skin. Its dead black eyes were empty of pupils or irises. Elongated canines poked out of its red mouth. It hissed at them, repulsive and pitiful.

Daksh flicked his wrist and spoke a complicated phrase that Katyani couldn't catch. Several aerial roots jerked down from the tree, transforming into thin, silver ropes as they snapped around the creature, binding its limbs. It howled in pain and anger.

"How did he do that?" asked Katyani in awe. She'd never seen such a cool bit of magic. Every time she thought she knew the extent of his powers, Daksh proved her wrong.

"It's a mantra known only to the Acharya and his sons," said Varun, a bit wistfully. "He can transform even grass into those ropes. Nothing can escape them."

Daksh withdrew a gourd from his knapsack and sprinkled a few drops of water from it onto the ground. He murmured under his breath, reciting the last rites for the soul trapped in the dead body before them.

The vetala stopped struggling against its bonds and smiled at them.

Somehow, that smile was worse than its howls. "Good evening, gentlemen and lady," it said in a velvet voice. "I am privileged to have such company grace my humble tree."

Katyani started. She knew vetalas could speak, but they rarely did.

"I see one among you whose blood my kin have tasted." Its inhuman eyes fixed on Irfan. "Very sweet it was, my kin told me."

Irfan took a step forward. "I'm not afraid of you," he said through gritted teeth.

"But if I were not bound, and you were alone, you would be." The vetala looked at Daksh. "I see one among you that is a liar. Even as he recites the funerary rites, his mind is elsewhere."

Daksh stumbled on his words, then continued whispering the last rites. What did the vetala mean? What was Daksh thinking about, if not the vetala?

The vetala looked at her. "I see one who is doomed. Lady, you will suffer so much. Why not let me take away the pain before it comes?"

Oh, great. A vetala had looked into her future and found pain. What a lovely thing to look forward to. She thought back to what the Acharya had said about the queen, the questions he'd asked about her family, and a deep unease took hold of her.

Irfan grabbed her hand. "Don't listen to it."

"Why not?" said the vetala. "You know I cannot lie. Let me give you another gift. You will be king one day, and yet, you will not get what you truly want."

"Shut up already," snapped Irfan.

"Calm down," said Varun. "It tries to agitate us, to delay its own demise."

The vetala looked at Varun. "I see one among you who will never amount to anything. You will live your life out in mediocrity, and when you die, no one will mourn."

Varun could not suppress a gasp.

Daksh shot them a look of warning and continued with the last rites.

"The day is coming soon when she will get what she desires," said the vetala, peering up at Daksh. "On that day, you will become an orphan. On that day, you will long for oblivion."

The daayan, thought Katyani, her stomach twisting. *It means the daayan.*

But this time, the words did not appear to affect Daksh. He walked closer to the vetala and threw a few drops of water at its face. It cringed, as if the water hurt its dead skin.

Yet, at that moment, something in its expression changed, becoming craftier, almost triumphant. Its eyes flicked up, a minute movement that would have eluded Katyani except she'd been watching for it.

Her gaze shot upward. She saw the *other* vetala just before it fell on Daksh.

She threw herself forward with a wordless cry, knocking Daksh to the ground and rolling away. The vetala landed beside them, hissing in frustration at the near miss. It launched itself on her and pinned her to the ground, talons digging into her arms. A red, rotten mouth with glistening canines opened in a snarl right above her face, nearly knocking her out with its disgusting stench. She wrenched her face away as it swooped down on her neck. The first vetala, still bound in silver ropes, began to laugh, a dry, hacking sound that set her teeth on edge.

A golden sword pierced her attacker's throat. The vetala went limp, collapsing on top of her. She gagged at the reek and feel of its blood, trickling down her body. Daksh kicked the vetala aside and pulled her up, his face distraught. "Your sword!" he shouted, and she was galvanized into action.

Around them, *five* more vetalas dropped to the ground, uttering warlike shrieks.

Irfan and the others fell into the sword dance, hacking at the monsters. Vetalas were hideously strong and difficult to kill.

"Katyani," cried Daksh from the other side of a prop root where he was fighting off two vetalas at once. "Watch out!"

She thwacked a vetala on the side of its head with the flat of her blade, stunning it, and leaped aside as yet another vetala dropped down from the tree, its talons out, its canines gleaming in the moonlight. How many of the bloodsuckers had hidden in the banyan, lying in wait for them? It growled and slashed at her face, scratching her neck even as she stumbled away from it.

Pain seared her throat; she gasped and gripped her sword, waiting. As the vetala flew toward her with inhuman speed, she stabbed it in the chest with all her strength. The blade went through it and came out the other side. The vetala struggled on her sword, its pale hands wrapped around the blade. She hung on in desperation, her arms twisting, trying to keep the vetala off.

The creature grinned, blood dripping from its mouth. "You will lose all you love," it rasped. "You will long for death. You will forget who you are. You will remember me then."

Her insides shriveled at its poisonous words. She jerked her blade out and staggered back. Dark red blood gushed from the vetala's ruined chest. It fell to the ground, still giving her that ghastly grin.

She dropped to her knees, exhausted, supporting herself with the sword, trying to get her breath back. Trying to unhear what she had heard.

Around her, the fight continued. Three vetalas lay unmoving on the ground. A fourth had pinned Varun to the banyan's gnarly trunk and was about to latch on to his neck. Daksh's blade glinted in the moonlight and decapitated the vetala in one swift stroke. On the other side of the tree, Irfan and Sagar were battling the two remaining vetalas.

Katyani hauled herself to her feet and rushed forward to help them. She stabbed one of the vetalas in the back—a cowardly move, but she was past caring about such niceties, and it wasn't as if they were alive to begin with.

The last vetala leaped on her back, toppling her to the ground. She fell face-first, tasting dirt, as the creature wrapped its long fingers around her neck and squeezed. The sword dropped from her hand. She grabbed the cruel fingers, trying to pry them away from her neck. But the vetala was too strong for her; she choked and gagged, struggling to free herself, struggling to breathe as panic roiled through her.

The golden blade flashed again, and the vetala's head rolled away. She sat up, taking huge gasps of air, her hand on her neck. Daksh stood above her, looking both disapproving and concerned. "You shouldn't have thrown yourself on me," he said in a stern voice. "Very risky."

Impossible creature. Couldn't he say *thank you* like a normal person and then she could thank him back? She swallowed and managed, "Oh? So you wanted me to let the vetala kill you?"

He sheathed his sword. "I had things perfectly under control."

"Yeah, right." She didn't even have the strength to roll her eyes. "Is everyone else alive?"

There was a chorus of moans and grunts as the disciples picked themselves off the ground. Irfan was bleeding from multiple wounds—they all were, except Daksh. Even Varun was battered and entirely speechless for once. No one had expected an entire community of vetalas in the banyan tree.

"Time to do the last rites," said Daksh grimly. "Varun, Sagar, help me."

It took over an hour to do them all. Daksh tied up the remains of the vetalas with his magic ropes, including the heads and limbs he had chopped off. The senior disciples went around, sprinkling water and murmuring ritualistic words over the grisly tableau.

Irfan and Katyani sat some distance away, watching. Daksh had killed most of the vetalas, and yet he barely looked winded. His hair was mussed up, but that was it. Even his robes were still more or less clean. Katyani gazed at him in mingled admiration and envy. Her robe was soaked in vetala blood and some of her own as well. Her face and neck were puffy and raw. Her arms, where vetala talons had dug into them, were red and swollen. Irfan looked as terrible as she felt.

"So did you learn anything?" she asked him, trying not to scratch her face.

"Yeah," he muttered. "I learned I'll never get what I most want."

"At least you'll be king," she said. "That'll soften the blow. I'll just suffer pain. That's it, that's my fate." That was the prophecy they had all heard; only she had heard the damning words of the second vetala.

"You know they don't tell everything, right?" he said. "Not even the most important stuff."

She didn't answer. *You will lose all you love,* it had said. That was pretty unambiguous. She thought of Ayan, Bhairav, Revaa, Hemlata, and Jaideep. Her family, her home, her life. And she thought of that other family she had lost, the one she'd never asked the queen about until the Acharya needled her with his pointed, painful questions and she was driven to write that letter—a letter that remained unanswered.

She'd already lost everything once. How could anyone lose everything twice? There ought to be a karmic law against it.

Daksh and the senior disciples finished the last rites and dragged the vetala remains further away from the tree. At a word from Daksh, the bodies caught fire. He looked at her then, as if to check on her, and she tried to smile, but it probably came out more like a grimace.

They stayed to make sure the bodies burned properly and no stray embers ignited the underbrush or the trees. When nothing but ash and bone fragment was left, they turned homeward. Dawn broke, fingers of light shooting across the eastern sky. She'd never been so grateful to see morning before.

They started back for the gurukul, and she found herself walking with Daksh behind the others. She stole a glance at his face, but it was once again a serene mask of indifference. Well, she knew how to get a reaction from him at least.

"Airya Daksh?"

"What?" he said, not looking at her.

"I made you break your vow of silence."

"No, you didn't," he said. "That was because of the vetalas."

"You're a liar," she teased. "That's what it called you. What are you lying about? Maybe you secretly like me after all."

Daksh shot her a look of loathing and strode ahead to join Varun. She would have laughed then, but her face hurt too much.

CHAPTER 7

JUST BEFORE ŞHRAAVANA, IN THE CUSP BETWEEN SUMMER and monsoon, Acharya Mahavir set the first-year pupils a test. They had to go into the forest, seek a place of solitude, and meditate without food or water for three days. Apparently, this would boost their spiritual power no end.

"Is he human?" asked Bhairav. "I mean, he does remember *we* have human bodies?"

It was afternoon, the time of rest between classes. They were lying inside the hut, recovering after a strenuous sword fighting class.

"I think he's forgotten what it's like to have an ordinary body," said Ayan. "The senior disciples say he can go weeks without food and water. Like one of the legendary Astomi who could survive by smelling flowers and apples."

"Well, I can't," said Bhairav. "I need to eat the flowers and apples. You'll have to tell the queen I failed."

"It's only for three days, Bhav; you can do it," said Katyani, thinking of Hemlata. Had she received Katyani's letter about what the Acharya had said? Why hadn't she responded? She'd replied to the first letter quickly enough. What was going on in the palace?

As time passed, the Acharya's questions about her family had taken root in Katyani's mind and grown larger, more insistent. If only the queen would reply with some simple answers. Tell her, *This is your surname. This is why you have no cousins, no uncles or aunts. This is why no one else in the palace talks of them.* Then she could finally let it go. Her tattoo itched, and she got up, restless.

"The monsoon is nearly here," said Ayan. "If it rains, water's sure to trickle into our mouths through *no fault of our own.*"

"What about vetalas and yatu?" demanded Bhairav. "Suppose they attack while we're meditating?"

"That's part of the test, right?" said Ayan. "Anyway, we've had plenty of practice."

This was true. The Acharya had given them both theoretical and practical lessons on vanquishing a variety of monsters. Even Bhairav had been dragged to a vetala hunt and a preta-expelling ritual. Pretas were invisible ghosts, more to be pitied than feared. They generally didn't interfere much with humans, beyond trying to impede them from achieving their goals. But their presence reduced the power available to a spiritual warrior. It was important to learn how to sense and banish them. The only monster they hadn't covered was the pishacha, a creature so rare it hadn't been glimpsed in decades.

"Think of it this way," said Katyani. "Pass or fail, we just have a few weeks left. Then we can go home and forget this place."

"I'll never forget it," said Bhairav. "I'll have nightmares for years."

Katyani chuckled and strolled out to sit on the porch. She could fool the princes, but she couldn't fool herself. She wouldn't forget this place either. Or its people. Well, *one* person in particular. Part of her was relieved to be returning to the palace soon. She wanted to reconnect with her spies and grill them on the progress they'd made in uncovering the assassination plot. Until it was solved, she wouldn't be at ease.

She was also looking forward to being reunited with the queen. Hemlata would not be able to avoid answering her questions when they were face-to-face. And the bond would not allow the queen to hide her emotions for long. Besides, Ajaigarh was *home*. The prospect of catching up on court intrigues, seeing Chaya again, having a proper bath, and eating her favorite foods filled her with pleasurable anticipation.

But another part of Katyani was loath to leave. She'd never get the chance to come back. The stark simplicity of gurukul life had grown on her, despite the ridiculous bath times and rigid rules. The past few months had flown by faster than she would have believed possible. The training had been hard but fair. All of them were tougher, mentally and physically, than when they had started out. Her swordswomanship had improved, as had her kalari.

Irfan hadn't stopped flirting and trying to find ways of being alone with her, but because of Nimaya, they had become friends. Once they left the gurukul, she doubted she would see either of them again.

Daksh remained . . . Daksh. Scarcely speaking, never smiling, always perfectly self-contained. She loved cracking that cool, collected exterior of his and took the chance whenever she got it. That morning during spearplay, he had helped them adjust their stances under the Acharya's eagle eye, and she had asked him innocently to show her the correct pose. He couldn't ignore her then; he had to demonstrate the pose and move her limbs when she failed to copy him. He had been perfectly courteous about it, but the tips of his ears had gone red. She'd given him a big wink at the end when the Acharya was looking elsewhere, making him drop his spear, which had delighted her.

Once, she'd seen him sitting under the peepal tree in the courtyard, jotting notes in a bundle of parchment corded together like a book. Consumed by curiosity, she'd inched up to him from behind the tree trunk, congratulating herself on her excellent spying skills, when he'd snapped his notebook closed and said, in a smug tone, "Do you always sneak up on people so loudly?"

It must have been the gurukul robe she was wearing that alerted him. It *swished*. "What are you writing?" she'd asked point-blank, but he hadn't answered, just given her a superior smile and tucked the notebook in a pocket, making her wish she could pounce on him and snatch it away.

After that, she kept trying to get a glimpse of its contents, sidling up to him whenever he took it out. One afternoon, he was distracted by another pupil while it was open in his hand, and she craned her neck forward and caught the words "wood ear" in his small, neat handwriting, which made no sense. He closed it at once, giving her a reproving look, and her curiosity remained sadly unsatisfied. It must be a secret diary of some sort. She spent hours daydreaming about its contents, wondering if she featured in it at all.

A month of training left, and they would be gone. She would miss Daksh. Yes, why not admit it to herself? She would miss this beautiful, shy, aloof man whose gaze could turn her insides molten. Her lips twitched as she wondered how he would react if she told him that. Go the color of beetroot, probably.

A shadow fell on her, and she looked up. Talk of the devil. Daksh stood before her, blocking the sun. "Yes, Airya? To what do I owe the pleasure of your regard?"

"Tomorrow's test is an important one," he said, his face serious. "You should meditate today in preparation."

She peered at him. "I should meditate to prepare for meditation? You're joking, right? Oh, wait. You don't joke. In that case," she grinned and patted the porch next to her, "meditate with me."

He lowered his gaze and turned away.

Don't go, she thought.

"You should visit our palace when our training is complete," she said to his back. "The princes and I will show you our favorite haunts. The Ajaigarh street food is fantastic, and our festivals are the talk of Bharat. I may even take you to the temples of Khajuraho, if that doesn't disturb your state of brahmacharya." She snapped her mouth closed, surprised at herself. What had made her blurt out such an invitation?

"I'll never leave the gurukul," he muttered, still facing away from her, his back rigid.

She bristled. "Oh? Why not? Is the world too evil for you?"

"I have my duty," he said in clipped tones, and walked away.

Duty. Weren't they all burdened by it? The king and queen, with the weight of a kingdom on their shoulders. Ayan, with the prospect of a future crown. Herself, charged with the safety of the royal family. Daksh and Uttam, tied to the gurukul and their father as surely as she was tied to the queen.

She remembered the daayan and the words the vetala had spoken to Daksh: *The day is coming soon when she will get what she desires. On that day, you will become an orphan. On that day, you will long for oblivion.*

He'd never brought it up—none of them had. But what must have gone through him to hear the fate of his father laid out in such cold, clear terms? Her chest tightened in sympathy.

That night, they had what would be their last meal for the next three days. Senior disciples watched them with sharp eyes to ensure they didn't overeat or steal any food. But the rules had been drilled into them long enough that Katyani didn't dream of slipping a flatbread into her pocket. It had been months since she'd felt compelled to do that. Even Bhairav ate just slightly more than usual. It was quite a feast: chickpea curry, flatbread, eggplant, nuts, yam chips, and steamed rice with mango pickle.

At the end of the meal, the Acharya rose to give them their instructions. "You will leave at five in the morning," he announced. "All fifteen of you must set off in different directions. Walk for an hour or ten, however long it takes for you to find your spiritual center. Whether you choose a tree, a cave, or a water body, make sure it is unoccupied. Do not disturb any nature spirits. If a yaksha is present, beg forgiveness and seek another spot. Sit in the lotus position and meditate. You must not eat or drink or speak. Return when three days have passed."

"How will we know when three days are over?" asked Katyani. Daksh, standing behind the Acharya, looked up at the sound of her voice. "Time passes differently in a trance." Not that she intended to meditate and starve for three days. Nor did she intend to let the princes wander off in a different direction from her if she could help it.

"We will find you," answered the Acharya. She opened her mouth to argue, but Nimaya dug an elbow into her side, and she fell quiet.

It was a subdued group that went back to their huts that night. The three-day test designed by the Acharya had the highest accident rate of all gurukul activities, including the monster hunts. Someone or other needed urgent medical attention every year.

"We've got to stick together," Katyani told Ayan and Bhairav. "We'll pretend to go in different directions, but I'm going to walk due north eventually. You come find me, okay? All you have to do is follow the stream that heads north from the bathing pool."

Ayan shook his head. "Won't work. The senior disciples will be keeping an eye on us. They may cast spells to see where we all end up. If we're too close to each other, we'll fail the test."

"How am I supposed to protect the two of you if I cannot even be near you?" she demanded.

Ayan squeezed her arm. "Maybe realize we don't *need* your protection?"

"I'll head north even if he doesn't," said Bhairav, chewing his lip.

"I'll walk for three hours and wait for you," said Katyani. She wasn't overly worried about Ayan. He could take care of himself, and the gurukul had toughened him further. He was one of the best students in the class in both weapons and kalari. It was Bhairav who concerned her. The training had been good for him, but he'd been on a much lower baseline than the others to start with. The incredible fight with the yatudhani must have been a fluke, because he hadn't shown that level of skill again.

The next morning, all fifteen pupils gathered in the courtyard, armed with swords as well as bows and arrows. Acharya Mahavir blessed them one by one, sprinkling their heads with water and uttering a chant to keep evil spirits away.

Daksh was among those who would be keeping an eye on the pupils. She hoped he didn't come anywhere near them, or Bhairav would have a hard time following her.

"All the best." She patted Ayan's back and gave Bhairav's shoulder a squeeze. They saluted and set off, among the first batch to leave.

Nimaya crossed her arms, her face tense. Vinita talked to her, reminding her which trees were likely to be free of both monsters and nature spirits and which kinds of bodies of water to avoid.

"My dear cousin, you'll be fine," said Irfan. "No spirit will want to occupy the same space as you."

Vinita frowned at him. "This is not the time for frivolity, Prince."

Irfan mumbled an apology. As he set off with the second batch toward the gate, he turned to give them a cocky wave. Katyani waved back, hoping he would be all right. She knew he was putting on an act to hide how nervous he was, both for himself and for his cousin. He'd confessed to her, after their vetala-banishing expedition, that he was still afraid of the monsters.

At last, only Katyani and Nimaya were left.

"As the two women of the class," said the Acharya, "I grant you an exemption. You may each ask for something to help you in your task."

No wonder some of the male disciples were hung up about women. They got their patriarchal ideas from *him*. "No, thank you, Acharya," said Katyani. "I don't want anything the others do not have. It would be unfair."

Nimaya hesitated, then nodded her agreement.

The Acharya looked pleased. "Very well. I wish you all success."

They bowed and turned to go.

"I should have asked for a gourd of water," muttered Nimaya. "I'm going to regret my pride, aren't I?"

"I don't know about you, Princess, but pride is part of who I am." A prickly feeling of being watched stole over her, and she glanced back. Daksh was still standing there, looking at her. The others had already turned away and were talking amongst themselves. Warmth spread through her chest, and she brought her fingers to her lips and blew him a kiss.

His expression didn't change at all.

Gah. So disappointing. Didn't she scandalize him anymore?

"Well, this is it. Good-bye, Katya. Stay safe." Nimaya reached out and hugged her—something she'd never done before.

Katyani hugged her back, surprised and touched. "You too, take care. See you in three days."

She walked past the vegetable plots into the forest, picking a route parallel to the stream. Thankfully, monsters weren't usually active before dusk. She didn't have to worry about them for several hours yet.

She hadn't been alone in the forest before, and it was a fine feeling to walk under the ancient, stately trees, most of which must be older than the gurukul itself. The forest was a vast green temple. If she'd been the introspective type, she might even have relished the prospect of meditating here for three days. But she wasn't. She intended to find a nice, quiet spot with abundant fruit and water that could easily be defended against monsters. Then she would wait for Bhairav to show up.

When she judged three hours had passed, she slowed and began to hunt for a likely place to hole up. To her satisfaction, the stream widened at a point where there was a large, flat rock in the middle, ideal for sleeping on. Vetalas didn't like crossing water, so this was a safer spot than a tree.

She bent down and scooped water into her mouth. *Ah, delicious.* All that walking had made her thirsty. She drank her fill, wondering how Bhairav and Ayan were getting on.

"Just a few hours, and you've already failed the test," came an icy voice.

She jerked around, heart thudding, her dagger in her hand. "*You.* Why are you here?" She sheathed her dagger, groaning at her luck.

It was Daksh, of course. He stood behind her, a disapproving look on his face. "I found Bhairav following you and sent him in a different direction. Varun is making sure he doesn't break any more rules. It would be a pity for a prince of Chandela to be sent back in disgrace."

"Yes, but it doesn't matter if a *bondswoman* of Chandela fails, does it?" she remarked.

He hesitated. "I shouldn't have called you that, should I? What should I have said instead?"

She stared at him, biting her lip. He looked perfectly serious. "Just say I have a magical bond," she said at last. "To call me a bondswoman is to define me by the bond, and I am more than that."

He nodded. "I will remember. Thank you for telling me."

She grinned and took another long draft of water. "You're welcome."

"You're not even trying to pass the test," he said with such disappointment that she looked up in surprise.

"Why should it matter to you?" she asked, wondering at his loquacity. These were more words than he normally spoke to her in a week.

"I am one of your teachers," he snapped. "Your passing does matter to me."

"It's an arbitrary standard which I do not accept," she said loftily, perching on a rock by the edge of the stream.

"You will gain spiritual power from it! And it's the standard set by the Acharya of this gurukul, whom you are sworn to respect and obey while you are here."

"Huh. Respect and obedience." As if respect and obedience were the most important things in the world. She untangled a twig from her hair. "Do you love your father?"

He frowned. "What kind of question is that?"

"A simple one. I may be bonded to the queen of Chandela, but I also love her. My respect and obedience to her come naturally." *Even though she hasn't replied to my letter,* she couldn't help thinking.

"It's not a love you chose," he countered.

She shrugged. "We don't choose our parents either, Daksh."

"You called me by my name," he said. *Without the honorific,* he did not need to add. He didn't sound mad about it, more curious.

She sighed. "We've known each other for months. We hunted vetalas together. We saved each other's lives. We are quite close in age. I think we can dispense with honorifics, at least when we're alone. If you let me call you Daksh, I will let you call me Katya."

"Katya," he said, tasting the unfamiliar word on his lips.

Warmth flooded her from the tips of her toes to the roots of her hair. Her name in his mouth sounded both sweet and intimate, as if it belonged there. *Say it again,* she wanted to tell him. But she wasn't that foolish.

"I should go," he said. "Don't drink or eat for the next three days."

She rolled her eyes. "I will have to eat. I'm hungry. In fact, I'm going to eat right now. I see a juicy mango hanging above you."

He looked up. *"Don't."*

She picked up her bow and nocked an arrow on it. "Want to bet I'll get it on the first try?"

"Stop," he warned, his hand on his sword, as if he were going to stab her for eating a forbidden mango.

She focused on her target. The arrow zinged through the air and knocked the mango to the ground. She pumped her fist, crowing, "My archery skills have improved in the last few months, wouldn't you say?"

"You disobedient . . ." he sputtered, at a loss of words for once.

She grinned in delight. That reaction alone was worth failing this test. "Excuse me, I have a mango to devour. I don't intend to share it with you either."

He reached for the golden-yellow fruit, but she dashed forward and snatched it off the ground.

"You, you . . ." He took a step toward her, furious.

She backed away, laughing at his expression. "Oh, Daksh, why are you angry? It's just a mango. I'll get you another one, I promise, if you let me eat this."

"You're not supposed to eat at all!" he shouted.

She calmed herself with difficulty, giggling and wiping her eyes. "I'm going to eat it right in front of you." She bit off the top of the peel and spat it out. "Watch me."

"Oh no, you're not." Daksh flicked his wrist. Blades of grass whipped up from the ground, transforming into silver ropes as they flew toward her. In her shock, she dropped the mango. The ropes tightened around her wrists, binding them securely behind her back.

She froze, all hilarity gone. "Airya Daksh," she said, emphasizing the honorific, "do you intend to keep me tied up for three days?"

"For as long as it takes." He stepped closer to her and kicked the mango. She watched it roll away with a pang. There went her lunch.

"Surely you have to keep an eye on the other pupils," she argued. "More important ones than me."

"All students are the same in the eyes of their teacher," he said serenely. Now that he had her at a disadvantage, his calmness and self-control had returned. Insufferable man! She wasn't going to let him get away with it.

"This is all just an excuse," she said, matching his tone. "You've been wanting to tie me up like this right from the beginning."

He blinked. "What? No."

She went on, determined to push her advantage and crack his facade. "I wonder why? What exactly do you wish to do while I'm tied up and helpless before you?"

"Nothing," he said, looking at her mouth.

"*Liar,*" she said, and smiled.

What happened next was *not* what she had predicted.

Daksh closed the distance between them in one step and brushed her lips with his fingertips. "I'd like to kiss you," he said, his eyes burning into hers. "May I?"

She looked at him, flabbergasted. Her mouth opened and uttered the first thing that entered her brain. "Sure, if you even know how?"

In answer, he tilted her chin and brought his lips down on hers. Soft and yielding, they curved in a perfect bow over her own. His warm breath caressed her cheeks, as intimate as the kiss itself.

Katyani's thoughts ground to a halt. Her heart was pounding so hard, she was sure he must hear it. She closed her eyes, giving in to the incredible sensations washing over her, astounded both at herself and at him.

He slid one hand behind her head and the other to her bound wrists, encircling them, anchoring her to himself. The kiss became deeper, more demanding. She made a tiny sound in her throat, and he responded by pressing her body closer to his. She could feel every contour of his lean, muscled form. Just when she thought she must stop and take a breath or fall apart, he broke the kiss and released her. He stared at her, breathing hard, his face open and alive with warmth and ardor, no trace of the coldness left. As if he had been wearing a mask all along and taken it off for her.

She was shaken to the core. Her lips were bruised, her pulse rate in the stratosphere. She couldn't speak or think clearly except she knew she wanted him to kiss her again. She'd wanted him to do this for a long time without acknowledging it to herself. She'd goaded him into losing control and now that he had, she was terrified. Terrified he would regret it, that *she* would regret it. That he would see how much she wanted him and be repelled by it. He was out of her reach, and she'd be a fool to make herself vulnerable in front of him.

In the maelstrom of emotions churning her insides, one thought rose clearly above the rest: she couldn't let him see how much the kiss had affected her.

She took a great gulp of air and said shakily, "Not bad. But I've had better."

He pressed his lips together and took a step back, the mask of coldness back on his face. Despite her resolve, a wave of hurt rose within her. How did he do it? She would love to hide her true face from the world like that.

Her bonds loosened and fell away. She rubbed her wrists, not looking at him, already regretting her words. But what else could she have said? *Oh, Daksh, kiss me again and don't let go, never mind that your father is a powerful sage who dislikes women in general and probably me in particular, and never mind that I am bonded to the queen of Chandela and any sort of romantic relationship between us is impossible.*

Yeah, that would have been perfect.

"I'm sorry," he said in a cool, detached voice.

It was the indifferent tone that pushed her to speak, to lash out at him and hurt him the way she was hurting. "For what? Kissing me? Or not making it better?"

His eyes widened.

Damn. She was making everything worse and worse. She needed to shut up.

"Just go," she said, managing to not let her voice break. "Please."

He turned and left without another word.

Only then did she let the tears fall. When she was all cried out, she crossed the stream to the rock in the middle, sat in the lotus position, and tried to empty her mind.

Darkness fell, and owls hooted from the trees. The night breeze prickled her skin. She did not move until her limbs gave out and she fell down in a half-sleep, half-trance state that felt weirdly like being drunk. She watched the stars wheel across the sky and thought of how Daksh would look up at the same sky every night as long as they were both alive.

She would never see him again once she left the gurukul. This was for the best; their separate worlds could not possibly intersect. Until he kissed her, she hadn't even been aware that she *wanted* them to intersect. *Foolish Katya. Wanting the moon.*

Soon, she would go back to her responsibilities in Ajaigarh. Daksh would continue his life of exemplary celibacy until he was twenty-five. Then, possibly, his father would arrange a marriage for him. He'd move smoothly from one phase of life to another, following the advice of ancient texts.

She, on the other hand, would stay single. Even when she was released from her bond, it was unlikely she would find someone who was her equal in the things that mattered, and who wouldn't care about her background.

And was it so bad, the life she had? The luxuries she enjoyed that none of the gurukul dwellers did? What did it matter that she didn't remember her parents or have any living relatives? She had purpose and duty; wasn't that more important?

The seed of uncertainty the Acharya had planted sent forth wormlike roots of doubt into her gut. Purpose and duty were all very well, but hadn't she paid her blood debt, as Daksh had pointed out, many times over? Why had Hemlata not released her?

Try as she might, Katyani could not suppress the questions roiling her insides. For the first time in her life, she longed to be free of the bond.

Katyani woke from a trance to hear someone calling her name. She opened her eyes and tried to focus through a fog of hunger and fatigue. Varun was standing at the edge of the water, looking irritated. It appeared to be dawn, judging by the light.

"At last!" he said. "I've been here for several minutes."

"Is the test over?" she asked, her tongue thick in her mouth. Her sense of time was shot, but it didn't seem as if three days had passed.

"It is for you," he said. "The Acharya wants you back in the gurukul. You've been summoned to Ajaigarh."

Katyani woke all the way up. Dread seized her. "Is everything all right in the palace?"

Varun shrugged. "I don't know. But there's a letter for you, so you'll find out soon enough."

She tried to move and keeled over.

"I hope you don't expect me to carry you," he remarked.

"I'd rather be carried by a vetala," she muttered, hauling herself up with difficulty. She waded across the stream to the bank where Varun was waiting.

He offered her a gourd. "Mango lassi to keep you going."

She accepted gratefully and drank, the cool sweetness reviving her. "The princes?" she asked, wiping her face with the back of her hand.

"Two other disciples have been dispatched to fetch them," he said.

She hesitated. "And Airya Daksh?"

He seemed surprised by the question. "At the gurukul, of course. Why?"

Her face flamed. "No reason." She'd just wanted to know he was all right.

Varun struck southward through the forest, and she followed, trying to match his pace. Why had they been summoned back to the palace before their studies were complete? It had to be serious; the queen would never interrupt their training for anything less. Various scenarios flitted through her mind, each worse than the last, making her stomach churn.

Varun was useless; he couldn't answer any of her questions. By the time they arrived at the gates of the gurukul, a couple of hours later, she'd worked herself into such a state of anxiety that any news would have been a relief.

Ayan and Bhairav stood underneath the peepal tree, their unshaven faces tense. No one else was in sight; the other junior disciples would still be in the forest. She scanned the courtyard, but Daksh wasn't there either. He must be with his father—something she was thankful for. She didn't want to make a fool of herself in front of him again. She made a beeline for the princes, and Varun went to the main building to report to the Acharya.

"Finally!" said Bhairav. "We've been waiting for an hour."

"Here." Ayan thrust a parchment into her hands. "It's in the code you share with Ma. It came with a cover letter for the Acharya, which said we needed to return at once."

Katyani snatched the parchment and unrolled it with shaking hands. As she decoded it, a mix of relief, unease, and confusion filled her. She translated aloud for the princes' benefit.

"The situation here has deteriorated. Paramara forces have attacked one of our border outposts and stolen weapons and horses. The army has been mobilized across the kingdom. Tensions at the border are high, and war is imminent. Please return at once. Don't worry, there is good news too. There was another assassination attempt, but this time the culprits have been captured—"

"What?" Bhairav interrupted, looking stunned. "How is that possible?"

"I left my spies working for Tanoj," said Katyani. "They must have figured it out together." She couldn't wait to debrief them and get more details from her boss. He had succeeded where she had failed. She should be happy about this, and she *was,* but she couldn't help being puzzled too. How had he managed it?

"What else does she say?" urged Ayan.

Katyani scanned the rest of the letter. "Not much. Just to be careful on the way back." She didn't tell him the queen's last line, which was meant only for her: *Katya, I'm sorry the Acharya upset you with his questions about your family. When you return, we'll talk further.* It wasn't the answer she'd been waiting for, but it was something. An acknowledgment and a promise of future clarity, at least. Most likely, Hemlata didn't want to put such personal matters down in writing but preferred to discuss them with her face-to-face. Despite the storm clouds hovering above the kingdom, Katyani's heart lightened.

Ayan exhaled. "We'll leave at dawn tomorrow."

"Let's hope we haven't survived the Acharya just to be killed by something as ordinary as war," said Bhairav.

"At least it's the kind of thing we're familiar with," said Ayan. "Humans are way easier to kill than monsters."

She had to agree with him there. Humans were sadly easy to kill.

Early the next day, they said farewell to the Acharya and his senior disciples. Daksh stood silently with his brother, eyes lowered. He did not look at her or speak. Part of Katyani was hurt by this; did their moment of intimacy mean nothing to him? Did he not care she was leaving, that he might never see her again? That her kingdom was on the brink of war and she and the princes were heading into danger?

But another part was relieved he did not so much as glance at her, because if their eyes had met, he would have seen through her own facade to the roiling mess of emotions beneath. And that would have been disastrous. The memory of the kiss, her ill-chosen words, and above all, his own loss of self-control, must embarrass him deeply. He probably wished he'd never laid eyes on her.

Well, she'd soon be out of his life, and the gurukul would once again be the peaceful, predictable place he knew and loved.

They bowed to the Acharya, and Ayan asked him what he wanted as his gurudakshina. As their teacher, the Acharya could claim anything, even their kingdom, and the Chandela princes could not refuse. That was the unbreakable rule of the guru-shishya tradition. But the Acharya's answer surprised Katyani.

"I'll think about it," he said gruffly. "I wasn't expecting you to leave so soon."

"But Acharya—" began Ayan.

"Go," he ordered. "I'll claim my payment in the future."

It was disturbing, to say the least. They were in the Acharya's debt. It would hang over their heads until it was paid, but there was nothing they could do about it.

As they mounted the carriage outside the gates, Katyani made the mistake of turning back for one last look at the gurukul. Daksh was standing in the courtyard behind his father, his face open and unguarded, with an expression of sadness that smote her heart. She nearly leaped off the carriage to run back to him, to say she was sorry, sorry for having entered his life only to cause him pain.

Bhairav pulled her inside, and Ayan clicked his tongue at the horses, and the carriage rolled away down the uneven path, away from the gurukul, away from Daksh.

CHAPTER 8

IT TOOK THEM FOUR DAYS TO REACH AJAIGARH, AVOIDING THE main roads, taking lesser-known routes through villages and fields. Each time they stopped near a village, Katyani made a quick foray to buy food and get information from the locals. Everywhere she heard alarming rumors of the latest atrocities committed by the Paramara forces. Shamsher's men had captured villages, killed Chandela soldiers, stolen livestock, kidnapped women, and drafted young boys into their own army. People were hoarding grain and lying low, preparing for worse to come.

A part of her was glad of the distraction, because nothing less than the threat of war could drive Daksh from her thoughts. Every moment she didn't spend planning their route, calculating risks, and interacting with others was spent thinking of him: the touch of his lips, the warmth of his gaze, the sadness in his eyes when they were leaving. The nights were the worst; she stayed awake while the princes slept, and there was nothing to occupy the hours. She sat on the driver's seat, her senses alert for danger but her mind on Daksh, reliving every moment they'd spent together.

When they entered the city of Ajaigarh, the butterfly on her neck fluttered, as if waking up after a long nap. Katyani started, her hand going to her throat. It felt like an intrusion, and she wanted to tell the butterfly to go back to sleep. After months of silence, the space within her was once more occupied by the queen. Hemlata was pacing the palace corridors, tense but safe. "The king and queen are fine," Katyani told the princes, and the two smiled in relief.

The familiar walls of Ajaigarh Fort loomed above them. They discarded the carriage at the foot of the hill, knowing it would be collected later and the horses taken care of. Katyani rubbed her tattoo, puzzled why she was not happier to be back. Perhaps it was just odd—and *noisy*—after all this time, to be connected to the queen again. Hemlata had sensed their return, but her mood was an ambiguous gray. Maybe that was why Katyani felt gray too. Or maybe it was the Acharya's questions, coming back to haunt her now that she was close to answers.

It was late afternoon, but already quite dark. The sky turned an ominous steel as they climbed the steps up to the fort. Ayan chattered nonstop, clearly thrilled to be back, but Bhairav was quiet—worried, she thought, about the approaching war. Thunder boomed, and a breeze shivered through the trees on the hillside. Monsoon was about to break over the city. *Good.* The wet season was a hell of a time to try to invade a kingdom. Torrential rains made chariot wheels stick in the mud, quenched enemy fires, rotted the food, and brought a plague of mosquitoes on camping armies.

The fort gates were closed and heavily guarded, but they were identified at once. A shout went up, and the gates were thrown open.

"Falgun?" said Katyani, recognizing the stocky young guard from Garuda. He was wearing a gate captain's uniform. "Have you been transferred?"

Falgun saluted. "Yes, my lady. Sir wanted a man he'd personally trained in charge of the gatehouse."

That made sense. Tanoj was paranoid about security, and this was a good time to be paranoid. "How goes the preparation?"

"We're doing our best," said Falgun. "Guards have been doubled and a cavalry battalion dispatched to every town in Chandela. Kalinjar is on high alert. The feudal lords have been commanded to mobilize their forces."

Even if they mobilized all their forces, would it be enough to repel the might of Paramara? She went hot and cold at the thought of Chandela overrun by enemy forces. At least the onset of monsoon would stall them.

Thunder boomed again, and the first drops of rain fell. A waiting carriage took them across the courtyard and past the gardens to the palace. The roses had withered in the summer heat. Bhairav had been right; they wouldn't smell these blossoms again until next spring. Unless the Paramaras sacked Ajaigarh and destroyed the gardens along with everything else.

She pushed that thought aside. Ajaigarh Fort had withstood invaders for centuries. No matter how badly the war went elsewhere, the fort itself was impregnable.

The queen met them in the entrance hall of the palace, as regal and lovely as ever in a richly embroidered pink sari and silk blouse with intricate stone work. A complex mix of emotions washed over Katyani at the sight of her: joy and relief, tempered with misgivings. If only the Acharya hadn't made her see the strange gaps in her life. If only she hadn't kissed Daksh, if only she didn't want him so badly she was ready to lose her bond with Hemlata to have a chance, however slight, of being with him.

Ayan and Bhairav bent to touch Hemlata's feet, and she blessed them. "Ayushmann Bhava." *May you have a long life.* Around them, palace staff bowed to the princes, murmuring excitedly to have them back.

The queen pulled Katyani into a hug. "It's good to see you. I'm sorry your training was cut short, but I couldn't bear to be parted from you one minute longer."

"Are you all right, Your Majesty?" Katyani drew back to examine Hemlata from top to toe. "You were not hurt?"

The queen smiled. "Not a bit."

"You said there was another assassination attempt," said Ayan, accepting a cup of mint tea from a server. "What happened? Is my father okay?"

"The king is fine," said Hemlata. "There was enough poison in our dinner to kill an army. Thankfully, Tanoj got wind of the plan in advance, and he laid a trap for the poisoners." Her eyes became flinty. "They are in the dungeons, all five of them."

Five? "The food taster?" asked Katyani, coldness pooling in her stomach. It was a man she'd picked and interviewed herself.

"Was in on it," said the queen. "Do not look anxious, children. Tanoj has replaced all the kitchen staff, and we have two new food tasters."

"Poison in the food," said Katyani, taking a cup of tea herself. "It seems so . . . *ordinary.*" She sipped the tea; it was cool and delicious.

"Yes, it's not in the pattern of the previous attempts," said the queen, her brows knitting. "A deadly riddle, which I can't figure out."

"We're glad you're okay, Your Majesty," said Bhairav.

Hemlata's face relaxed. "We're lucky to have Tanoj to take care of our safety. He has interrogated the prisoners and confirmed they were working for Malwa. He said it would be better if you all returned now that we've caught the culprits. The kitchen staff—who could have imagined it?"

"I should speak with my father," said Ayan.

The queen nodded. "Soon. You may rest today, but from tomorrow, we expect you to attend all the council meetings in the king's private audience chamber. Your father has recalled his ministers and meets with them daily."

"We heard reports of villages being sacked on the way," said Ayan. "People being killed or drafted into the Paramara army. Is it true?"

"Some of the settlements on the border have indeed been attacked," said Hemlata. "But you know how things grow in the telling. You'll get a more accurate picture at the meetings."

Katyani's gaze was snagged by a plump, royal figure clad in a blue lehenga at the top of the grand staircase of the entrance hall. "Revaa!" she called, her heart filling with gladness. "We're back."

Revaa glared at her and stalked away, vanishing into a corridor without responding. Katyani suppressed a sigh. The princess must still be angry with them for leaving her behind.

"What's wrong with her?" asked Bhairav, frowning.

"The silly girl has been pining for you all, and now you are here, she doesn't want to speak to you. Never mind, she'll come around," said the queen. "Go to your rooms and freshen up. You smell like the stables."

"You said we would speak when I returned," Katyani reminded her.

Hemlata's face closed. "Later, Katya."

The queen was worried about multiple things she wasn't divulging. Katyani sensed the stress behind her calm facade. There was no point trying to push Hemlata now; there would be time enough for a quiet conversation later. But doubt and disappointment gnawed at her as the queen swept away, followed by her retinue.

Palace servants led the princes up to their rooms, chattering with delight. Ayan was their favorite; he never ordered them about like the rest of the royal family did. He didn't have to; everyone tried to anticipate his wishes and make him happy. He would make a great king one day.

Katyani headed to her own room in the west wing. Even at half the size of the princes' quarters, it was still quite large and richly appointed with silk drapes, wall hangings depicting Chandela history, and carved teak furniture. A four-poster bed with an embroidered quilt occupied one side of a wall. To its right, a series of lattice windows usually let in light and air. Someone had prudently closed them today. Rain battered the palace walls and streaked down the windows. An oil lamp burned on her desk, alleviating the dark.

On the wall opposite her bed was an alcove with a wooden tub. A fragrant bath had been drawn for her, a testament to the speed and efficiency of the palace staff.

She'd always taken her luxurious quarters for granted. But after four months of sleeping on a grass mat in a hut, this room felt unreal. Like the two could not—*should* not—exist in the same world. Perhaps that was the actual reason the queen had sent them to the gurukul. A prince who had experienced only the luxury of a palace would never know how the ordinary people of his kingdom lived.

But this was still the room she'd lived in since she was a child, and gradually the strangeness fell away, replaced by a sense of homecoming. She stripped off her sweaty clothes, dumped them on the floor, and stepped into the bath. Fresh clothes were already waiting for her, neatly folded on a low table. She sank into the water and hummed in pleasure. It was cool and fragrant, perfumed with rose essence. The tiredness leached away from her bones. This was one thing she had definitely missed in the gurukul. The occasional dips in the stream had been too hurried and too outrageously early in the day to satisfy her. She remembered her encounter with Daksh on the first night and grinned. Poor Daksh, he needed a luxurious bath like this to relax his muscles and take the tension away from his ramrod-straight back and rigid shoulders.

But the image of Daksh naked in a scented bath took her mind to all sorts of places she'd rather it wouldn't go, heating her skin until she thought the water would boil around her. She counted her breaths, emptying her mind until she'd cooled down once more.

Chaya came bustling in a little later. "Welcome home, my lady." A small, plump, efficient woman who had been Katyani's personal maid for more than five years, she wore her trademark yellow blouse and sari, her hair pinned in a neat bun.

The familiar sight filled Katyani with gladness, and she blew Chaya a soapy kiss. "I missed you, Chaya. My hair missed you even more."

The maid squatted behind Katyani. "I have brought coconut oil, my lady." She massaged Katyani's head, the heavy scent of coconut permeating the air.

Katyani groaned as Chaya's hands worked their magic on her scalp. "That feels heavenly."

"You must not have combed your hair the whole time you were away," said Chaya, trying to untangle the locks with her fingers.

"I combed it every day," protested Katyani. "It's not my fault it's like this."

Chaya gave a disbelieving snort and continued to work out the tangles. When she pronounced herself satisfied, Katyani rose from the bathwater and dried herself. It was nice to not have to count the pieces of clean underwear she had left. She finished dressing, and a serving boy entered, wheeling a small cart filled with aromatic dishes. There was a steaming cup of masala chai and plates of diamond-shaped almond sweets, spicy kebabs, and crispy samosas. She ate her fill while Chaya brushed her hair into submission and arranged it in a plaited bun.

A runner arrived with a message from Tanoj as Chaya was putting the final touches on her work. Katyani's boss wanted to see her as soon as possible. She gulped down the rest of her tea and stood.

"My lady, please allow me to finish," said Chaya.

Katyani peered at her reflection in the wardrobe mirror. "It looks fine to me."

Chaya held out a wreath of jasmine. "I need to pin this to your bun."

Katyani rolled her eyes. "Have I ever allowed you to put flowers in my hair? Honestly, I should shave my head. All this hair slows me down."

Chaya's eyes went round with horror. Katyani made her escape before her maid could start berating her. Poor Chaya, she should have been in

Queen Hemlata's entourage, or at least Revaa's. Instead, she had been assigned to the least ladylike woman in the entire palace.

Tanoj was waiting for her in the Garuda office, a small, nondescript room at the base of the eastern tower. As soon as she entered, he stood and threw her a sword, which she caught easily. "Show me what you've learned," he barked.

Katyani bowed. "Yes, sir."

The office wasn't the best place for a duel, but an actual fight would not take her preferences into account. She gripped the sword in both hands and fell into stance.

His attack was immediate and intense. It took all she had to parry his blows. She danced behind his desk, grabbed a brass inkpot, and threw it at him. Ink spattered everywhere: his face, his clothes, his sword. She took advantage of his momentary surprise to leap on the desk and smash her sword down on his, knocking it out of his hand.

"Yield," she snapped, her blade at his throat.

He gave a raspy laugh. "Good job. I see you've not forgotten my training in that fancy gurukul."

She put down her sword and grabbed a small linen cloth. "You were my first teacher, sir. I'll never forget your most important lesson."

"And which one is that?" he said as she dabbed his cheeks with the edge of the cloth. "Katyani, are you trying to spread ink all over my face?"

"Sorry, sir," she muttered, tossing the cloth away. "You may need a bath. The lesson is *use what you have*."

"Of which you have given an excellent demonstration," he said. "There's another lesson, though, a more advanced one. I'm not sure you've learned it yet."

"Which one, sir?" she asked, puzzled.

He grinned, revealing a row of broken teeth, currently ink-stained. "I'll let you know when it's time." He perched on his desk, waving her to the seat opposite. "The queen would have told you how we foiled the assassination attempt."

Katyani sat down. "Yes, sir. Congratulations on capturing the perpetrators. I assume there are things she hasn't told me?"

"Too damn right," he said. "All four of your palace spies have gone missing."

"What?" She stared at him, her gut clenching. "You think they've been compromised?"

He pressed his lips together in a grim line. "If it was one or two of them, I could have argued with myself that they were lying low. But all four? I'm afraid they've been killed or captured by Malwa."

Katyani leaned back, her head reeling. "When?"

"A month ago, just before the attempted poisoning," he replied. "I've started training a couple of new ones."

The news made her sick to her stomach. Training a spy took years. "Did you ask the prisoners about them?"

"Of course. They haven't said much yet, but they'll spill the beans eventually." His eyes narrowed. "I'll squeeze them for everything and make them beg for death before I slit their throats."

His words chilled her. Tanoj had taught her special interrogation techniques that involved knives, nails, water, and a lot of screaming. She'd never had the chance to use them, nor had she wanted to. "Who's the leader?" she asked. "One of them must be adept at magic."

"We'll find out," said Tanoj. "It's just a matter of time. The human body can only take so much."

She took a deep breath. "I should interview them, too. Or at least accompany you."

His mouth twisted. "Are you sure? They're not pretty."

She imagined sunken, starved faces, digits missing from hands, nails embedded in flesh, and shuddered.

"Give it a few days," said Tanoj. "Let me soften them up for you a bit more."

She nodded, and they discussed the more mundane matters of Garuda: the new recruits, the retiree, the one who was ill with stomach poisoning, the one whose lovesickness had rendered him worthless, and Falgun, who'd been promoted and transferred to the gatehouse. She left a little later and headed for Revaa's suite of rooms, taking a route through the whispering gallery she loved.

Revaa was getting ready for bed, enduring the combined attentions of three maids as they tugged off her elaborate clothes and removed the ornaments from her hair.

"You have ink on your face," she said when Katyani entered.

"Hah, this is nothing. You should see Tanoj," said Katyani, relieved that Revaa had thawed enough to talk with her.

"Have you come to apologize for leaving me?" demanded Revaa.

Katyani sat next to her on the divan and kissed her cheek. "Even better. I've come to tell you all about our awful adventures."

"As if I care," sniffed Revaa, but she dismissed her maids to an adjoining room and turned to Katyani, her face full of anticipation. Katyani launched into a description of the more interesting parts of her stay at the gurukul, leaving out her encounter with Daksh that first night. And the kiss, of course. No one must know about that, ever. These memories were too precious, too intimate to be shared with anyone else.

And yet, something in her tone and expression must have betrayed her.

"This man Daksh, you like him, don't you?" said Revaa when she had finished recounting the vetala-hunting expedition.

"I never said that," said Katyani, annoyed at her perceptiveness. She could barely admit the force of her feelings to herself; to have them picked up by the princess discomfited her.

"You didn't have to say it in words." Revaa gave a smug smile. "I just know it."

"He's okay," said Katyani in an offhanded tone. "Not bad with a sword. But he's pretty cold."

"And you'd like him a bit warmer, eh?" said Revaa slyly.

Katyani threw a silk-tasseled cushion at her. The princess dodged, cackling in a most unprincesslike way.

"I wish I'd met him," she said when her laughter had subsided. "I wish I'd gone with you to the gurukul."

"The queen——" began Katyani.

"I know," said Revaa. "But I'm meant for so much more than *this*." She pointed to her gold-embroidered silk nightgown.

Katyani squeezed her hand. "Still two years until your wedding. Anything might happen before that."

Revaa made a face. "Help me run away if nothing does?"

Katyani laughed. "Your aunt and uncle would kill me." She rose from the divan. "Time for your beauty sleep, Princess. I'd better go."

To her surprise, Revaa didn't try to delay her, just nodded in a distracted way. She was planning something. Hopefully, it wasn't something dangerous. Katyani checked to make sure Revaa's usual bodyguards were on duty outside her rooms before she left.

CHAPTER 9

IT RAINED FOR FOUR DAYS STRAIGHT. KATYANI TRAINED INDOORS with the princes, attended council meetings in the evenings, and tried to pin Hemlata down for their promised conversation.

But Hemlata evaded her; she was always too busy or too tired. It had never been hard for Katyani to get her alone before.

She tried to make excuses for the queen. The kingdom was on the brink of war. The angst-laden questions of a bondswoman regarding her family history were not a priority. Still, Hemlata's callousness hurt. She would know how much this meant to Katyani, how the Acharya's questions troubled her, and yet, she did not make any attempt to seek her out or put her at ease.

On the fifth day, the sun came out, and so did the people of Ajaigarh. Ayan made his first public appearance in months, riding in an open carriage with select courtiers and bodyguards, throwing coins to the adoring crowds that lined the streets. It was risky, given the situation with Paramara, but Hemlata decided the people of Ajaigarh needed to see their crown prince. It was good for morale.

On the sixth day, a messenger arrived from Prince Okendra in Kalinjar Fort, reporting an enemy troop buildup a few miles to their northwest. Bhairav volunteered to go with a cavalry unit to provide support to their twin fort. At first, Jaideep was disinclined to send him, but Bhairav assured him that the months of training at the gurukul had improved his skills no end. At last, the king agreed to let him go.

"Don't be a hero," Katyani told him before he left, early the next morning. They were waiting in the entrance hall for the king and queen so he could take their blessings.

He laughed. "I'll leave that to the crown prince of Chandela."

"I can't believe you volunteered," said Ayan. "Try not to get killed, okay?"

Bhairav gave a mock salute. "As you command, Your Majesty."

But there was an undercurrent of tension in his voice that didn't escape her. Katyani couldn't help but worry about him. Bhairav was third in line to the throne, a natural choice to send to Kalinjar. But he was more of a scholar than a warrior, and she wished he had not volunteered to go.

The council meeting that evening was held as usual in the king's private audience chamber: a long, narrow hall with a painted ceiling and lush, tapestry-covered walls. There was a throne at one end for King Jaideep, a lower one on each side for the queen and crown prince, and two rows of cushioned seats stretching before them. A thick wooden door with an iron bolt was the only entry point, guarded by members of Garuda. Hemlata sat to the left of the king, Ayan to his right. Bhairav was conspicuous by his absence. Katyani sat beside Nanuk, the stick-thin, hawk-eyed minister of defense, and tried to concentrate on what he was saying. She needed to pay extra attention because Tanoj was missing, and she'd have to fill him in later; he'd excused himself to attend to security details of the fort.

"Paramara forces have attacked Guna and Lashkur," said the minister, naming two towns at the border with their aggressive neighbor.

The king frowned. "I am more concerned about the forces near Kalinjar. Any movement?"

"None reported, Your Majesty," said Nanuk. "We will engage them at dawn tomorrow."

Katyani's heart constricted. Bhairav would be in that attack force.

"I don't understand their strategy," said Jaideep. "Why have they stopped? Why not advance on the forts if they have come this close?"

"They know the forts are impregnable," said Waran, the grizzled general of the king's army, who was seated opposite Katyani. "Especially Ajaigarh. They wish to draw us out on open ground."

"Then we shouldn't give them what they want," said Jaideep. "We must concentrate our forces within and around the forts and towns."

"And let them desecrate our motherland with their filthy boots?" snapped the minister of agriculture.

The debate raged on, devolving into the nitty-gritty of troop numbers, weapons, and horses, and where best to position them, like chess pieces on the rain-soaked board of Chandela. Ayan suppressed a yawn, grinning as he caught Katyani's disapproving eye. A server stationed in the room poured fresh mint tea for everyone from a silver teapot.

Midway through, a disturbance sounded in the corridor outside: running footsteps, clashing swords, and a series of screams, choked off. The door thudded as something was thrown against it from outside.

Katyani grabbed her sword and shot to her feet, heart thumping. Around her, others did the same, their expressions wary.

"Surely it's nothing," said Hemlata. But she rose from her seat, her hand on her dagger, her eyes cold.

Katyani caught a glimpse of movement behind a carved wooden screen in one corner and put a finger on her lips. The others watched as she stole toward the screen and, in one swift movement, threw it aside.

The screen clattered across the room. Behind it cowered Revaa in spy mode, dressed in black and devoid of jewelry, her eyes wide and scared. Katyani stared at her, aghast, not knowing whether to laugh or cry. Revaa had put her lessons on eavesdropping to practical use. Katyani knew she should be proud of her pupil, but all she wanted was for the princess to be safe and sound in her room, surrounded by bodyguards.

"What are you doing here, Princess?" inquired the queen in icy tones.

Something powerful battered the door, and everyone jumped. Revaa gave a little scream and shrank against the wall.

Katyani's stomach seized. The guards would not have let anyone approach the door if they were still conscious. She cut her eyes to Revaa. *"Hide."*

"There's nowhere to hide," Jaideep grated. "That door is the only entrance or exit. This is my private audience chamber. I thought it was the most secure room in the palace. But even my niece can steal into it unseen."

Katyani snatched the wooden screen she had thrown across the room and set it upright in its original position. "Stay behind it," she ordered Revaa. "No matter what happens. Promise me?"

Revaa nodded, swallowing visibly.

"Do you have a weapon? A knife?" asked Katyani.

In answer, Revaa withdrew a dagger from her robes.

"Good. But you're not to use it. Not unless you're found, and then you'll stab to kill—base of the skull, carotid, or lungs, like I've taught you. Understood?"

Revaa nodded again, gripping her dagger and melting behind the screen.

Boots thudded in the corridor outside. The battering ceased, and there were shouts mixed with crashing noises, clanking armor, thumps, and growls.

"What was that?" asked the minister of trade and foreign affairs in alarm, but no one had an answer.

Katyani advanced into the room, adrenaline accelerating her pulse, taking stock of their pitiful forces. Eight ministers of the inner council, nearly the entire royal family, one bodyguard, and one terrified-looking server armed with a teapot. *Pathetic.* Most everyone had a sword, but less than half could wield it well. The queen had her daggers as well as Chentu; she was equally skilled with both.

"Spread out, please," Katyani told the ministers in clipped tones. "Give yourselves space to use your swords." *And present a more diffused target,* she did not add.

They fanned out obediently, but Waran blocked the king and queen with his body. "Stay behind me, Your Majesties."

Jaideep gave a grim laugh. "I didn't fight multiple wars hiding behind you, General."

"But my king!"

"If the door doesn't hold, we'll need every sword we have."

Ayan, signaled the queen, and Katyani went to stand beside him in the middle of the hall. She exchanged a glance with him, and he gave a sharp nod, falling into stance, his sword held ready in his hand. They would fight together, as they had fought the yatu in Nandovana. Whatever was behind the door couldn't be half as fearsome as that monstrous horde.

The relentless hammering started again. It sounded like a battering ram. But how was that possible? The palace was crawling with soldiers. It stood in the middle of one of the most secure forts in Bharat.

With a tremendous crash, the door splintered.

"Hold your weapons," snapped the king as one of his ministers whimpered. "Stand with me."

Crimson waves of alarm rolled through Hemlata, and Katyani's feet started toward her of their own accord. The queen held up a hand, stopping her, controlling herself. "You will protect the crown prince," she commanded.

"I can protect myself," protested Ayan.

"We're a team." Katyani gripped his shoulder, trying to anchor both him and herself. "The two best swords in this room, and stronger together. I need you to work with me, okay?"

Ayan took a deep breath, his eyes on the door. "Okay."

Katyani fell back into stance next to him. Her nerves thrummed with anticipation. She'd been training for something like this her whole life. She knew her priorities: Ayan, Hemlata, and Jaideep. Everyone else was a distant second. She'd attack whatever came through that door, cleave a path of safety, help the royal family to escape, and then think of the rest.

There was another crash, and the door collapsed inward, splinters flying everywhere. A tiny piece struck Katyani's cheek, but she barely noticed. She tightened her grip on her sword and tensed, ready to attack.

There was a hideous roar of triumph, and several yatu squeezed through the door and lumbered into the hall.

For a moment, Katyani was too shocked to move. This couldn't be happening. The fort was warded against monsters. Yatu should not be able to enter. They hadn't even been seen in Chandela in years.

She sensed what she had missed earlier: the thrumming of broken wards, like a wind of cut glass blowing over the fort. The queen realized it in the same instant she did and uttered a small cry of horror. Katyani swallowed the cold panic in her throat and rapidly counted the monsters. At least twenty yatu filled the hall with their guttural cries, their unbearable stench, their wicked maces and nail-studded clubs. Two remained at the door, blocking their only escape route.

The lead yatu—a seven-foot-high monster—grabbed the minister of trade and foreign affairs and ripped off his arm. The minister dropped to the floor, blood fountaining from his severed arteries, shrieking with agony.

"Ripples in the Steel," shouted Katyani, and sprang forward, Ayan at her heels. This was a basic attack technique when confronted with a large number of foes. Katyani would be in the lead, and Ayan would follow her moves. If she was cut down, he would leap to take her place. It would be her life on the line before his. He might not like it, but he would not disobey her at such a time.

She summoned every bit of her spiritual power and swung her blade, decapitating the closest yatu. Ayan sliced the throat of another yatu who had the finance minister in his talons.

Katyani sensed the queen unfurl Chentu and lay about her with the whip, clearing a space around herself and the king. Waran went down fighting in the middle of a trio of yatu, his head wrenched, his neck broken. The server cowered in one corner, his eyes tightly shut, disregarded for the moment.

She steeled herself to ignore the plight of the ministers, focusing on Ayan, Jaideep, and Hemlata, trying to keep them all in her sight. A yatu grabbed the king's sword, trying to wrench it out of his grasp.

"Oh no, you don't," she snarled, leaping on his back. She drove her dagger into the monster's thick neck and twisted with all her might. Gray fluid gushed out, almost choking her with its noxious odor. She jerked out her blade, pushed herself off the yatu, and sprang back to Ayan's side, just in time to block a monster from clubbing his head. Behind her, the queen shrieked in rage and triumph as she whipped Chentu around a yatu's neck and stabbed it in the liver.

Katyani blinked back sweat and fought on, stabbing, swinging, parrying with her sword. There were too many yatu. She couldn't keep track of them all. Around her, the ministers fell one by one, their limbs torn, their heads smashed, their intestines spilling out. The server was finally noticed. A sword pierced his chest and came out the other side. The floor became slippery with blood and guts. Ayan took a mace blow to his left arm. It hung limp and useless down his side, but he continued to fight.

A yatu snatched Chentu from the queen's grasp, uttering an agonized cry as it burned his hand. Another smashed a mace into her back, driving her to the floor.

White-hot pain flooded Katyani through the bond. She flew toward the queen in a panic, hacking a yatu that stood in her way. She had to get Hemlata out of here, had to get her medical attention right away.

Hemlata raised her bleeding face, anguish and determination in her eyes.

Ayan! You must save Ayan.

Katyani sobbed and turned around, unable to resist the command, torn between her need to protect them both. She dived down to cut off the feet of a yatu that held Ayan's throat in his grip. The monster crashed to the floor, releasing the prince. They fell back into Ripples in the Steel, striking at the monsters that surrounded them.

Jaideep leaped in front of the queen to defend her, his sword flashing as he lopped off the head of the snarling yatu who had snatched the whip from her. He held back three yatu, blocking their clubs and stabbing their chests, his feet dancing from one stance to the next.

But two more yatu threw themselves on him from behind, bearing him down. Before Katyani's horrified gaze, they tore his sword from his hand, grabbed his head, and twisted it with a sick crunch. The king's head lolled back, sightless eyes staring blankly at the ceiling.

"Jaideep!" Hemlata wailed and stretched an arm toward him. But the yatu who had hit her with the mace grabbed her by the hair and dragged her to the door. Terror and pain spilled into Katyani, her own as well as the queen's. Before she could move, Ayan broke the formation they were in.

"Ma!" he shouted, darting forward.

"Ayan!" Katyani screamed. "Stay with me!"

But he did not listen. Before he could reach Hemlata, a yatu swung a club at the side of his face. Ayan stumbled and fell. The yatu kicked his sword away, and another brought a mace down on his head.

Hemlata locked eyes with Katyani, the shock in them reflecting her own. The yatu dragged her out of the hall, out of sight of the terrible things that lay within.

Ayan lay unmoving on the floor, awash in his own blood.

No, no, no.

Katyani ran to Ayan and bent over him, her trembling fingers trying to feel the pulse in his throat.

But there was nothing. Ayan was dead, his eyes empty, the side of his head caved in. She touched his face in a daze and looked at the blood on her shaking hands.

Blood on her hands.

Ayan was her charge, her prince, her duty. But more than that, he was her brother, her friend, her sparring partner. The hope and future of Chandela, and she had allowed him to die.

The sword dropped from her hand. She rocked back on her heels, the cold blade of grief stabbing her heart. A keening voice rent the air; she scarcely recognized it as her own.

Let them kill her now. She wouldn't fight back. Death was preferable to the agony searing her insides.

A hood dropped on her face, and a strange chemical smell invaded her nostrils. She coughed and swallowed.

Before she passed out, she remembered Revaa, hidden behind the screen. With her fingers, she spelled out her last instructions to the princess.

Stay hidden. Stay safe.

CHAPTER 10

CONSCIOUSNESS RETURNED IN SLOW, NAUSEOUS WAVES. KATYANI opened her eyes and wished she had not. Her head throbbed, and her mouth felt like sandpaper.

Above and around her was gray canvas. A tent? A lantern set on a stool next to her gave off a dim, wavering light. She was lying on a rug on the floor, her hands folded neatly one over the other.

Someone had done that. Someone had laid her out on the rug and folded her hands. The thought made her skin crawl.

Memory returned, and pain twisted like a knife within her. The councilors—dead. The king—dead. The crown prince—dead.

And the queen? Katyani reached out to her through the bond, her heart in her mouth, desperate to connect. What she sensed made her shudder in distress.

Hemlata was alive, but she was a roiling mass of grief and agony. She had lost her only child, the heir to the Chandela throne. *You must save Ayan,* she had exhorted Katyani. And Katyani had failed. She gulped back a sob.

"Ah, you are awake."

The voice startled her. Deep and gravelly, it put her in mind of empty wells and echoing canyons.

She struggled to sit up, get her bearings, and assess the speaker, but her head swam.

"Here." A hand supported her back, and a cup appeared at her lips. "Drink."

She pressed her lips closed and turned her face away. Even that tiny movement made her dizzy.

"Come, Ambika. It's only water, mixed with antidote. It will make you feel better."

"Poison," she whispered through cracked lips, wondering why he was addressing her by that name. Had he kidnapped the wrong person?

There was a gruff laugh. "If I wanted to kill you, child, you would certainly not still be alive."

What she'd meant was, even water offered by an enemy was akin to poison.

But the alternative was quite likely fainting. As long as Hemlata was alive, and as long as she could hope that Revaa had escaped, Katyani still had a duty to fulfill. She turned back to the cup and drank, the cool water reviving her. Then she raised her gaze to the man standing above her.

He appeared to be in his sixties, trim and fit-looking, with a neat gray moustache and beard, hooked nose, and deep-set eyes. He wore the dark green tunic and pants of the Paramara army, brown knee-length boots, and several ribbons and medals hung with gold chains. A senior officer, perhaps even a general.

"You don't know who I am," he stated.

Katyani curled her lip. "You are my enemy." It hurt to speak.

"I am the enemy of the Chandela kingdom. I am not *your* enemy."

"You killed them all." Her voice broke. She looked at her hands, fisted in her lap. She'd never spar with Ayan again, never hear his boyish laugh as he teased her. She wouldn't get to watch his coronation or be his most trusted advisor. Her eyes blurred, and she swallowed. She would not cry in front of this man who had torn her world apart. She would wait for an opportunity and kill him.

"I did not do it lightly," said the man in a calm voice. "They got what they deserved."

So will you. What were her chances against him right now? He had a sword on his belt and at least one dagger that she could see. She just needed her limbs to feel less heavy, her head to stop spinning. Then she would leap on him, snatch his sword, and drive it through his murderous heart.

The man dragged up a folding chair from the side of the tent and sat beside her. "Ambika, there are things I need to tell you."

"My name," she said through gritted teeth, "is Katyani." Her throat burned and her limbs ached. She would have liked another glass of water. But she'd die before admitting it.

He made a dismissive gesture with his hand. "That is the name *she* gave you. The lying, thieving queen of Chandela. Your birth name is Ambika. I should know. I named you, after all."

She stared at him. *Water,* she thought. Maybe whatever he'd given her was making her hallucinate. Because she thought she knew who this man was. She remembered him from a painting in a book about the rulers of Bharat. Except, in the picture, he had looked crueler. His eyes had been colder, his mouth a sneer—the outside mirroring the inside.

"Shamsher Singh," she said slowly. "Regent of Malwa."

He smiled and bowed. "At your service, granddaughter."

Granddaughter? Her head reeled. She clutched the side of the rug, leaned over, and retched. Nothing came out.

He patted her back. "The effects of the gas should wear off in an hour or so. I would have waited to speak with you, but time is of the essence."

She wiped her face with the back of her hand and leaned against the canvas wall, trying to breathe. "You called me granddaughter."

He nodded, watching her. "You are my son's daughter. My son, who was killed in an attack on our palace along with his wife and sister fifteen years ago."

"No." She massaged her forehead. Why was this man lying to her? What did he hope to gain? "My parents died fighting for Chandela."

"I don't know what is worse," he said, glaring at the butterfly tattoo on her neck. "The lies you were brought up to believe, or the abominable bond she placed on you, making you her lifelong hostage."

Katyani put a hand in front of her eyes, as if by blocking his face she could also block his words and unhear what he had said. "She did it to save me. I was so ill, I nearly died."

He grasped her hand and gently pulled it down. "Ambika, look at me. I am sorry. I have waited fifteen years for this moment, and I cannot give you even one more hour to recover. Do you know why I had to wait this long to rescue you? Because the bond she placed on you is unbreakable until you come of age. Not until you crossed eighteen did I have any hope of freeing you."

She snatched her hand away from his. This was some kind of cruel mind game. She'd studied methods of emotional torture that left prisoners unable to comprehend what was real and what was not. She just had to figure out his motive.

"You don't believe me." He sighed. "I should have anticipated this. She took you, took your memories, made you her *bodyguard*. What did they tell you about the war, Ambika? That the Paramaras were greedy and wanted Chandela territory? Look at the prewar maps that exist anywhere else in Bharat, and you will know the lie. Guna and Lashkur used to belong to us."

"You're lying." She hugged herself, trying not to shake. "Why have you captured me alive? What do you want?"

"I want to take you home," he said simply.

"You *destroyed* my home." Images of torn limbs and blood fountaining from severed arteries flashed before her eyes. The sick crunch of broken bones, the thud of clubs landing on defenseless heads. And Ayan's lifeless eyes, staring emptily up at her from an unrecognizable face. She bit down a sob and tried to focus. "You brought yatu into the palace. How did you get them to work for you? How did you break the wards?"

"There will be time for explanations later. First, we must free you from that woman." He rose and snapped his fingers.

The entrance flap of the tent was pushed aside, and two soldiers in the Paramara uniform entered. Between them, they dragged a woman across the floor, hauling her by her bare arms. Her head lolled forward, and her hair was matted with blood. Her sari hung in limp rags; all her elegant jewelry was gone.

Katyani struggled to her feet, choking off a cry. She rushed forward and knelt beside the queen, cradling her bruised face. "Your Majesty." She blinked back tears. *I failed. I'm sorry.*

Hemlata raised her head and fixed burning eyes on Katyani. *Then make it right.*

"Release my granddaughter from the unholy bond you have placed on her," came Shamsher's cold voice. "And I will let you live."

Hemlata gave a half laugh, half sob, a grating sound Katyani had never heard from her before. "You killed my son. Do you think I'll let you have her back?"

Katyani rocked back on her heels, shock coursing through her. "It's not true." She stumbled over the words. "I'm not. Not his. Tell me it's not true, Your Majesty!"

"I am sorry for what this woman has done to you," said Shamsher. "She raised you to think of your family as your enemy, and your enemy as your family."

But Ayan *was* her family. So were Hemlata, Revaa, and Bhairav. The only ones left alive. *If* Bhairav survived the dawn assault. *If* Revaa remained hidden. *If* Hemlata could escape this man.

This man, who was the regent of Malwa and the murderer of her king, her prince, and the entire council of Chandela. This man, who claimed to be her grandfather by blood.

But blood didn't make him her kin. It didn't, it didn't, it didn't. The words rose inside her like a scream that threatened to tear her apart.

She swallowed it down. "If she releases me from the bond, do you swear to let her go?" she asked, enunciating each word with care, as if they might change shape on her tongue.

"Of course," said Shamsher with a chilly smile. "Let her live with the death of her son, as I did."

Katyani grasped the queen's arms, releasing her from the grip of the soldiers. "Your Majesty," she said, trying to keep her voice steady. "Please dissolve the bond. This will ensure your safety."

The queen smiled, showing bloodstained teeth. "Oh, Katya. Do you think I care for my safety, now that Jaideep and Ayan are gone?"

And me? Did you ever care for me? Katyani pushed aside the thought that made her want to cry. She couldn't break down, not now. Not in front of *him*. "Please, Your Majesty, an entire kingdom depends on you."

"The kingdom will survive. Malwa has not the capacity to rule Ajaigarh, and he knows it well." Hemlata looked up at Shamsher, standing behind Katyani. "I refuse. Kill me if you wish. See what it does to her."

"I do not plan to *kill* you, thief," said Shamsher. "I plan to keep you alive for a long, long time in the dungeons of my palace. You will wish for death to find you. You will beg for release. You will dissolve the bond. And then, perhaps, I will grant your wish." He nodded to the soldiers. "Take her away. We'll leave for Malwa now."

"Wait," said Hemlata. Her entire demeanor had changed as the regent talked, becoming fearful and apprehensive. Katyani sensed this was a facade. Whatever complex emotions roiled through Hemlata—anger, grief, regret—fear wasn't one of them. The worst thing that could happen to her had already happened. If Shamsher had truly wanted a hold over her, he should have kept Ayan alive. Then the queen might have bargained with him honestly.

But Shamsher could not know this. He did not know Hemlata the way Katyani did, as intimately as a lover. She was torn between admiration for the queen and uncertainty over what she intended.

Hemlata sat up with difficulty, head lowered, hands on her lap—the picture of frightened misery. "I . . . please don't torture me. I will release her."

"Is she speaking the truth, Ambika?" demanded Shamsher.

Katyani stared at the queen, her eyes burning with unshed tears, thinking of the conversation they'd never had, the questions Hemlata had refused to answer. *What game are you playing, Your Majesty? What am I to you? You lied to me all my life. Should I lie now for you?*

Hemlata raised her head and locked gazes with her. *I have always loved you, Katya.*

And that was true, even if nothing else was.

"She is," said Katyani. Two words, and such a little lie, but it felt momentous, as if her future hung in the balance.

"All right," said Shamsher. "What do you need?"

"A knife," said Hemlata, calm now. "A bowl. A mirror. That is all."

Shamsher waved a hand, and one of the soldiers bowed and left.

Katyani tried to sense what Hemlata was planning, but her intentions were opaque. The queen was in so much pain, it blocked everything else. The mace blow to her back had broken several ribs. The flange at the end had penetrated her flesh. The wound needed immediate attention, or it would kill her even if Shamsher didn't. She'd also received numerous blows on her head and face, either during the fight with the yatu or after being captured.

The soldier returned with a kitchen knife, an earthen bowl, and a small mirror, such as men used for shaving. He set the items down in front of the queen and stepped back.

"You have your implements, witch," said Shamsher. "Cast your spell."

Hemlata bowed obediently and set to work, her hands trembling. She took the knife, held it against her palm above the bowl, and sliced into her skin, right where the blue butterfly was located.

Katyani suppressed a wince of pain, curling her hand into a fist. She could scarcely bear to watch. Right that minute, she could scarcely bear to exist. The inside of her chest was hollow, as if everything had been cut out. All the good things she'd known, the duties and ideals she'd lived for, were gone. Her home was destroyed, her brother was dead. And now the queen was releasing her from the bond, one of her last remaining anchors to her previous life—except she wasn't, not really.

Blood dripped into the bowl. The queen began to chant under her breath. A tiny wisp of smoke curled away from her palm—another drop in the sea of pain she was enduring right now.

Katyani's butterfly tattoo tingled. She put a hand on her neck, as if that would still it. Fear wrapped its icy fingers around her heart. What was Hemlata trying to do?

The queen placed her bleeding palm on the mirror and looked into Katyani's eyes.

Forgive me, Katya.

She picked up the mirror and smashed it on the floor.

The pain was so intense, Katyani screamed. She clutched her neck and keeled over, gasping. Shamsher gripped her shoulders, his bony hands digging into her flesh.

Before her, the queen continued to chant. But Katyani could no longer sense her. The bond that had always alerted her to Hemlata's presence and mood had broken.

It hurt more than Katyani would have believed possible. Not just physically, but psychically, like a butterfly-shaped piece of her soul was being torn apart.

The queen stopped chanting. She gathered the broken pieces of mirror, poured them into the bowl, and turned it upside down. She looked up with a victorious smile. "I'm done."

"Ambika, are you all right?" asked Shamsher, still gripping her shoulders.

No. I'm not.

Katyani tried to breathe. Inside her, the piece of her soul that had been ripped apart re-formed into a raven and flew out of her grasp. With a sudden, devastating sense of being *pulled,* the bond settled onto someone else. Someone familiar and yet unfamiliar, dark and complicated and full of pain. In place of the blue butterfly, a black raven tattoo dug its talons into her neck as if it would strangle her.

Shamsher grabbed her hand and pulled it away from her neck. His eyes bulged with horror as he beheld her new tattoo.

"What have you done?" He rose and kicked the queen with his booted foot. Hemlata collapsed on the floor, laughing soundlessly, unrecognizable from the person Katyani had known and loved all her life.

"It was all for nothing," she said, between painful gasps. "Everything you did. All your waiting and planning and murdering. The blood on your hands, the laws you broke. She will never be yours. The bond has passed from me to my heir."

Katyani shriveled at her words, at this final betrayal from the woman who had raised her, loved her, and used her.

Shamsher kicked her again, this time in the face. Still, she did not stop laughing. At last, he unsheathed his dagger and plunged it into her throat.

Katyani cried out and crawled to her, shivering and sobbing. She clutched Hemlata's hand and squeezed it. The queen's mouth shaped words, but Katyani could not hear them, could not understand what she was trying to say.

She died choking on her own blood, smiling to the last.

CHAPTER 11

THINGS BLURRED AFTER THAT. KATYANI SAT IN A STUPOR, holding the dead queen's hand, while Shamsher issued orders to his men. Finally, he grasped her arm and pulled her up.

"We have to leave," he said. "The bond has passed to her next of kin, which means Bhairav can track us."

Katyani came out of her daze. "He's alive?"

Well, of course he was. She'd sensed him. Except he didn't feel like the Bhairav she knew. There was too much pain, too much anger, even at this distance. On the surface of it, that wasn't hard to grasp. He must know of the mayhem in Ajaigarh by now. But Bhairav's hurt went deeper, older than that.

"I gave no orders for him or his sister to be killed." Shamsher gave a grim smile. "I'm not a butcher, no matter what you may think of me."

"Really? There was enough poison in the food to kill an army," she said, remembering Hemlata's words.

He knitted his brows. "What poison?"

She didn't respond; she couldn't. Soldiers were dragging the queen's body out of the tent. Katyani watched them, her heart clenching. Hemlata had been so regal in life, so magnificent. She'd commanded the hearts of an entire nation of people. In death, she was treated worse than a traitor.

Forgive me, Katya, she'd said. But for which particular transgression had she been asking forgiveness? For what she'd already done, or what she was about to do?

Katyani summoned words. "You should leave me here, if you don't want to be tracked." Surely self-preservation would persuade him, if nothing else could. She'd find her way back to Ajaigarh, make sure Revaa was all right, and get Bhairav to break the bond. She hadn't asked for this, but neither had he. She was done being bonded to anyone, subject to the worst of their impulses. The bond pulsed, and she shivered with distaste.

"The aim of this entire campaign was to rescue you," said Shamsher. "I will not leave you here, no matter what the cost."

His words stabbed her. *She* was the reason Ayan was dead, and Hemlata, Jaideep, and the entire council. She, Katyani, member of Garuda, one-time bodyguard, sworn to protect the royal family of Chandela. Darkness came before her eyes, and she swayed, feeling faint.

Shamsher gripped her arm. "Stay strong. There are men of power in Malwa who may be able to break the bond."

A soldier entered and saluted. "The horses are ready, Your Majesty."

"Let us go." Shamsher led her out, never relaxing his grip on her arm.

Outside, it was pitch dark, alleviated by the occasional wavering glow of a lamp. Trees clustered thickly around them, and the air smelled damp. They appeared to be in a wood on the outskirts of Ajaigarh. The ground was still squelchy from the rain of the past few days. Men worked in silence, packing tents, loading carts, saddling horses.

No yatu were in sight; the monsters had camped elsewhere or taken a different route. She hadn't heard of yatu working with humans before. *Eating* humans, yes. Helping them, never. Even in Nandovana, Varun had told her, yatu generally kept to themselves. What hold did Shamsher have on them?

She caught sight of Hemlata's corpse and came to a grinding halt. The queen's body hung from the branch of a peepal tree, swaying in the breeze. She had been stripped down to her underclothes, her feet bound and painted with sigils to prevent her vengeful spirit from chasing them.

"You said you weren't a butcher," she said, speaking with difficulty.

Shamsher glanced at the body. "That is merely a message. They will find her and give her the last rites. If I were truly vindictive, I'd cut her into pieces and hide the parts, trapping her spirit in the mortal plane forever. Can you ride?"

Katyani swallowed and dragged her gaze away from the awful sight. "Yes." She could make a break for it on horseback.

But Shamsher asked her to mount his own horse—a huge white

stallion—and swung himself up behind her. She sat rigid, clutching the pommel, loathing the nearness of him.

Grandfather. What a horrible joke. Perhaps she could kill him with the sheer mental force of the hatred that rose in black waves within her.

But was not the Chandela queen equally culpable? *I have always loved you,* she'd said. But her hate for Shamsher had been greater than her love for Katyani. The queen had made her a pawn in the deadly game between two kingdoms. Grief and anger warred within Katyani. No, she could not forgive the queen, even though she'd give anything for Hemlata to still be alive. Anything, to be able to look her in the eye and shout: *You lied to me. You used me. Why? Why? Why?*

Shamsher barked an order, and the horses cantered away. They emerged from the wood just as a crescent moon peeped out from behind a cloud. Katyani saw that the company was not big—perhaps fifty armed men and as many horses. The regent of Malwa had relied almost entirely on the yatu for his raid. He had kept his human force small and nimble to get past Chandela forces. But how had the yatu approached the fort unseen? How had they broken the wards? And why had they agreed to help Shamsher?

They crested a rise, and a red glow lit the horizon. Was that smoke she smelled?

Realization came as a sick punch to the gut. "You set the city on fire."

"We had to keep the garrisons busy while we attacked the palace," he said.

"How many people died tonight for your revenge?" she asked, her voice cold and flat.

"There won't be many civilian casualties," he said. "The roofs are still damp, and the fires did not spread widely. It was meant as a distraction."

"Even one innocent life lost is too much," she spat. "You will be judged for it."

He sighed. "Ambika, I did it for you. To bring you back home to your family."

That's not my name, she wanted to scream. *You attacked my home. You killed my family. Don't pin the blame for your murders on me.*

Tears fell from her eyes and dried on her cheeks as the wind picked up. Despite her turmoil, she filed away details of the terrain as they traveled. They were heading northwest of Ajaigarh, toward the border with Malwa.

The bond sat uncomfortably on her skin. She'd barely noticed it when she was bonded to the queen, perhaps because she was used to it. But Bhairav was a stranger to her, not the boy she'd grown up with. She tried to reach out to him, but it was like falling into an ice-cold well of anger and contempt, and she recoiled from it in fear. She couldn't understand it. What had happened to make him like this? Where was the book-loving, bantering brother of her childhood?

The further they went, the weaker the bond became, until she could no longer sense him. The silence within her was a welcome relief. When she'd left the palace for the gurukul, she'd missed the connection with Hemlata for weeks. But she was glad to lose it with Bhairav. He could still track her, but at least she didn't have to feel his pain and resentment. Her own grief was enough. She couldn't handle his right now.

"Where are we going?" she asked. If she knew, she could plan her eventual escape.

"Malwa," answered Shamsher. "But not to the capital, Dhar, not yet. It's a five-day journey at this pace, and we cannot keep it up. We'll have to take refuge somewhere in the middle. I have a stronghold near the border we should be able to reach tomorrow night. A place I can defend while I summon my troops."

She would have to make her move before they reached Dhar. The cool night air had dissipated the remnants of whatever drug they'd used to knock her out, but she had a pounding headache, and her limbs ached. She had no serious injuries, though. He must have instructed the yatu not to hurt her and to capture the queen alive. What kind of man could make yatu do his dirty work for him?

They rode until dawn, then rested the horses in a secluded glade. She thought of her sword, abandoned in the audience hall, and wished she had it with her. They'd even taken her obsidian knife. Could she steal a sword? How closely would Shamsher watch her? She had to wait for a moment when he let down his guard. Nothing good would come of staying with him.

But Shamsher did not relax his guard. Three or four of his soldiers always had their eyes on her, although they weren't obvious about it.

Next day, late in the evening, they arrived at the foot of a grassy hill. On top of the hill was a ruined fort—abandoned, by the looks of it. The setting sun cast its dying rays on the half-crumbled buildings, enveloping them in an eerie red glow.

"That's your stronghold?" Katyani eyed the broken battlements as they climbed up an overgrown path.

"This is Rajgarh," said Shamsher. "It was destroyed in a previous war with Chandela. It's time I reclaimed it."

"How do you plan to defend broken walls and smashed gates with fifty men?" she inquired.

Shamsher smiled. "Give me some credit, granddaughter. All I need to do is buy some time until my main troops arrive from the capital. Messenger pigeons have already been dispatched. They should be here in two days."

Her bond gave an unpleasant little throb. Tentatively, she reached out to check on Bhairav, and retreated almost at once. He was on the move, coming closer, although still far away. It was only a matter of time before he found her. The thought should have reassured her, but it didn't. She was too tense, too exhausted to figure out why.

They passed the rubbled walls of the fort, the horses picking their way through boulders and fallen masonry. The courtyard inside was overgrown with weeds. Tree roots had cracked the stones; vines had climbed up the walls and through the windows, invading the unseen rooms. Wind whistled through the courtyard, and the vines rustled. A feeling of being watched crept over her, and she averted her gaze from the windows. A haunted place, if ever there was one.

Shamsher dismounted, and she followed suit. "Stable the horses," he told the men. "Make sure you keep them away from the yatu."

The yatu were *here*? She wheeled around, scanning the ruined buildings. A cloud of bats poured out from one of the gaping windows and flew over the fort, toward a thicket of trees. A hyena called, a series of hysterical chuckles that made the hair at the back of her neck stand on end. But she saw no sign of monsters.

The wind changed direction, and the familiar stench of yatu assaulted her nostrils. She gagged and stepped back. No wonder Shamsher was confident about keeping Chandela forces at bay.

The regent continued giving instructions to his soldiers. "Stay away from the palace and the temples. The stables and storehouses are relatively safe. Sleep in groups of five. No cookfires."

As the men dispersed, leading the horses, she asked, "Safe from *what?*"

"Pretas," he answered. "Ghosts trapped in this plane by karmic misdeeds. Some are my ancestors; some are likely from the Chandela army that attacked this fort all those years ago."

"You could lay your ancestors to rest by performing the right rituals," she pointed out.

"Why should I? They deserve their fate. And they give this place a reputation that keeps my enemies away. Only a Paramara citizen can survive a night in Rajgarh."

"That means I will die tonight," she said.

He frowned. "As the granddaughter of the regent of Malwa and the cousin of the crown prince, you will certainly be safe."

She started. She hadn't thought she had any other relatives.

"His name is Aditya," said Shamsher, watching her. "He's looking forward to meeting you. You were born just four days apart and were raised together. He is the elder by four days, but you were the more aggressive. You often snatched his toys and rattles, but when he cried, you always returned them. You learned to walk before he did, and the first thing you did was to go to him and pull him up so he could walk beside you."

She turned away from him, her eyes stinging. *Lies,* she thought fiercely. Lies to manipulate and weaken her. It was Ayan she loved, good-natured and handsome, the darling of his people, the crown prince of his realm. Ayan she'd grown up with, Ayan she'd sworn to protect. Who was this man to tell her she'd been nothing more than a hostage? Was her loyalty so cheaply traded?

"Your father was a good, brave man," he continued. "He died trying to protect your mother and aunt."

"Stop," she said, her voice sounding strange and harsh to her own ears, like the caw of the raven tattooed on her neck. She couldn't bear to hear about her birth family. It was a betrayal of the one that had raised her.

A hulking yatu emerged from one of the dilapidated buildings, carrying a lantern, and Shamsher walked over to speak with him. Katyani watched him go, relieved at the interruption.

Man and monster met as equals. There was no sign of deference from the yatu or fear from Shamsher. The yatu towered over the regent, at least a foot taller and twice as wide. With his curving tusks, huge moustache, and crimson skin, he was a caricature of his kind. How much of the blood in the audience hall had been shed by him?

Her hands clenched and unclenched. Again, she thought of her sword, abandoned in a moment of despair. If only she held it in her hands.

They both glanced at her and continued talking, as if discussing her. It gave her a sense of dissonance she could not shake off. Monsters and humans weren't meant to be allies.

She turned away from them and leaned against a crumbling wall, still warm from the sun. The courtyard had transformed into a hive of activity while Shamsher talked. The soldiers lit oil lamps and unpacked bedrolls and provisions. The smell of pickles mingled with the smell of horses, a peculiar mixture that reminded her, inexplicably, of home.

Farther down the courtyard, near the broken, rusted gate that led to the interior, was an old stone well. She walked up to it, meaning to see if there was a bucket she could use to draw water. A soldier who must have been keeping watch ran up to her.

"Please don't go there," he warned. "The well is haunted and the water unclean."

She gazed dispiritedly at the well. They'd watered the horses at a river not too far off and replenished their gourds. She should have washed up there when she had the chance. "I need a drink."

"Take this." He removed the stopper from a gourd and offered it to her. She took a long swallow, sparing a few drops to wipe the dust off her face.

Shamsher returned, and they ate a frugal meal by lamplight, sitting a little way away from his soldiers. The yatu remained out of sight, for which she was grateful. She had no appetite, but she had to eat something to regain her strength. Still, it was hard to sit next to the man who claimed to be her grandfather, to eat flatbread and pickles with him as if he were not Ayan's murderer.

Was there anyone in the world she could still trust? She thought of Daksh, and her heart gave a swoop of longing. The Acharya and his sons were noble, upright people, but also impractical and unrealistic. How would they react to her current situation?

With horror and pity, most likely. Neither were helpful, and she was glad they weren't around to witness her fall.

After eating, they spread mats and bedrolls on the open ground. Three yatu emerged from the same building as the first one had, carrying clubs on their shoulders. No one gave them a second glance. They lumbered past the courtyard and climbed the broken battlements—to keep watch, Katyani deduced.

She lay on her back and watched the stars peep out of the inky sky. A new moon night, perfect for escaping. There were three soldiers on a rotational watch, circling the courtyard, and she could easily slip past them. But the yatu were a different matter. She was debating whether it was worthwhile to take the risk of being caught and ignominiously hauled back when exhaustion overwhelmed her, and she fell asleep.

She woke with a start sometime later. The night was quiet but for the chorus of crickets and the occasional snore and snuffle from the sleeping men. From the position of the stars, she judged two or three hours had passed.

Katyani, came a cold, yearning whisper of a voice.

She sat up, instantly awake, fear pooling in her stomach.

Katyani. We are so thirsty. Will you not draw water for us?

She jumped to her feet and looked at the well, heart pounding. Pale shapes hovered beside it, ghostly in the pitch dark. Were those pretas? Humans weren't supposed to be able to see them. She certainly never had before, not even when she'd learned to expel them in Acharya Mahavir's gurukul.

She walked toward the well, itching for a weapon, even though weapons were useless against pretas. She stopped a cautious few meters away and strained her eyes in the dark.

We won't eat you, Katyani. We only crave water, and we never get to drink it.

The pretas resolved into view—three of them, each more frightful than the last. Pale-skinned and humanlike, they had huge, distended stomachs that drooped over spindly legs. Their twig-thin necks could barely support their misshapen heads. The skin stretched tightly over the prominent ribs in their concave chests: a mark of their perpetual hunger. They were condemned to an eternity of suffering unless their descendants performed the right funerary rituals to release them from this state. Why did Shamsher think they deserved this?

We betrayed Malwa, one of them whispered. *Because of us, Rajgarh was lost.*

Turncoats. No wonder Shamsher hated them. But even turncoats didn't deserve to suffer for eternity.

Will you give us water, Katyani? a second pleaded.

Unease rippled through her. "Why me?"

There is no one else here who will give us even one drop.

That was probably true. She looked at their scrawny necks. "Will you be able to drink it?"

If you draw it for us, we will, said the third.

She shivered as the full meaning of those words hit her. They would be able to drink it because *she* was drawing it for them. That meant she was a descendent of theirs, no matter how distant. She could deny Shamsher, she could call him a liar, but she couldn't deny these pale, wretched ghosts.

She approached the well and peered inside. Water gleamed in the starlight, far below. A bucket hung from an old, rusty chain on a simple pulley. She lowered the bucket, hoping the chain would hold. The pretas crowded around her, murmuring in anticipation. When she judged the bucket was full, she turned the wheel and hauled it back up. She offered it to the pretas, but they shrank back.

You must bless it before we can drink it, one of them explained.

She stared at the bucket. She was no priest. She didn't know any blessings.

But bits and pieces of old Sanskrit shlokas from the Rigveda came back to her.

"Apvantram amritamapsu," she said, stumbling over the unfamiliar words. *Water is nectar, water is medicine.* "Apah sarvasya bheshjh." *Water is the cure for all diseases.*

That would have to do. She held out the bucket once again, and this time, one of the pretas accepted it. He tilted the bucket over his mouth and drank greedily, water splashing over his face and neck. The other two watched, the longing on their repulsive faces making them almost human. Pity washed over her at their plight. Here were beings who were infinitely worse off than her.

When the first preta was done, she hauled up a second bucket for the next preta and repeated the blessing. She did it again for the third. She thought that would be it, but they begged her for a second bucket each, and then a third. By that time, her arms were cramped and aching. Where were they putting the water away?

"You can do this forever, and it still wouldn't quench their thirst," came a harsh voice from behind her. She nearly dropped the bucket she'd been hauling up for a fourth round.

Shamsher stood with his arms folded, watching her with flinty eyes. The pretas moaned and cringed.

She pressed her lips together and turned back to the ghosts. "Is there anything I can do so you don't feel thirsty again?"

Make three clay mounds, said the first preta eagerly.

Offer them a pot of water and three rice balls every morning at sunrise for a month, said the second.

Then, for three days, feed three mendicants in our name, said the third.

Fast on the fourth day, said the first.

Utter the last rites over the clay mounds on the fifth day, said the second.

This will free our spirits from the mortal realm, concluded the third, stretching his mouth in a ghastly grin.

Shamsher gave a dry laugh. "You think my granddaughter has nothing better to do with her time?"

She threw him a defiant glare. "I'll do it," she told them. "If ever I get out of this." *This* being her present situation. She didn't have to spell it out for them. Pretas saw almost as much as vetalas did.

Then we will give you a gift, said the first preta, excitement crackling through his whispery voice.

A token of our thanks, added the second.

"Don't listen to them," Shamsher warned. "All such gifts must be paid for, much more than they're worth."

Consider the payment made, said the third preta. *The nine buckets of water, a drop in the ocean of our thirst. An hour of your time, a moment in our eternity.*

"I didn't do it to get anything back from you," she said.

We know, said the first preta. *That is why we offer this.*

There will come a time when you suffer great pain, said the second preta.

She stiffened, thinking of the vetala's prophecy.

Think of us then, and we will absorb your hurt, said the third.

One drop in the sea of our suffering, said the first. *Do you accept?*

"I do," said Katyani, mostly because Shamsher wished her to say no, but also because she pitied the pretas. She wanted them to know she didn't look down on them the way the regent did.

The pretas bowed and faded away, nudging each other in delight.

"That was unwise." Shamsher regarded her with thin-lipped disapproval. "Pretas are not to be trusted."

"Neither are yatu," she pointed out. "Yet you use them."

"Yatu are the closest to humans among all monstrous beings," he said.

She grimaced. "They *eat* humans."

"But they are capable of surviving on animal flesh, and many choose to," said Shamsher. "Like the band that is working with me. It doesn't make them any less deadly, however, so I would advise you not to try to escape. Now, if you will excuse me, there is one hour of sleep left before dawn."

He walked back to his makeshift bed.

Too restless to lie down again, Katyani circled the courtyard, keeping a wary eye out for yatu. The raven flapped its ungainly wings; Bhairav, reaching out, trying to find her. He would be here in a day or two. But what he intended to do after that was opaque to her. Except it couldn't be anything good, not with him feeling all bitter and vengeful.

She rubbed her neck. There was nothing she could do about how the bond made her feel. All she could do was hope that when they were face-to-face, she would find again the brother she had grown up with. She'd already lost Ayan; the thought that she might have lost Bhairav too was unbearable.

The next day passed in slow, agonizing anticipation. Shamsher's forces were on their way, as was the Chandela army. The only question was who would arrive first.

CHAPTER 12

O N THE MORNING OF THEIR THIRD DAY AT RAJGARH, A SCOUT returned to the fort to report that a cavalry regiment flying Chandela colors had been spotted an hour's ride away.

Katyani rose from the ground where she'd been doing a series of sun salutations, her ears pricking up. She'd spent the last two days exercising, trying to get her strength back.

"How many?" asked Shamsher.

"Between five and six hundred, Your Majesty," the scout replied between gasps. He'd ridden hard to deliver his news.

Shamsher issued curt orders to his human and yatu troops. Although this was not the news he had been hoping for, he didn't betray any unease or disappointment. Katyani wiped her hands on her kameez, watching the preparations.

Men armed with bows and arrows stationed themselves next to the window slits on the broken ramparts. The yatu concealed themselves around the courtyard. Close combat was their strength, and each one of them would be a match for ten ordinary soldiers.

Shamsher turned to Katyani. "You will stay inside until this battle is over. You are a noncombatant for all intents and purposes."

"I am one of the best fighters in Ajaigarh," she said. "I will not be viewed as a noncombatant by either side."

"Yet, this is not your battle," he said. "I don't expect you to fight for Malwa. I know how conflicted you must be. But I cannot allow you to endanger my men. Give me your word you will stay out of it."

"Why would I do that?" She cast her eyes about. A soldier passed her, hurrying to his assigned position. She grabbed his sword and unsheathed it. It wasn't as light and fine as her sword, but it felt good to have a weapon in her hands again. She twirled it before the discomfited soldier's eyes. "Perhaps I will fight you, *grandfather*."

Shamsher gave a thin smile. "When we get back to the palace, you may challenge me to a duel if you wish. But for now, please return the sword and take shelter. Or I will have to ask one of the yatu to tie you up and throw you into the dungeon with your new friends, the pretas, for company."

Reluctantly, she returned the sword to the soldier. She didn't want to go anywhere with Shamsher, but she couldn't help a spark of curiosity about the cousin she supposedly had and the palace where she should have grown up.

Another scout ran into the courtyard. "Four riders with white flags are approaching the fort," he reported.

The raven on Katyani's neck clacked its beak. One of the riders was Bhairav. Her pulse quickened.

Shamsher frowned. "A truce? That's not like the Chandelas. But allow them to enter unharmed. Be alert in case it's a ploy." He pointed at Katyani. "Inside."

She went to the nearest building, which the men had converted to a stable. The smell of horses was overwhelming but also comforting. She patted a few friendly noses and positioned herself next to a window so she could see what was going on. Shamsher was right; the white flag was definitely *not* on Chandela's list of ways to respond to the murder of their king, queen, and crown prince. This was a trap of some kind.

A few minutes later, the riders entered the courtyard and dismounted. The sun glinted on their shields and Katyani blinked, trying to make out their faces.

One of them turned to the window, locking eyes with her, and she shrank back against the wall. *Bhairav.* Why was her heart beating so fast? This was her adopted brother. The need for vengeance burning inside him was surely not directed at her. He must know she had nothing to do with the massacre, that she'd tried her best to protect the royal family. Then why was he so bitter and confused when he looked at her?

"Shamsher Singh," came a gruff, familiar voice. Shock coursed through Katyani, and she whirled back to the window, uncaring of who saw her.

"Acharya Mahavir," said Shamsher coldly. "What a surprise. I thought you were above the petty politics of the kingdoms of Bharat."

"I am here," said the Acharya, "because some actions are so despicable, they demand my intervention."

He stood in the middle of the courtyard, an erect figure clad in white, staff in hand. Two men flanked him, one on each side. Katyani's stomach clenched as she recognized Daksh and Uttam. What were they all doing here? The gurukul had a policy of noninterference. The Acharya was famous for not taking sides in any war.

"That's not what you said fifteen years ago," said Shamsher. "I came to you for help; have you forgotten?"

The Acharya made a cutting gesture. "I have not forgotten. If you had waged war against Chandela, I would not have interfered. Your cause is just. But your methods are not."

"You question my methods?" Shamsher gave a harsh laugh. "You are aware of what the Chandela queen did to my granddaughter. Did you question *her* methods?"

Katyani went hot and cold. The Acharya had known. All the time she'd been in the gurukul, he had *known* her true lineage. *Ask your queen who you really are,* he had said. Why hadn't he told her himself? Not that she would have believed him.

"I accepted your granddaughter in my gurukul to see if I could remove the bond," said the Acharya. "Unfortunately, I did not succeed."

"Your attempt to help came fifteen years too late," said Shamsher. "You have always claimed to stand with justice, but when it counted most, you failed."

The Acharya bowed his head. "I accept the accusation. But my failure to help you then cannot be used as an excuse to break the rules of ethical warfare."

"The rules of ethical warfare?" cried Shamsher. "Can you hear yourself, Acharya? The Chandelas kidnapped my granddaughter. After fifteen long years, I managed to get her back. It's as simple as that."

Bhairav cleared his throat. "Not quite." He'd been standing behind the Acharya and his sons, but now he stepped forward. He was dressed for battle in chain-link armor, sword and shield in hand, a bow on his back.

Beneath that competent facade roiled a sea of complex emotions Katyani could not gauge.

"The queen passed the bond to me upon her death." He turned to the window. "Come out, Katyani."

Even had she wanted to, she could not have disobeyed a direct command. She bit her lip until it bled.

It's okay, whispered a voice. *I'm with you.*

"Ayan?" she breathed. There was no one besides her in the stable—just the shadows thrown by the horses and the occasional snort and stamp of hoof.

But it was his voice. She hadn't imagined it.

A hand clasped hers. She dared not look around, because she couldn't bear for the illusion to break.

But as she pushed open the door and stepped out, his comforting presence evaporated. She would have cried then, except for the eyes on her.

Stay well, brother, she thought. *I'm sorry I could not save you.*

She straightened her back, hardened her face, and walked toward the group. Shamsher's men were stationed on the ramparts, awaiting his instructions. The yatu were invisible, although the wind carried a whiff of their rank smell, betraying their presence.

Bhairav's hand went to his sword, as if he feared she would attack him. Could he not sense her as the queen used to? Surely he realized the depth of her grief? He had lost family, yes, but so had she.

All of them stared at her like she was some strange species of animal. The most painful gaze belonged to Daksh. His eyes seared her as if they would burn the tattoo on her neck; she was laid bare before him, unable to hide the terrible things that had happened. She wished he would look away. She wished he were not here at all. She longed to feel Ayan's hand in her own again. Even if it had been an illusion, it had been a fine one.

"I told you to stay inside," snapped Shamsher.

"And I told her to step out," said Bhairav. "But you can return to the shadows if you wish, Katyani."

She said nothing, keeping her gaze fixed on the ground. She couldn't read him at all now. He had blocked himself from her.

"Is this ethical?" Shamsher appealed to the Acharya. "Are you not going to instruct him to release her?"

The Acharya's forehead creased, and he looked at the prince.

"I will," said Bhairav. "But not right away. She is the only survivor of the massacre in Ajaigarh, and she must be questioned. Moreover, my aunt's last act was to transfer the bond to me. I have to honor her sacrifice. There must have been a reason for what she did."

"Hate was the only reason," spat Shamsher. "You will be honoring her hatred."

"For a year and a day," said Bhairav, as if the regent had not spoken. "Until the mourning period for my aunt, uncle, and cousin ends, Katyani will stay in Chandela. At the end of that time, I will release her, provided my other conditions are met."

"What other conditions?" said Shamsher suspiciously.

"Half your kingdom," said Bhairav. "Disbanding of your army. Execution of the yatu that killed my family. And a complete disclosure of how you were helped, and by whom." He looked at Katyani as he said that.

Shamsher burst into mocking laughter. Daksh and Uttam stiffened beside the Acharya. Katyani's face burned. Bhairav had set peace terms the regent would never accept.

"Shamsher Singh," said the Acharya in chilly tones. "For what you have done, you must pay. Let no one think they are above the laws that divide good from evil."

"Do you think yatu are evil and men are good?" asked Shamsher. "Is the world that simplistic for you?"

"No," said the Acharya. "But the use to which you put them is evil. They committed murder in your name, at your command. This is not something which can be forgiven, in this life or the next. But you can begin the process of atonement by making reparations to the kingdom of Chandela."

"I don't regret what I did," said Shamsher. "The queen of Chandela deserved to die. I refuse these unfair terms."

"I will ask you once more," said the Acharya. "Accept these terms and surrender. Return in peace to your palace. Your granddaughter will be freed at the end of the mourning period and returned to you. I will personally ensure this."

"Will you?" said Katyani. "How?"

They all started, as if they had not expected her to speak. But her blood was boiling. She longed to stab them all.

"What do you think I am?" she inquired. "A pawn to be moved across your heartless chessboard?"

The Acharya frowned. "We will speak later, child."

"I am no longer a child," she snapped. "I was once, and you could have helped me then, but you didn't. I have been wronged, and you know it."

"Please, listen to her," said Daksh to his father.

Be silent, Katyani.

"Why, Bhairav?" she asked. "Why should I be silent? My world has been torn apart, my brother killed before my eyes. Everything I thought to be true turned out to be a lie. Am I not allowed to express my anger and my pain?"

"This is not the time and place for it," said the Acharya, a note of warning in his voice.

"I reject you," she said coldly. "All of you. None of you have any moral authority over me. I am free, as of this moment. Let me go."

"A year and a day," said Bhairav, matching his tone with hers. "Those are my terms. The palace was your home for fifteen years. Why are you reluctant to return to it? What has changed in your heart?"

"The people who made it home are dead." Her stomach twisted, and she fought down the grief that threatened to overwhelm her. She hardened her voice. "It's not my heart that changed. It's yours I no longer recognize. Who the hell are you, and what did you do to my brother?"

"Enough." The Acharya raised his hand. "Shamsher Singh, the army you called for will never arrive. It was intercepted by Chandela forces early this morning. Do you agree to the terms of truce?"

The regent bowed his head. For a moment, it looked like he was reconsidering his options. Then he raised his head and snapped his fingers.

Dozens of yatu poured out from the buildings where they had been hiding, armed to the teeth. The courtyard vibrated with the thud of their hideous feet as they surrounded the group, weapons raised. The soldiers on the ramparts nocked their arrows.

Steel clanged as Daksh, Uttam, and Bhairav withdrew their swords and fell into stance. The Acharya did not move. "This is your answer?" he said, sounding tired. "We bear the white flag."

"Forgive me, Acharya," said Shamsher. He uttered a guttural word in an unfamiliar tongue.

The yatu attacked. From the Acharya's staff, thick gray smoke curled up into the air. Arrows fell toward him from the ramparts but were diverted by an invisible force, falling harmlessly to the ground.

Katyani felt exposed and defenseless without a weapon, but she rushed into the fray. Daksh and Uttam fought back-to-back, their blades cutting through the yatu like scythes through stalks of wheat. They could take care of themselves. It was Bhairav she made a beeline for.

But Bhairav was fighting in a way she'd never seen him fight before—except once. She remembered how he had fought the yatudhani in Nandovana. He moved now with the same speed and grace, savage and elegant, slicing off yatu limbs and dancing out of the way of their clubs and maces. He'd been holding back all these years, allowing Ayan to outshine him. Pretending to be weaker, less accomplished—but why? So he wasn't deemed a threat? She sensed his fierce joy in the battle, his pride in his skills, and was struck again by the confusion and conflict that had overwhelmed her when the bond transferred to him.

Still, there were far too many yatu for three men to beat, no matter how exceptional their swordsmanship. Why was the Acharya not helping them? She leaped on the back of a yatu and grabbed his neck, trying to twist it. It was like trying to twist an iron bar.

The archers on the battlements aimed their arrows outward as the Chandela cavalry thundered up to the broken gates. The smoke from the Acharya's staff must have been a signal. Shouts and screams rang out as dozens of arrows found their mark among the cavalry. But fifty men would not last long against five hundred.

The Acharya raised his staff and tapped the ground with it thrice. Streaks of white lightning crackled from the tip of the staff and struck a group of five yatu. They fell to the ground, writhing, and the nauseating smell of burned yatu flesh invaded Katyani's nostrils. She managed to snatch a dagger from the belt of the yatu she was grappling with just before he threw her off his back.

Shamsher sprang forward and slashed his sword down on the Acharya's staff. Even before the two connected, Katyani knew which one would prevail. The staff was a powerful spiritual weapon. Shamsher's sword, no matter how sharp, could not cut it.

There was a terrific *clang,* and the regent's sword clattered across the courtyard. Shamsher was thrown back with the force of the blow. A yatu bent to pick him up but dropped to the ground with a roar of agony as the Acharya tapped his staff again.

Shamsher struggled to his feet and threw his dagger—not at the Acharya, but at Bhairav. Katyani didn't pause to think; her body moved of its own accord, propelled by the need to protect the brother she'd grown up with—so different from the man she was bonded to. She flung herself forward and blocked the dagger with the one she'd snatched from the yatu. Shamsher's weapon spun away, and he gave her a look full of sadness and betrayal, as if he knew it was over, and was only going through the motions for the sake of appearances. The Acharya's involvement had shifted the balance. Shamsher was doomed to defeat.

While he was standing there, still looking at her with that lost expression that would haunt her dreams in the nights to come, an arrow flew through the air and pierced his chest. He staggered back, clutching the shaft. Blood seeped from the wound and stained his tunic. He fell, and this time, no one rushed to his side. The yatu were already dead or driven away. His soldiers still fought the Chandela horsemen, although the battlements had been breached and the cavalry was among them, stabbing them with maces and swords.

Nightmare. It was all a nightmare. She'd wake up and none of this would have happened. Everyone would still be alive.

The dagger dropped from Katyani's hand. She walked up to Shamsher and crouched beside him, a wave of contradictory emotions washing over her. He deserved this end, and yet, it hurt. She'd only just found out she had a grandfather, she'd barely accepted the horrific truth, and he was already lost to her. One more person who might have been family in a different life, different circumstances. One more wound in her soul. Blood dripped from his mouth, and he struggled to speak.

"Hush," she said. "It's over. You can rest now."

"What . . . irony," he gasped. "Dying . . . like this."

If he had spared Ayan, she could have found it in her heart to sympathize with him. But he was a cold-hearted murderer and did not deserve her compassion.

Yet, his cause had been just. She would not withhold him a sliver of comfort in his dying moments. She grasped his hand and held it between her own. "The soul is neither born, nor does it die, nor once having been does it cease to be," she whispered, repeating words she remembered from a lesson on the Bhagavad Gita. "It is unborn, eternal, immortal, ancient. It cannot be killed, even when the body is killed."

He relaxed and smiled, despite his pain. "Call me grandfather before I go."

She took a deep breath. "Grandfather, if you see my parents, say hello to them from me."

Shamsher returned the pressure of her hand and closed his eyes. It took a few minutes for him to die—the longest minutes of Katyani's life. She wanted to focus her thoughts on him, to recite another line from the Gita, but her mind blanked, and she was too aware of the men who surrounded her. They stood some distance away, obviously waiting for the dying to be over with so they could proceed to the next item on the agenda. Namely, her.

A tiny rattle sounded in Shamsher's throat, and his breath stopped. She removed her hand from his, feeling empty. She'd known him for just a few days, and she'd hated him for most of it. She still hated what he'd done, and she'd never forgive him the death of Ayan. But, like a preta, he was more to be pitied than hated.

"A better death than he gave my aunt," said Bhairav, coming closer, his voice flat and emotionless. He'd blocked himself from her again, but she sensed, behind the wall he'd raised, a shiver of triumph.

She rose and faced him, summoning her inner strength. "He's dead. You no longer have reason to hold me hostage for a year and a day."

"Hostage?" Bhairav shook his head. "There will be an investigation into what happened. Your presence will be critical. We also need to ensure your cousin's cooperation in meeting the terms of the truce."

"The crown prince of Malwa does not remember who I am," said Katyani. "He won't care what happens to me."

"But I do," said Bhairav, changing tack. "Come home, Katya. Do you not wish to see Revaa?"

"Of course I do," she said, even as her heart swelled in mingled gladness and shame. The princess was alive; how had Katyani not thought of her until reminded? "You don't need to *bind* me for that. Or for anything else. I will go with you; I will help in your investigation. But I am not your bondswoman, Bhairav. I never will be."

Daksh made a small movement, as if he would go to her, but his father gave a minute shake of his head, and he subsided.

Bhairav opened his palm and blew a soft breath on it. She shuddered as the raven on her neck beat its wings. "I didn't ask for this either, Katya. How about this: you return with me, and let us complete the investigation. I will research how to remove the bond, and you can decide where you want to go next."

That sounded reasonable, but she could not read him, could not be sure of his true intentions. There was no objection she could make to his words, though.

"Now that Shamsher and his yatu are dead, we can be flexible in how we deal with Prince Aditya," said Uttam in his calm voice. "He studied at the gurukul two years ago. He is an honorable young man, and it is likely the regent acted without his full knowledge."

"I agree," said the Acharya. "Do not carry your hatred into the next generation, Bhairav."

Katyani sensed a frisson of displeasure from Bhairav, but he bowed and murmured, "Yes, Acharya."

A Chandela soldier hurried up to them. "All Paramara soldiers have been killed," he reported.

The Acharya winced. "None surrendered?"

"No, Acharya, they fought to the death."

"Loyalty to the wrong man, the wrong cause," mused the Acharya. "I am reminded of why I stay away from the affairs of Bharat's kingdoms."

Katyani managed to stop herself from shouting that he should have interfered years earlier, when she still had a chance at a normal life. The massacre in the audience hall would never have happened, and Ayan would still be alive.

Bhairav bowed. "Thank you for your help today, Acharya Mahavir, Airya Daksh, Airya Uttam. I will be forever grateful."

The Acharya waved a hand. "It was our duty."

"Are you all right?" Daksh blurted out to Katyani, the first words he had spoken to her.

She had avoided looking in his direction, but now she was forced to. It wasn't any easier than it had been during their last meeting. The kiss might as well have happened a lifetime ago. She could hardly recognize herself as the girl who had teased him in the gurukul. He, on the other hand, looked the same as ever, handsome and pristine, barely disheveled from the fight. His eyes were warm with concern, his jaw tense as he regarded her.

"I am physically uninjured," she said, which was not exactly an answer to his question, but would have to suffice. Anything else would have been a lie.

"Then let us return to Ajaigarh," said Bhairav briskly. "I will be honored if you accompany us to the palace, Acharya."

"We must return to the gurukul," said the Acharya. "I need to recover my strength and get back to my students." He looked exhausted. Using the staff must have depleted his spiritual reserves.

"I have to give the regent a funeral," said Katyani.

"I will ask my men to give the last rites to everyone who died here," said Bhairav.

"See that you do," said the Acharya. "We don't want their spirits trapped in these ruins."

"What about the yatu?" asked Bhairav, eyeing the corpses in distaste.

"They have their own death rituals," said the Acharya. "I will send word to a yatu band in Nandovana to collect them."

It felt wrong to leave Shamsher's body in the courtyard for strangers to pick up. But it felt wrong to leave his dead soldiers too.

At least he wasn't alone in death. So many men and monsters had died for him. What kind of person could inspire such loyalty? She'd never know. She remembered how she'd shut him down when he tried to talk of her parents, and regret stabbed her.

Her dead outnumbered the living. If not for Revaa, she would have longed to join their ranks. Bhairav no longer regarded her as a sister to rely on. But there was still one person left in the world who depended upon her. She would not fail Revaa, as she had failed everyone else.

CHAPTER 13

THE ACHARYA AND HIS SONS PARTED WAYS WITH THEM HALF-way through the journey back to Ajaigarh. A couple of times, Daksh maneuvered his horse so he was riding next to Katyani, but he did not speak to her, and she was glad of that. What could he have said that would have made the slightest difference?

Yet, when he was gone, she missed him.

They rode in silence the rest of the way to Ajaigarh at the head of the Chandela cavalry. She felt like an enemy captive, for all that her hands were untied. Their return to the capital was greeted with subdued cheers. People came out on the streets to throw flowers at them, as if they had won a great victory. What kind of rumors had been circulating about the Paramara invasion and the deaths of the royal family?

A current of jubilation ran through Bhairav, but he kept his face solemn as he waved at his subjects. *Acting like a king already,* she thought, watching him. Why did it hurt so much? Yes, it should have been Ayan, but Ayan was gone, and people would look to Bhairav now. That was only natural.

They dismounted at the foot of the hill and climbed the steps to the fort, followed by a company of ten soldiers.

"There were dead bodies all over," said Bhairav. "Took the whole day to clean up."

Katyani's stomach dropped. Of course, the casualty rate in the fort must have been high. Her own Garuda unit must have suffered terrible losses. "How did the yatu enter the fort?" she asked. Not that she expected Bhairav to know, but he might have some theories.

"I was hoping you could tell me that." He gave her a sidelong glance.

She shook her head. "The regent didn't tell me."

The walk up to the fort was unreal. The thick, humid air of Shraavana sat on her skin like a living thing, enveloping her in its familiarity. Here were the same steps, the same trees there had always been. And yet, nothing was the same, nor would it be again. She remembered how care-free she had been walking down these steps with her brothers on their way to the gurukul and choked back a sob.

The gates were thrown open, and they entered. She didn't recognize any of the guards at the gatehouse. Were the old ones dead or injured? She hoped Falgun had survived the attack. A good, brave man. Weren't they all? Didn't they deserve to be remembered as such?

"When are the last rites for the king and queen?" She swallowed a lump in her throat. "For Ayan?"

"Tomorrow," answered Bhairav. "We'll cremate them by the banks of the Ken and float their ashes down the river."

At least she'd have a chance to say good-bye. It was a small comfort, but it wasn't nothing.

An open carriage was waiting to take them to the palace. Bhairav dis-missed the soldiers and the two of them climbed in. As they crossed the outer courtyard and passed the temples and gardens, Katyani saw in her mind's eye the trail of dead bodies and broken limbs the yatu must have left behind. No trace remained of them now. Servants must have carried away the bodies, and perhaps rain had washed away the blood.

In the entrance hall of the palace, two servants waited for them with fresh towels and drinks of cool lemonade. "Where's Revaa?" she asked, accepting a glass with gratitude.

"In seclusion," said Bhairav. He stared at the glass in his hand, not meeting her eyes. "The events have traumatized her."

"I will go to her at once." Katyani drained her glass and set it down.

"Later," said Bhairav, putting his own glass away untouched. "You should go to your room and rest. I'm sure you're tired."

Her head did feel heavy. One of the servants led her up the stairs to her room. She dragged herself up, clutching the bannisters. Too late, she realized that the lemonade had been spiked. She had antidotes to almost every kind of drug, but she was in no shape to fetch any of them. She barely made it to the bed before blacking out.

When she woke, it was pitch dark outside, although a lantern had been lit in her room. A tray with a plate of food and a cup of water sat on a table by her bedside.

She waited for her head to stop spinning and crawled out of bed. Her stomach hurt, but whether from hunger, nausea, or the drug she'd been given, she couldn't be sure. She went to her medicine cabinet, supporting herself by clutching the furniture and leaning against the walls.

It was empty. All the dried herbs, tinctures, pouches of powdered leaves and petals—all gone. She felt along the edges of the shelves, but not even a sachet remained. Someone had been quite thorough.

She went back to the table, picked up the cup of water, and sniffed. It didn't smell of anything. There was no way to be sure it wasn't drugged too, but it was difficult to poison water without leaving some minute trace in its smell or taste.

After she'd drunk, she felt better. She went to the windows and twitched the curtain aside. Two guards paced the length of the courtyard beneath. She grimaced. Bond or no bond, Bhairav wasn't taking any chances.

He'd said the last rites would be "tomorrow." Had tomorrow already come and gone? Had she missed her chance to say good-bye? Bitterness and sorrow surged through her, leaving her racked by sobs; why would he deny her this small comfort? Did he hate her that much?

What happened to you, Bhairav? What happened to me?

After a while, her head felt heavy again, and she lay down. She woke to bright sunlight, a fresh tray of food and water, and a bath laid out for her, which she gratefully sank into at once. But no Chaya came to do her hair or chatter with her. Was she one more innocent victim of the palace massacre? The thought was agonizing.

She dried herself, dressed, and drank the water. The food looked and smelled delicious, but she couldn't bring herself to touch it.

The door to her room slammed open. She whirled around, heart jumping. Five guards, none of whom she recognized, entered. The one in the lead said, "Please follow us to the audience hall. The trial is about to begin."

"Whose trial? For what?"

But the guard did not answer. A cold pit opened in her stomach as she followed them out. She suspected whose trial this might be, given her treatment, but hoped she was wrong. She was glad to at least escape the confines of her room. Perhaps she'd glimpse someone she knew and be able to question them.

But none of the faces she saw were familiar. Strange servants hurried past, not paying her any attention.

"Is Chaya okay?" she called out a couple of times, but no one answered.

The main audience hall was the largest chamber in the palace. It occupied most of the ground floor behind the entrance hall and was reserved for the king's weekly audiences with Chandela citizens. The other days of the week were designated for more formal trials.

The hall today was packed and noisy. A narrow corridor of space led from the door to the dais where the judges sat, dressed in black robes, looking like a line of crows. Each side was roped to prevent people blocking the path. Katyani walked down the corridor, flanked by guards as if she were a public danger. A hiss rose on both sides. Men and women broke off their chatter to make the sign to avert the evil eye as she passed.

Her heart sank. What stories had been circulating about her the past few days? She'd always been a popular figure before, the royal family's confidante and bodyguard. Of course, things could not continue the same way with the deaths of those who'd been in her charge, but she'd hoped that people wouldn't blame and hate her to this extent. Had her kinship to Shamsher already been leaked to the general public? Would they hold it against her, even though she could not help it?

The guards escorted her to a box before the dais and pushed her in. *The prisoner's box.* She'd already guessed she was the one on trial, but until she was in the box, it didn't hit home. How many times had she sat on the dais with the king and queen, trying not to yawn as court assessors debated the evidence and prisoners begged miserably for clemency? Now she was the one in the box. A bitter laugh welled up inside her; she suppressed it and turned her attention to the judges.

There were thirteen of them, all men. The gender flexibility in professions and social mores did not extend to a court of law in the Chandela kingdom. Odd how she'd never noticed it before, but she and Hemlata had always been the only women on that dais.

Bhairav sat in the middle, simply and soberly dressed like an ordinary litigant, facing east as prescribed by the law. He did not glance her way, but her bond gave a dark little throb of tension. He was stressed about the trial but also confident of the outcome, a strange mix she could not parse.

Flanking him were the chief justice, priests, and councilors who would hear the evidence and debate her case. She recognized around half of them. There was her old nemesis Shukla, the chief royal priest. She tried to catch his eye, but he kept his head lowered. Was he ashamed? He should be. She'd been his student once.

Off to one side stood the dandanayaka, the chief punishment officer. She'd sparred with him in the training ground a few times.

Next to him was Tanoj, looking his usual self with no injuries. Relief welled up in her at the familiar sight. She curbed her desire to shout and wave at him. *It's me, sir. Glad you're okay.*

He must have sensed her regard, for he glanced at her. His face twisted in pain and disgust before turning away.

Her stomach flipped. What was *wrong* with him? He'd known her for years. How could things change so much in just a few days? She'd been snatched from her universe and thrown into a different one where everything was upside down.

At a desk opposite her sat the court scribes and messengers. Bhairav gave a regal wave of his hand, his face stern and sad, behaving like the king he already was in everything but name. One of the scribes got up to ring a silver bell, indicating the court was now in session. Everyone fell quiet. Katyani tried to slow her pulse. Whatever happened, she would not let them see her distress.

One of the court assessors bowed before the dais and began to read from a scroll. She ignored the initial part, which was an exhortation to the court to follow the path of dharma, a reminder to the king of his moral and ethical duties to his people, and a command to ordinary citizens to follow the rules of proper conduct.

When he had dispensed with the preliminaries, the assessor cleared his throat and said, "We come now to the case that stands before us today." Everyone perked up. "Katyani, second-in-command of the royal Garuda unit, stands accused of conspiracy to murder King Jaideep, Queen Hemlata, and Crown Prince Ayan."

A part of her had expected it, and yet the words stunned her. She felt sick and dizzy. Here was their unjust suspicion given voice and power and formalized in a court of law. She willed Bhairav to turn his gaze on her, but he refused to look in her direction.

"Call the first witness," said the chief justice, a sleek man with an oiled moustache.

The assessor bowed. He called the captain of the gatehouse to give an account of the yatu attack on the fort. Falgun walked up to the dais, his arm in a sling, his face bruised and haunted. Katyani's gladness at seeing him alive soon evaporated at his words. It was difficult to listen to him. He related how all his men had died defending the gate, their necks twisted, their torsos trampled in blood and dust. He kept his voice low, his gaze on the floor, but when his statement had ended, he cast a hate-filled glance at her.

It's not my fault, she wanted to tell him. But he wouldn't believe her. And wasn't it at least partially her fault? Shamsher had done it because of *her.* The weight of this knowledge bowed her back and silenced her voice.

Next, the assessor called a couple of servants who had survived the attack. They described scenes of horror in the palace, of hiding behind furniture and armor while their friends and colleagues were brutally maimed and killed before their eyes. Katyani listened to their testimony, her eyes burning with unshed tears of guilt and grief. All told, nearly a hundred people died that night. This figure did not include those in the king's audience chamber.

The assessor unfurled his scroll further. "We now come to our most important witness: Princess Revaa."

Katyani gave a shaky sigh of relief. At last, she would lay eyes on the princess and be assured she was okay. Revaa would tell them Katyani had fought against the yatu and been dragged away against her will. That *she* had been the one to tell the princess to stay safe and stay hidden. She was surprised the court had summoned the princess at all, but it gave her hope that the process would be a fair one and she would be acquitted.

Revaa entered the hall through a private door behind the dais, flanked by several members of her retinue. Katyani put a hand on her mouth, trying to hold herself in. *Thank the goddess you're all right, love.*

She wore mourning white, like Bhairav, but still managed to look every inch the princess with her pearl necklace and elegant ivory sandals. Her hair had been piled up on her head; it made her look vulnerable, as if her neck could not bear the weight of all that hair. She kept her eyes on the floor, but it was clear to Katyani she'd been crying. Revaa's nose always went red at the first hint of tears. Katyani longed to comfort her.

"Princess Revaa," said the assessor kindly, "we know this is a difficult task for you. But justice must be served. Please tell the court what happened the night the royal family was murdered."

"I wanted to attend the council meeting, but the queen wouldn't allow me," whispered Revaa. "So I decided to—"

"I request you to speak louder for the benefit of the court," interrupted the assessor.

"I decided to eavesdrop," said Revaa, making her voice stronger. "I entered the king's audience chamber before anyone else and hid behind a screen."

"Please tell us what happened," said the assessor.

"Shortly after the meeting began, someone rammed the door. A few minutes later, the door broke and yatu entered. They killed everyone except the queen and Katyani."

"Did anyone know you were hiding behind the screen?"

"No," said Revaa.

What? Katyani gripped the walls of her box, dark confusion coursing through her. That wasn't true. She had found Revaa and told her to get back behind the screen when the door was rammed.

"Please describe Katyani's actions during the attack," said the assessor.

"She . . . did nothing to help the royal family," said Revaa tonelessly. "She stood aside while the yatu killed everyone. Then she led the wounded queen out of the room."

Hubbub broke out across the court. The court messenger rang his bell for silence.

Blood pounded in Katyani's ears. Revaa had lied. Revaa had implicated her in the deaths of the king, queen, and crown prince.

But *why?* She loved Revaa like a sister and had always believed the princess felt the same way about her.

The testimonies continued. Katyani listened in a daze, no longer able to make sense of the words being spoken. Her chest hurt, as if there were not enough air left to breathe in this hall, in this entire world. She'd been accused of murdering the royal family, and the one person who could have saved her with the truth had condemned her with a lie. The one person she'd thought was still family, the one person she'd thought still cared about her and needed her. Katyani's eyes blurred as she looked at Revaa standing next to the dais, her face puffy, her hands clenched together.

The last person to testify was Bhairav himself. His grieving, exhausted voice commanded complete silence in the court. He told them how he had sought the help of Acharya Mahavir to confront the regent of Malwa and discovered that the person he'd always thought of as his adopted sister was actually Shamsher's granddaughter. After listening to his sister's testimony, he'd come to the reluctant conclusion that Katyani was a traitor who had betrayed the king and queen to take revenge for Malwa's defeat fifteen years ago. The most damning piece of evidence was the fact that only Queen Hemlata had known how to break the wards that protected the palace from monsters. As her bondswoman, Katyani would have had access to this crucial piece of knowledge.

Look at me, thought Katyani, staring at him, trying not to shake. *You know none of this is true. That's not the way the bond works. Why are you doing this?*

But he did not look at her, and he did not allow her into his mind.

Shouts broke out among the citizens gathered in the court.

"Drown her in boiling oil!"

"Cut off her limbs one by one."

"Chop off her head and hang it by the city gate!"

Bhairav raised a hand, and they fell silent. "Let the judges decide if she is guilty or not," he said gravely. But his gravity was a sham; he knew what they would decide, had known it before the trial started, had known it back in Rajgarh itself when he had offered to let her go after the "investigation" into the massacre. He'd lied to her, lied to the Acharya. Katyani's hand clawed her neck as if she could tear the raven out, tear *him* out of her. If she could, she would have erased every memory she had of him in that moment.

It didn't take the judges long. The men on the dais went into a huddle and whispered together. Scant minutes later, the chief justice rose. "Your Majesty, we have arrived at the conclusion that the defendant is guilty of the heinous crime of conspiring to murder the royal family."

The words barely registered with Katyani. She leaned on the wooden walls of the box, willing herself not to pass out.

Bhairav looked at her for the first time. "Do you wish to confess?" he asked, his voice icy. "Confession is the first step toward atonement."

His eyes were cold, emotionless orbs of judgment, as if he *believed* in her guilt. *What an amazing act you're putting on, Bhav. But you can't fool me, and you can't fool yourself.* "I won't confess to a crime I did not commit," she spat.

"Your guilt has already been established," he said. "Your punishment will be less severe if you make a full and heartfelt confession."

Katyani shifted her gaze to Revaa, who was standing in a corner surrounded by her retainers. "Why did you lie, Princess?" she asked, keeping her voice even.

Revaa gave her a quick, frightened glance and lowered her head.

Bhairav frowned. "Silence! There will be no manipulation of witnesses in this court. Hear my verdict. I will spare your life, for all the years of service rendered to Chandela, even if it was a lie. Nor will I have you thrown into the dungeons."

There were murmurs of disappointment and outrage. Of course, he could not have her executed while she was bonded to him. He would have to break the bond first. Pain, though, he could inflict on her at will without hurting himself. She glared at him, unable to guess what he intended. Nothing good, from the dark satisfaction seeping through the bond. Everything had gone as he planned. But *why* had he done it? Was her lineage enough to make her the enemy in his eyes?

"For the crime you have committed, you will pay," he continued. "I give you twenty-five lashes of Chentu if you will confess to your crime. I give you one hundred lashes if you do not. Which will it be?"

A hundred lashes from Chentu? Katyani thought she must not have heard right. The maximum sentence meted out was usually not more than fifteen or twenty. Each lash eroded both spiritual power as well as memory. By the middle of a lashing, even the most hardened criminals wept for forgiveness. By the end of it, they forgot their names. A hundred lashes would shred her soul to pieces.

And yet, she would not confess to something she had not done.

"I did not conspire to kill the royal family," she said, loud enough that even people in the back could hear her. "Revaa lied. I fought the yatu and was overpowered."

"So be it," he said calmly. "A hundred lashes." He beckoned the dandanayaka.

"No, please!" Revaa screamed. "A hundred lashes is too many. Bhairav, you promised!"

Bhairav made a sharp gesture with his hand, and guards surrounded the princess. They carried her out of the back door, struggling and sobbing, "Let her go! Please let her go."

He passed a weary hand over his eyes. This, too, was an act. Was there anything left in him of the boy she'd known? "I apologize to the court. This has been too much for the princess. As you all know, she regarded Katyani as her elder sister. I promised to spare Katyani's life, but I cannot be lenient in the punishment. I owe it to the people of Chandela to make an example of the person who is responsible for the deaths of the beloved royal family."

"I didn't do it," shouted Katyani in desperation, clutching the walls of the prisoner's box. But did anyone hear her? Did it matter? In their minds, she was guilty. They needed a culprit, someone to blame and punish. She was the perfect candidate.

Bhairav tossed Chentu to the dandanayaka. "One hundred lashes. Then you may carry her body to the healing station."

The world grew dark before Katyani's eyes. She dug her nails into her palm, focusing on the pain to stay conscious. *It's me, Bhairav,* she wanted to scream. *We grew up together. I considered you my brother.*

But no sound emerged from her parched throat. Drums sounded as guards pushed her out of the box and down on the floor in front of the dais. The dandanayaka walked toward her, swinging Chentu. He'd always been deferential to her in the past. Hadn't they all? Yet now they bayed for her blood, cheering as the dandanayaka flicked the whip in his hand.

"Uncover her back," he ordered.

Katyani wrenched away from the grasp of the guards holding her down. "I will uncover my back myself," she said, her voice loud and firm. The hall fell silent, amazed at her audacity.

Before Bhairav could issue any order to the contrary, Katyani unbuttoned her waistcoat and shrugged it off. A collective sigh went through the court. She tugged her kameez over her head, fury overriding every other emotion inside her.

Did they expect her to remove her bodice as well? She left it on. It was only a strip around her chest anyway. If they wanted to expose her breasts, let them say so aloud with their evil tongues.

She knelt on the floor and bowed her head. "Dandanayaka, what are you waiting for?" she snapped.

There were whispers of astonishment and disapproval. *Good.* Let them remember her voice before it broke. Let them remember her body, unblemished by the whip. One day, she would come for them; she would make them regret what they'd done.

"Begin," said Bhairav, sounding annoyed. She looked up, met his eyes, and showed him her teeth. *I'll remember this,* the smile said. *Even if I forget everything else.*

Chentu sang through the air and slashed her back, delighted to have found a new victim.

"One," said the dandanayaka, his voice flat.

For a moment, she felt nothing. Then the pain hit her, a trail of fire from her shoulder blades to the base of her spine.

What shall I take? mused Chentu in the smoky, oily voice only its victims could hear. *That memory of beating up Ayan for the first time when you were ten, and stealing mangoes for him from the orchard to make him feel better.*

She gasped and shuddered as the whip whistled its way down for the second slash. The memory vanished, a piece of her heart falling into shadow.

"Two," said the dandanayaka.

This time, some of that power you're so proud of, said Chentu.

She curled her fists around her knees, trying to hold herself in as the third lash struck at the core of her being, eating into her spiritual power. She would not cry; she would not give them the satisfaction of breaking down.

I am not enjoying this, Katya, Bhairav sent. *But it is necessary. Your body will heal, eventually.*

Burn in hell, Bhairav.

The whip came down yet again.

"Four," said the dandanayaka. And: "Five."

She bit her lip to keep from screaming. Blood trickled down her back. Memories flared and died, and spiritual power drained away from her.

In a haze of agony, she remembered a ghostly voice.

There will come a time when you suffer great pain. Think of us then, and we will absorb your hurt.

Pretas, she thought, *if you can hear me, this would be a great time to show up.*

Chentu came down for the tenth slash. But this time, it landed on the back of a ghastly, pale-skinned creature with a distended stomach and misshapen head. She sobbed in relief at the sight. Someone still cared enough to come to her aid.

The whip screamed its frustration. *This is not allowed. You're cheating!*

The dandanayaka continued to beat the preta, unaware that his victim had changed.

The preta's back split open, and it whimpered in agony. A dark, stale smell of something rotten stole into the air. With every lash, the preta seemed smaller, diminished.

Katyani extended a trembling hand to the suffering creature. *Enough,* she whispered. *Save yourself.*

It turned its white, pupil-less eyes on her. *Remember us the way we remembered you.*

Chentu came down again, ferocious in its thirst. Before her horrified gaze, the preta turned to dust and blew away.

At last, said Chentu in triumph. But before the whip could slash her back, another preta appeared to take the place of the one that had been devoured. *No,* she tried to say. *Don't, please don't.*

But the preta did not leave. Five lashes, ten, fifteen, and it crumbled to dust like the first.

The third and last preta appeared. Katyani bent over, coughing blood.

"Fifty-five," said the dandanayaka as the last preta vanished. Her stomach clenched in sorrow. Even with their help, there were still forty-five lashes to go. She would not survive this. The pretas' sacrifice would be in vain. Who would remember them? Who would offer rice balls for a month to free their trapped souls?

"Fifty-six," said the dandanayaka, and Chentu landed on her back with a screech of victory. She lurched and fell forward on her stomach. Her back was a river of pain. Again and again the cruel whip came down, peeling off her skin, exposing the red, raw flesh, draining her power until she could barely raise her head or remember who she was. Blood spattered the white marble floor.

The vetala's words came back to her. *You will lose all you love. You will long for death. You will forget who you are. You will remember me then.*

Did she long for death?

Yes, in that moment, she did. Anything to be free of this unbearable pain. She'd lost everything worth living for. She sobbed and scrabbled at the floor, wishing for the blessed darkness of oblivion.

Heavy footsteps strode down the hall. A gruff voice commanded, "Stop."

The dandanayaka paused.

"Who dares interrupt the king's court?" Tanoj stepped forward, his hand on his sword.

"Who dares raise his voice at me?" came the gruff voice. "Tell me your name so I can curse you, your family, and your entire lineage for generations to come."

There was pin-drop silence. The raven fluttered in alarm. A curse delivered by someone with the actual power to wield it would finish off Tanoj and his entire clan. It would rebound on Bhairav too. With enormous effort, Katyani raised her head to look at the owner of the voice.

A tall, bony man in ivory robes, his white hair wild and uncombed, his face thin and ascetic and, right now, bearing a thunderous expression.

From somewhere within her, Katyani dredged up his name.

Acharya, she tried to say. *Acharya.*

He gave her a quick glance, and his expression became even darker. Behind him stood a much younger man in sky-blue robes who did not look her way at all. He had the same ascetic face, drawn in taut lines. A silver scabbard was tied to his belt. His hand trembled above the hilt of his sword, as if on the verge of unsheathing it.

Daksh. She longed for the earth to swallow her up. *Why, Goddess, why? Why did you have to make him see me like this?*

Bhairav stood and bowed. "Acharya," he said in a conciliatory tone, hiding the anger Katyani knew he was feeling, "please forgive my bodyguard. He does not know who you are. Kindly overlook his ignorance. Please also forgive the lack of a reception from myself. I thought you were back in your gurukul."

"Hah, I surprised you, didn't I?" said the Acharya in a satisfied voice. "I am here for my gurudakshina, the payment due to me for teaching you, your cousin, and your adopted sister. I have immediate need of it."

"Of course." Bhairav hurried down the steps of the dais. "Would you please wait in a guest room while we finish up here? As you can see, a punishment is in progress. Katyani has been found guilty of conspiracy to murder the royal family and sentenced to a hundred lashes from Chentu."

Daksh grabbed the hilt of his sword and took a step forward, his face almost unrecognizable in its snarl. The Acharya held up a hand, and he froze. Katyani looked away from them, choking with rage and humiliation. She would make Bhairav pay. She would make them all pay for this spectacle they had made of her.

"I cannot wait for my gurudakshina," said the Acharya. "You are halfway to destroying it."

Bhairav looked at him, confused. "Whatever you ask for shall be yours, Acharya."

"I want her," said the Acharya, pointing to Katyani's bleeding, broken body.

Incredulity coursed through her, both her own as well as Bhairav's. The Acharya was asking for *her* as payment?

"What?" Bhairav sputtered. "But Acharya, she is my bondswoman."

I'm not, she thought fiercely.

"Why else am I asking you for her?" the Acharya snapped. "You must transfer the bond to me."

As if she were some kind of package. She knew why the Acharya was doing it, but it still cut to the bone.

"Acharya, she is a criminal." Bhairav tried to speak in a reasonable tone. "She has been found guilty of *murder*."

"Sixty lashes of Chentu did not kill her," said the Acharya. "That means her fate lies elsewhere. Transfer the bond to me!"

"I don't know how," said Bhairav, his voice rising, panic stirring inside him as control slipped away.

"I will guide you," said the Acharya. He pointed his staff at a guard, who shrank visibly. "You! Fetch a pot of water, a mirror, and a clean knife."

The guard looked helplessly at Bhairav.

The chief justice rose and said in an oily voice, "Acharya Mahavir, you are famous in all of Bharat for your knowledge of the ancient texts. Prince Bhairav will shortly be crowned the king of Chandela. Surely the king is the highest judge in his own kingdom. He has been quite merciful to this cold-blooded traitor."

The Acharya banged his staff on the marble floor. The ground shook as if there were an earthquake. People screamed and cowered. Katyani bit back a cry as the vibrations jarred her back. "Let me not wish such mercy on my worst enemies," he said, his voice like granite. "I am disappointed in you, Bhairav. You forgot the virtue of compassion. It is a failure of your character or my teaching. Which is it?"

Bhairav wisely kept his mouth shut. She sensed the frustration roiling his insides. Everything had been going perfectly, and the Acharya had to turn up and spoil it all. Even through her pain and nausea, Katyani wanted to laugh. A whimper emerged from her instead.

For the first time, Daksh looked at her. In his eyes was bright, burning rage.

"Give me my gurudakshina," said the Acharya coldly. "I have no wish to linger in this impious hall."

Bhairav licked his lips; confusion and uncertainty filtered through the bond. The raven squawked, looking for a place to hide. "May I ask what you intend to do with her?"

"You may not," said the Acharya. "But I don't mind telling you. She was my pupil once. She has useful gifts. I intend to make her work in my gurukul."

"Of course, Acharya." Bhairav nodded to the guard, who ran out of the hall as if chased by hungry tigers.

Katyani thought of the pretas. *Thank you for saving my soul. I won't forget you.*

There was no glimmer of response. Chentu had eaten them. But she would free them one day. She would destroy Chentu and liberate the souls it had sucked into its void.

The guard returned with the requested items. The Acharya instructed Bhairav to cut his raven tattoo out of his hand, dripping blood into the pot of water. Onlookers watched in terrified fascination. This was a story they would tell for generations to come.

Katyani laid her cheek against the floor, exhaustion and relief seeping into her. No matter what happened next, she would be free of Bhairav. She tried to remember how she'd felt when the queen transferred her bond to him, but she couldn't—one of the many things she'd lost in the last hour. She would not miss that particular memory.

But it would have helped prepare her for what happened next. Something dark and raven-shaped within her twisted, tore away, and re-formed into a white dove.

Don't go, she thought, writhing in agony. *You belong to me.*

The dove circled above her once, as if to comfort her, and flew away. She watched it go, her heart wrenching at the loss. The tattoo on her throat pulsed cold fire as it reshaped itself. Once again, her bond had passed to someone else, and she'd had no say in it. But this would be the last time. She didn't know if that was the Acharya's thought or her own, but it lessened her pain.

"It is done," said Bhairav, his voice shaking.

"I know," said the Acharya, giving his right hand a disgusted glance. "We'll go now."

Bhairav straightened and smoothed his expression, trying to regain his poise. "Load her into a carriage," he instructed the guards.

Katyani cried out as rough hands grabbed her shoulders and yanked her upright.

"I will take her." Daksh pushed aside the guards and caught her arms. She stared up into his grim face, too stunned to protest.

"But Airya, you will get blood on your robes," said Bhairav.

Daksh did not answer. He bent his knees and pulled Katyani on his back, placing her arms over his shoulders. Every movement sent fresh spasms of pain through her, but she pressed her lips together, determined not to make a sound. She crossed her arms around his chest, and he grasped her wrists and straightened up. He was carrying her like this so he would not touch her ruined back and hurt her. *So thoughtful and gallant to do this at his father's bidding.* She knew she should be grateful, but all she felt was shame and anger at having to be carried.

They made their way down the hall, the silent crowd parting for them like a river. Katyani gave a sickly, bloodstained grin to whoever was unlucky enough to catch her eye. They averted their gazes hastily, making the sign to ward off evil.

But evil would come for them. It already had. They just didn't know it yet.

Daksh carried her down the carriageway and through the palace gates, past the gardens and into the outer areas of the fort. Guards, maids, gardeners, clerks, and priests stopped to stare at them. She gave them the same sickly smile she'd given the crowd inside the hall; they recoiled and hurried away. No one tried to stop them. Bhairav must have sent a runner ahead to keep the gates open and the Acharya's path unimpeded.

It had grown cloudy in the past hour; a soft breeze sprang up, drying the sweat on her forehead. "I can walk," she said, the words slurring into each other.

Daksh did not deign to respond. The Acharya said, "Put aside your pride and let him carry you. It is good karma to carry the weak."

Carry the weak, my ass. She licked her parched lips and wished for water. The sky rumbled and it began to rain—not entirely unexpected, for it was the monsoon season, but it still felt like a gift. She turned her face up, letting the drops fall on her lips. They trickled down her back as well, stinging her wounds, washing away the blood.

Warm, sweet rain—how she'd loved to play in it as a child. Ayan and Revaa had enjoyed it too, but Bhairav had hated getting wet. They'd often teased him, dragging him out into the garden as the rain poured down and the maids gave chase, shouting at them to come back *right now*.

Hell of a thing to remember. She wished Chentu had taken that memory. She wished Chentu had taken them all: the good and the bad, the bitter and the sweet. None of it was real.

They crossed the outer courtyard and exited the fort through the serpentine gates. Over a mile, and he'd carried her the entire way. But he would not be able to navigate the slippery steps with her on his back.

"I can crawl down," she said, trying to make her voice strong and confident. It came out as a husky whisper.

"Shut up," said Daksh, tightening his grip on her wrists.

"Daksh," said the Acharya, his voice full of reproof. She sensed his displeasure through the bond.

"I'm sorry," said Daksh after a moment. "I meant to say, please do not distract me."

Oh, is that what you meant? Katyani bit her lip and said nothing. They began their descent. Every moment, she expected him to slip and fall down the rain-slickened steps, taking her with him. There were six hundred of them, after all. He only had to trip once. A fall from this height would injure him badly. And it would be *her* fault. She squeezed her eyes shut, unable to bear the tension.

But he didn't fall—a miracle in itself. They made their way safely down the hill even as the rain picked up its pace. The Acharya held his staff above them, diverting the water so it looked as if they walked in a moving chamber with invisible walls.

A gurukul coachman and carriage were waiting at the base of the hill. Acharya Mahavir climbed in and helped Daksh lay her on the grass-covered floor of the carriage, facedown. She inhaled the scent of the grass, feeling dizzy. Daksh got in, and the horses set off. *Good-bye, Bhairav,* she thought. *Good-bye, Revaa.* Her heart squeezed. *Betrayal must run in the family.*

"That wicked, murdering——" began Daksh.

She turned her head to look at him sideways, taken aback at his words and the passion in his voice. Daksh was always cool and collected. Except that once . . .

"Quiet," said the Acharya, a note of warning in his voice. "Focus on the task at hand."

What task, she wondered.

Hands loosened her bodice, and she stiffened. "Clothes," she said, her voice cracking.

"You will wear the robes of our gurukul henceforth," said the Acharya. "We must treat your back, so please stay still."

She tried, but it was hard. A cool, numbing liquid poured over her back gave momentary relief, but then Daksh began to swab it, and she had to bite her knuckles to stop from screaming.

"Some pain is good," said the Acharya. "But too much pain is bad. I can lessen it temporarily. Look at me."

She raised her head and gazed into his dark, fathomless eyes.

"Sleep," he said, and she slept.

CHAPTER 14

WHEN KATYANI WOKE, SHE FOUND HERSELF WRAPPED in bandages like a mummy. Over the bandages was a loose blue robe. Thankfully, she had retained the lower half of her clothing. She was still on the floor of the carriage, on her side, with a soft cushion beneath her head. Her back throbbed, but in a distant way, as if it belonged to someone else. That only made the pain inside her heart sharper in comparison. She tallied all she'd lost—home, family, name—and was surprised she still lived and breathed, like a reed persisting after a storm had destroyed the trees around it.

"This is why I hate to meddle," came the Acharya's crabby voice. "Once I start, I can never stop." A gray wave of exhaustion washed over him. He had overextended himself against the yatu and still hadn't fully recovered. The earthquake display in the audience hall had cost him far more than it should have.

The carriage swayed, and she winced, trying to hold herself still.

"We're entering Nandovana," said Daksh.

"At last." The Acharya sighed. "I don't feel safe in Chandela anymore."

You and me both, Acharya.

"The forest isn't exactly safe for you, Father."

"It's safer than the Ajaigarh palace. Katyani will attest to that, won't you?"

Katyani opened her cracked lips. "Snakes," she whispered. The palace was filled with beings that looked human but had the hearts of snakes.

The Acharya understood, of course. He'd have understood even without the bond, because he knew that what distinguished humans from monsters lay beneath the skin.

It felt both like and unlike the bond she'd had with Hemlata. The Acharya did not try to hide himself from her. Rather, he trusted her to maintain the proper psychic distance from him. She sensed that he considered it an abomination and hated having to resort to this to save her life. What would he tell everyone back at the gurukul? What would *she* tell Irfan and Nimaya?

She fingered the tattoo on her neck. The blue butterfly had transformed into a black raven had transformed into a white dove. When would she be rid of it once and for all?

The Acharya bent forward. "When we reach the gurukul, I will remove it."

She licked her lips. "Debt."

"You will find a way to pay it," he said. "And maybe you won't have to. All of this is at least partly my fault. I am sorry I arrived so late."

Daksh uncovered a gourd of water and held it out to her, his brow furrowed, his eyes full of concern.

Why, Airya, are you worried about me? Her lips twitched, and her heart lightened. She sat up and drank until the gourd was empty. Then she leaned her shoulder against the seat, trying not to let it touch the wounds on her back. Her head spun, but she had too many questions to stay silent.

"How did you know of the trial?" she asked.

"An anonymous letter," answered Daksh. "We started from the gurukul as soon as the messenger pigeon arrived."

"I didn't expect the prince to seek vengeance on you," said the Acharya. "And definitely not so soon, or I would not have left you with him at all."

"What about fifteen years ago?" she asked, not looking at him. Not wanting to feel his guilt, but letting him feel her anger.

The Acharya shifted in his seat. "What is past is past. I cannot change it."

"I just want to know what happened," she said.

"Of course," he said. "Your grandfather approached me and said you'd been kidnapped by his enemies, the Chandelas. We didn't know about the bond until much later. We weren't even sure if you were still alive. Malwa and Chandela were at war, and I decided not to interfere."

"Why did they kidnap me?" asked Katyani. "What did they hope to gain?"

The Acharya shook his head. "I don't know. Perhaps initially they meant to use you as a hostage, and later on the queen changed her mind. I did not investigate, and I regret this. But I have always kept out of politics. I maintain neutrality, and all the kingdoms vie to send their princes to me for education. This enables me to instill the gurukul's ethical values into future rulers. In this way I hope, with each succeeding generation, to lessen the warfare that brings so much misery to the common people of Bharat."

"Is it working?" she asked, not bothering to disguise the sarcasm in her voice.

He considered. "It is difficult to say within my lifetime. When my sons take over the gurukul, they will be in a position to judge."

Katyani glanced at Daksh. His face was unreadable once more. The man was a cipher. He'd carried her on his back in the pouring rain, down several hundred slippery steps. Yet, she understood the Acharya better than she did him, and the bond was the least of it. *What are you thinking, Daksh? What do you want? You were so angry on my behalf. Was that only your sense of justice, or was it something more?* She wished she knew the answers to her questions. She wished it was as simple as grabbing him by the collar and demanding answers.

The carriage came to an abrupt halt, and the coachman screamed.

Katyani was overcome with déjà vu. A few months ago, she, Ayan, and Bhairav had been attacked by yatu on the way to the gurukul. It felt like a lifetime ago. She'd still had both brothers then, and she hadn't even known how rich she was.

Daksh leaped out of the carriage, and she heard the clang of a sword being unsheathed. The Acharya followed, using his staff to help himself to the ground. "Stay inside," he ordered before slamming the door shut.

Like hell she was staying inside. She dragged herself across the floor, pushed open the door, and poked her head out.

An astonishing sight met her eyes.

A lovely young woman stood in front of the carriage. She had rippling black hair, large, lustrous eyes, smooth olive skin, and plump red lips that were curved in a come-hither smile. She wore a silver nose ring, a red sari that exposed her flat midriff, and a thin, strapless blouse that left little to the imagination. *Not* the kind of person that would make a man scream. Except, perhaps, in pleasure, if he was very lucky.

Which made the reactions of the three men in Katyani's company puzzling. The coachman had scuttled below the carriage and was reciting a prayer in a feverish voice. Daksh stood in a defensive stance, gripping his sword in both hands. The Acharya, standing behind him, clutched his staff like a drowning man embracing a log. Katyani sensed his fear, which was the oddest thing of all. The Acharya wasn't afraid of anyone or anything. Except, apparently, sexy women.

"It has been so long since we met, Mahavir." The woman's voice was honey and silk. She pouted, looking, if anything, even more gorgeous. "And here you are, being a stranger. Aren't you even going to say hello to me?"

"Hello," said Katyani, when it was clear the men were too petrified to reply.

The woman transferred her gaze to Katyani, and an expression of delight crossed her face. She clapped her hands. "Oh, this is a surprise. Who do we have here?"

Go inside, Katyani.

She fought against the Acharya's order and crawled out of the carriage, supporting herself by holding on to its walls. "My name is Katyani," she told the woman. "I don't believe I have the pleasure of your acquaintance."

It's the daayan, you fool! Now go back.

Oh. *Oh.*

The woman threw her head back and laughed. Her mouth was red, the teeth white and pointy. "Mahavir, darling. Your concern is misplaced. I would never hurt an innocent girl, especially not one with such an auspicious name. You, on the other hand, I've been waiting for."

"My time is not today, not tomorrow, and not for many tomorrows to come," said the Acharya grimly. "Begone!"

"You're so mean," the woman complained. "What about a smile, or"—her tongue darted out of her mouth—"a kiss?"

The Acharya gave a convulsive shudder. "Take your true form, daayan," he commanded, and he banged his staff on the forest floor. A streak of white lightning zigzagged from the staff and struck the woman's chest. She stumbled back a step, and for a moment, Katyani was afraid she might be hurt.

But she laughed again, her smile twisting, her teeth extending. "Do you love my true form better than this one?" she asked, her voice becoming deeper, almost a growl. "Then you shall have it, Acharya."

Her body unfurled, stretching so she towered above them. Her skin darkened, and her hair gathered in a thick plait that reached the forest floor. Her nails elongated to black, curving talons, and her eyes deepened to red. Her feet turned backward and hovered a few inches above the ground.

The daayan loomed before them in her true form, ebony-skinned and crimson-eyed like her patron, Goddess Kali, and just as fierce. Fear pulsed through Katyani's veins—not for herself, but for Daksh and his father. Would the daayan have her revenge today?

The Acharya raised his staff, but Katyani could have told him it was no use, that he should join the coachman under the carriage, for the goddess loved and protected her monstrous followers.

The daayan's long plait whipped out and knocked the Acharya's staff from his hand. Before either of them could react, the plait snagged Daksh's sword. He hung on to it grimly, determined not to let go, but the plait wrapped itself around his midriff and threw him across the clearing.

Katyani's stomach seized. Was he hurt? She hobbled toward him, biting down her own pain. He stirred and moaned, but before she could grab him or tell him to hide, he staggered to his feet and rushed past her toward the daayan, toward certain death.

Terror surged through her. "Stop, Daksh," she tried to scream, but it came out as a whisper. Even if he had heard her, he would not have stopped. The daayan's powerful hands closed around the Acharya's neck. She dangled him above the ground, an expression of gloating delight on her fearsome face. His feet jerked as he struggled to free himself from her grip.

Daksh brought his sword down on the daayan's plait, but it snaked out and lashed him across the face. He cried out and stumbled back. The plait snapped around his neck and squeezed, choking him.

Katyani couldn't believe it. Both men were dying before her eyes. The white dove tattooed on her neck gasped for breath. Daksh's sword had fallen to the ground; his hands desperately tried to pry the plait away from his throat.

She fought the panic that threatened to overwhelm her. It was up to her to save them. *Calm down,* she told the dove. *I have an idea.*

She dropped to her knees before the daayan and bowed her head.

"My lady, I beg a minute of your attention," she croaked.

"Speak, child," said the daayan, not loosening her grip at all. The Acharya's face had purpled, and his struggles were weakening.

"If you could please spare the lives of these two men, I will be grateful. I have a bond with Acharya Mahavir, a result of his saving my life. I owe him a blood debt. If you kill him now, my debt will never be paid. My soul will remain bonded to his, and this is terrible for me to contemplate. Whereas, if you spare him because of my intervention, the debt will be paid. The bond will dissolve, and I will be free of him forever."

Katyani didn't know how true that was, but the thought of the Acharya dying while she was bonded to him was horrifying; it would be like dying herself, except without the release at the end of it.

"Hmm." The daayan's grip slackened, allowing both men to take a ragged breath. "What of my vow?" she demanded. "Long have I waited to suck the life force from his miserable body. Am I not to be satisfied?"

"Of course, my lady. This is his fate, and he knows it well," said Katyani, weak with relief that the daayan was listening to her. "But perhaps not today? After all, what is time to such a one as you, who follows the mighty Goddess Kali?"

The daayan grinned and dropped the Acharya. He fell to the ground in a trembling, moaning heap. Behind her, the plait released Daksh and swept him out of the way. Katyani almost wept in gratitude. Was Daksh all right? She squashed her impulse to check on him. "Thank you, my lady, for your benevolence."

"Oh, I am not benevolent, not in the least," said the daayan, inspecting her talons. "But you please me. You are named after my beloved goddess. How can I say no to you? But I have one condition."

"Please tell me," said Katyani, her heart sinking. What would the daayan demand of her? *Careful, Katyani,* the Acharya sent, still gasping for breath.

"Nothing difficult," said the daayan, her grin widening. "Only that you must not come between me and my prey again. The next time I attack the Acharya, you will not come to his aid."

"I accept," said Katyani, knowing she had no choice in the matter, and this was only fair. In truth, she was relieved. The daayan could have asked her for anything.

"Then free yourself from him quickly, child, because the next time I see him, I will certainly kill him."

Wait, that wasn't all. There was something important she needed to clarify with the daayan. "If you could please spare the life of his son," she said in a humble tone, "I will light a diya to the goddess every night for a year and a day." From the corner of her eye, she saw Daksh prop himself against a tree trunk and fix his gaze on her. Her skin burned at the touch. *Look away,* she thought fiercely. *Pretend you cannot hear.*

"He does not matter to me one way or the other," said the daayan. "Does he matter to you?"

Katyani froze, trapped. The daayan would remember what she said now. So, unfortunately, would Daksh. She longed to flee from the intensity of his gaze. The Acharya, she noted, was listening with unbridled interest despite his pain. Her insides roiled with embarrassment.

"I would like the opportunity to find out if he matters," she said carefully. Daksh made a small sound of startlement.

The daayan cackled. "What an answer! Come, let me bless you."

Katyani quailed. The blessings of a daayan were not so different from curses. She crawled forward on her knees and bent her neck.

The daayan brought down her monstrously clawed hand and rested it heavily on top of Katyani's head. "What shall I wish for you?" she mused. "The blessings of priests are boring and worthless. Like, may you be the mother of a hundred sons. What woman in her right mind would want that? Or, may you have a long life. What use is a long life if you don't do anything interesting with it?"

"A long life is acceptable," said Katyani, beginning to sweat.

"Yes, but what do you most want out of it?"

Katyani thought of all the men on the dais and in the court—the guards, the dandanayaka, the assessors, the so-called judges—and their avid expressions when she disrobed for her punishment. "I want justice. I want revenge."

"Ah. But justice and revenge are not the same. What does your blood hunger for?"

Tanoj, turning away from her in disgust. Revaa, lying in the court, sealing her fate. Bhairav, passing judgment, when he knew she was innocent. The chief justice, calling a hundred lashes of Chentu *merciful*. People she'd trusted. People she'd loved. People who had taken an oath to serve justice and done the exact opposite. The blood thundered in Katyani's ears. They had to pay for what they'd done.

The daayan gave a happy sigh. "A child after my own heart. So be it. May you get the revenge you seek or die in the attempt."

The weight on Katyani's head vanished. She looked up.

The daayan was gone. Daksh sat with his back against the tree trunk, cradling his sword, regarding her with a thoughtful, puzzled expression that made her squirm. He appeared unharmed, which was the main thing.

"I only said it to save your skin," she told him, her voice flat. "Stop looking at me like that." She struggled to her feet, trying not to wince. Her back was on fire. The bandages stuck to her flesh, wet and revolting. She limped toward the Acharya, still heaped on the ground, and poked his shoulder. "I know you're alive, Acharya. Please get up, because I don't think I can carry you."

Daksh leaped to his feet. "I will do that," he said in a hoarse voice.

"No need." The Acharya pushed himself up on an elbow, massaging his neck. "I still have the use of my legs."

Daksh helped him into the carriage and went to retrieve his staff.

Katyani peered underneath it and spotted the coachman. "You can come out now. She's gone."

He crawled out, shaking. "You were so brave," he quavered. "I have never seen anyone face down a daayan before."

"Face down?" she scoffed. "Don't be ridiculous. I just appealed to her better nature."

The coachman gave her a look that told her plainly he thought she was the one being ridiculous. He climbed up on his seat, casting nervous glances over his shoulder.

Daksh returned with the staff and stood before her.

"What?" she said, unsettled.

He hesitated. "May I help you climb in?"

"No." She turned away so he would not see her expression and clambered inside. The Acharya sat near a window, his face pensive. Daksh followed her in and placed the staff next to his father. The carriage jerked to a start, and they trundled away from the scene of their near-death encounter.

Daksh offered her another gourd of water; she drank it, then sat sideways, leaning against the wall of the carriage. Black spots danced before her eyes. It was four days since she'd eaten. Her spiritual power had burned down to an ember. There were gaps in her memory: precious moments that Chentu had stolen. Evil thing. She quivered with anger as she remembered its gloating, chilly voice. She would have her revenge on it. Such a weapon should not exist in this world.

"You have paid your debt," said the Acharya. "It is time to dissolve the bond."

"It can wait a day or two," said Katyani. *Until I've eaten some food, changed my bandages, and feel stronger.*

"As soon as we return to the gurukul," said the Acharya forcefully, "I will invoke the fire."

"If you're sure," murmured Daksh, his forehead creasing.

"What fire?" asked Katyani, sitting up.

"Of course I'm sure," the Acharya snapped, ignoring her. "I can feel it trying to get out. It's horrible. I'm too sensitive for this sort of magic."

"I miss my sword," said Katyani. "Any time someone used to annoy me, I could point my sword at them and make them stop."

They looked at her, their faces slack with surprise. "What fire?" she repeated, pleased she'd gotten their attention.

"The bond was created by a sacrifice of spiritual power," said the Acharya. "I must make a similar sacrifice to dissolve it."

"The queen always said we'd both know when it was time to let go," said Katyani.

The Acharya made a dismissive gesture. "She lied to you. You owed her nothing, and yet she kept you, year after year."

His words burned through her like acid. Yes, the queen had lied to her. But surely not about everything. The part about the bond having saved her life, for instance. The queen might have kidnapped her to hold her hostage—a despicable thing to do. But she'd created the bond to save Katyani, or it would never have been so strong to begin with.

Or perhaps that was just what Katyani wanted to believe. Whatever the truth, it had died with Hemlata.

After a while, the Acharya fell into a doze, leaning his head against the window frame. There were red marks on his neck where the daayan's long fingers had squeezed it. Katyani could feel the ghost of that pain in her own neck. She gave him zero chances for survival in his next encounter with the daayan.

Daksh dug into a knapsack and produced oranges for them to eat.

Katyani gave him an accusing stare. "You had this all the time? I'm starving."

His lips twitched. "You were asleep until a couple of hours ago." He peeled one and handed it to her. "And I wasn't exactly thinking of refreshments when the daayan was trying to kill us."

She popped an orange section into her mouth. The heavenly sweetness exploded on her tongue. She'd never tasted anything so good. She inhaled the rest of it and stole another peeled orange from his hand just as he was about to eat it.

"You're welcome," he said, raising his eyebrows.

"I didn't thank you," she said indistinctly, her mouth full of orange.

"I imagined you did. I always imagine you far more polite than you actually are." His gaze traveled over her, as if imagining a lot more than that.

Her insides heated. "I can't think why," she said, keeping her tone flippant. "Politeness is overrated. I miss my sword. Did I already say that? This is the moment I would have pointed my sword at you and demanded all your oranges."

He choked on a section of orange and had to pause to drink water from the one remaining gourd. He picked up his sword and held it out to her. "Here, borrow mine."

What? Spiritual warriors like Daksh and Uttam were jealous of their weapons, never letting anyone else handle them. And Daksh's golden sword was famous in all of Bharat. She couldn't believe he was offering it to her. But he looked perfectly serious about it. She took it from him gingerly and ran her hand along the silver scabbard, carved with shlokas. A shiver ran through her. It was as if she were touching *him*. She withdrew it an inch, just enough to see its fiery glow, then sheathed it again and returned it.

"You don't wish to unsheathe my sword?" he said, sounding disappointed.

She bit down a laugh. Laughing would shake her body worse than the moving carriage and make her cry in pain. "There are so many terrible jokes I could be making right now," she said. "But I won't, not because I don't enjoy seeing you blush, but because I am in no condition to laugh."

He looked at her, puzzled, then at his sword, as if the secret to her mirth lay there.

It was almost too much to bear. She clamped her lips together, but a snort of laughter escaped through her nose. She crossed her arms and stared at the sleeping Acharya until she felt sober enough to look at his son again. He was eating a section of orange with the same earnestness he did everything else.

"What is funny?" he asked, his brows knitting.

"You," she said, trying to control herself.

"You're impossible," he said. "Can you never be serious? You've suffered terrible wounds and confronted a daayan. You must be in a lot of pain. How can you still laugh?"

"Imagine, Airya, I've gone through so much, and you can still make me laugh. It's a rare gift you have."

"Daksh," he said.

"What?"

"You can call me Daksh."

She stared at him. He'd asked her to drop the honorific. Did he remember the day she'd done that? He'd kissed her, as if the formality of address had been the only barrier holding him back. The kiss was branded on her lips; she could taste him still. Her fingers flew to her mouth. Her cheeks warmed, and she was furious with herself. *She* was the one to fluster *him*. Not the other way around.

The Acharya stirred. "How far are we?" he murmured. Katyani dropped her hand and turned away, taking a deep breath of mingled relief and annoyance at the interruption.

"I'll check," said Daksh with alacrity, and he leaned out to talk with the coachman. "Three hours," he reported a minute later, "unless we run into more trouble."

The Acharya sighed. "Nothing else in Nandovana can trouble me."

Katyani stole a glance at him. Had the daayan really been his mistress? Had he promised marriage to her? Or led her to believe that marriage was a possibility? She sensed his ambivalence, guilt, and sadness when he thought of the daayan. But she'd never know, not unless he told her, which was as likely as the sky falling on their heads.

The rest of the ride was blessedly uneventful. Vetalas and yatu might be no match for the Acharya and his son in ordinary circumstances, but the attentions of the daayan had depleted them both, and Katyani could barely sit up straight.

They arrived at the gates of the gurukul late in the evening. The air was thick with the scent of ripening fruits and vegetables, damp with the promise of rain. The light of the setting sun glinted on the pagoda of the main building. It was as if she'd gone back in time.

Here was a place she could be safe—a place where she could recover and plan the revenge the daayan had blessed her with. She didn't care, anymore, about the rigid rules and ludicrous bath times. Of all the places in Bharat, this was the only one left where she might, however tenuously, still belong. The Acharya would try his utmost to remove the bond safely, and she would be free at last. *Free.* The thought made her feel as if she were floating several inches off the ground.

A crowd of senior disciples surged forward to greet them, Varun at their head, looking as thin and solemn as ever.

"Is everything all right, Acharya?" he asked, darting a quick glance at her and the white dove tattooed on her neck. The other disciples bowed to the Acharya and gazed at her with a mixture of concern and curiosity.

"Everything is perfectly fine." The Acharya scowled, wringing his hand as if shaking off a spider. "Why are you looking at me like that?"

"I don't see any of the first-years," said Katyani, saving Varun from having to reply to this. Obviously, the Acharya was not going to tell them about the daayan.

"I sent them home early," said the Acharya. "We didn't know how long we'd be away or in what condition we'd find you."

Katyani exhaled, her anxiety ebbing. She'd been dreading meeting Irfan and Nimaya and dealing with their questions.

"Prepare the sacrificial fire," the Acharya ordered. The disciples scuttled away, and Daksh took Uttam aside, probably filling him in. She imagined their conversation:

Daksh: Father nearly got eaten today.

Uttam: Oh no, what happened?

Daksh: We met the daayan.

Uttam: How come you're both still alive?

Daksh: Katyani postponed our consumption by promising the daayan she can snack on Father next time. She got an exemption for me by hinting she is interested in me.

Uttam: Interested how?

Daksh: I don't know. My sword?

Katyani suppressed a giggle and tried to keep up with the Acharya's long strides as they entered the familiar courtyard of the gurukul. Ahead of them, a disciple was stacking wood in the firepit before the main building. Varun was bent over the ground, sprinkling something on it. Sagar stood behind him, holding a basket of fruit. *The sacrificial fire.* Her stomach churned with a mixture of fear and hope.

"Will it hurt?" she asked the Acharya.

"Yes," he said. "Prepare yourself."

Oh, great. As if she hadn't borne enough torture for an entire lifetime.

Had it hurt when Hemlata created the bond? Katyani had no memory of it. Perhaps forgetfulness was a blessing.

Atreyi came forward to meet them, forehead creased in worry. Katyani bowed to her, taking care not to bend too much for fear she would topple over.

"Welcome back, child." Atreyi laid a hand on her head. "I did not expect to see you again so soon. Consider this your home as long as you need it."

Tears pricked Katyani's eyes at the kindness. She blinked them back and tried to smile. "Thank you, Airyaa."

Atreyi turned to the Acharya. "What happened?"

As succinctly as possible, the Acharya filled her in on the trial, the punishment, and his intervention.

Atreyi put a gentle hand on Katyani's shoulder and glanced at her back. What she sensed through her spiritual power must have alarmed her. "I need to see to this immediately."

"The fire first," rasped the Acharya, cradling his right hand in his left. "Or I might be tempted to chop my hand off."

The right palm was where the tattoo of the white dove would be. "It's nothing to do with your hand," said Katyani. "That's just the place where it manifests itself. It's a *soul* bond."

"You think I don't know that?" he snapped. Katyani kept quiet. The bond disturbed the Acharya more with every passing minute. It was forbidden magic, after all, and the Acharya had spent his entire life harping about ethics. The bond must be hurting him at his very core.

Varun hurried up to them. "Acharya, the preparations are complete. I instructed them to use a mixture of sal and sandalwood. Who will light the fire?"

"I will." The Acharya strode toward the firepit. It had been filled with twigs of fragrant wood. Around it, Varun had constructed a hasty altar, outlining the square with white rice and marigold petals. Sal leaf plates full of fruit, flowers, leaves, and nuts were arranged around the pit. *Fast work,* thought Katyani. They must be used to the Acharya's sudden demands.

Varun lit a sandalwood twig and handed it to the Acharya.

"Back away, all of you," the Acharya commanded. "Not *you*," he added in irritation as Katyani made to follow the others.

Daksh and Uttam drew up behind them. "Can I be of any help?" asked Daksh.

"No, you can't." The Acharya took a deep breath. "If this incapacitates me for any length of time, I pass the guardianship of the gurukul to my elder son, Uttam, until I recover. Follow him as you would me."

The disciples murmured their assent, unease on their faces. Katyani's heart leaped into her mouth. She'd been worried about the pain she might undergo; she hadn't thought there was any danger to the Acharya. She should have remembered what he'd said: he'd have to make a sacrifice to dissolve the bond.

"This will hurt you?" she asked, her voice tentative.

He snorted. "Not doing it will hurt me far, far more. Now be quiet."

As the sun sank below the horizon, he leaned forward and lit the fire, chanting mantras. The twigs crackled, and the fragrance of burning sandalwood rose in the air, overwhelming the senses.

"Sit," he ordered, and Katyani complied, sitting cross-legged by the altar. He sat opposite her and continued to chant, alternately throwing grains of rice into the fire and sprinkling drops of water on it.

Katyani stared into the flames, thick waves of fatigue rolling over her. The white dove on her neck fluttered in anxiety. *Soon,* she told it. *Soon you will be free. And no one will ever take you from me again. They'll have to kill me first.*

She'd been kidnapped, bonded, and passed around like a pawn. But no more. No one would use her again. She thought of the blue butterfly, flighty and fickle; the raven, dark and dangerous; the dove, pure and peaceful. All different, but also, all *her.* When the bond broke, finally, they could come home to her.

Twilight deepened to night. The Acharya droned on. Did he deliberately elongate rituals and lectures to torture everyone? Katyani suppressed a yawn. She was so exhausted, she might fall asleep right now. She'd have to be careful not to fall face-first into the sacrificial fire. That would anger the Acharya no end, besides peeling the skin off her face.

Just when she'd decided she could close her eyes for a bit without nodding off, the Acharya plunged his right hand into the fire.

The pain was immediate. She clutched her throat and tried not to scream. The white dove soared above the flames, beating its wings in panic, looking for a place of safety.

Here. She held out her palm. *You belong to me.*

The white dove plunged toward her and crashed into her palm, a bundle of soft feathers with a wildly beating heart. She cupped it in both hands, her eyes blurring. *At last.* The piece of soul that had been stolen from her in infancy had returned. She was free. *Free.* She wept, her tears falling on the little dove. There was a hint of black beak, a flash of bright blue wing, and the bird dissolved into her palm.

The world outside swam back into focus. The fire leaping in the dark. The tense figures that surrounded them. Daksh, leaning toward her, his face a mask of anxiety. The Acharya, withdrawing his burned and withered right hand from the flames.

And the pain in her back, a screaming, screeching pain that obliterated everything else. She fell to the ground, limbs shaking, unable to breathe.

She realized what the Acharya had meant, what he had done. All this time, he had used the bond to absorb some of her pain. With the dissolution of the bond, that shield had vanished, and she felt the full impact of what Chentu had done.

She curled up in a fetal position, biting her wrist to stop herself from crying out. Strong, gentle hands picked her up and carried her away from the fire. Someone put a fragrant cloth before her nose. And then there was nothing. Not for a long, long time.

CHAPTER 15

DAYS PASSED. THEY WERE EASIER THAN THE NIGHTS. THE darkness was when the beast visited, crouching on her back and clawing it open until she sobbed in agony. Sometimes she managed to sleep, only to dream of Ayan, standing on the opposite side of a fissure in the earth. She reached her hand out to him, but the fissure widened to an abyss, swallowing him before her horrified gaze. He fell in slow motion, his eyes full of hurt and bewilderment. *How could you let me die?*

She woke sweating and shaking from these visions, reaching for a cup of water if she could, often not able to keep it down. In an ironic twist, she'd been given the same hut she'd lived in with the princes. Despite Atreyi's misgivings, the Acharya had insisted she be granted a private space to heal. She was grateful to him for that. She didn't want to disturb the women every night with her cries.

Daksh came by often. Each time, she told him to leave. She didn't want him to think her broken and hurt. Her pride would not allow it, and pride was all she had in this world now.

Once, she surfaced from a mid-afternoon doze to find him leaning against the entrance, drenched. It was raining, warm sheets of water blowing across the courtyard, bringing the smell of wet earth into the hut. He was looking outside, oblivious of his dripping robes and hair.

"Why're you here?" she asked, her tongue thick and unnatural in her mouth. Her back was a mass of pain, her clothes sticky with sweat.

He turned and gave her a tentative smile. "Gulmohar is in bloom. The forest looks like it's on fire, even with the rain."

"Go 'way," she mumbled. She hated him to see her like this, sick and weak and without clever repartee of any kind.

He nodded. "I'll return tomorrow."

"Don't bother," she said, but he was already gone.

Only then did she notice the branch of flame-colored flowers on her windowsill. Gulmohar, the rain flower, which bloomed in the heart of the monsoon season. It brought a bit of color to her dull, dark room, raising her spirits. A world that had flowers so bright—and someone like Daksh to bring them to her—wasn't all bad.

She lay on her stomach on the pallet, a thousand needles pricking her flesh, enveloped in silence—a forever silence no one would disturb again. No one's voice in her head, commanding her against her will. No one watching her every move, her every thought. No one manipulating her from within. That was worth all the pain in the world.

Atreyi came by every day to apply healing salves and change the bandages on her back. She had explained it would take several weeks for Katyani's back to grow new skin. Meanwhile, it would itch and burn, and she had to avoid both sunlight and rain.

Vinita visited to tell mythological stories, which would have been interesting but for her inflectionless voice and grim demeanor, as if this were part of Katyani's punishment. Shalu and Barkha brought food, which mostly stayed uneaten. At Katyani's request, they also brought diyas. No matter how she was feeling, she lit a diya every night in the name of Goddess Kali. She hadn't forgotten her vow to the daayan.

Once, Shalu brought her the most awful soup Katyani had ever tasted: a mixture of bark, grass, petals, and what looked like clumps of worms but were apparently mushrooms. She took a cautious spoonful and nearly spat it out. "You're trying to poison me," she accused.

Shalu grinned at her expression. "It's a special medicinal soup to increase both physical and spiritual strength. I have been instructed to stay here until you consume every spoon of it."

"No, no, please, I beg you . . ."

But Shalu was adamant. She made Katyani eat it all, chivvying her as if she were a disobedient toddler. It tasted horrible, but Katyani did feel better after eating it. Part of that was probably just relief it was finished.

She asked after the Acharya, but all anyone would say was that he was recovering. The memory of his withered hand haunted her. Had he sacrificed his hand to dissolve the bond? Or was that the physical manifestation of a deeper loss?

Time ceased to have meaning. She lost count of the days. Rain flooded the courtyard, and the chirping of frogs and insects filled the night air. She continued to dream of Ayan, sometimes of Hemlata and Shamsher too. They stood behind a barrier of thorns, their enmity forgotten, smiling at her. No matter how hard she tried, she could not reach them.

The day came when Atreyi said bandages were no longer required. Katyani's back had healed, and she was free to step outside.

Katyani refused to leave the hut. A terrible fatigue came over her, as if nothing she did could possibly matter. Eating food was a chore. Even lighting the diya was a chore. She couldn't understand what was wrong with her. But the thought of trying to return to the outside world made her feel as if she carried stones inside her chest.

After a few days of this, the Acharya visited her. He looked old and thin. His right hand was wrapped in a white cotton glove.

"Acharya." Katyani sat up, hoping she looked presentable—or at least, fully dressed. "Someone should have warned me. I'd have tidied up."

He glowered at her. "This hut smells." His gaze strayed to the gulmohar on her windowsill, and his brow furrowed.

"I've been unwell," protested Katyani, hoping he wasn't going to ask about the flowers. She never saw Daksh put them there, but there was always a freshly blooming branch of gulmohar on her windowsill.

The Acharya snorted. "Excuses. When do you plan to step out?"

"Soon," she prevaricated. "I need to avoid sunlight."

"Like a vetala? Very well. It is cloudy today. Neither rain nor sun." He held out his uninjured hand. "Come on."

Katyani got up reluctantly. "Suppose I faint? I feel quite weak."

"The weakness is in your mind." The Acharya twitched the grass mat aside and strode out.

Katyani followed, annoyed at him and a bit unsteady on her feet. To her surprise, her head cleared as she stepped from the porch into the courtyard.

The evening sky was a washed-out steel gray. The ground was wet, the air thick with the promise of more rain. The peepal tree shivered in the breeze, showering raindrops on a group of disciples standing below it. They laughed and scattered. Others sat on the steps of their porches, chatting with each other. It was a homey scene, and it lifted her heart. Monsoon had always been her favorite season. She loved how it annihilated the heat and dust of summer and made everything green and new.

"Well? Feeling human again?" barked the Acharya as they took a slow circle around the courtyard. "I expect you to attend meditation at seven in the morning tomorrow. There will be an ethics discussion at ten. You will eat your meals in the dining area from now onward. You don't have to spar if you're not up to it yet. But please have a bath. You smell terrible."

She glared at him. "I've been regrowing skin."

"Atreyi says your back has healed," said the Acharya. "The scars you have will stay forever. Bear them with pride."

And the scars inside, would they ever go away? Or were they also something to be proud of?

She took a deep breath. "What about your hand? Has it healed?"

"As much as it ever will," he said. "Go to the cleansing pool. The water has medicinal properties. I will give orders you are not to be disturbed."

"The first time I went during off-hours, Airya Daksh caught me." Her hand flew to her mouth. What was *wrong* with her?

The Acharya gave a dismissive wave. "I know. He will not do so today."

"What? How do you know? Did he tell you?" Katyani was mortified.

"Very little in my gurukul escapes me." He paused and added, "My sons are quite different in temperament. Uttam will succeed me one day. I have no worries about him. But as for Daksh, he has always been rebellious. He will make his own fate."

Rebellious? Had she heard right? "But Acharya, he does everything you say."

"In the things that matter, it seems I end up doing what *he* says." The Acharya gave her a sharp look. "When the pigeon arrived with the message that you were to be put on trial, it was Daksh who insisted on going to Ajaigarh, Daksh who argued it would be an unfair process and the prince would use it to trap you. I had better hopes of Bhairav. But my son persuaded me to intervene. If I had not agreed, he would have gone without me. So you see, he can be quite stubborn sometimes."

Goose bumps prickled her skin at the thought that Daksh would have defied his father for her. She remembered the look of rage in his eyes when he entered the audience hall, as if he wanted to burn the entire palace down. Good thing the Acharya had agreed to go with him.

"Do you regret your intervention?" she asked, looking at his hand. She wouldn't blame him if he did.

He sighed. "I should have intervened a long time ago, as soon as I heard rumors of the bond. But I told myself I must not interfere in the political affairs of kingdoms. Once I start, where do I draw the line? I am paying the price now for my inaction."

Katyani imagined how her life would have turned out if she had been freed from her bond as a child and returned to Malwa. Ayan would still be alive. So would Hemlata and Jaideep. She would be living peacefully in the palace at Dhar with her cousin and grandfather. The Acharya had a lot to answer for. But she wouldn't blame him for the evil others had done.

"Do not regret the past or worry about the future," murmured the Acharya, as if he had read her mind. "Stay in the present, which is happening now."

Easy to say, hard to live by. Katyani did not answer, and after a minute he left to lead an evening meditation for the senior disciples.

She went back to her hut, grabbed clean clothes and a washcloth, and headed for the waterfall behind the gurukul. She was glad the Acharya had dragged her out of the hut, out of whatever dark mood she'd sunk into. She did feel better now. Her back hurt much less. She was a bit wobbly on her feet, but that was only to be expected. She'd go to the dining hall for the evening meal. The Acharya was right; it was high time she stopped being a burden on everyone around her, especially the women who had taken care of her during the worst of her illness. She wondered if Daksh would still leave branches of gulmohar on her windowsill.

Probably not. They were likely a "get well" kind of thing.

Rain had swollen the waterfall; the placid pool had become a river. But Katyani could swim, and the banks were not far apart. The night-blooming jasmine was still in flower; its sweet, familiar fragrance permeated the air, reminding her of that first night, eons ago. She undressed, feeling self-conscious, even though there was no one to see her apart from a frog or two. As she stepped into the warm water, the past sloughed away like dead skin. She closed her eyes and immersed herself, emptying her mind.

When she emerged for a breath, she imagined Daksh standing behind her. She jerked her head around, as if to catch him in the act.

But there was no one. A koel called, and the evening thickened. She rose from the water until her scarred back was visible from the neck down to the hip and lifted her hair out of the way.

"What do you think, Daksh?" she asked. "Isn't my back spectacular?"

He didn't even have to be there for her to know how he would respond.

Shameless, he would say, and avert his eyes. Keeping her, however, in his peripheral vision.

So you don't think my scars are beautiful?

I didn't say that!

You called me shameless. You think I should be ashamed of them.

That's not what I meant.

What did you mean, Daksh?

And he would look at her, tongue-tied and furious. She giggled as she waded out of the water and dried herself. He could make her laugh even when he wasn't around.

She managed to make it through the evening meal, sitting next to the women disciples. She even managed to eat. Daksh sat beside his father and brother as usual, but he looked at her from time to time with a small, pleased smile as if her recovery were entirely his doing.

Afterward, she went to the kitchen and made the oddest request they'd received in a while: three rice balls, every morning at sunrise, for the next month. Oh, and a lump of clay, please.

That night, she molded the clay into three separate mounds and placed them below the window of her hut. If it was sunny the next day, she'd put them on the windowsill to dry. She hadn't forgotten her vow to the pretas. They'd saved her life and been swallowed by Chentu as a result. She was going to do her best to drag their souls out from that evil weapon. Meanwhile, she would give them the rites they'd asked for.

Slowly, she fell back into the routine of meditation, ethics, weapons, and martial arts. The interval between her first stay at the gurukul and the present receded like a nightmare. Only the presence of the scars and the absence of the bond made it real.

She'd never belonged wholly to herself before. It gave her a sense of equilibrium, as if the scales within her were balanced. The room that the queen had occupied and Bhairav had invaded was finally hers again. No matter what happened in the future, no one would control any part of her. She would recover her strength and return to Ajaigarh tougher than ever.

It was hard at first. She'd lost a lot of spiritual power to Chentu, and only the guided meditations of the Acharya helped her regain it, bit by bit. He told her it might take a year of regular practice to reach her previous level. Although she chafed at the delay, she knew she had to be at her strongest when she confronted her enemies.

She thought back to the events that had brought her to this time and place. They were like jagged pieces of a jigsaw puzzle, refusing to fit together. Months of assassination attempts followed by a massacre led by monsters working for the regent of Malwa. Were the two connected? She had thought they were. Hemlata had quoted Tanoj as saying that the captured prisoners were working for Malwa. But when Katyani had mentioned the attempted poisoning to Shamsher, he had acted surprised. Nor was the poisoning in keeping with the past assassination attempts.

Another piece that didn't fit was the yatu themselves. Why had they helped Shamsher kill the royal family? How did they get past the wards into Ajaigarh Fort? Only someone adept at magic could have broken the wards for them. And only someone who knew the palace inside out could have led them to the audience hall. Shamsher must have had help from within. Who had betrayed them all?

The third piece that didn't fit was the most painful. Why had Bhairav and Revaa set her up? Was it just that she was the granddaughter of the regent of Malwa? Was that enough to brand her a traitor in their eyes?

Katyani didn't have answers to any of her questions. But she did have access to an entire library of books. She needed to find out more about the yatu. That was the first step toward understanding why they had allied with Shamsher. She requested permission from the Acharya to visit the library for "research purposes." To her surprise, he assigned Daksh to accompany her.

As expected, Daksh had stopped leaving gulmohar on her windowsill. She missed his floral offerings, and was annoyed at herself for missing them, for wanting more than he seemed willing to give.

"What kind of research do you wish to do?" he asked, leading her up the winding steps to the library one afternoon.

"I just want to read up on monsters," she said, keeping her answer vague. She didn't want to reveal her true purpose, not yet.

He sat in the lotus pose in the middle of the library, eyes closed, while she wandered around, peering at the titles on the bookshelves and trying not to sneeze. In the end, she borrowed seven books on a variety of monsters so as not to give herself away. Two of the thickest were about yatu. A quick glance was enough to tell her that yatu-human interaction was far more common than she had supposed.

Monsoon gave way to the coolness of autumn. She spent her days training, using her time between classes and after meals to read her library books, and the evenings with the women disciples. They sat together on the porch listening to Atreyi's stories, strumming the sitar, or playing Pachisi. Their warm companionship healed her as nothing else could.

In the second half of the month of Ashwin, a visitor arrived at the gurukul and asked to see her. *Alone*. When she heard who it was, she was flummoxed. But the Acharya sent a message through one of his disciples, requesting her presence in the visitor hut, and, of course, she obeyed.

CHAPTER 16

I T WAS EVENING, THAT FLEETING MOMENT BETWEEN SUNSET and dusk when the day seemed suspended, unable to advance or retreat. Katyani hurried across the courtyard to the visitor hut, both looking forward to the meeting and praying it would be short so she didn't miss the evening meal.

She pushed aside the grass mat at the entrance, prepared to find all sorts of changes in her erstwhile classmate now that he had been anointed the crown prince of his realm.

But Irfan looked exactly the same, tousle-haired and bright-eyed, casually dressed in a yellow kurta and white pants. He even had the same grin on his face as he rose from his chair—only the visitor hut in the gurukul had actual chairs—to greet her.

"Katyani, it's wonderful to see you." He walked up to her, his arms outstretched as if he expected a hug. *That,* she would certainly not give him.

Katyani took a careful step back and bowed. "Crown Prince Irfan." His smile slipped at the formality of her address.

Why had he asked to see her alone? And why had the Acharya granted his wish? She now had the status of a semi-permanent disciple of the gurukul; at least, no one would kick her out unless she managed to seduce Daksh and ruin his state of celibacy, as she so often dreamed of doing. Irfan, on the other hand, was an outsider, for all that he had once been a pupil here. At the minimum, Atreyi should have been present at this meeting as a chaperone.

"Katya," he said, a note of appeal in his voice, "we were students here together. You don't have to stand on ceremony."

"Crown Prince Irfan," she said, emphasizing his title, irritated that he'd called her *Katya,* "we are not students together anymore. I heard you had your coming-of-age ceremony and are now officially the crown prince of the Solanki kingdom."

"Well, yes, that was bound to happen sooner or later unless I really messed up." He took a step forward, as if he wished to close the distance between them. "Nimaya sends her greetings."

Katyani perked up at the mention of her friend. "How is she?"

His face became serious. "Worried about you. You left so abruptly, and the Acharya wouldn't tell us anything."

"Please tell her I'm fine, and there isn't anything to worry about."

"Isn't there?" He tilted his head. "I heard what happened in Ajaigarh. I'm sorry I wasn't there to help. I came as soon as I could make up a reason to leave Patan."

Katyani frowned. "But why are you here?"

He leaned forward. "To make you an offer."

"What offer?" She narrowed her eyes at him. "I was injured, Crown Prince. I have a fraction of the power I used to. I wouldn't make a good bodyguard right now, even if you were willing to overlook the whole 'conspiracy to murder the royal family of Chandela' thing."

"A setup." He banged a fist on his palm, startling her. She'd never seen him angry before. "You loved Ayan. He was like a brother to you. You'd never hurt him. Anyone who knows anything about you would know that."

She bit her lip. True words, and they helped a little, but they also hurt. Why had no one at her trial shouted these words in her defense?

He cleared his throat. "Anyway. I didn't come here to buy your services. I came with an offer of marriage."

Her jaw dropped. "Whose marriage?"

"Yours. And mine." He raised his hand as if to touch her, but she crossed her arms, and he thought better of it. "As the wife of the Solanki heir, you will be under my protection. No one will dare raise their voice against you, ever again."

Had he taken leave of all good sense? She'd known he had a crush on her, but a crush was one thing and marriage quite another. Especially for a crown prince of the realm.

"Crown Prince Irfan, thank you for your offer," she said. "But I must decline."

Irfan stared at her in open-mouthed shock. He probably imagined that any normal woman would leap at the chance to marry him. But if he put Katyani in that category, he knew her less than he thought he did. "I realize this is . . . ah . . . sudden," he said, fumbling for words. "And girls are shy about such things."

"I'm not," she cut in. "You told me I should not stand on formal ceremony. I'm going to take your advice and speak frankly. You are the heir to your kingdom. Your parents have surely already arranged your marriage to a suitable princess."

"A prince may have more than one wife—" he began, but she interrupted.

"No king will marry their daughter to you if you take me to your palace. Set aside marrying, you cannot even hire me as your bodyguard. No, Irfan, let me speak. You will be tainted by any association with me. Your father, the king, would never stand for it. If you persist in your foolishness, he will pass the crown to your younger brother. Fond as you are of your brother, he is a wastrel and a womanizer, unfit to rule." She knew this from the many details provided by her spies over the years.

Irfan winced and ducked his head. She took a deep breath and continued, "Your kingdom will fall into chaos if your succession is threatened. You must return at once. Tell your parents and advisors you were here for a private meditation lesson, or to ask the Acharya some urgent question on good governance."

"What about you?" he burst out, raising his head. "What do you want? Are you content to hide in this gurukul forever? I thought you detested this place."

"We are not children, Crown Prince," she said, keeping her voice even. "It does not matter what we want. It matters what we do."

"It matters to me." He gazed at her with moony eyes like a lovesick calf, making her squirm. "I know the rules and conventions. But with you by my side, I would fight them all."

An offer of marriage and a declaration of love from the crown prince of one of the most powerful kingdoms in Bharat. She should feel something other than exasperation and embarrassment. But all she could think of was Daksh. She hoped fervently he didn't know why Irfan was here. She imagined him listening to this conversation, and her stomach shriveled. Really, it was the Acharya's fault. He should never have allowed it. At least, he should have insisted on someone else being present at this meeting. Irfan would not have been quite so dramatic.

"Crown Prince Irfan," she said, "I would not come with you even if you were not the heir to the Solanki throne. I need to stay here at the gurukul and recover my power."

"There are learned men and women in our kingdom who can help you," said Irfan. "We have a peace treaty with the Chandelas, and they would not dare attack us. The gurukul, on the other hand, is just a gurukul. The Acharya, no matter how powerful he is, cannot stop an army by himself."

Her stomach flipped. She hadn't dreamed she was endangering the gurukul with her presence. She cursed Irfan for this unwelcome thought.

"Don't you think it's better for them if you leave?" He watched her, eyes wide and innocent. "We needn't get married right away if you don't want to. Or at all, in fact. But I could give you a safe place to stay."

But she would be dependent on his goodwill for her safety, and she would never put herself in such a position. It would be like the bond all over again. She'd earned her freedom too dear to risk it.

"If I must leave, then I must," she said. "But I will not go with you."

"Why not?" he appealed. "Do you dislike me that much?"

"I don't *dislike* you," she said. "But it wouldn't be right for me to go with you. And right action is all that's in our hands."

"Now you sound like one of the Acharya's lectures," he complained.

"Yeah, the more time I spend here, the more I sound like him," she said. "He's like a disease of righteousness. Why don't you ask him for an audience and catch some of it?"

Irfan gave a brittle smile. "I came here for nothing."

"No journey is for nothing," she countered. "A private meditation lesson with the Acharya would benefit the future Solanki king."

He caught her hand as she moved toward the entrance of the hut. "If you stay, you risk your own safety as well as the gurukul's. If you leave—where would you even go? Who will give you shelter?"

"There's a daayan in the forest who's taken a shine to me." Katyani pried her hand out of his and stepped back from him. "You said what you came to say, and I gave you my answer. Respect it."

His face fell. "It's just as the vetala predicted. I will be king one day, but I will not get what I truly want."

She was what he truly wanted? "If this is the extent of your problems, you are fortunate indeed," she said dryly. "I'm sure you will have a perfect harem of wives one day. The Solankis are not known for their restraint."

The grass curtain at the entrance was pushed aside, and Varun poked his head in. "If you are done, Crown Prince Irfan, the Acharya wishes to see you before the evening meal."

Katyani had never been so happy to see Varun before. "Go on, Prince," she prodded. "You can say good-bye to me before you leave."

Irfan gave her a beseeching look and left with Varun. She followed them out, meaning to head for the dining hall, but stopped short at the sight of Daksh, sitting on the steps of the porch, a marked lack of expression on his face.

Her toes curled. "What—what are you doing here? Have you been listening?"

He frowned. "I came with Varun. I was waiting for you."

How long had he and Varun been outside while she tried to persuade the Solanki prince to see reason? Her face heated at the thought of how much they might have overheard.

Daksh laid his sword on his knees and studied her as if she were an insect. "He asked you to go with him, didn't he?"

"If you know, why are you asking me?" she snapped.

"You seem upset," he said, his voice even.

Katyani took a deep breath and tried to calm herself. "Am I endangering the gurukul with my presence?"

"Is that what he said?" Daksh shook his head. "He's more manipulative than I gave him credit for."

"Answer my question!"

"You should ask my father that," he said mildly.

"No matter how strong he is, he cannot stop an entire army if it attacks the gurukul." Katyani bit her nails, imagining the gurukul on fire, the walls crumbling, the staff running, the disciples screaming from the pain of poison-tipped arrows.

"Why would Bhairav risk his soldiers and his reputation?" said Daksh. "He has just been crowned king. I don't think the people of Chandela have an appetite for military adventures right now, not so soon after losing their royal family. Besides, my father has taught many of the kings and princes of Bharat. They won't stand aside and allow Bhairav to destroy this place. It would dishonor them. Whereas, if you go with the Solanki prince, Bhairav will have a clear target. No one will interfere if he attacks Patan for harboring you. You should stay here."

What he said made sense. But people were often guided by their emotions, not their sense. Irfan was a case in point. Bhairav had a great deal of anger and ill will toward her. She didn't know why, but it made him dangerous and unpredictable. She couldn't afford to confront him until she had regained every bit of the power she'd lost. Nor could she endanger anyone else with her presence. The sooner she was able to leave the gurukul, the better for everyone.

Daksh stood. His voice gained an edge. "Unless, of course, you have a different reason for going with Irfan."

Surprise bloomed like a butterfly in her stomach. Men could be incredibly dense. "Why, Airya, are you jealous?" she teased.

He threw her a cold look and stalked away from the hut, toward the peepal tree. *Aha,* she had annoyed him. She followed him, perking up. "You should not be jealous. After all, you have seen me bathe, and he never will."

"That was an accident," he snapped.

"Was it? The more I think about it, the less sure I am," she continued, enjoying herself. "You could not have missed my clothes, lying on the rock."

They reached the shade of the peepal tree's vast canopy. Daksh wheeled around, his face taut. "Why did you refuse to go with him?"

So he *had* heard at least part of the conversation. And it had upset him, or he wouldn't be talking like this, showing lowly human feelings. She was gratified by the display, but she quenched her mirth.

"For exactly the reasons I gave the prince," she said. "I was charged with conspiracy to murder the royal family of Chandela. The Acharya can get away with associating with someone in my position. A crown prince of Bharat cannot. Irfan's father would never stand for it. He may even pass the crown to the younger son, who is an absolute jerk."

His lips pressed together. "So you were guided by your concern for Irfan."

"*And* his entire kingdom." She tilted her head. "Were you expecting a different answer?"

"You make decisions with your head, not your heart." He plucked a leaf from a branch and crumpled it in his fist, as if it had wronged him in some way.

"Sometimes, the head and the heart agree." She grinned. "Now, if it was *you* asking me to run away, I'd have a tough time deciding what to do."

He gave her a reproachful look. "Be serious!"

Her eyes widened. "I *am* serious." *At least a little bit.* "You were bringing me all those flowers when I was sick, like you were wooing me. How could my poor, weak heart resist?"

His lips quivered, and she congratulated herself. He deserved to be teased, not for bringing her flowers, but for *stopping*.

"Anyway," she continued, taking pity on him, "I'd rather not be the cause of any more murders."

"Surely you do not blame yourself for what happened? None of it was your fault." He tossed the crumpled leaf and stepped toward her. "If anyone is to blame, it is the queen of Chandela and the regent of Malwa."

She sighed and looked up through the branches of the peepal tree. Dusk had fallen while they talked, and a flock of starlings flew in formation across the sky. Going home.

Home: a time and place she could never return to. The palace with its labyrinth of corridors, the magical whispering gallery, the rose gardens, the games of hide-and-seek they'd played as children—all these things were gone from her forever.

"Does it matter whose fault it was?" she said. "In the eyes of the world,

I am to blame. Do you know, it's the time of the autumn harvest? There will be four days of celebrations in Ajaigarh: wrestling, singing, dancing, boat racing in the Ken. And lots of delicious food. Puffed rice, samosas, laddus, pakoras. I remember eating these things, but I've forgotten what they tasted like." Chentu had stolen these flavors from her—among the many things she'd lost. Her heart ached as she counted them all.

"You'll taste them again," said Daksh, closing the distance between them. "You'll clear your name one day."

Warmth flooded her at his words. He was standing right next to her, his eyes holding her in their intense regard. She tried to smile. "You have such faith in my abilities?"

"I do." He grasped her wrist and squeezed gently. His fingers were light and strong and warm. She wanted him to never let go. Nothing bad could happen to her while he was holding her hand. She closed her eyes, unable to bear the intensity of his, and felt his hot breath in her hair.

She shivered at his nearness, his touch. "Daksh?" she whispered.

"Hmm?"

"You know when I said I'd had better? I lied."

Oh no, what had possessed her to tell him that? She cringed, wanting to run away and hide.

He tilted her chin, forcing her to meet his gaze. In the darkness below the tree, his face shone like a lamp. "I know," he said simply.

Her insides roiled in mingled indignation and embarrassment. "You know nothing! Maybe I didn't lie then. Maybe I'm lying to you right now."

His gaze dropped to her mouth, and he caressed her cheek with his fingertips. "Should I make a second attempt so you can make up your mind?" His voice was soft, yet compelling.

She stared at him, her mouth half-open, a molten pool of desire spreading through her body. *Yes.* She wanted him to kiss her again. She wanted to slide her hands up his chest, tangle them in his hair, run them down his back. She wanted him to encircle her in his arms and—

"I'm glad you decided to visit, Irfan," came the Acharya's brusque voice from behind the tree. "Princes sometimes forget their teachers when they take on royal duties."

"I will never forget you, Acharya," came Irfan's dutiful response.

Daksh gave an annoyed huff and dropped his hands. She stepped back from him, trying to still the hammering inside her chest. Goddess, that had been close.

The Acharya appeared from around the tree, Irfan by his side, surrounded by a group of senior disciples. His brow furrowed as he spotted her and Daksh. "What are you two doing here? You're late for the evening meal."

"Waiting for you, Acharya," said Katyani with as much sincerity as she could summon. Irfan threw her a soulful look.

"Well, let us go to the dining hall," said the Acharya. "Crown Prince Irfan will join us and stay the night."

Daksh fell in step beside his father; she walked behind the group so no one would notice her flustered expression.

Had the wily old man allowed Irfan to meet her in the hope that she would be tempted to go with him and leave his son alone? Poor Acharya Mahavir, he was stuck with her for the time being.

Irfan left the next morning. He bid her a halting good-bye, his eyes lingering on her. Before he boarded his carriage, he said, "If you need anything—anything at all—please think of me."

"Good-bye, Crown Prince," she said formally, aware of Daksh's hot gaze on both of them.

The carriage rolled away, and Daksh murmured, "Good riddance." She looked at him, startled, but he had already turned away and was walking back inside with the other disciples.

But she hadn't imagined his words. She hadn't imagined the almost-kiss either. If the Acharya hadn't interrupted them, he would have kissed her again. It meant he did not regret the first time he'd done it. She touched her cheek, remembering the feel of his fingertips against her skin, and smiled. She kept smiling for the rest of the day, including the meditation session, and even the Acharya's scolding voice couldn't wipe it off her face.

CHAPTER 17

AS THE WEATHER COOLED, KATYANI'S STRENGTH GRADUALLY returned. She threw herself into martial arts practice and sword fighting. Uttam summoned her one day to the armory, a long, narrow building opposite the dining hall, its walls adorned with swords and shields. He took down a sword encased in a black wooden scabbard and presented it to her.

She unsheathed it and gasped at the dark glow emanating from the blade.

"It reminds me of . . ." She hesitated. "Your brother's weapon."

Uttam ran a thumb along the flat of the blade. "And mine. They were part of a set. My sword is silver, my brother's is gold, and this one, you can see, has a bronze aura. Darker, but it suits you, I think. It used to belong to my father when he was younger."

Her breath caught. "This was the Acharya's sword? I can't take it!"

Uttam smiled. "It was my father who suggested I give it to you. Wield it well."

She left the armory, her head in the clouds. Of course, it would take some getting used to. It was heavier and not as flexible as her old sword, but it had a heft and decisiveness she liked. She cleaned and polished the blade every day and oiled it once a week. She slept with it next to her pallet, her hand on its hilt. The more time they spent together, the better it would respond to her wishes.

She finished reading the books about the yatu and returned them to the library. She'd discovered that many kingdoms in Bharat, including Malwa, had ancient land and resource agreements with the yatu to avoid conflict. Even the Acharya had an agreement with them inherited from *his* father, who had given them refuge when they were driven out of Chandela. Then why had she been brought up to believe they were vermin to be killed? She thought back to what she'd been taught, of how Chandela used to be infested by the monsters until they were expelled from the kingdom. What was the truth? Had Chandela had an agreement with them too, one that had been erased from history books?

She began asking for assignments outside the gurukul, hoping to learn more. The Acharya often dispatched senior disciples in response to petitions that came from various kingdoms, requesting help in dealing with monsters. Such groups were usually headed by Uttam, Daksh, Atreyi, Varun, or Vinita. Depending on the seriousness of the threat, the Acharya might lead the expedition himself, but this had become rarer over time. In fact, she hadn't seen him leave the gurukul once since the attack by the daayan. Was this to do with the injured right hand he kept hidden in a glove? The injury was her fault, and she longed to be of use to the gurukul, to pay her way so she wouldn't be a charity case.

At first, the Acharya demurred, but she pointed out that she was one of the few people in the gurukul who had experience with all four of the major monster types that infested Bharat. She was also well on her way to recovering her former spiritual power.

Her first foray into practical monster-banishing was a two-week-long assignment with Atreyi, Vinita, Barkha, and Shalu to a group of tribal forest villages south of Nandovana, bordering the kingdom of Chalukya. Misfortune had struck them in the form of a persistent preta infestation. The pretas had latched on to a returning traveler and gradually spread into every nook and cranny of the villages, summoning their ghostly kin from far and wide.

The villagers had fallen into depression and ennui, to the extent that people had stopped working, talking, and eating. They sat on their charpoys, empty-eyed and hollow-cheeked, waiting, it seemed, for death. Katyani could not see the pretas, but she could sense them, wrapped around the humans, draining their will to live. The Acharya had taught them to use spiritual power like a lens to detect invisible monsters.

The women wasted no time in setting up their preta-expelling rituals, but it was several days before the villages were cleansed of ghosts and it was safe to leave.

Despite the hardship of travel, the frugality of the food they carried, and the dangers of the forest, Katyani enjoyed the mission. The women were efficient, kind, blunt, and easy to be with, unlike some of the male disciples. They gossiped over cups of weak tea and dried fruit, and the two younger ones ribbed her about Daksh. His gifts of the gulmohar had not gone unnoticed.

"The gulmohar is called the flame of the forest," said Barkha with a sly wink as they sat around a fire one evening. "It can also mean flame of the heart."

Katyani's cheeks warmed. "There's nothing like that between us."

Well, maybe there was. But a serious relationship between the two of them was out of the question, no matter how much she longed for it. She might be free of the bond, but her path was set in blood, and it was not a path Daksh would approve of, to say nothing of the Acharya. She'd best not let rumors of romance taint his saintly reputation, or they'd be sure to get back to his father.

"He's never given flowers to anyone before," said Barkha, throwing a few twigs into the fire, making it crackle. "No matter how sick they've been." She turned to Shalu. "Remember the time Varun got cyclical fever? He was practically at death's door. Not a blade of grass did he get from Airya Daksh!"

"It's not the flowers but the soup that cinches it," said Shalu, nudging Katyani with her shoulder.

"What soup?" asked Katyani, confused.

"The medicinal soup you said tasted horrible?" Shalu gave her a knowing grin. "Airya Daksh had it made especially for you."

"He fancies himself a bit of an herbalist, like his mother used to be," explained Barkha. "Have you not seen him with his notebook? He uses it to jot down ideas and ingredients for recipes. But you're the first person he's actually experimented on."

That was a *recipe* book? And here she'd been thinking it was some sort of secret diary!

"He must either like or dislike you very much," added Shalu, and they both giggled.

"Stop it, you two," said Vinita in a quelling tone, and they fell silent. Thankfully, they didn't broach the topic again. That didn't stop her thinking about it. *Do you like or dislike me, Daksh?* she imagined saying to him when they returned. *After all, I'm the first person you've tried your awful recipes on.*

But when they returned to the gurukul, Daksh was more aloof to Katyani than he had ever been. When they made their report to the Acharya in the lecture hall, he stood beside Uttam, his face closed, his body tense, even as his brother and father questioned them. Katyani had been away from the gurukul for two weeks, and he would not even look at her.

His coldness hurt, and she was angry with herself for letting it hurt. After all, she'd said it herself. There was nothing between them. Best not to imagine there was. One kiss and one almost-kiss didn't count for much—not for *him*.

She threw herself back into training and plotting her return to Ajaigarh. She wanted to leave the gurukul before the next batch of students arrived in the spring. A plan took shape in her mind, audacious, tenuous, but better than simply storming the palace with her new bronze sword. She had to find out who in the palace had helped Shamsher. That person was the true culprit behind the killing of her family.

The month of Pausha ended, and Magha began—the last month of winter. Uttam led an expedition to a town in the Yadava kingdom to deal with vetalas who had abandoned the forest for a more urban lifestyle, attracted by the abundance of prey. Varun was tasked to visit the Kalachuri court to root out a persistent preta. Katyani's days turned into a peaceful routine, one she knew could not last forever, but all the more precious because of it. The only thing that marred her peace was Daksh, who continued to avoid her like the plague. Had she done something unspeakably awful she had no clue about?

One afternoon, when she was in the middle of a group meditation session, she was summoned to the Acharya's presence in the lecture hall. When she entered, she found him sitting on a mat, Daksh to his right. Both heads were bent over a parchment. No one else was in the room.

The Acharya raised his gaze to her. "King Aditya of Malwa has written, requesting mediation with a group of yatu on the outskirts of Dhar." He waved the parchment in his hand. "He has specifically asked for you."

Katyani's heart jumped. Aditya was her cousin. *King* Aditya. She would finally get to meet him. "Malwa has a treaty with the yatu, right?"

The Acharya gave her a sharp-eyed look. "I see you've been reading up on them. Many kingdoms have such treaties. I believe even Chandela once had an agreement with them."

Her stomach knotted. Here was her suspicion given voice and form. "I was brought up to believe Chandela has never negotiated with monsters."

The Acharya frowned. "Remember, history is written by people to propagate certain ideologies. The truth is more nuanced, always, but you have to dig deeper to find it."

The Acharya was right. And this mission was her opportunity to dig deeper. "Why do you think Aditya has asked for me?"

He stroked his beard. "Perhaps he wants to see you. You are cousins, after all."

"You don't have to go," said Daksh. He rose from where he had been sitting next to his father and paced. "It could be a trap."

A frisson ran through her at the sound of his voice. They were the first words he had spoken to her in weeks. A mix of emotions roiled within her: hurt and anger at his coldness, relief that he was speaking to her again.

"I can't hide here forever," she said, her voice even.

"You're not *hiding*." Daksh wheeled around, his face taut. "Everyone knows you're here." The Acharya cast him a warning glance.

But it was true. Reports of the trial, her punishment, and the Acharya's intervention had spread far and wide.

"He has asked for me, and I would like to go," said Katyani firmly. "I'm not afraid." She needed to know more about the yatu in Malwa, their relationship with her grandfather, and why they had helped him.

"You should be," said the Acharya. "Fear will make you more careful, less likely to get killed."

Katyani swallowed. "Do *you* think it's a trap?" she asked the Acharya.

"I don't know," he said. "The yatu have a decades-old agreement with the Paramaras. Why would they need our help in mediation?"

"Maybe I should go alone," said Katyani. "Not risk anyone else."

The Acharya snorted, and Daksh threw her an incredulous glance. "You have learned very little of our ways if you think that is an acceptable suggestion," said the Acharya. "I would have sent Uttam, but he will not be back for another week at least. Next to him, Daksh has the best yatu-subduing skills. Daksh, take any two disciples of your choice. Request Atreyi to join you as well."

As a chaperone, no doubt. Katyani would be glad of Atreyi's solid, sensible presence on this assignment. The senior-most woman disciple had over thirty years' experience dealing with both men and monsters. Daksh might be the superior yatu-killer, but when it came to diplomacy, Atreyi won hands down. Katyani had a feeling this mission would require more of the latter than the former.

Daksh picked Sagar and Lavraj to accompany them. They set off for Malwa the next morning, all five of them on horseback. If they kept up their pace, they would reach Dhar in four days. The city of her birth, according to Shamsher. One more place that had been her home and no longer was. She tried not to think of it: the missed years, the broken relationships, the lost memories, the stolen lives. But the closer they drew to Dhar, the more sadness weighed on her until she could scarcely bear it.

"What ails you, child?" Atreyi finally asked the night before they were to reach their destination.

They were in a woodland on the northwestern edge of Nandovana and had stopped by the banks of a rippling stream. Moonlight filtered through the trees, making shadows dance. The air smelled of rich earth, rotting leaves, and tomorrow's rain. They had just doused the fire after a frugal supper and were preparing to sleep. Daksh was on first watch. He sat in the lotus pose, his back to them, his eyes closed. Sagar and Lavraj were making beds of dried grass covered with light canvas.

"Just nerves," said Katyani, trying to smile.

"Do pranayama," advised Atreyi. "It never fails to calm me."

But Katyani could not focus on her breathing. When the others had settled in to sleep, she walked some distance away and sat on a rock at the edge of the stream, trailing her hand in the limpid water. What would her cousin be like? Why had he asked for her? Would he want her to stay? Did he think of her as family? Would she find answers to any of her questions?

A soft footfall alerted her to Daksh. She willed herself not to turn around.

"You're worried about tomorrow," he said.

She made a noncommittal sound.

He perched beside her on the rock, leaving an inch of space between them. She inhaled the clean, masculine scent of him, and her breath hitched.

"I will be with you," he said gently, placing a hand on her back. "You will not be alone at any time."

His words and touch almost undid her. What a changeable creature! Did he or did he not care for her? He blew hot as fire one moment, cold as a vetala's heart the next. And now he was being warm as sun-drenched honey. She wanted to shake him until his teeth rattled. Why hadn't he spoken to her for so many weeks? She sat up and faced him. "Airya, I can take care of myself," she said in a cutting voice. "I am used to it. Please do not concern yourself with me."

His brows drew together. "You *are* my concern. Everyone on this assignment is my concern."

So she was no different from everyone else? Had he been kissing them all? She clenched her teeth, trying to keep her temper. "Suppose we were attacked by vetalas and you had to choose just one of us to save. Who would you choose?"

He tilted his head, regarding her with puzzlement. "I would kill all the vetalas and save everyone, of course."

A curse on him and his useless gulmohar. "Go away," she said, turning back to the water. "This is *my* rock."

"Actually," said a silvery voice, "it is mine."

Katyani leaped to her feet, her hand on her sword. Behind her, Daksh did the same.

A ravishing woman with red lips and large, lustrous eyes hovered above the stream, scarcely ten feet away from them. Her full breasts were bare, her waist narrow, her ample hips scarcely covered by a filmy white robe.

Her pearly skin glowed in the moonlight, and her hair shone like a dark waterfall. *Love me, touch me, worship me,* said that voluptuous form.

Yakshini. Katyani was torn between admiration and alarm. She had never seen a nature spirit before.

Daksh made a strangled sound in his throat, and the yakshini's smile deepened. Katyani took a deliberate step back and stamped on his foot as hard as she could.

"Ouch." He sat on the rock and clutched his foot.

Katyani bowed to the yakshini. "Greetings, my lady. We did not realize the stream was occupied, or we would have camped elsewhere."

The yakshini waved a slim, graceful arm. "No matter. Since you are here, you can stay."

"Thank you, my lady, we deeply appreciate it." Katyani grabbed Daksh by the arm and hauled him up from the rock. They needed to wake the others and move away from the stream. Yakshinis were mostly harmless, but they could be mischievous at times. They only showed themselves to humans when they wanted something, and she suspected she knew what this one wanted.

Sure enough, the yakshini said in a petulant voice, "You didn't let me finish. You can stay if you can pay."

Katyani's heart sank. "I'm afraid we're incredibly poor. I doubt we can afford to stay here. I'll tell the others to move, shall I?"

"You shall not," said the yakshini, sounding even more miffed. "You have already sat on my rock. That is my favorite rock. And you have *seen* me." She gave a coy smile and cupped her breasts. "Am I not lovely?"

Katyani groaned mentally. "You are gorgeous, my lady."

"Why is *he* not saying anything?" said the yakshini, craning her slender neck to peer at Daksh. "Why is he hiding behind you? Am I so repulsive, Airya, that you do not wish to lay your eyes upon me?"

Daksh said not a word. He stood with his back to the water, his hands clenched and trembling. Katyani would get no help from him.

"To lay eyes upon you would be to ruin his state of brahmacharya," explained Katyani. "His father would punish him severely."

The yakshini pouted. "His thoughts are not those of a true brahmachari."

"How can anyone restrain their thoughts after looking upon your beauty?" said Katyani, her desire to shake Daksh until his teeth rattled going up tenfold. "You would evoke lust even in a stone." Why did it make her so bitter that the yakshini had evoked lust in *him*? It was only natural, and yet she burned with jealousy.

The yakshini smiled in delight. "Ah, you do not know? His thoughts were not those of a brahmachari even before I manifested myself."

What? The only person here with Daksh before the yakshini appeared was . . . Katyani. Her stomach fluttered.

"Silence!" snapped Daksh, his body tensing. "Do not test my patience."

"Such harsh words," said the yakshini, her eyes narrowing. "This is my domain, and you entered without my permission. You owe me payment, and I will have it, or I will curse you."

"Please don't curse us," said Katyani hurriedly. "And please forgive my friend. Tell me what would be a fair payment in your view."

"A fair payment for *all* of you sleeping safely in my domain would be for *one* of you to sleep with me." The yakshini giggled at Katyani's expression of open-mouthed horror. "But I will not insist on it. I can see where someone's preferences lie. No, I shall be content with a single kiss."

"I would not kiss you if my life depended on it," said Daksh through gritted teeth. Katyani's urge to hit him faded somewhat.

The yakshini stuck her tongue out, looking, if anything, even sexier. "Did I say I wanted to kiss you, Airya? Such presumption! No, I want to kiss your lady love."

"What?" said Daksh.

"I'm not his lady love," said Katyani. She processed what the yakshini had said. "What?"

"A kiss," said the yakshini. "Isn't that the extent of your experience? Allow me to show you how it's done. Airya can watch and learn something."

Daksh swung around and unsheathed his sword, looking furious. The golden flash of the blade fell on the yakshini's face, making her seem, for the first time, inhuman. Katyani grabbed hold of his arm. "Don't do anything foolish," she implored.

The yakshini showed her teeth, perfectly white and slightly pointy. "Swords are not the answer to everything. You think you can frighten me?"

In response, Daksh drew a line in the sand with his sword, reciting the words of a spell. Smoke curled up from the sand, and the yakshini drew back, her hand flying to her chest.

"You cannot cross this line," he growled, his face like thunder, reminding Katyani, just for a moment, of the Acharya. "Let us go in peace. I want no quarrel with you."

"I only asked for a kiss," said the yakshini, her eyes huge and distressed. "One little kiss in exchange for sleeping on the banks of my stream."

"It's inappropriate!" Daksh grabbed Katyani's hand. "Let's go."

"Are you sure, Airya?" said the yakshini. "Your boundary might stop me, but it cannot stop my curse."

Katyani tugged her hand away from Daksh. They couldn't afford to be cursed by a yakshini. Their curses were rumored to be as powerful as the Acharya's. "I'll do it," she blurted out.

The water spirit clapped her hands in delight.

"Katyani," urged Daksh. "You don't have to."

She gave him her sweetest smile. "But I want to."

His eyes widened in hurt; his mouth opened, but no words came out. His expression gave her such a pang, she almost changed her mind. But a kiss was only a kiss, whereas a curse could be their collective downfall.

"I'll be fine," she told him. She stepped over his line and stood at the water's edge. "I'm ready."

The yakshini floated toward her. Up close, she was even more stunning. She looked and smelled like a water lily, delicate and fragrant.

"Are you watching, Airya?" she called over Katyani's shoulder. Whatever she saw in his face seemed to give her great amusement, for she held a hand over her mouth to stifle a giggle. Then she looked into Katyani's eyes, her gaze both tender and fiery.

"What a lovely girl you are," she whispered. She smoothed Katyani's hair back from her forehead and caressed her face with soft yet sure hands.

"Hurry up, yakshini," Daksh bit out. "Do you plan to do this all night?"

The yakshini shook her head sadly. "One of the problems with human men is how little they last, like dry leaves going up in flames. A woman is like a candle; she can burn all night long." She traced Katyani's lips with her fingertips. "Will you burn for me, pretty girl?"

"Don't answer," warned Daksh. "Don't say anything."

But his voice seemed to come from far away. The yakshini's eyes held Katyani in their warm embrace. Her hands slid down Katyani's arms, giving her goose bumps. Could she touch the yakshini back? Was that allowed? Did she even want to?

What the hell, thought Katyani, and she slipped her arms around the yakshini's graceful neck.

The yakshini touched the tip of her tongue to her lips. "Now?"

"Yes," breathed Katyani, scarcely able to get the word out.

The yakshini drew her arms around Katyani and brought her lips down on hers. They were soft and sweet and intoxicating, like a full-blown rose at the end of spring. The yakshini tugged Katyani's lower lip with her teeth, and Katyani opened her mouth, wanting to taste all of her at once. The blood pounded in her ears, and she closed her eyes.

How long did the kiss go on? The yakshini broke once to whisper in her ear, to tell her everything she wanted to do to her, to tug her earlobes with her teeth, to lick the hollow of her throat. Katyani would have fallen then, but the yakshini held her in her arms, strong yet gentle.

After an unknowable length of time, Katyani became aware that she was lying on the bank of the stream, her lips sore, her heart thudding inside her chest.

"And that, Airya, is how you kiss a woman," came a cool, amused voice.

Katyani gave a tremulous sigh. She could still feel the yakshini's lips on hers. If she never kissed anyone again, the memory of this kiss alone would be enough to carry her through a loveless life. She would make up songs about it and sing them in the street for coin.

Cold water drenched her face.

She sat up, sputtering. Daksh crouched beside her, his face anxious, ready to throw more.

"How dare you," she croaked.

He sat back, his expression changing to relief. "You're awake."

He caught hold of her arm as she struggled to rise. She pushed him away in irritation, but to her surprise, she was barely able to walk straight. Her head swam as if she'd drunk liquor. She tottered to the rock and sat down, rubbing her forehead.

"Not here, please." Daksh tugged her hand. "Let's walk to where the others are, and then you can sit, okay?"

She allowed him to lead her away from the stream. "That was some kiss," she mumbled. Why did her head feel heavy?

"That was a yakshini," said Daksh grimly.

"You've got to learn how to kiss like that," she said. "What teeth!" She'd meant to say technique, but "teeth" was an equally good choice of word.

"And you are an excellent judge of kissing, are you?" he said, glancing at her, his voice flat.

"A better judge than you," said Katyani. "I want to jump into the stream and beg her for more."

"Fool," he muttered.

"You're just jealous she kissed me, not you." She gave a drunken giggle.

"Hush," he said. "We're here."

They had arrived at the spot where the other three slept, oblivious of the world-changing kiss she'd experienced.

Daksh made her sit down under an acacia tree and drink a gourd of water. Then he tapped Atreyi's arm, waking her. Katyani was too woozy to hear what he told her, but Atreyi came to her at once and knelt beside her. She touched Katyani's forehead and chanted under her breath.

"What are you saying?" Katyani wriggled to get more comfortable against the knobby trunk.

"The words of a healing spell." Daksh leaned over them, his face intent. "Be still."

She stuck her tongue out at him, but he didn't even react.

Sagar and Lavraj had woken up too. At a signal from Daksh, they gathered all their belongings, loaded the horses, and led them away.

Gradually, Katyani's head cleared, and she returned to herself. She no longer felt like jumping into the stream. Not *particularly*.

"Let's go," said Atreyi in clipped tones. "The more distance we put between ourselves and the yakshini, the sooner you will recover from her glamour."

"She was very beautiful," Katyani informed her.

"I am sure," said Atreyi dryly, getting up. "Can you walk?"

She rose, clutching the tree trunk for support. "Yes, of course. I'm fine."

"You are luckier than many have been," said Atreyi as they walked away from the stream. "Yakshinis sometimes suck spiritual power from humans. This one didn't. Quite the opposite, in fact. She seems to have *given* you a small power boost. It is a rare gift and will stay with you forever. The only harm she did was to enthrall you, and that is temporary."

"I can't believe you wanted to kiss her," said Daksh in a disapproving voice.

"I can't believe you wanted to be cursed by her," she retorted. "Surely a kiss is less harmful than a curse?"

"You should have been on your guard," said Daksh, hectoring her as if they were back in the gurukul and he'd caught her making a rookie mistake. "Then she would not have been able to affect you so much."

"Yakshas and yakshinis are not in the gurukul curriculum," she said heatedly. "I think they should be."

"I'll take it up with the Acharya," said Atreyi in a placating tone.

They arrived at a small, moonlit clearing where Sagar and Lavraj had tied the horses.

"Check the trees," said Daksh, circling the clearing, glaring at the undergrowth as if he expected it to grow fangs.

"We already did," said Sagar. "There is no one."

Daksh looked up at the sky. "Three hours till dawn. I'll take watch. You'd all best get back to sleep."

Only three hours? "How long was I with the yakshini?" she asked.

"Two hours," he said.

She was stupefied. "No way we were kissing for two hours."

"That's how long it felt to me," he said, and his mouth quirked.

Had he made a joke? She wasn't sure. He kept revealing startling new sides to his personality. She spread her sheet under a tree next to Atreyi and leaned against the trunk. The yakshini had said something about him that surprised her, but she couldn't remember what it was.

At least Daksh was back to his normal self. She didn't know why he had been so cold to her the past few weeks, but the encounter with the yakshini had thawed the ice between them. Melted it. *Steamed* it.

She fell asleep thinking of the kiss. *Kisses.* In her dreams, Daksh and the yakshini got jumbled up. The first kiss and the second kiss blurred until she was no longer sure which was which and who was kissing whom.

CHAPTER 18

THEY ENTERED MALWA EARLY THE NEXT MORNING, CROSSING the great Narmada River on a barge. Malwa was drier than Chandela, and the trees were different, gnarled and twisted with spiky leaves and long green pods. Jagged brown hills rose in the distance and fallen boulders forced them to take detours from the main road. They arrived at a military camp on the outskirts of Dhar in the evening and asked for directions to Biaora, the village they had been summoned to.

A couple of cavalrymen escorted them there. It turned out to be a row of mud-walled huts along a dirt street, a stone well, enclosures full of grazing goats, and tiny vegetable plots. They were put up in the village council house, the sole building made of brick. It was a roomy, pleasant house with a porch, a large central courtyard with a pump, and a row of pallets in the back room.

They washed up at the pump and ate a simple meal of yogurt, flatbread, and ripe yellow bananas, delivered by one of the village women. Afterward, they rested in the courtyard as stars peeped into the sky. Katyani stretched her legs on the still-warm stones, trying to relax.

"I don't see any signs of yatu," said Atreyi to Daksh. "Have we been called here for nothing?"

He frowned. "We have been treated with courtesy so far. I will give Aditya the benefit of the doubt. But we must stay vigilant. Sagar and Lavraj, take first watch. Katyani, you and I will take the second."

Katyani thought she wouldn't be able to sleep from the tension, but after four nights of camping on the open ground, the pallets in the council house were a luxury, and she slept like a sloth. When Sagar woke her at three in the morning for the second watch, she nearly kicked his face.

She rubbed the sleep out of her eyes, buckled her sword to her belt, and went outside to the porch. Daksh was already awake, sitting on the steps, sword across his knees. The village was silent, the moonlit street before them empty but for a couple of pariah dogs, sleeping nose to nose. She leaned against a porch pillar to his right, trying not to yawn, giving him sidelong glances. He was quiet and still, like a beautiful statue in the moonlight, his expression contemplative.

"Do you think there are any yatu in the vicinity?" she asked him. "Or was that all a bunch of lies?"

"My sword tells me there are," he answered. "But where, and how many, I can't say. Only the morning will tell us why we're here."

"Why haven't you been speaking to me?" she blurted out.

Oh no. She writhed in embarrassment. She hadn't intended to say that aloud. It made her sound needy, as if she craved his attention.

He turned to her, eyebrows raised in surprise. "I am speaking to you right now."

She scowled. "I meant before yesterday—ever since my return from the mission with the women disciples. Were you mad at me about something?"

He dropped his gaze. "No, it's nothing like that."

"Then what?" She sat beside him and poked his shoulder. "Tell me."

"It is unimportant," he said in a low voice, staring at the ground.

It's important to me, she wanted to scream. She pressed her lips together and regarded his immovable profile, the straight back, the strong yet elegant hands that rested on his sword, and, with great difficulty, held her tongue. If he wanted to tell her, he would, and if he didn't, he wouldn't. She might not like it, but she couldn't change it. If she pushed him, he would clam up. It was deeply frustrating—just like him.

They sat in silence for a few minutes, Katyani thinking of and discarding a great many one-liners that would have gotten a response, but perhaps not the one she wanted.

He looked up at last, shifting slightly so he was facing her. "While you were away, my mother's death anniversary came by. I lit a diya for her and put offerings of fruit and flowers beneath the peepal tree. They were gone the next morning. In their place was a palash leaf inscribed with the words 'thank you.'"

Cold fingers skittered up her spine. Those who'd had the last rites weren't supposed to linger in the mortal plane. "You think it was *her*?"

He shrugged. "I don't know. I didn't tell my father. If it was my mother, it means she's still around, waiting for him. She hasn't moved on yet. If it was *not* her, then it could only be the daayan, making mischief."

She exhaled. "Surely the daayan's power cannot extend into the gurukul."

"I thought so too, but I am no longer sure."

"You should tell the Acharya," she said.

"There's nothing he can do about it. I don't want him to worry about my mother. And I don't want him to seek the daayan out. That will only hasten his own end." His mouth twisted in a half smile. "I couldn't talk about this with anyone, not even my brother, for Uttam would have told our father. I wished you were there, for you have met the daayan, and you would have understood."

All the anger she had felt toward him melted in the wave of compassion that washed over her. Her arms itched to hug him, but she managed to restrain herself. "Why didn't you tell me earlier?" she asked.

His lips tightened, and he lowered his gaze again. She wouldn't get any more words from him. But the ones he'd offered had been enough. They sat in companionable silence as the moon moved across the sky.

A sense of weightlessness came over her, as if all her burdens had slipped off her shoulders. *I am happy.* What an odd feeling to have in such a place and with such a person. Were they friends? Did he have any others? Most likely not. If he did, he would have been able to confide in that person the way he had confided in her. It must be hard to make friends if you were the Acharya's son. Duty and responsibility took the place of friendship and just about every other human relationship. Year after year, pupils arrived at the gurukul and left. Daksh could not leave; what a strange, painful twist of fate that had brought her back to him and made this moment possible.

Dawn lightened the sky, and a cow mooed from a shed down the street, breaking the spell the night had cast. Sagar came out on the porch and bade them good morning. Daksh gave her a small smile before rising and issuing instructions for the day. She stretched her limbs, wishing the night had lasted a little longer. At least she was no longer anxious about the day ahead.

A couple of village women came by with bowls of sweet porridge and a basket of dates. They ate in the sunny courtyard, under the shade of an overhang, to the sound of birdsong and the distant lowing of cows. They had scarcely finished when a group of armed soldiers entered the courtyard and took up stations along the walls.

Sagar leaped to his feet, his hand going to his sword, but Daksh shot him a glare, and he subsided.

"Our presence here was requested to deal with yatu," said Daksh, addressing the soldiers. "Where are they?"

"In a field adjoining this village," came a smooth voice. A young man clad in the dark green Paramara uniform walked into the courtyard. "They don't enter human habitation if they can help it. Apparently, humans smell bad."

Daksh rose and gave a slight nod. "King Aditya." The others rose as well.

Aditya? This was her *cousin*. Katyani stared at him, her skin tingling. He was tall, slim, and clean-shaven, with Shamsher's deep-set eyes and air of command. Did he look like her in any way? Shamsher had said they were born four days apart. He had the same tawny brown skin that she did, the same unruly black hair, except his was cut short.

He gave Daksh a warm smile. "You look well, Airya. It's good to see you. And you, Airyaa Atreyi. Thank you all for coming. How is Acharya Mahavir?"

"He sends his blessings," said Daksh. "What problems are you facing with the yatu? The Paramara kingdom has an agreement with them, yes?"

"My *grandfather* had an agreement with them," corrected Aditya. "I do not. But I hope to, with your help."

"You asked specifically for Katyani," said Atreyi. "Any reason for that, King Aditya?"

Aditya's smile vanished. "The yatu insisted on her presence."

"Why?" asked Katyani, bewildered.

Aditya's expression could have frozen a hot spring. He looked away from her, addressing Daksh and Atreyi. "According to them, any agreement must be made with all members of the current royal generation to be valid. That means both myself and Princess Ambika must be present during the discussion."

A bitter taste filled her mouth. He'd called her by a title she didn't want and a name she didn't remember having. "My name is Katyani."

"For the purpose of this discussion, you are Princess Ambika of Paramara," said Aditya, his voice hard. "If you have a problem with that, take it up with the yatu who lost their kin in Ajaigarh and Rajgarh."

Katyani's mind flashed back to the massacre in the audience hall: the blood, the torn limbs, the screams of dying men. Hemlata, being dragged away by her hair; Ayan, running after her, only to be cut down. Nausea gripped her stomach. She breathed deeply, trying to return to the courtyard.

"The yatu he used were from Malwa?" asked Atreyi when it became clear that Katyani wasn't going to speak.

"Only a few. Most were from Nandovana," answered Aditya. "I wasn't involved, so I don't know why they chose to help him or what he promised them."

Shamsher's yatu were from *Nandovana*? This meant it had nothing to do with the traditional relationship they had with Malwa and everything to do with their own goals. Many of the yatu who lived in Nandovana were refugees, or descendants of refugees, from the Chandela kingdom. Had they helped Shamsher to get revenge on the Chandelas?

"Now the local yatu have encroached on human territory, and cattle and goats have started vanishing," Aditya continued. "How much longer before people start vanishing too?"

Atreyi nodded. "It's a good thing you called us. Your grandfather's death has left a power vacuum. You must be seen to fill it."

Daksh stepped toward Katyani and grasped her wrist. "Can you do this?"

Aditya's cold, indifferent gaze returned to her. She swallowed her nausea. "Of course I can do this." *Be someone else. Answer to a stranger's name. Sit next to monsters whose kin helped kill Ayan.* Her stomach knotted again, and she thrust away the traumatic memories. She had to focus and stay in the present as the Acharya had advised. She would regard it as an information-gathering session. What kind of agreement did men make with monsters?

"Then let's get it over with." Aditya strode out, followed by his retinue of soldiers.

Katyani sighed. "He hates me, doesn't he?" It shouldn't have mattered to her—he was a stranger, after all—but it did. A part of her had hoped for something more.

"He is grieving," said Atreyi. "Now that Shamsher is gone, he has no close relatives left alive." *Except you,* she did not say.

"Think of this as a test like any other," said Daksh. "The difference is, we'll all be there to help you pass."

She shot him a grateful look. "I won't fail." He squeezed and let go her hand.

"Of course you won't," said Atreyi briskly. "I have complete confidence in you."

And yet, when they were outside, they walked with her in the middle, as if they were afraid she'd run away or keel over. Their concern might have irritated her once; now it warmed her, chasing away the last of the coldness in her stomach. They followed Aditya and his cohort down the dusty street, awestruck villagers lining up for a glimpse of their king. Beyond the village, they struck out across a field of threshed wheat.

A group of five yatu sat beneath a crooked sheesham tree, waiting for them. Any hopes she had that these yatu would look different from the ones in Nandovana or Ajaigarh vanished the moment she laid eyes on them. They were the same hulking monsters with curving tusks and bloodred eyes, clubs and maces resting on their shoulders. Katyani kept her outward calm, but her hand twitched over the hilt of her sword. It was hard to think of them as anything but enemies, hard not to be reminded, yet again, of the massacre in the audience hall.

One of the yatu lumbered to his feet and spoke a few guttural words to Aditya. To her surprise, Aditya responded in kind. Introductions were made, and all the yatu fixed their crimson gazes on her, making her wish she could disappear.

They sat down, and the process of negotiation started. They spoke in a Paramara dialect that was unfamiliar to her but had some similarity to

Hindavi. She gleaned enough to know that these five were representatives of the local yatu. They discussed rights and responsibilities, conflict management, territorial boundaries, and reparations for those lost in Shamsher's bloody campaign. Despite herself, her interest grew as she listened and tried to understand. It was the kind of discussion two warring tribes might have with each other if they wished to avoid fighting.

From time to time, she was asked whether she agreed or disagreed on certain points, and she followed Aditya's lead in this. She didn't want to mess up the negotiations for him. More to the point, Aditya's arguments appeared both reasonable and compassionate. He impressed her with his calm demeanor and rationality. It must have impressed the yatu too, for they arrived at a working agreement a couple of hours later. It would be formalized at a ceremony on the next new moon night. To her relief, she didn't have to be present for that.

They bowed to the yatu; the yatu bowed back and trudged away into a thicket of trees at the edge of the field.

As they walked back to the village, Aditya thanked them again for coming to his aid.

"You didn't need much help," said Atreyi in an approving tone. "You did well."

Katyani, walking beside her, silently agreed. She was glad the session was over and she was no longer forced to be in the monsters' reeking presence. But she was also glad to have witnessed the discussion. It was a side of the yatu she'd never seen before. Although she'd read about the treaties they had with humans, it was one thing to read about it and quite another to see the negotiation for herself. She would have to try to separate them in her mind—those who had massacred the royal family and those who were simply trying to live in a land dominated by humans.

"Your presence was critical," Aditya assured Atreyi. "The Acharya is famed throughout Bharat among both humans and nonhumans. Now they know I have your support, despite what happened in Rajgarh, and they will be less inclined to break the agreement."

"My father will be glad to hear of your progress," said Daksh. They arrived at the council house, and he looked up at the sky, calculating. "There are still many hours of daylight left. We should start back."

Aditya turned around to face them. A muscle twitched in his jaw, betraying tension. "Before you leave, I wish to talk with my cousin in private."

Katyani's heart jumped. Why did he want to speak with her alone? He'd already made his dislike abundantly clear.

Daksh glanced at Atreyi, and an unspoken message passed between them.

"You may talk with her in my presence," said Atreyi. "The rest will wait outside."

"She is my cousin," said Aditya, an edge in his voice. "Surely you do not expect me to harm her."

"She is a disciple of my gurukul," said Atreyi firmly. "If you wish to speak with her, you must follow the gurukul rules." She beckoned Katyani and walked into the house. Katyani followed, grateful for her presence. Aditya entered behind them, frowning.

Atreyi headed for the courtyard and sat in the lotus pose under the shade of the overhang. "Pretend I am not here, children," she remarked, and closed her eyes.

Katyani walked to the other side of the courtyard and faced Aditya. "You wished to speak with me."

He raked her with the eyes that reminded her of Shamsher. "I wanted to examine the face of the person responsible for our grandfather's death."

Her insides twisted. One more death unfairly laid at her door. She'd been a pawn, nothing more. Why did he blame her for the wrongdoing of others? She clamped her lips together to stop herself saying something she might regret.

"Tell me how he died," grated Aditya.

She took a deep breath and tried to remember the events without re-living them. Once again, she saw Shamsher stagger back, an arrow piercing his chest, blood darkening his tunic, a look of hurt and betrayal on his face. "An arrow," she said, keeping her voice even. "I don't know whose. The Acharya had just disarmed him. Your grandfather struck first," she hastened to add. "He told his yatu to attack even though the Acharya came to Rajgarh bearing a white flag."

His lip curled. "You said *your* grandfather. Not *our* grandfather."

She flushed. "A fact I knew for all of three days before he died."

Aditya bowed his head. "He meant everything to me. He was my father, my mother, my guru, my advisor."

A pang went through her. She'd lost her family, but so had he. She wanted to say: *He was the grandfather I didn't know I had, the person who should have raised me.* But she didn't grieve him the way Aditya did, and it wouldn't have been right. "I'm sorry," she said instead.

He raised his head, nostrils flaring. "So am I. I'm sorry you exist. I'm sorry you didn't die in that bloody war that took our parents. Then he would still be alive."

Her stomach dropped. The virulent words should not have shocked her. What did this man care for her? He was mourning, like she was. But she would not bear his unfair accusations in silence. "The regent of Malwa died because of his own actions," she said. "You cannot blame me for his karma. He reaped as he sowed."

"Did you not help him?" he demanded. "Were you not the one who gave him the idea to use the yatu and guided them into Ajaigarh?"

"No!" She dug her nails into her palms, trying to focus on what was important. "Are you saying it *wasn't* his idea?"

He narrowed his eyes at her. "He told me someone had suggested he use the Nandovana yatu to carry out his attack. I thought it must be you."

A chill went through her. Here was confirmation that there was indeed a traitor in Ajaigarh. "I guessed he had help from within the palace, but it wasn't me. I would never have helped someone murder my own family."

"Your family?" he sneered. "The ones who killed our parents, kidnapped you, and made you a bondswoman?"

"The ones who raised me." She swallowed the painful lump in her throat, angry at herself for letting him hurt her, for having hoped for anything better. "What makes family, *cousin*? If it was blood, you would be embracing me as your long-lost sister, not making accusations against me. *Our* grandfather murdered the royal family of Chandela. He got the end he deserved."

"Even now your sympathies lie with them?" A note of wonder crept into his voice. "After everything they did to you? To *us*?"

"No." She showed him her teeth. "I'm a free agent. The only loyalty I currently harbor is to Acharya Mahavir."

"Then it was all for nothing, what he did, what he endured."

"Untrue," she said. "I am no longer in Chandela, no longer bonded to anyone."

"You think that's worth his life?" He gave her a disbelieving glare. "I tried to stop him. He refused to listen to me. He told me stories of how it was when we were kids, how it would be when you returned. How I would no longer be alone. I begged him not to risk everything for you. I told him he was enough family for me, that I didn't need anyone else. The truth is that *I* wasn't enough for *him*. He couldn't stop thinking about you, talking about you, Princess Ambika of the Paramara dynasty."

Every word was a twist of the knife in her heart. "That person does not exist," she said, keeping her voice flat, her face blank.

He gave a harsh laugh. "Oh, she existed all right. She existed in his imagination. I'm almost glad he's dead. Even if he'd managed to bring you here, you would have been a disappointment, a failure of his dreams. At least he didn't live to see that."

"Enough," said Atreyi, rising. *At last.* Relief flooded Katyani.

"Have a nice life, *cousin*," said Aditya. "Remember him sometimes, the man who loved the idea of you more than he did the reality of me."

"Don't blame me for whatever was lacking in your relationship with him," she shot back, the facade crumbling. "I didn't ask for any of this. I was *three*."

"You aren't a child anymore." He took a deep breath. "What happened in Ajaigarh? If not you, then who was it that tempted my grandfather to his death?"

"I don't know," she said, her voice shaking at last. "But I'm going to find out, and I'm going to destroy them."

He gave a thin smile. "Good luck. The first step on your path to atonement."

"I have nothing to atone for," she said, staring at the ground. "I've always tried to do the right thing."

"Did you try to save him?" he countered.

Save him? The man responsible for the carnage at Ajaigarh? He deserved to die.

But Aditya would refuse to see that. For him, Shamsher was a different person. It was no use arguing with him. It would only hurt them both even more.

"Come on, Katyani." Atreyi walked to the door that led to the main room. "Let's go."

She turned to follow Atreyi, her heart squeezing in a fist of pain.

Aditya caught hold of her hand, stopping her. "Ambika," he whispered. "I remember you from before. Don't you remember me?"

Her eyes blurred. If only he'd started on that note, this conversation would have gone differently. "The bond with the queen erased my memories. I don't remember you. I wish I did." She freed her hand and went outside. Daksh and the others were waiting, horses saddled, bags and water gourds loaded. Daksh gave her an encouraging smile, but he asked no questions, for which she was grateful.

They mounted their horses. Aditya came outside to watch them, his shoulders bowed, his face drawn in tight lines, but he said nothing, nor did he try to stop them from leaving.

Katyani's heart ached, both for herself and for him. But the pain of this mission had been worthwhile. She now had proof that Shamsher had been helped by a traitor from Ajaigarh. And she had gleaned an important piece of information. The yatu Shamsher had used were from Nandovana. Her next clue lay walking distance from the gurukul itself. The bold plan that had taken shape in her mind earlier solidified.

CHAPTER 19

A FEW DAYS AFTER THEIR RETURN FROM MALWA, THE Acharya summoned Katyani to the lecture hall and told her to stay in the gurukul and avoid meeting any outsiders. Daksh and Uttam concurred. They sat beside their father, identical expressions of concern on their faces. Atreyi must have told them everything Aditya had said to her.

"I should leave before your next batch of pupils arrives in spring," said Katyani, sitting opposite them. "People will be reluctant to send their precious heirs to a school that harbors a known criminal."

The Acharya bristled. "I do not harbor criminals. Those who know me will also know there is an excellent reason for what I did."

"Still, all kinds of rumors will have spread about me after the trial." Her mouth twisted. "I am possibly the most infamous person in Bharat right now." It was a stomach-curdling thought.

"This is not far from the truth," said Uttam. "Even in Devagiri, people talk about you." Devagiri was the capital of the Yadava kingdom.

"What do they say?" asked Katyani.

An expression of distaste crossed his face. "Many false things. I do not wish to repeat them."

"Let me help you, Airya," she said. "They say I committed mass murder. I led monsters into Ajaigarh and slaughtered my own family. I escaped punishment for my crimes by fooling the Acharya into thinking I was innocent. Have I captured the general feeling?"

"If you know, why do you ask?" snapped Daksh. He was angry not at her, she knew, but at her situation.

"Daksh." Uttam laid a calming hand on his shoulder.

She gave them a brittle smile. "To remind you why I need to leave."

"Where will you go?" asked Uttam.

She shrugged. "I'll figure something out. My name might be infamous, but my face is not. Few people outside Ajaigarh know what I look like."

"You are a disciple of my gurukul," said the Acharya. "As long as you are here, no harm will come to you."

His words warmed her. "Thank you, Acharya." She was more concerned about the harm that might come to *him,* but she left that unsaid.

The only way for her to clear her name was to discover the real culprit behind the bloodbath in Ajaigarh. Her confrontation with Aditya had cemented her resolve to bring the betrayer to justice. She hadn't forgotten her treatment in the court either: Revaa's lies, Bhairav's cruelty, and Chentu's lashes, cutting her back open.

The daayan had blessed her with revenge. It would be disrespectful not to pursue it. She had worked hard to regain her spiritual power and even obtained an added boost from the yakshini she had kissed. She had no excuse to continue hiding in the gurukul.

She would miss Daksh. Her heart ached, thinking about it. It wasn't just his touch she craved; it wasn't just how he made her laugh without meaning to; it wasn't only his confidence in her or the odd moments of tenderness they'd shared. It was all these things and more. When he was with her, she felt no fear, as if nothing truly bad could happen in his presence.

She had best get used to being without him. Unless she could prove her innocence, she was a danger to those who sheltered her. And she wasn't going to endanger the few people she had left: Daksh, the Acharya, Atreyi, Shalu, and all the rest. No one had questioned her innocence, her right to be here. They'd simply accepted her as part of the gurukul. She wasn't going to repay them by risking their reputations and their lives.

Late that night, while the gurukul slept under the light of a gibbous moon, she snuck out of her hut, the bronze sword at her belt and a knapsack on her back. The courtyard was quiet and peaceful. She paused at the gate and gave a last look back at the place where she'd lived for nearly a year. The pagoda-topped main building where she'd endured innumerable lessons on ethics. The peepal tree, beneath which Daksh had almost kissed her a second time. The little hut where she'd recovered her strength. The women's dormitory where she'd found true friends.

This is my home. These people are my family. The realization made her heart soar. To find family again after losing everything in the world was both a reason to live and a reason to leave, if that was what it took to keep them safe. *Stay well,* she thought to them, blinking back tears.

She set off, heading east. She would take the path through the forest that led to the kingdom of Chandela—not that she was going there right away. The trees clustered around her, whispering in the wind, moon-dappled branches framing the winter sky. The air was cool and fresh, the ground dry and easy to walk upon.

She inhaled the rich, loamy scent of the forest, calm spreading through her body. After all these months, Nandovana held no fear for her. She knew how to deal with most monsters by now. If she encountered a coven of vetalas, well, that was good-bye, Katyani. She'd come back as a vengeful spirit and haunt the Ajaigarh palace.

After a few minutes, a sound intruded in her thoughts—a sound that didn't belong to a creature of the forest. She stopped and listened.

There it was again, that soft footfall, that crunch of leaves.

Seriously? She hadn't dropped the slightest hint she was leaving tonight. She'd made it sound as though she would wait till spring. Certainly there had been no one in the courtyard to watch her leave.

She put her hands on her hips. "Daksh? Come out."

He stepped out from behind a tree. His sword hung on his belt, and he carried a bow and quiver on his back, as if he were going into battle.

"Why are you following me?" she asked, not knowing whether she was happy or annoyed to see him. Her lips twitched. Was she *smiling?*

He lowered his eyes and said nothing.

"Please go back," she said. *Stay with me,* she thought.

He raised his gaze to her. "The forest is not safe at night. How do you think my father would feel if something happened to you?"

"Tell him I'd come back as a daayan," she said.

He gave her a reproachful look, and her hand flew to her mouth. She shouldn't joke about daayans, not with him. "Don't be flippant."

She sighed and dropped her hand. "Look, I have a *plan*. I'm not even going to Ajaigarh. Not yet, anyway."

"Then what are you doing out here? You know we're not supposed to leave our rooms at night."

Him and his rules. "This is an essential activity." She turned and continued down the path, ducking under an overhanging branch.

He fell in step beside her. "What is the plan?"

She glanced sideways at his stern, handsome profile. As always, his nearness sent a shiver through her. She'd been aching at the thought of life without him, and here he was, by her side once more. *Just for a little while,* she told herself. *What harm can it do?* "I'll tell you if you promise not to try to stop me."

"Hmm." He pushed aside a curtain of ropy vines blocking the path, casting a sharp gaze upward.

It was not an affirmation, but she plunged ahead. "I want to find a yatu to interrogate."

He frowned but said nothing. Encouraged, she continued, "The only people who can tell me what really happened back in Ajaigarh are the yatu who attacked it. Aditya said Shamsher used yatu from Nandovana. Many of them died in Rajgarh, but a few must have escaped. If I can find one of the survivors, I can question him about what happened." She nearly tripped over a tree root.

"That is not a bad plan," he said, grabbing her arm to steady her.

She sucked in a quick breath. "It's not? I mean, of course it's not bad. It's the best I can come up with. Have you ever spoken to a yatu in this forest?"

"A couple of times," he said. "They have their own tongue. A few of them speak Hindavi, but they usually choose not to converse with humans."

"They spoke to Shamsher," she said. "He had an alliance with the yatu, and I don't mean the kind of agreement Aditya negotiated. Do you know of any yatu haunts in Nandovana?"

"They move frequently, but there is a cave behind a waterfall where the maternal head of one of the clans is often to be found. My father has forbidden us to go anywhere near it."

Her heart sank. "So you cannot take me there."

They walked in silence for a minute, Katyani racking her brains for a way to persuade him to tell her where it was.

"I will take you there," said Daksh, glancing at her, his face resolute.

What? Katyani gazed at him in astonishment. "Did I hear right? You're going to break the rules for me?" He'd broken the rules when he'd kissed her, of course, but *this* was premeditated. His father would have a fit.

"Rules are made to be followed," he said. "They should only be broken for a higher purpose."

"Like that time I bathed during the night," she said, knowing she was blathering but unable to stop. "I had the higher purpose of getting clean."

He gave her a withering look. "You reduce everything to a joke. No, don't speak! The cave is a two-hour trek from here. The going will be difficult. Watch the trees."

She bit her lip and unsheathed her dagger. Daksh led her away from the trail and into the thick underbrush, using his sword to clear a path for them. Behind them, the bushes closed up again as if by magic. Branches whipped her face, and vines wrapped around her neck. She slashed them with her dagger, her throat tight.

"They don't want us here," she muttered.

"No." Daksh struggled to keep his balance as vines snaked around his feet.

"I thought the Acharya controlled the entire forest."

"It is under his guardianship. The trees and nature spirits owe him their allegiance. He does not *control* them."

"What's the difference?"

"Think for yourself."

She rolled her eyes but kept her silence. Slowly, they made their way through the underbrush. Daksh swung his blade in a grim rhythm, hacking a path open. The moonlight was a blessing; at least they didn't have to struggle in pitch dark.

After a couple of hours, the undergrowth thinned, and they entered a moonlit clearing alive with the sound of water. An ancient mango tree held court in the middle; behind it loomed a jagged cliff with a waterfall tumbling down its steep sides. No one was in sight, but the unmistakable sensation of being watched prickled her shoulders. Fumes lingered in the air, as if a fire had just been put out. To her right, a pit full of chopped wood still smoked.

"Is this it?" she whispered. "Where is everyone?"

"Follow my lead." He sheathed his sword and laid it on the ground, then shrugged off his bow and quiver and put them down as well.

How could he disarm himself? His famous golden sword was the only thing the yatu were afraid of.

Oh, right. She put her sword down beside his and stepped away from it.

"Your daggers too," he said.

Reluctantly, she withdrew two daggers and tossed them on her sword.

Daksh raised his hands, palms out. "Greetings," he said in a loud, clear voice. "We apologize for disturbing you. We are in search of information and would be grateful for the chance to talk."

A massive, hunched figure moved out of the darkness behind the mango tree. Moonlight fell on the hideous face of an elderly yatudhani: white-haired, bulbous-nosed, and wrinkle-skinned. A single yellow tusk curved out of her mouth; a jagged shaft was all that was left of the second. She was clad in leaves stitched together and bits and pieces of human clothing. Katyani squashed the urge to grab her sword and run.

Daksh joined his hands together and bowed low. "Vilamba, please accept my greetings."

"You killed my kin," she growled in a guttural voice. "You have some guts showing up here."

"I am sorry for your loss," said Daksh, as if he were talking of some natural tragedy and not his sword. "But I am bound by rules, as are you. Had your kin not eaten the human, I would have let them live."

"Rules!" The yatudhani gave a dry half laugh, half cough. "We also have rules. And the first rule is, defeat your enemies."

"Not *eat* your enemies, right?" said Katyani, her stomach seizing as she spied a ring of yatu around them, keeping to the shadows. "It's a joke," she added, trying to grin, when the two of them glared at her.

"Shut up," hissed Daksh. He turned back to the yatudhani. "Please forgive my companion. Her sense of humor is a bit misplaced."

"No, it's right here," said Katyani. She knew she needed to stay quiet, but talking was a way to still the churning in her gut. The yatu around them were deathly silent. Moonlight glinted on the steel of their maces. If they attacked now, not even Daksh's sword would save them.

Daksh gripped her forearm, as calm as ever. "It's all right. Trust me." Her terror had finally gotten through to him, or he had noticed the circle of yatu too. She took a deep breath, her terror receding. Of course she trusted him.

Vilamba squatted among the twisted roots of the mango tree and beckoned with one clawed finger. "You. Girl. Here." Her voice was deep and cracked, like the roots of the tree itself.

Katyani shrugged off Daksh's hand and walked forward, chin high. *Don't show your fear, don't show your fear. . . .*

"I can smell your fear," remarked Vilamba, giving a terrifying, black-toothed grin.

Katyani knelt in front of her. "I can smell *you*," she retorted. "So I guess we're even."

"Katyani!" said Daksh in a strangled voice.

Had she gone too far? Katyani joined her hands and bowed. "I'm sorry. Please, Vilamba, we are in need of information."

"Why should we help you?" demanded Vilamba. "You are from the kingdom of Chandela, our sworn enemies. Well I remember the day your evil-hearted king drove us out from our territory. Many of us died, young and old. Nearly forty years, and we have not recovered."

"*Your* territory?" Hollowness grew in her chest. "King Jaideep told us his father expelled the yatu from Chandela land."

Vilamba's red eyes flamed with anger. "We had an ancient agreement with the kings of Chandela. We had our own territory within the kingdom, near the banks of the Ken River." She snapped off a twig and drew a few lines in the earth. "See? This is Ajaigarh. That is the gorge that marked the boundaries of our land. We would not harm humans outside of it, but anyone venturing inside was fair game. Men challenged each other sometimes to cross over, because men are foolish that way, and we would get the flesh we craved. But mostly, we kept to ourselves and ate a vegetarian diet of deer, boar, and hare."

"What changed?" asked Katyani.

"A group of hunters entered our territory, chasing a wounded deer. Among them was a distant cousin of the king. We were well within our rights to eat the trespassers, but the king used this as an excuse to attack us. He did not even spare our children. Two-thirds of us perished that day. The Chandela king broke his peace treaty with us, and for that, we cursed his lineage."

Katyani exhaled. "I didn't know this. Thank you for telling me." Her suspicions had proved right. There had been an agreement between the Chandelas and the yatu, which the humans had broken. The yatu had helped Shamsher because their goals had temporarily aligned. Both had sought revenge on the Chandelas for past crimes.

"Is this the information you sought?" asked Vilamba. "I think not."

Katyani inclined her head. "You are right. Please allow me to introduce myself. My name is Katyani. I was bonded to the Chandela queen until her death. I thought I belonged to Chandela but recently discovered that I am Paramara by birth. I have been accused of conspiring to murder the royal family of Chandela. Vilamba, you must know that a group of yatu from Nandovana invaded Ajaigarh and murdered the king, queen, and heir. They had help from within the palace. I need to find out who it was so I can clear my name."

"I heard of these events," said Vilamba. "It is our curse that bore this deadly fruit. But no one in my clan was involved in the attack on Ajaigarh."

"Surely you must know someone who was, or someone we can speak with," said Daksh, coming closer to stand behind Katyani. "If you can guide us to them, we would be grateful."

Vilamba tapped her long fingernails on her knees. "Why should I? Every word I have given you thus far is a gift, but anything more must be paid for."

Katyani's muscles tensed. Everyone was driven by self-interest; in this, the yatu were no different from humans. "What would be a proper price?"

"Restitution," said Vilamba. "We want our land back."

"It is a fair ask," murmured Daksh, resting a hand on Katyani's shoulder.

"You know it's not up to me," said Katyani.

"But one day, it might be," said Vilamba. "On that day, you must vow to return what was stolen from us."

"*If* I am ever in that position, which I doubt," said Katyani. "Moreover, you must make a vow of your own to become wholly vegetarian. No eating anyone who wanders into your territory."

Vilamba waved a hand. "The details can be worked out later. It is enough for me if you give your word to follow up in good faith."

"I give my word," said Katyani. It was easy to promise something she was sure would never materialize, but the yatudhani gave a cackle of triumph, as if it were in the bag.

Vilamba issued a guttural order. An enormous yatu lumbered up to them, mace resting on his shoulder. "This is my grandson, Tarak. He will take you to a cousin who knows someone," she told them.

A "cousin who knows someone" didn't sound terribly promising, but it was still a lead. They bowed their thanks to the yatudhani, gathered their weapons, and followed Tarak out of the clearing. The more Katyani found out about the yatu, the more ambivalent she felt about them. They were monsters, yes—vermin, no. *Dig deeper,* the Acharya had said, and she'd discovered that history had lied to her.

Tarak's presence made their journey through the forest easier. The underbrush parted before his heavy tread and his mace like butter under a knife. Around an hour before dawn, he slowed and motioned for them to stop. They stood before a huge, spreading banyan tree that filled the night air with creaks and whispers. Tarak sniffed the air, his body tense.

"Vetala?" whispered Katyani, her hand going to her sword.

"I think not." Daksh examined the knotted branches and ropy aerial roots. "This is a yatu hideout."

Tarak uttered a series of throaty grunts that sounded as if he were choking to death.

A smaller yatu—who was still as tall as Daksh and twice as wide—dropped down from the tree. Unlike Tarak, he was clean-shaven, his hair tied back in a ponytail. He still looked ferocious, but kind of neater, as if he didn't want hair falling on his face while he was chomping his luckless victims.

The two yatu gripped each other's shoulders as if they were attempting to break them. A conversation of grunts and snorts ensued. Katyani wished she knew what they were talking about.

"You should have learned Yatu," she told Daksh. "I'm surprised your father didn't make you. Would have been dead useful right now."

"They do not teach their tongue to outsiders," he said.

The smaller yatu—whom she nicknamed Ponytail—beckoned them. They looked at Tarak, but he simply pointed at the other yatu and left.

Their latest guide led them down a narrow path that wound through a grove of acacia trees. It was scarcely wide enough for them to pass; they kept having to duck overhanging limbs and push aside prickly bushes that had encroached on the path.

Dawn was breaking by the time they arrived at the base of a thickly forested hill. Ponytail squeezed into a narrow gash in the hillside, which turned out to be the opening to a cave system. Katyani found herself in a vast, firelit cavern that smelled damp and musty, like a flooded cellar.

Ponytail held up a clawed hand, stopping them, then ducked into a dark opening. They heard him grunt at someone. A little later, he emerged and gestured them over. They followed him through a narrow passage that stank of unwashed yatu and stale blood. Katyani breathed through her mouth, hoping she wasn't going to pass out from the stench.

Light glimmered at the end of the passage. They emerged in a cell lit by a single torch. In one corner was a bed of rushes, and on the bed was a yatu. *Part* of a yatu. One tusk was missing; so was an arm. His skin had lost its crimson luster and was a dull reddish gray. His chest was covered in an ointment made of crushed leaves and bark. It rose and fell with his labored breathing.

"Princess Ambika," he said in a cracked, hollow voice. "What a surprise."

There was that name again, rising up like a ghost from the past to taunt her. She suppressed her desire to correct him. He was more likely to help a Paramara than a Chandela. He spoke Hindavi, and that was all she needed. "Do I know you?" she asked, kneeling beside him.

"To humans, all yatu are the same," he said. "My name is Durbhag. You cut off my arm."

Her stomach clenched. "You were part of the group that attacked Ajaigarh?"

"Yes. I was ordered not to hurt you." He reached forward and gripped her elbow with his bony fingers. She tried not to flinch. His skin was hot and dry to the touch, his claws as sharp as needles. "I could have killed you with one blow. But I didn't, and I lost my arm."

She closed her eyes and a shudder racked her body. Again, she saw the bloodbath of the audience hall: the broken necks, the torn limbs, the twisted bodies.

Daksh squeezed her shoulder. "Katyani," he said, his voice warm and reassuring.

She exhaled and opened her eyes. "I lost a lot more than you that night," she said, keeping her tone even. "You killed my family."

The yatu released her. "I followed orders. And it is no more than the Chandelas deserved."

Ayan didn't deserve to die, she wanted to scream. Only Daksh's presence and her own need for information prevented her from falling on him with her sword. "Whose orders?"

"My clan leader. He died in Rajgarh, trying to protect the regent of Malwa."

Katyani leaned forward, thrumming with anticipation. "How did you get into the Ajaigarh palace?"

"You gave your word." An ember sparked in his pain-fogged eyes. "You will give us back our land."

"*If* I am ever in the position to do so, yes, I will."

"Then listen. We entered Ajaigarh through an underground passage from Kalinjar Fort."

Katyani sat back, stunned. She'd always thought the stories about a secret passage between the two forts to be just that—stories. No one in living memory had seen the mythical passage. She had spent many happy hours with Ayan, Bhairav, and Revaa, trying to locate it when they were children. They used to pretend Ajaigarh was besieged, and they had to escape using the secret passage. It had been one of their favorite games.

She recovered her voice. "What were your entry and exit points?"

"We entered the passage from a temple in Kalinjar. Below the main idol is a slab which can be moved. Steps lead down to the passage. It is a dark place, damp and haunted."

Katyani shivered. The yatu were creatures of the night. For *him* to call it a dark place meant that it was evil.

"We are strong," continued Durbhag, "but it took us nearly the entire day to reach the end of the passage and enter Ajaigarh. We emerged in an underground place filled with water."

He meant one of the underground water tanks. Katyani thought back to the testimony she'd heard in the court, and a jolt went through her. Falgun had said all the men at the gate died defending it. But that couldn't be right. The yatu had emerged *within* the fort.

"How did you get into Kalinjar?" asked Daksh. "Were the gates not guarded?"

"We came over the walls during the night," he said.

Of course. Kalinjar had no magical wards. And the wards on Ajaigarh were meant to keep monsters away from the walls. There was nothing that could harm a monster that was already inside. Their sheer presence would have broken the logic of the spell. That was one riddle solved.

"Who showed you the secret passage?" she asked.

"A man in gray of medium height and heavy build," said Durbhag. "I do not know his name or what he looked like, for he wore a mask. The regent of Malwa told us he would guide us to Kalinjar and through the passage."

A man in gray. The uniform of Garuda was gray. Falgun? He'd been in Garuda, and he'd lied during the trial. But why had he turned traitor? How had he found the passage? There had to be someone behind him.

"Patches, weapons, insignias of any kind?" she asked.

"No. The clothes were plain, good for hiding in the shadows. He had a sword, but he did not unsheathe it." Durbhag added, "He was a brave man, not afraid of us and not afraid of the darkness underground."

"He brought yatu into the palace to slaughter the royal family," Katyani bit out. "It was an act of cowardice, not bravery."

"Perhaps we measure such things differently," said Durbhag. "His task was to take us through the secret passage and guide us to the palace. Our task was to kill the king and the crown prince, and to capture you and the queen."

"Until we find out who the man in gray is, we cannot find his cocon-spirators either," said Daksh.

"Oh, we have a suspect," said Katyani. "The yatu entered Ajaigarh through a secret passage. Yet, during my trial, the captain of the gatehouse claimed that all his men died defending it."

"He lied," said the yatu. "There was no one at the gatehouse when we left Ajaigarh. The gate was open and unguarded."

Katyani shot a triumphant look at Daksh. His lips tightened. "We have a liar who will be made to tell the truth." He turned to the yatu. "Thank you for all your help. We won't forget it."

"The promises of men," murmured Durbhag. "What are they worth?"

"You are safe in Nandovana as long as you do not attack any humans," said Daksh. "That is my grandfather's promise to you, my father's, and mine too. If you ally yourself with evil men to commit evil deeds, you have only yourself to blame for your injuries."

"My injuries are nothing," said Durbhag. "But one of the swords that touched me was tipped with poison. I am dying slowly."

So are we all, Katyani nearly said, but managed not to. Durbhag had been a tremendous help, and he'd suffered enough. She rose. "Thank you for the information you have given us."

"Good-bye, Princess Ambika."

They exited the passage, and Ponytail led them out of the cave system. They emerged into a bright, sunlit morning filled with birdsong and the chittering of squirrels. Katyani took deep breaths of the fresh air, her knees weak with relief. Her risky plan had paid off, thanks to Daksh. They followed Ponytail away from the hill, back down the narrow, twisting path they had come.

"Can you put me on the path to Ajaigarh?" she said, plucking Daksh's sleeve. She couldn't wait to renew her acquaintance with the treacherous Falgun. She was looking forward to introducing him to her dagger. He would spill his guts to her, if it was the last thing he did.

"You'll be caught if you go to Ajaigarh," said Daksh, knitting his brows. "Let's go back to the gurukul and tell my father what we've learned. He's sure to have some advice for you."

"He'll punish us both for staying out all night," she pointed out.

"Yes, but *after* that he will help us. Trust me."

He looked so earnest as he said that. How to tell him, *Thank you, Airya, for everything you have done for me and for being the person that you are. But this is not your war; I cannot endanger you or the gurukul.*

"I know you want to help," she said. "But you and your father have already done enough. He cannot be seen to take sides."

"Politically, no. But my father will always be on the side of what is right and good. What happened in Ajaigarh was wrong. He'll want the perpetrators punished as much as you do." She frowned, about to demur, when he added, "Please. Give it a day. See what he has to say."

And partly because she knew what he said made sense, and the Acharya probably *would* have good advice for her, but mostly because she couldn't bear to say good-bye to Daksh, not yet, she agreed to go to the gurukul.

CHAPTER 20

THE ÁCHARYA SAT UNDER THE PEEPAL TREE IN THE COURT-yard, radiating a cold disappointment that cut to the bone. Katyani and Daksh stood before him, heads hanging, while the rest of the disciples watched from a safe distance.

"Uttam," barked the Acharya. "List the rules they have broken."

His elder son regarded the duo with resignation. "First, you left the gurukul without permission," he said in his calm voice. "Second, you were out during the nighttime. Third, you went to a yatu haunt where we are forbidden to go."

"You're forgetting one," rasped the Acharya.

Uttam bowed. "You went together, without chaperones."

Katyani resisted the urge to scream. Of course, unmarried young men and women of the gurukul weren't allowed alone together, the flawed reasoning being that it was impossible to maintain brahmacharya in the face of feminine temptation. And he hadn't even kissed her this time.

"I am sorry, Father," said Daksh, sounding as calm as his brother.

"Sorry?" The Acharya gripped his beard as if he would tear it off. "*She* is an outsider, but *you* are my son. You were born and brought up in this gurukul. The other disciples look up to you. How could you have violated so many rules?"

"I accept any punishment you deem fit," said Daksh, staring at the ground.

"Of course you accept it, or how can I maintain discipline in the gurukul?" The Acharya rose. "Let it not be said that I showed partiality to my son. You will bear ten lashes of the whip for every rule you broke."

Katyani's throat clogged. *Ten lashes for every rule?* "That's not fair," she said, stumbling over the words. "It was my fault. I made him do it."

"No one can *make* him do anything," said the Acharya with asperity. "He could have brought you back to the gurukul, persuaded you to see sense. Instead, he facilitated your rule-breaking."

He helped me because it was the right thing to do, she wanted to shout. *You can't punish him for doing the right thing.* She hugged herself, trying not to shake. "Let me share the punishment. Twenty lashes each. How about that?"

"You try to bargain with me?" The Acharya's bushy eyebrows rose in incredulity. Beside him, Uttam gave a tiny shake of his head. *Stop talking,* he mouthed.

If she stopped talking, she'd start screaming. "It's only fair," she argued. "I ought to share in the punishment."

"Your punishment will be to watch him bleed," said the Acharya. "Varun! Fetch the whip."

No, this punishment was too cruel. She would not survive it. Her back burned, making her tremble. "We'd never have found out what we did without breaking the rules," she said, willing her voice not to break. "Now I have a solid lead in who was responsible for the murder of my family."

"Information that you could have gained by asking me for permission," said the Acharya.

"Would you have granted it?" she asked.

The Acharya was saved from having to reply to this by the arrival of Varun, bearing a nasty-looking whip made of twisted rope.

Katyani swallowed, feeling sick. How easily she had assumed Daksh would help her, how little she had thought of the consequences. But he would have known. And yet, he had broken the rules for her. Tightness grew in her chest until she thought it would burst.

The Acharya grabbed the whip from Varun. "What are you waiting for?" he demanded.

Daksh turned away from her, untying his outer robe, revealing his straight, unblemished back.

"Wait. Stop," she cried.

But Daksh did not acknowledge her in any way. He knelt on the ground before his father, folding his outer robe neatly and placing it out of the way.

The Acharya's expression hardened. He raised the whip and brought it down on Daksh's bare back. "One."

Katyani gasped. The world swam before her eyes. She was back in the Ajaigarh audience hall. Once again, Chentu slashed her skin and seared her soul.

"Two."

Twin red lines tracked down Daksh's back. He hadn't even made a sound.

"Three."

Her feet propelled her forward, and she flung herself on him in time to catch the fourth blow. Her back stung, and she cried out, but whether from pain or the memory of pain, she did not know.

"Katyani," said Daksh through gritted teeth. *"Move."*

"I won't." She locked her hands around his waist. He was so warm to the touch. She trembled against him, trying not to press against the welts on his back.

"A spiritual warrior accepts his punishment with the same indifference that he accepts his reward," said the Acharya. "Why do you deny him this opportunity to prove himself?"

"Because this punishment is unjust, and you teach us to fight against injustice," she shouted, losing control of her voice.

Atreyi stepped forward from the crowd of disciples and laid a hand on her shoulder. Katyani flinched at the touch. "Child, come away from here. If you cannot bear to watch—"

"I cannot bear for him to be punished at all!" Katyani took a deep, sobbing breath. Everyone she cared about ended up hurt or worse, all because of her. "I said it was my fault."

"And the Acharya told you what your punishment must be," said Atreyi.

"Then I am punished twice, for I feel every lash upon my own skin." The tears she'd held back from Chentu spilled from her eyes. "And have

I not been whipped enough to last a lifetime? How much should I bleed? Until nothing is left?"

"Katyani," said Daksh, his voice gentle. "Remember where we are."

"I was about to leave for Ajaigarh." Her voice wobbled. "Daksh persuaded me to return here. He said you would have good advice for me. What is your advice, Acharya? To be punished? I am sick of being punished! It's time we hunted down and punished actual evildoers."

"Father," said Uttam. "Please . . ."

"So today you have all decided to go against me?" The Acharya threw the whip across the courtyard. It came to rest several meters away and burst into flames. Katyani watched it burn, the tears drying on her cheeks, light-headed with relief. It couldn't hurt Daksh now.

"Father," said Daksh in a choked voice.

"If I cannot punish you, I cannot punish anyone." The Acharya turned and stalked away.

"Let go, Katyani," said Daksh.

She released him, dazed, her back still stinging.

Daksh stood and reached for his robe. The three angry red lines on his back had swollen, although the skin hadn't broken. A spasm of pain went through her at the sight.

She wiped her face with a sleeve and rose. "You need healing. A neem paste and—"

"It can wait." He pulled on his robe and gazed at her, his eyes full of concern. As if *she'd* been the one whipped, not him. "Are you all right?"

"I was protected by my robe," she said, which was not what he meant, but there was no other answer she could manage right now.

Daksh made to follow his father, but Uttam put a hand on his shoulder and shook his head. "Go," he told the disciples, and they dispersed. At last, only Atreyi was left.

"I'm sorry," said Katyani in a small voice.

"For what?" said Atreyi. "Flouting the gurukul rules? Or flouting your guru?"

Katyani winced. "Both. Neither. I don't know. I had better go speak to him."

"What will you say?" asked Uttam.

"That I am leaving. I have brought you all nothing but ill luck. It's time I left before something worse happens."

"You will not go alone," said Daksh.

Look what happens when you don't let me go alone, she almost shouted. She pressed her lips together. "You won't accompany me this time."

"You mistake me," said Daksh. "My father will not let you go alone. You are his pupil, and you saved his life. That is why he threw the whip away."

"You are wrong," said Atreyi, her face softening. "He threw the whip away because he loves you and could not bear to punish you. Katyani gave him an excuse to stop."

"Beg pardon, Airyaa," said Uttam. "But I disagree. We have both been disciplined by him innumerable times. He threw the whip as a gesture of surrender."

"I don't think so," said Katyani. "He threw it in anger."

Uttam smiled. "No part of this was unforeseen by him. Go, Katyani. I think he expects you."

Katyani gathered her courage and made her way to the lecture hall. She had defied the Acharya in front of his entire gurukul. How would he punish her?

The Acharya was seated in the lotus pose in his customary place in the center of the hall. She knelt opposite him and waited, quaking inwardly.

His eyes flew open. "You must keep your promise."

"Which one?" she asked, flummoxed.

"All of them." He fixed her with a penetrating stare. "Your promise to the yatu. Your promise to the daayan. Your promise to Daksh."

"I don't remember making any promises to Daksh," she protested.

"Oh? You think leaping on him to save him from his own father wasn't a promise?"

"Er . . . what was I promising?" she managed to ask.

He snorted. "Figure it out, since you're so clever."

"I'm not so clever," she said. "I've figured *that* out."

"Then you have learned." His lips twitched, then pressed together. "There was a promise I made once which I did not keep. I have regretted it ever since."

She went cold. "You mean . . ."

"The daayan, yes," he said. "Who was once an empathic, accomplished woman called Devyani. My promise, much like yours, was implicit rather than explicit. That does not make it any less real." His tone softened. "I want you to live your life without the kind of regret that has darkened mine."

Her mouth had gone dry. "I'll remember."

He nodded. "Take care of Daksh when I am gone."

Her stomach fluttered. What did he mean? "But you're right here," she stammered.

"Did I say take care of him *now*?" he demanded. "I said, when I am *gone*. That is the gurudakshina I ask of you."

She stared at him, her thoughts in turmoil. Had he seen into her heart when she'd built such thick walls around it? Or had her leaping on Daksh to save him from a whipping betrayed her feelings to everyone? A hot wave of embarrassment washed over her.

"Are you going to gape at me like a fish or give me an answer?" said the Acharya irritably.

She bowed her head. "Of course, I cannot say no to anything you ask of me as gurudakshina."

"Excellent." The Acharya rose. "Then we are ready to go."

She stood, confused. "Go where?"

"To Ajaigarh. Do you not have a witness to interrogate?" He strode toward the door.

She followed him out of the hall, warmth radiating through her chest. "You're coming with me?"

"No. You're coming with me." He paused at the door and shot her a reproving look. "What were you planning to do, invade Ajaigarh on your own?"

"I thought I'd—ah—capture Falgun," she admitted. That had been the extent of her "plan."

"My way will be easier," he said. "Less likely to get you killed. Look forward to punishing *actual* evildoers." He gave her a harsh smile.

"But Acharya, you do not interfere, as a rule," she protested.

"I have been lied to and taken advantage of," said the Acharya. "What we need is evidence, and I have no doubt your dishonest captain will provide it."

Her heart felt as if it would overflow. No matter how he put it, he was bending his rules for her. With the Acharya by her side, she could take on all the Falguns of this world.

The Acharya ordered a carriage to be made ready and gave Uttam instructions for taking care of the gurukul in his absence. Daksh assumed he was going with them, and the Acharya did not forbid him, which gladdened her heart. Despite the drama of the last few hours, Daksh seemed the same as ever, although she caught the whiff of neem paste from his robes. *Good*. That would prevent any infection.

They boarded the carriage, surrounded by disciples who had gathered to see them off, the last light of the evening falling on their serious faces.

"Be safe and return soon," called Atreyi as the coachman clucked to the horses.

The carriage trundled away from the gurukul, into the waiting forest. Opposite Katyani, Daksh sat with his eyes closed, his sword on his lap, his bow and a quiver full of arrows at his feet. Katyani had her bronze sword and a couple of daggers as well. It felt good to be armed. It felt even better to not be alone. The moment of reckoning had arrived. *Time to punish evildoers.* She tingled in anticipation.

Why had the Acharya asked her to take care of Daksh? And what did it mean, to take care of someone? She had been Ayan's bodyguard, and she'd failed miserably to take care of him. It could even be said he'd died because of her. Her chest constricted. She didn't want anyone else to die because of her. She gazed at Daksh, willing him to stay alive, stay safe.

Daksh opened his eyes and caught her gaze. She looked away from him and out the window, trying to rein in her feelings. Dusk had fallen. Fatigue stole over her. They'd missed an entire night of sleep.

"Rest," said Daksh in a low voice. "I'll keep watch." The Acharya had already dozed off beside him.

"Wake me in a couple of hours, and I'll take a turn," she said.

He nodded, and she curled up on the seat, placing her sword on the floor. The movement of the carriage was soporific, and she was asleep in moments.

She woke in the middle of the night to the sound of voices. The carriage had stopped. Moonlight filtered in through the window. Opposite her, the Acharya still slept, his eyes closed, his face relaxed. But Daksh was missing. The hair on the back of her neck rose.

She slid off the seat, buckled her sword to her belt, and slung Daksh's bow and quiver on her back. She crept out of the carriage, ready for anything. A whiff of smoke caught her nostrils.

The coachman was gone. The two horses cropped grass, unperturbed by the presence of the daayan. She loomed before Daksh in her monstrous form, swinging her thick plait in one clawed hand. Daksh was unarmed; he had laid his sword at her feet. Katyani's heart shriveled at the sight.

"Please," he said. "A life for a life."

The daayan grinned, her teeth gleaming in the moonlight. "It's not your blood I crave. But if that girl hiding in the shadows agrees to it, I will grant your request."

Daksh swung around. Katyani stepped forward and bowed low. "Greetings, my lady."

The daayan raised her right hand in benediction. "Are you off to seek the revenge I have blessed you with?"

"I am," she said. "What request has he made?"

"Katyani . . ." said Daksh, a note of appeal in his voice. She ignored him, intent on the daayan.

"He has offered his life in exchange for his father's," said the daayan. "Do not blame him too much. He will accumulate great merit through this action."

Her stomach seized. The Acharya's time had come. *Not yet. Oh please, not yet.*

But who could she have made that appeal to? She was bound by her word to the daayan, and the Acharya was bound by his fate. Daksh could not change it——not for the better.

She cut her eyes to him. "Of all the selfish things to do," she grated.

"My father is the most powerful spiritual warrior in Bharat," said Daksh, his words stiff, his body tense. "Think of the good he can do with the remaining years of his life."

"What about you?" shouted Katyani, wanting to hit him. "Are you incapable of doing good?"

Daksh lowered his eyes. "I cannot hope to match him, not in this lifetime."

"Then try harder," she snarled. She turned to the daayan and bowed again. "My lady, please forgive us and ignore this man's foolish request. It would break his father's heart."

"And yours?" said the daayan slyly.

"My heart says it is wrong for a son to offer his life in exchange for his father's," she said, ignoring the implication. "My heart says it would be a punishment worse than death for the Acharya."

"You have no right to interfere in this," said Daksh.

"Oh? So I mean nothing to you?" If not for the monstress, watching them with every evidence of enjoyment, Katyani would have slapped him.

"I did not say that," he muttered, his eyes shifting away from her.

"That is what you implied. However, even if I mean nothing to you, I have the right to interfere, and that right was given to me by your father himself."

"What do you mean?" he snapped, finally losing control.

"She speaks the truth," said a voice behind them.

The Acharya emerged from the carriage, using his staff like a walking stick. He looked old and tired, as if he should be in bed rather than the middle of the forest.

Daksh grabbed his sword from the ground and took a step back, shielding his father from the daayan.

The daayan smiled. "Mahavir. It is time."

"Already?" he said. "I had hoped to do a few more things before I died."

"There will always be more things to do," said the daayan. "Choose your weapon."

The Acharya grasped Daksh's shoulder and pushed him out of the way. "You cannot protect me today, son."

"I can die trying," said Daksh, his voice hard.

"Who will help Uttam run the gurukul and protect Nandovana?" asked his father.

"Uttam does not need my help." Daksh unsheathed his sword. "He would do the same in my place, and you know it."

"Daksh, *don't*," pleaded Katyani. But he would not listen to her, not when his father's life hung in the balance. She would have to stop him herself. Her muscles tensed, waiting for the right moment.

"So be it." The daayan uncoiled a curving sword with a whip-like blade from a pouch that hung at her waist. Katyani's heart lurched. This was an urumi, the deadliest sword in all of Bharat. Without a shield, there was no hope of countering it.

"Spare him, Devyani," said the Acharya.

"You dare call me by that name?" raged the daayan. "Devyani is dead. Her blood is on your hands. And your blood will be on mine."

She raised her urumi and rushed forward with an ear-splitting screech. Katyani threw herself on Daksh, knocking him out of the way. The smell of smoke grew stronger. Daksh pushed Katyani aside and struggled to his feet. She grabbed hold of his legs, hanging on like grim death. "Let me go!" he shouted.

Steel thwacked against wood. The Acharya's staff gleamed in the moonlight as he sought to parry the daayan's flexible blade. But the urumi wrapped around the Acharya's staff and snatched it out of his hand.

Daksh finally succeeded in freeing himself from Katyani. Her heart leaped into her mouth as he ran toward the monstress. The daayan's plait whipped backward and bound Daksh's arms to his waist. At the same time, her urumi struck the Acharya. Blood trickled down his face and neck, and he staggered back. Katyani went cold. *Help him,* screamed a voice within her. Her hands ached to unsheathe her sword and run to his defense. She wrapped her arms around herself, shuddering. "I can't." Why had she made such a promise? It had seemed easy, then. Easy, too, to promise to take care of Daksh.

"Help him!" cried Daksh, echoing her inner voice, struggling to free himself from the daayan's plait.

"I made a vow." Katyani rocked herself, her eyes blurring.

The urumi slashed open the Acharya's chest, and he fell to the ground. "Acharya," she sobbed, feeling the cruel cut in her own chest. Daksh let out a groan of agony.

The Acharya gasped, "Devyani. Have I earned the right to call you that now?"

The daayan bent over him and caressed his blood-soaked cheek. "Mahavir," she said, her voice tender, "are you ready to go?"

"My . . . son . . ." he said.

The daayan released Daksh from her plait. He toppled to the ground and lay there, unmoving. Katyani's gut clenched in terror. She ran to him and bent over to check his pulse. It beat faint but steady. She sat back and drew a shuddering breath.

"I did not harm your son," said the daayan. "He will draw the lines of his own fate. You cannot help him now."

"Katyani . . ."

Katyani went to her wounded guru and knelt beside him. His chest was reduced to bloody ribbons, and his voice was a husky whisper. But his eyes shone with light and clarity. He extended a hand to her, and she clutched it as if she were drowning. The greatest spiritual warrior in Bharat—her *teacher,* the man who had saved her—and she had not lifted a hand to help him. Her heart ached.

"Thank you," he whispered.

"For *what*?" She blinked back tears. "Letting you die?"

He squeezed her fingers. "Keep . . . promise." His hand fell away, and his eyes lost their focus.

"Acharya!" Katyani bent over him, laying her fingers on his throat.

There was no pulse. He was gone.

The world spun and slowed. She could not breathe. The daayan was saying something, but Katyani could not hear her.

Gone. An abyss yawned before her; she teetered at its edge, flailing, darkness before her eyes.

Keep . . . promise, came the Acharya's ghostly voice. She blinked and swallowed, backing away from the edge. *I will,* she thought. *I swear it.*

She knew which promise the Acharya meant. It was not the one to the yatu, the daayan, or even to Daksh. No, it was the implicit promise she had made to the Acharya when he rescued her. He had risked his reputation and his gurukul to break the bond and give her the freedom to be the mistress of her own fate. It was time she repaid him by acting like it.

The daayan gripped her arm. The pain brought her back to the present. The smell of smoke was so strong she coughed.

"The forest is on fire," said the daayan, pointing to the east.

She stared at the monstress, falling back into herself. Smoke. Fire. Forest. Gurukul. Daksh.

She wheeled around. Daksh was still lying on the ground, unmoving.

"He's fine," said the daayan. "Go, put out the fire."

Katyani looked eastward. There was a distant red glow above the trees. Why was the forest burning? Surely there were wards in place to protect it.

The daayan rose and began dragging the Acharya's body away.

Her throat tightened. "Where are you taking him?"

"To give him the last rites," said the daayan. "To free him, free his wife, and free myself." Her skin sloughed off, and her plait retreated. Katyani blinked.

The daayan was gone. So was the corpse of the Acharya. In their place, a man and two women clad in sky-blue robes were walking hand in hand, their backs to her. A peal of laughter came from one of the women.

"Acharya?" She took a step forward, wonderstruck, and the vision vanished. There was no one and nothing between herself and the night. She swallowed the terrible sense of loss that threatened to engulf her, and tried to concentrate.

Daksh was unconscious. There was only herself to stop the fire. No time to search for the coachman or run to the gurukul. No time to even worry about Daksh. Here, now, she had to act, or everything would burn.

She unslung the bow from her back and moved toward the red glow on the horizon, her hand reaching for an arrow. She emptied her mind.

Your aim must be true and your intent pure, the Acharya had said.

Katyani mustered her spiritual power and recited the mantra to summon water. Then she bowed her head, aimed the arrow at the sky, and closed her eyes. Her intentions were as pure as the River Ganga. She wanted to save the forest and its denizens. She sent a quick prayer up to the goddess and let the arrow fly.

Nothing happened. The smoke thickened. Grass crackled and branches snapped, thudding to the ground. An animal screamed, its cry of agony shredding her veneer of self-control. She fell to her knees. Her heart wanted to leap out of her chest. *Why me?* she wanted to shout. *Why now?*

But there was no one to hear, no one to help. The crackling became a roar, and the hellish red glow drew closer, a monster eating the forest, heading their way.

She got up, swallowed her fear, and took another step. Once again, she nocked an arrow on her bow, recited the mantra, and released it.

Still nothing.

The heat of the advancing fire burned her skin. Smoke rose in a dense black cloud above the burning trees, making it difficult to breathe.

Were her intentions not pure? Was her aim untrue? Was she unworthy to summon such a weapon?

She knelt on the ground, heedless of the heat, the smoke, and the rapidly approaching flames. The tears dried on her cheeks. *The mantra is embedded in your mind,* the Acharya had said. *You must summon the weapon with your soul.*

She took a third arrow from the quiver and nocked it on her bow.

Here is my soul. My flawed, needy, lying, selfish soul. The real reason I saved Daksh is because I cannot bear to live in a world without him. I have already lost everyone else. And I would break every promise, every oath, to keep him alive. Do you hear me, arrow? I want you to save his life or take mine.

She closed her eyes and rose to her feet. The arrow felt heavy in her hand, as if it didn't want to go anywhere. She pointed it at the sky and drew back the string so hard it cut her fingers.

Be what I need.

She let the arrow fly and held her breath.

Nothing. She opened her eyes and looked skyward, trying to hold despair at bay.

Lightning split the heavens, dazzling her. A loud thundercrack shattered the night, followed by a rolling boom that set her teeth on edge.

She blinked, unable to believe what was happening. A *storm.* She'd summoned a blessed storm. She slung the bow on her back and waited for the rain with bated breath.

The first drops fell, slow and hesitant at first, and then faster, heavier. In a minute, the drizzle had turned into a deluge. The smoke, the smell of ash, and the roar of the fire were drowned in the furious flood of rain. Gratitude filled her heart. *Thank you, Acharya, for teaching me this mantra. Thank you, arrow, for deeming me worthy.*

She staggered back to where she had left Daksh, going by instinct since she couldn't see a thing in the darkness and the rain. Her feet sank into the mud, and she had to lean against the tree trunks for support and shelter. She railed against her slow progress. Was Daksh all right in this rain? Had he regained consciousness?

After a while, the fierceness of the storm abated. Thunder boomed again, sounding further off. She walked faster, then ran, consumed by anxiety.

At last, she came upon the clearing where she had left the carriage and horses. There was no sign of Daksh.

"Daksh?" she called, going cold.

No one answered. Fear bloomed inside her. Had he been swept away in the deluge? *Drowned?*

She climbed into the carriage and took down a small oil lamp that hung from the ceiling. Her hands shook, and it took three attempts before she was able to light it. She climbed out and circled the clearing, calling Daksh's name. A fist of panic closed around her chest.

On her second circle of the clearing, he stepped out from the forest directly onto her path. She bit back a scream, almost dropping the lamp. *Alive.* A wave of relief rushed over her.

His hair was plastered over his face, his robes clung to his skin, and his eyes were wild with grief and anger. He grabbed her wrist. "Where is he?"

"She took him," said Katyani, finding her voice.

"You let him die, and you let her take him." His grip tightened. "Did you hate him so much that you would not even leave us a body to burn?"

His words were a punch to the gut. She freed herself from his grasp. "I did not *hate* him. He was my teacher. You're being unfair to me."

"When you prevented me from saving him, were you being fair?" he bit out.

I did the only thing I could to protect you. "You could not have saved him," she said. "You could only have died with him."

"Perhaps I should have," he said, glaring at her.

She swallowed the painful lump in her throat. *He's grieving,* she told herself. *He doesn't mean it.* She stared at the rain-soaked ground, wishing she could comfort him, knowing he would not welcome it.

"What right did he give you to interfere?" he demanded. "Tell me!"

She raised her gaze to his with difficulty. It was hard to look at him, harder to answer. "As his gurudakshina, he extracted a promise from me to look after you."

His lips pressed together. "When was this?"

"Just before we left the gurukul."

"So he knew. He knew she'd be waiting for him!" Anguish twisted his face. "If only we'd stayed in the gurukul, he'd still be alive."

His grief smote her. "This is my fault," she said, a hollow ache in her chest. "I'm sorry." *Sorry I could not save him. Sorry you lost your father. Sorry I lost my teacher.* Sorry, sorry, sorry . . . a useless word that did not change a thing.

The rain had slowed to a light drizzle. The dim light cast by the carriage lamp fell on his face, full of fatigue and sorrow. "My father is dead. You are free from any promise you made to him." He turned away from her.

"Wait, please." She couldn't bear him to leave like this, all angry and bitter. And there was something she needed to ask him. "You smelled the smoke, right? Has Nandovana ever caught fire?"

He turned back to her, brows knitting. "No. Our father laid wards to protect it from natural hazards and human accidents."

"Then it was set on fire deliberately." She hugged herself, coldness spreading inside her. Who could have committed such a crime? And *why?* "I got the rain to put it out, but some roots and trees may still be burning from the inside. Please warn everyone at the gurukul. You and Airya Uttam may have to patrol the forest and summon rain."

His gaze went to the bow slung on her back. "Is that what you did?"

"Yes."

He folded his arms and regarded her with narrowed eyes. "In the gurukul, you could not summon even a drop."

"The gurukul was not on fire," she retorted. Why was he bringing this up? Did he think she was lying?

"I find it difficult to imagine someone could have set Nandovana on fire," he said, his voice flat. "The forest has ancient protections. Only someone with great spiritual power could have done it."

He didn't believe her. It cut to the bone, but she tried her best to ignore his tone, ignore her own hurt. "Someone did. You will see the evidence while you are patrolling. Perhaps you will find clues as to who it was. This is important, Daksh. That person tried to destroy the forest."

"I will talk to my brother. Now that our father is gone, the burden of the gurukul rests on his shoulders." He bent his head, his fists clenched, his lips tight. Then he squared his shoulders and raised his gaze again, the mask of indifference back on his face, as if it had never left. As if they'd never shared anything but the most superficial of interactions. "Where will you go now?"

"Ajaigarh. Where I should have gone months ago. All this could have been avoided." She gulped back a sob. "I'm sorry, Daksh. I cared for him too."

"Do not apologize to me," he said, every word falling like a chip of ice. "I cannot forgive you."

She lowered her eyes so he would not see the pain in them. The last person left in the world who had believed in her, cared about her, and she'd lost him, like she'd lost everyone else. If not for all her promises, she would have broken then. She blinked back tears and summoned her strength. "I don't need your forgiveness to do what I believe is right."

She hefted the bow on her back and walked away. Each step felt like the slow piercing of her heart with a needle.

Perhaps, she thought, he would try to stop her. Take back those unkind words. Give her a chance to explain.

But he didn't. She turned around for a last look behind, only to find him gone.

CHAPTER 21

KATYANI WALKED THROUGH THE DEVASTATION OF THE forest, which mirrored the desolation of her heart.

If she hadn't gone back to the gurukul with Daksh, the Acharya would still be alive. Daksh hated her now, and no wonder. She was responsible for his father's death, just like she was responsible for so many others. The names sounded in her head, one after the other: Ayan, Shamsher, Hemlata, Jaideep, Acharya. And those who were still alive, but gone from her all the same: Bhairav, Revaa, Daksh. *Daksh.*

You have such faith in my abilities? she'd asked him once. *I do,* he'd replied.

Who was there now, who had any faith left in her?

Keep . . . promise, came the Acharya's voice, breaking the dreadful litany.

"I will." She wiped her face with a sleeve. "I will, Acharya."

The path to Ajaigarh was blocked by burned and fallen branches. Whoever set fire to the forest had approached from that direction. It would take years to recover.

Who had committed this heinous act? A person of great spiritual strength, Daksh had said. Could it be a former pupil of the Acharya's? Was it related to her presence at the gurukul, a retaliation against the Acharya for sheltering her? In that case, her list of suspects narrowed to *one.*

She thrust aside her pain and focused her thoughts. Who were the people she knew who had lied? Falgun, Revaa, and Bhairav. Falgun had most likely guided the yatu into Ajaigarh. Perhaps he was involved in the assassination attempts, too. But the architect of the earlier attempts had great magical skills. That was why Garuda had failed to catch any of the attackers alive. Falgun was an ordinary man with low spiritual power and zero magic. Revaa didn't have any magical knowledge either. That left Bhairav.

Which didn't make any sense. He had skills, but not at *that* level. And why would he turn against his own family? She remembered the darkness and pain she had sensed through the bond, and a deep unease took hold of her. The thought that he might be the murderous mastermind was absurd. The boy she'd grown up with wasn't like that at all. Her head hurt just thinking about it. But who else stood to gain as much as he did?

She was making far too many assumptions to be sure of anything. She needed evidence. Her first visit would be to Falgun; her second would be to the dungeons to question the poisoning suspects. She hoped they were still alive.

She emerged from the forest into fields burned black. The spring crop had turned to soggy ash. The fire-setting arsonist had given no thought to the poor farmers who lived on Nandovana's borders. She came across the remnants of burned huts and sheds and hoped the villagers had managed to escape the flames. Anger built inside her at the sheer wantonness of the destruction.

In the next village, she bartered one of her precious daggers for a set of old clothes. Although her robe had dried, it was stained and filthy and, more to the point, advertised her as a disciple of the gurukul. Although it granted her a degree of automatic respect from people, she couldn't afford to be noticed, especially with the bow on her back and the sword at her hip.

Reports of the fire were everywhere. Refugees described waking up in the middle of the night to see flames exploding over the forest, setting their fields on fire. Katyani walked down the main street, barely able to contain her fury as she listened.

If you misuse this power, you will be cursed, the Acharya had said.

I am your curse, she thought. *I am the sword that will pierce your heart.*

Her first home had been destroyed. She'd lost everything, everyone. And now they were trying to destroy the gurukul too, which had become a second home to her. Her fury hardened to a cold resolve. She would protect the gurukul and its residents, the way she hadn't been able to protect Ayan.

She hitched a ride on a carriage going to Ajaigarh by intervening in a financial argument between the owner and his passengers, resolving it in the owner's favor. As the carriage rolled through the familiar, crowded streets of the city, she was seized by a homesickness so fierce it took all her self-control not to burst into tears.

They dismounted at a stable near the main marketplace. The owner folded his hands and bowed, and she blessed him. He was more than twice her age, but he seemed to expect it. Perhaps the Acharya's asceticism had rubbed off on her. She might discard the robes, but she was marked by the gurukul and all she had learned within its walls.

She walked through the busy market in the failing light of the evening, trying not to remember the past. But the past came crowding in, overwhelming her senses.

Lamps filled the air with smoke, and vendors called out to passersby to try their wares. People flocked around the stall of a man frying samosas in an enormous wok. On the steps of a tiny shop, a woman rolled betel leaves around chopped areca nuts, spices, and candied seeds, closing each leaf triangle with a clove, making small, delectable paans for a queue of waiting customers. Ayan had loved these after-dinner treats, even though Hemlata had forbidden them, deeming them unhealthy. Katyani's eyes filled, remembering how she'd sneaked them to Ayan on the sly.

Away from the market, the streets became progressively darker. Ayan had talked about introducing street lighting in the city to reduce crime and aid travelers—one of the many ideas he'd had to improve the lives of common people. Ideas he would never be able to realize.

She arrived at the foot of the hill that housed the fort and climbed the steps, listening for guards. It was a cloudy night, and the darkness was in her favor. Had Bhairav managed to reset the magical wards?

The smell of beedis and the flicker of lanterns warned her of the first checkpoint. She slipped into the thicket of tendu trees on the hillside to avoid it. There was one more checkpoint and then nothing but empty steps winding to the top of the hill. The walls of Ajaigarh Fort loomed before her. A lone lamp hung above the black iron gate, casting a small pool of light.

Skirting the gate, she followed the wall until it curved outward to accommodate one of the four towers. Between the curving tower and the horizontal wall was a dihedral space she could climb using her feet to push against the stone. Wall-climbing had been part of her training. Hopefully, her body remembered what it had learned.

She placed her right hand and right foot on the tower wall, and her left hand and left foot on the flat wall. The wards, she sensed, were still broken. It probably took far greater skill than Bhairav possessed to resurrect them. She pushed her hands hard against the walls and climbed, ignoring the scrapes to her skin and the ache in her legs.

A watchman called out when she was right under the battlements, and she nearly fell from the shock. She managed to grab a window slit just in time. She dangled, silent and panting, until the guard had passed. There would normally be ten guards making the rounds of the parapet, which meant she had a few minutes before the next one. She climbed the rest of the way up and squeezed herself in between the merlons.

A cool breeze sprang up, drying the sweat on her brow. She wiped her scratched and bleeding palms on her dupatta and ran toward the gatehouse, staying low to the floor. Was it too much to hope that Falgun would be on duty? She prayed to the goddess for luck as she snuck down the stairs from the parapet to the main courtyard.

Glass-covered lanterns stood on each side of the gatehouse and at various points around the courtyard. Her best bet was to hide in the shadows and wait for the changing of the guard at midnight.

She crouched behind the stairs and scanned the courtyard. Few people were up at this hour. All the shops were shuttered. A lone chaiwallah hunched over a pot, brewing fragrant tea over a coal fire for a few late customers. After a while, the customers dispersed, and the chaiwallah packed his pot and doused his fire. The courtyard emptied.

A sentry called the midnight hour, and the men filed out of the gatehouse, greeting their replacements.

"Remember, stay alert," said a man, and a sick jolt went through her. That was Falgun's voice—the very man she was eager to meet. "We might have an unwanted visitor."

"Tonight, sir?"

"Tonight, tomorrow, day after. One day, she will come. As long as she's alive, none of us are safe."

She tightened her grip on her dagger. They were talking about *her*. Unsurprising that she was being painted as a villain by someone who was a villain himself.

"Do you think the yatu will help her again?" asked a different guard.

"Nobody knows," said Falgun. "Anything is possible for her. She must have gained even more powers in Acharya Mahavir's gurukul."

Katyani's ears burned. The rumors about her had gotten worse, helped along by people like Falgun.

"I always thought the Acharya was a holy man," said the guard.

"She has fooled him like she fooled the poor king and queen for so many years," said Falgun. "Such a cruel, deceptive creature. She will bring ruin to whoever shelters her. I've received reports of a great fire in Nandovana a few days ago."

There were exclamations of astonishment and outrage at her treachery. Katyani seethed with anger. They were even pinning the blame for the fire on her. Meanwhile, the real culprit walked free, uncaring of the lives he had taken and the destruction he had wrought.

The guards dispersed to the barracks that lined the right side of the courtyard. The men slept in a dormitory, but the captain had better quarters, a room to himself. Katyani followed at a distance, taking care to stay out of the pools of light cast by the lanterns. She marked the door by which Falgun entered the barracks and waited until the courtyard had fallen silent again. Then she crept to the door and pushed. It didn't budge; he must have bolted it from inside.

The bolt turned, and she beat a hasty retreat. Falgun emerged, looking denuded in his undershirt, and made his way across the courtyard to the privy. Ayan had told her the men's privy was the nastiest place in the entire fort. They had much nicer facilities inside the palace.

He came back a little later, hitching his pants and humming tunelessly.

As he pushed open the door to his room, she raced up behind him and delivered a kick to his backside, sending him sprawling. She ducked inside and bolted the door shut behind her.

He tried to scramble to his feet, but she leaped on his back, grabbed his hair, and pulled his head up, sliding her dagger under his throat. The lone candle sputtered, making shadows dance on the walls.

"Don't move," she hissed. "Don't try to call for help. You'll be dead before the sound leaves your throat." She pushed the blade against his skin, allowing a trickle of blood to seep out.

He gasped and stilled, using his hands to support his arched back.

"I will ask you questions," she whispered in his ear. "You will answer with the truth. If I am satisfied, I may leave you alive. For every lie, I will cut you. Understood?"

He made a small, choked sound that she took for assent. He stank of sweat and fear. *Good.* Let him fear her.

"How many gatehouse guards died the night the king and queen were killed?" she asked.

"There were . . . eight . . . on duty," he gasped.

She pushed the blade a fraction deeper into his skin. The trickle of blood became a steady drip, and he uttered a strangled cry. "I hate repeating myself. I asked, how many died?"

"None," he moaned.

At last, the truth. The yatu had entered the fort via a secret passage. They had been nowhere near the fort walls.

"Who told you to lie during my trial?" she demanded.

"They'll . . . kill me."

"Choose between certain death now and an uncertain death in the future." She tightened her grip on his hair and jerked his head backward. "Which will it be?"

His feet drummed against the floor, and he struggled to break away. She almost stabbed him by mistake. Was he trying to get himself killed? "You don't understand," he gasped, trying to wrench his head away. "I can't speak."

"I understand you lied under oath," she said through gritted teeth, maintaining her grip on him with difficulty. "I understand you betrayed your king and queen. I understand you are a traitor. You deserve to die. But don't you want to take them with you?"

"I didn't know! He told me it was a trap, that *you* were the traitor!"

"Who told you?" She summoned all her spiritual power into the command. "Tell me his name."

"Tanoj," he said, and collapsed.

She let go his hair, and he fell forward on his face. She stared at the comatose man in disbelief. *No.* Not Tanoj.

She'd looked up to him all her life. He'd trained her, mentored her, bested her, and been bested by her. He was one of the few people who actually *knew* her, through and through—her faults, her weaknesses, her skills, her strengths. One of the few people who ought to have known she was innocent, trial be damned.

Turned out, she was the one who hadn't known him.

She prodded Falgun. "Wake up. I have more questions." When he didn't budge, she turned him over.

He was frothing at the mouth, and his eyes had rolled to the back of his head. His tongue was purple, his skin blue.

She scooted back in alarm. Had he poisoned himself? He hadn't appeared to be the kind of man who wanted to die for his beliefs. But all he had managed was one name before having a fit. Was this what he had meant by saying he couldn't speak, that he would be killed for it? What kind of dark magic could kill a man for speaking the truth?

The same kind that melted a man's face if his mask was removed.

The truth sank into her, cold and undeniable. The person behind the assassination attempts on the king and queen and the person responsible for Falgun's plight were one and the same. Not the boy she'd grown up with, but the man she'd been bonded to. She'd best accept it. But where and how had he learned all his wicked tricks?

A final spasm shook Falgun's body before he stilled. She felt for his pulse, but there was none. Her only lead, and he was dead.

But he hadn't died in vain. He'd given her the name of his handler. The night wasn't over yet.

She pulled open the door and stared into the faces of several guards, their swords drawn, their expressions alternating between terror and triumph.

"She's here!" shouted the one in the lead, pointing his sword at her.

"Good evening," she said, smiling sweetly. "Don't you all have mothers to go home to?" She plucked an arrow from her quiver and nocked it on her bow.

"His Majesty said we must take her alive," said another guard. Someone shouted for reinforcements.

Her luck was running out. "I'm going to summon divine fire," she told the guards. "The Acharya told me never to use it against someone of lower power than myself. So I'm warning you to back off now." She stepped outside the barracks, and the men retreated, fanning out around her, alarm on their faces.

"We have you surrounded," said the lead soldier, his voice trembling. "Drop your weapons and come quietly."

"In your dreams, little man." She drew back the bowstring. The mantra for fire burned through her brain, igniting her blood. Fire wanted to dance and destroy everything in its path. Rain had to be coaxed; fire was always there, waiting for a chance to bloom.

She pointed the bow upward and let loose the arrow into the sky.

A huge ball of fire exploded above the courtyard. Men screamed and ran for shelter as embers drifted down, setting hair and clothes alight.

She froze, awestruck by the fireball she'd summoned. An arrow grazed her shoulder, and she ran for the nearest stairs to the parapet. She didn't want to jump twenty feet if she could avoid it, but the gatehouse was out of the question. As she flew up the stairs, the heat of the explosion dissipated, replaced by cool rain. She glanced behind. Bhairav stood in the courtyard, bow in hand, an expression of thin-lipped anger on his face.

Her heart gave a painful twist. Her suspicion had been correct. Bhairav had the power to summon arrows of fire and rain. He had been the one to set Nandovana on fire. Did he hate her so much that he would burn down her every refuge?

Guards poured out of the barracks and spread out around the courtyard.

Others ran up to the battlements. Her narrow window of escape was closing. But they assumed she would try to flee the fort. They wouldn't expect her to go in the *wrong* direction, toward the palace.

She ran cat-footed over the parapet, her thoughts racing. To get into the palace, she needed a disguise.

A guard turned the corner ahead of her and came to an abrupt halt, staring at her, wide-eyed. He opened his mouth to deliver a warning shout.

Katyani kicked the side of his head, and he went down in a soundless heap. She dragged him around the corner of a curving tower wall and checked his breathing. Still alive—good. She didn't want to kill any of the guards. Concussing them in self-defense, however, was perfectly acceptable.

She stripped him of his blue outer tunic, turban, and boots. The tunic was too large for her, and the turban smelled, but she'd pass for a guard at a superficial glance. At least the boots fit.

The man stirred and moaned. She stepped over him and continued down the ramparts.

Tanoj. Betrayer. The attempted poisoning, his framing of the kitchen staff, his claim that they worked for Malwa—had it all been an elaborate plan to get her and the princes back to Ajaigarh in time for the massacre? A current of anger ran through her. She couldn't wait to confront him and get some answers.

The ramparts extended beyond the outer courtyard to encircle the entire fort. She took the stairs down to the orchard and made her way to the palace, keeping to the shadows cast by trees and temples.

The palace walls were ten feet high and easy to scale, being more for privacy than protection. She dropped down to the other side and stashed her bow and quiver behind a rosebush in the garden. Time to test her disguise.

She trotted up to the marble steps at the entrance of the palace and saluted the guards on duty. "Message for Captain Tanoj of Garuda from His Royal Highness," she said in as deep a voice as she could summon.

The palace guard closest to her frowned. "New, are you?"

"No, sir. I was a kitchen boy before this."

They laughed. "Not even a hair on your chin, and you think you can be a guard of Ajaigarh?" said one.

She forced her lips into a smile, mapping her escape routes in case they recognized her and attacked. "Please, sir, it's urgent. His Royal Highness wants Captain Tanoj right away."

One of the guards went inside to find him. Katyani retreated beyond the lamplight, lowering her head. Her skin tingled with anticipation. The guards continued to rib her, their empty words falling like dust.

The palace doors creaked open, and Katyani tensed. The guards straightened and fell silent.

"Where's the messenger?" demanded Tanoj, stepping out.

"Hurry, sir!" she choked out, squashing her first impulse to charge him on sight. She waved and turned around, jogging down the carriageway.

"Wait!" shouted Tanoj, hurrying down the steps to catch up with her. "Did His Majesty tell you what he wants with me? Has the intruder been caught?"

"Yessir!" Katyani turned right from the carriageway into the garden, passing through the grove of amaltas trees and skirting the lily pond in the middle. She headed for a small stone temple on the far side of the garden, making sure Tanoj could still see her. Taking him by surprise was the only way she could take him in silence.

"Where are you going? The gate's *that* way," he said, closing the gap between them.

When he was right behind her, she hooked her arm around his neck, flipped him to the ground, and smashed an elbow into his chest. He let out a grunt of agony. She dragged him behind the temple and slid her dagger under his neck, pushing its cold steel against his skin.

"Falgun's dead," she whispered in his ear. "Are you next?"

He steadied his breathing and relaxed his body. "Katyani. I thought it might be you." Calm, as if the blade between them were of no import, as if the years they'd worked together were nothing. As if he weren't a traitor who'd brought yatu into the palace he'd sworn to protect.

"You betrayed the king and queen. Why did you do it?" She crouched over him and glared at his face, familiar yet strange. *"Why?"*

"All my life, I have done evil at the behest of others," he said, still in that preternaturally calm voice.

She gritted her teeth, trying to match his calm. "You were my teacher. I looked up to you."

"And you were my pupil. Know why I saved your life?" His eyes burned into hers. *"Balance."*

"What do you mean? You didn't save me!" she snapped.

A slow smile spread on his face. "I warned the Acharya about the trial. I knew he would intervene. Same reason why I—well, you'll figure it out."

The breath left her body. *Tanoj* had been the one to send the anonymous note? She remembered how he had challenged the Acharya in the court, as if he had no clue who the guru was, and went hot and cold all over. "You should have let me die. You should have known I would come after you."

"That's why you had to live." He took a deep breath. "If he had spared Ayan, I might have forgiven him."

"Who? Name him," she rasped. "Who was behind the assassination attempts? Where did the dark magic come from?" She already knew, but she needed to hear it in his voice. Without his confirmation, there was no proof.

His mouth twisted. "I must keep my vow."

She tightened her grip on her blade. "What vow? Did you kill my spies? And the kitchen staff—did you frame them? Are they even alive?"

A spasm crossed his face. "I killed them in the most humane way possible. One thrust of a knife and they were gone."

So many innocent victims. Her eyes and throat felt hot and painful. "You're going to hell, Tanoj."

He gave a half laugh, half sob. "I'm already there."

"Who did you report to?" she demanded. "I want his name."

Something sparked in his eyes. "Do not hesitate."

"What?"

"When the time comes, do not hesitate to kill. The more advanced lesson. Have you not learned it yet?" Then, uncaring of the blade at his throat, he shouted, "She's here! Katyani is here!"

Her hand pushed the dagger into his flesh of its own accord. His voice died in a gurgle, blood spurting out of his slashed artery, spraying her face.

She wiped her face with a sleeve and backed away, numb with horror. She'd killed him. She'd wanted to keep him alive, force a confession in front of witnesses, send him to the dungeons. She'd wanted an answer to the question *why*. He'd taken her by surprise, shouting like that.

He'd told her not to hesitate. He'd practically asked her to kill him, and she'd fallen into his trap. He hadn't even named Bhairav. This was the worst failure of all.

Boots thudded up to the temple.

"She's here!" screamed a soldier, flashing a lantern at her face.

She got up and ran, retracing her steps to the rosebush to retrieve her bow and quiver. Guards poured into the garden from the direction of the palace, and bobbing lanterns threw pools of yellow light everywhere. She grabbed her bow and quiver and raced to the rear of the garden, heading for the palace walls.

A shout went up. "I see her. There she is!"

She lodged her foot into a crevice. If she could make it to the ramparts, she could leap off them and escape into the trees that covered the hillside.

Light flooded the palace walls, freezing her.

"Did you return just to murder my men?" Bhairav's voice rang out, as cold as a cave in winter. "Aren't you even going to say hello?"

She turned and faced him, her back to the wall, her heart thudding. A thick circle of guards surrounded her, arrows nocked on bows, swords unsheathed. At their head stood Bhairav.

"Greetings, Your Majesty," said Katyani, making her voice as cold as his. "You look well. Kingship appears to suit you."

"Are you envious?" he asked with a sneer. "Do you wish I had died too? There would be nothing to stop you being regent."

"How dare you accuse me?" she cried. "The trial was a sham. Falgun lied—"

"Falgun, whom you killed," he interrupted. "Was Tanoj your man too? Did you kill him to eliminate the possibility he would reveal your plot?"

Her head swam. "I didn't plot anything."

"Do you recognize this?" Bhairav unslung a whip from his shoulder, and a jolt of terror shook her.

No. Not Chentu. She couldn't bear the touch of that evil weapon. She flung herself up the wall, her feet darting from one crevice to the next. She was almost at the top when the whip whistled through the air and snagged her foot. She clung to the wall, her palms bleeding, panic scattering her thoughts.

Bhairav gave a hard jerk, and she fell to the ground with a painful thud, the quiver on her back smashing with the impact. Broken arrows dug into her skin. Her hand closed over her dagger, and it cut her palm. The pain snapped her out of her fog of fear.

Bhairav's face was a mask of fury. "You could have stayed away. But no, you had to come back. Tell me, would the Acharya approve of the murders you committed? Will he save you now?"

"Why did you burn Nandovana?" she shot back. "Was it not to flush me out?"

His lip curled. "I had nothing to do with that." He flicked Chentu, the movement so swift she barely raised her arm to her face in time.

The whip slashed her arm, leaving a searing streak of pain and a whisper of gloating delight. She wanted to run, to scream, but her limbs refused to move. Didn't she deserve to be punished? She had killed her teacher when he was unarmed and defenseless.

He was a traitor, said her voice of reason. *He killed your spies and the innocent kitchen staff.*

The whip lashed her again, and yet again. As her spiritual strength seeped away, a hand slipped into hers.

Ayan bent over her, a smile on his handsome face. *Get up, Katya. It's time to fight.*

I can't. I just can't, she sobbed. *I can't do this alone.*

You're not alone. I'm always with you. He tugged her hand. *Come on, where's the girl who could beat us with one hand tied behind her back?*

A memory arrived like a breath of fresh air in a bloodstained field. Her and Ayan and Bhairav in the training ground, age fifteen. Tanoj had made her tie one hand behind her back before she fought Bhairav to even out the difference in their skill levels. Ayan had crowed with laughter when she beat Bhairav. But then, she'd turned around and beaten him, too.

What a delicious memory. Chentu coiled around her neck and trailed her chest, leaving scorch marks. *It belongs to me now.*

No. She wouldn't let it take anything else from her. She grabbed the whip with one hand, taking Bhairav by surprise. Before he could jerk it away from her, she slashed it with the dagger hidden in her bleeding palm.

Chentu screamed, a squealing, high-pitched sound that nearly made her drop the blade. Grimly, she held on and cut all the way through until a foot of the whip fell twitching and wriggling like a snake on her chest. Repelled, she flung it away. It landed on the face of one of the guards. He shrieked and clutched his face, dropping his sword. The others gathered around him, shouting advice and instructions.

She tried to get up, hoping she could make a break for it while they were distracted, or at least unsheathe her sword. But Bhairav stepped on her forearm, his boot pinning her down, making her gasp in pain. He pointed his sword at her throat. "Don't move," he said, his voice ragged. "Or I'll kill you as you killed Tanoj."

"Do it, why don't you?" she taunted. "One more murder will make little difference to your ledger."

His eyes narrowed. Before he could say anything, lightning split the sky, making Katyani's hair stand on end. Thunder boomed, blasting their eardrums. Hail began to fall, lumps of ice smashing down on helmets and turbans, littering the courtyard. One of them landed on her chest, right where Chentu had burned it. She bit back a cry, staring up in disbelief. Hail was rare, and such large chunks nearly unheard of in this part of Bharat.

"Take her inside," barked Bhairav, stepping off her arm. She massaged it, hoping nothing was broken. Multiple hands grabbed her.

"I advise you to let her go."

Goddess. That voice. Katyani twisted around, her heart leaping.

Daksh stood on the palace walls, bow in hand, aiming at Bhairav. Hail fell around him as if deflected by an invisible shield. His face was as calm as ever, his body perfectly poised.

Katyani blinked back tears. All the hurts her body and spirit had suffered melted away as if they were nothing. She'd thought she'd never see him again, but he'd come back for her. She didn't care what happened now.

"Airya Daksh, what a surprise," Bhairav ground out as two guards rushed to hold an umbrella over him. "You are far from your jurisdiction. Does your father know you're here?"

"I don't have time for idle chatter," said Daksh with supreme indifference. "Let her go, and we'll be on our way."

"Does your gurukul have a new policy of sheltering murderers?" spat Bhairav. "She conspired to kill the royal family, and the Acharya prevented us from punishing her. Now she has returned and killed a key witness of the trial as well as the head of Garuda, who used to be our teacher. Tell me, Airya, what is the appropriate punishment for that?"

His words stabbed her. Twisted and untrue, except she *had* killed Tanoj.

Daksh's gaze did not falter, nor did his bow move an inch. "I will count to three. Before I finish, your soldiers will release her."

"Or else what?" demanded Bhairav. "What can you do?"

"The hailstorm was only the beginning," said Daksh serenely. "My next arrow will bring your palace down."

Daksh had summoned the hailstorm? She stared at him in awe, barely noticing when another icy lump whacked her shoulder.

"You wish to test me?" he continued. "Very well. ONE."

The soldiers backed away, faces contorted in fear. Bhairav stood his ground, looking like he would explode in fury.

"TWO."

The hands clutching Katyani trembled. The Acharya's powers were legendary, and his aura had rubbed off on his sons.

Daksh smiled a terrible smile. "TH—"

"Stop!" shouted Bhairav. "Take her and good riddance. I don't want anything to do with this murdering traitor."

The trembling hands let her go and the guards scuttled away in relief. She stood, trying not to sway, and sheathed her dagger. She picked up the broken bow and quiver, unable to bear leaving them behind. They were the only things of Daksh's she could lay any claim to.

"Come on, Katyani." Daksh tucked his arrow back into his quiver and held out a hand to her.

A small gesture, but it filled her with an indescribable warmth. She wiped her hands on her tunic, slung the bow and quiver on her back, and took the hand he had offered—not because she needed it to haul herself up the wall, but for the feel of it in hers.

They dropped over the palace wall. "What made you decide to follow me?" she asked, both dreading and needing his answer.

"Later," he said, his voice clipped, and she understood. They were in enemy territory, after all. She shook her hair out of the smelly turban, ripped off the rank tunic, and ran with him across the grounds. Hail clattered around them, making the going hazardous, but they made it to the ramparts without injury.

Daksh led her to the rear of the fort, pulling her behind the wall of a staircase to hide when a patrol passed. She stood with her back nearly touching his chest, his hand on her shoulder, his breath on her cheek, her emotions as tangled as her hair.

When the guards were gone, he ran to the parapet and bent over to check something. She followed him, puzzled. "Still here," he reported. "You first."

She peered down. Daksh had come prepared. He had thrown a noose around a merlon and used that to haul himself up. *Much* easier than what she had done. She lowered herself on the rope, going down in a series of short slides to minimize bleeding afresh. Daksh followed. By the time he reached the ground, the hailstorm had passed, although a sharp wind remained, whistling through the trees. She marveled anew at the power that had conjured such a storm.

"We cannot use the stairs," he said tersely, scanning their surroundings.

"I know another route," she said. "It'll take a while, that's all."

She took him through the forest on a goat path she remembered from her childhood. Overgrown with weeds and treacherous with loose stones, it snaked through the trees, cutting steeply downhill. The four of them had often played hide-and-seek here. She ached as she remembered those carefree times. Gone from her—all gone. At least she still had

Daksh. Strange to be walking down this path with him, haunted by the ghosts of the children they'd been.

Although the hail had stopped, it was still pitch dark. Daksh bumped into her and stammered an apology.

"Take my hand," she said, perking up. "We'll go faster."

Pity it was too dark to see his expression, but they did go faster after that. She held his hand tightly, wondering why he had come back for her. What had changed his mind?

A large white owl flew right past her face, and she almost fell. Daksh steadied her, gripping her shoulder.

"Are you all right?" he asked, his voice full of concern.

It was the third time he had asked such a question in a situation when she could not answer with any honesty, or it would burn his ears.

Daksh, I might be the unluckiest girl in the world, but when I walk with you, holding your hand, I wouldn't change my fate for anyone's.

"Owls are lucky," she said instead, tugging him along.

"I have not heard so," said Daksh gravely. "Does not superstition say the opposite? That when an owl hoots, it means impending death?"

What a killjoy. "*One* hoot means impending death, *two* hoots mean success," she said. "I heard two hoots."

"I only heard one," he said.

She wanted to shake him. Why were they talking of owls? She walked in silence for a minute, going over the events of the last few hours: the deaths of the two witnesses, the revelations from Tanoj, her confrontation with Bhairav, and the lack of evidence on his pivotal role. Right now, all she had to go on was her own deductive reasoning. "You didn't tell me why you decided to follow me," she said at last. She remembered the chill finality of his words: *I cannot forgive you.*

He exhaled. "We found the arrow that set fire to Nandovana. I came as soon as I could."

"Was it Bhairav's?" she asked at once.

"Atreyi is conducting a ritual to trace ownership. We'll know in a day or two."

Yes. This would be an incontrovertible proof, one that no one could deny. She imagined confronting him in a court of law, presenting the arrow as evidence to a group of unbiased judges—if such existed.

Daksh added, "But I knew the arrow wasn't yours."

She wheeled around, surprise coursing through her. "You thought *I* set fire to the forest?"

"I thought perhaps you made a mistake and lost control." He gazed at her, his face open and vulnerable in a way she'd only seen it once before. "But I'm the one who made a mistake. I'm sorry I doubted you. Losing my father—" He stopped, unable to go on.

She wanted to put her arms around him and squeeze him in a hug. She contented herself with squeezing his hand. "In your place, I would be angry too."

They continued down the path, still holding hands, although it was no longer strictly necessary, because they had emerged from the thicket and the clouds had dissipated.

She would have loved to rest and recover at some convenient guesthouse in the city outskirts before making the journey back to Nandovana, but Daksh insisted on leaving at once. He had stabled his horse at an inn, and he managed to rouse the owner and obtain a second horse for Katyani.

The journey back took three days. They stopped twice for food at a dhaba and once at a public well to replenish their water. Apart from that, they only stopped to sleep and rest their horses for short periods, taking turns to keep watch. Despite her exhaustion, the pain of her wounds, and the shock of recent events, she felt calm and unafraid, as she always did when Daksh was by her side. In his presence, all the troubles that blocked her path like boulders turned to dust.

He did not question her about the two deaths Bhairav had accused her of, but he deserved the truth. As they entered the burned and blackened trees on the borders of Nandovana, she told him all that had happened, holding nothing back. When he had heard her out, he said, "The answer to Bhairav's question is death by execution."

Her heart clenched. The question was: What was the appropriate punishment for the killing of a teacher?

Daksh glanced at her sideways. "But there are exceptions for self-defense. You acted in self-defense, and this does not violate the law of ahimsa. Moreover, he committed evil acts. Dharma says your duty to fight evil is greater than your duty to your teacher."

"He died by my hand," she muttered, unwilling to absolve herself, even if he was.

"Your hand or the hand of fate," he said. "Have you forgotten the daayan's blessing?"

A blessing she herself had chosen. "I should have asked for justice."

He did not say anything, but she knew what he was thinking. She couldn't change the past. The dead would not become the living merely because she regretted her actions.

They left the damaged part of the jungle behind them. It was a relief to breathe the fresh air of an unburned forest, to move under the dense green gaze of its ancient trees. She had a sense of homecoming, of things righting themselves in an upside-down world. She wished she could make the moment last and wrap it up to open later, like a present to herself. It would remind her that things were not wholly terrible; they only seemed so when she forgot the forest, the gurukul, and Daksh.

He rode beside her, his body relaxed, his face serene. She remembered the powerful hailstorm he had summoned and wished she had his level of elemental control. "What were you going to do if Bhairav had not obeyed you by the count of three?" she asked.

He gave a mirthless smile. "I don't know. I was bluffing."

Bluffing? "But . . . the hailstorm?"

"Our father taught us to control the elements," he said. "But he also taught us to use such powers sparingly in times of greatest need. The hailstorm was a coincidence."

Her mind reeled. He'd been faking it all along. If Bhairav had given his soldiers the command to attack, Daksh would have, at the very least, been injured. Her insides roiled at the thought. There had been over fifty guards surrounding her at the time.

He glanced at her. "If I can defeat someone with words, why use weapons?"

She recovered herself. "You have more layers than a cabbage," she said, a teasing note creeping into her voice. "I didn't know you were capable of deception."

"It was the lesser evil," he said seriously.

She curbed her desire to rib him further. Odd, how being in his presence elevated her spirits, even in the most awful circumstances.

They reached the gurukul late that afternoon and dismounted at the gates. A horde of disciples rushed forward to greet them, uttering cries of relief. A few even had tears in their eyes. She thought it must be because of the Acharya's death. The gurukul had lost its revered teacher and most powerful protector. Uttam might be capable, but it would be many years before he gained the renown and respect his father had commanded.

Shalu went up to Daksh and said, "*Never* do that again." Then she hugged Katyani and pulled her inside.

"Never do what?" asked Katyani.

Shalu cast a meaningful glance at Daksh, who lowered his gaze. "I'll let him explain. Are you okay? Do you need healing? Food?"

"It can wait," said Katyani with gratitude as they walked into the familiar courtyard with the peepal tree that stood in the middle like a sentinel. "Where is Airya Uttam?"

"My brother is in seclusion," said Daksh. "There are multiple rituals for him to complete now that my father is gone. The safety of the gurukul and everyone inside depends upon him. He must meditate to enhance his spiritual strength."

Atreyi hurried up to them. "There you are." She glared at Daksh. "You are not so old, child, that I have forgotten how to punish you." Daksh winced. Shalu bit back a grin, squeezed Katyani's hand, and retreated, shooing the other disciples away as well.

What had he done? Before Katyani could ask, Atreyi turned to her. "I have discovered whose arrow set fire to Nandovana. It was Bhairav's."

"Yes!" Knowledge brought no victory, only a hollowness in the pit of Katyani's stomach. "He denied doing it, but I guessed he was lying." Here, at last, was the first solid piece of evidence against Bhairav. He had set fire to Nandovana to retaliate against the Acharya for protecting her. What else had he done?

Everything, said her gut. He stood at the center of it all—the one who had most to gain, the one who had been lying to them all his life, the one who was most fascinated with the magical section of the library, and the one whom Tanoj had spent countless private hours training. She still didn't know *why* he'd done it, though. Was it only for the sake of king-ship?

"This is an act of war against us," said Daksh. His voice filled with cold fury. "My father would never have stood for it, and neither will I."

"What will you do?" asked Atreyi. "Uttam must not be disturbed. The rest of us, taken together, cannot match your father in strength or power. We cannot fight an army."

Katyani pursed her lips. They couldn't fight an army by themselves, but they didn't have to do it alone. "There are those who may help us. I could talk to the king of Malwa or the crown prince of the Solanki king-dom." She didn't know if her cousin would want to be involved, and Irfan might have conditions she couldn't meet. Neither was a sure bet.

"No," said Daksh flatly. "Once we ask for help from other kingdoms, we lose both our moral authority and our political neutrality. This is an internal matter of Nandovana."

Oh, was it? An idea blossomed inside her, one both daring and logical. "You're forgetting that Nandovana isn't just inhabited by humans."

Daksh frowned. "What do you mean?"

She gave them a triumphant smile. "You're forgetting the yatu."

CHAPTER 22

IT WAS AN AUDACIOUS SUGGESTION. AT FIRST, DAKSH AND ATREYI wouldn't hear of it. After all, the only reason the Acharya had intervened in the conflict between Chandela and Paramara was Shamsher's use of the yatu.

"But he used them to murder the royal family and councilors," argued Katyani as they halted under the peepal tree. "Whereas we will request them not to kill any humans, to act only in self-defense, so we can capture and question Bhairav."

"The rules of warfare state that the combatants must be human," Daksh pointed out.

"This isn't war," said Katyani. "Think of it as a reckoning."

His brows knitted. "No matter what you call it, we would be entering Ajaigarh Fort with yatu by our side."

"Something I have already been falsely accused of." Bitterness flooded her mouth as she remembered her trial. "Consider what Bhairav has done, what he yet might do."

"You're sure the wards are broken?" asked Atreyi.

Katyani nodded. "The yatu invasion destroyed the wards. It would take greater magical skill than Bhairav has to resurrect them. Not even Hemlata could have done it."

"I must ask my brother," said Daksh. "It's not something our father would have done."

"It's not something he would ever have needed to do," said Katyani.

"You're assuming the yatu will agree to help us," said Atreyi. "Every interaction they've had with humans has ended in tragedy for them."

"They'll agree to help us because without them, we have no hope of success," said Katyani. "I promised if I were ever in a position to do so, I would return their land to them. That can be one of our conditions for releasing Bhairav."

Varun stepped out of the main building and hurried over to them. "Airya Daksh, your elder brother wishes to see you."

"Has he come out of seclusion?" asked Daksh.

"Not yet, but he sensed your return," said Varun.

Daksh looked at Katyani. "You'd better come with me. You two as well."

As they walked toward the main building, Atreyi explained Katyani's idea to Varun. As expected, he was aghast. "The yatu are monsters," he protested. "We don't engage with them."

"The Acharya had an agreement with them," said Katyani. "The Paramara kingdom has a treaty with them. So did the Chandelas, until they broke it. No one was more surprised than me about that, but if you look up the history of Bharat, you'll find multiple examples of yatu-human engagement."

"They aren't saints," warned Daksh. "Quite the opposite. Think of them as our distant cousins, with all the faults that humans can have and ten times the strength. Remember this when you negotiate with them."

"And remember that for many of them, humans are basically a menu item," said Varun.

Katyani rolled her eyes. "I can hardly forget."

Uttam was seated in the lotus pose in the main hall, surrounded by flowers, swords, plates of fruit, candlesticks, and earthen cups of water. His face was etched with lines of grief and exhaustion.

The trio knelt and bowed to him.

"Airya Uttam, I am sorry for your loss," said Katyani. A spasm of pain went through her, both for him and for herself. The Acharya should have been here right now. The hall didn't look the same without his glowering presence.

Uttam gave her a tired smile. "Daksh told me what you did. Thank you for saving my brother's life."

She swallowed. "I allowed your father to die."

His forehead creased. "Could you have saved him?"

She shook her head. "I vowed to the daayan I would not intervene the next time I encountered her. That was the price I paid for being able to save him the first time."

"Then you did the only thing you could under the circumstances," said Uttam. "Our father would have understood this. Did he have any last words?"

"He told me to keep my promise," she said.

Uttam's face softened as he glanced at Daksh. "Anything else?"

She hesitated and plunged ahead. "I had a vision when he died. Both he and the daayan vanished. In their place, a man and two women clad in gurukul robes were walking hand in hand. They had their backs to me, so I could not see their faces."

Daksh exhaled. "You did not tell me this."

"I don't know if it was real or not," she said. Also, Daksh had been angry and grieving at the time, and she hadn't had a chance to talk about it. He might even have suspected her of lying to make him feel better. Now, in his brother's presence, was the right time to bring it up. "Perhaps I dreamed it. But it means they are at peace now—all three of them."

Uttam's eyes lit up. "That is something to celebrate."

"Forgive me if I don't celebrate being an orphan, Brother," said Daksh, his voice brittle.

His pain cut her to the heart. Uttam reached forward and squeezed his shoulder. "Death is the body's final truth. Do you think we will live forever?"

"He was a force for good in this world," muttered Daksh, lowering his eyes. "And now he's gone."

"Then we must make sure we are worthy to be called his descendants," said Uttam, his voice warm. "But come, you wish to speak to me of more practical matters."

"How much longer do you need to stay in seclusion?" asked Katyani.

"I do not know," said Uttam. "Some of the rituals are straightforward. I have just completed one to transfer the allegiance of all weaponry in the gurukul to myself. But others will take longer. The allegiance of the trees and nature spirits, for instance, is far trickier even at the best of times. The forest is in chaos right now. Many spirits are injured or in hiding. It will take a long time to regain their trust and get them to listen."

Atreyi leaned toward him, her face taut. "The arrow used to burn the forest was Bhairav's."

Uttam gave a heavy sigh. "I suspected it belonged to one of our disciples. I had hoped to be wrong."

"What should we do about it?" asked Daksh.

"You have already decided what you should do," said Uttam quietly. "Why ask me?"

"We will not act without your permission," protested Daksh. "But we must do *something,* or we would be failing in our duty to protect the forest."

"What do you propose?" asked Uttam.

Daksh looked at Katyani. He wanted her to speak. This was only fair, since it was *her* preposterous idea. She cleared her throat. "I thought we should ask the yatu to help us attack Ajaigarh Fort. Not to kill anyone, but to take Bhairav captive. It would be a lesson to everyone that Nandovana is off-limits. And we'll make him return the land that once belonged to the yatu."

"Is there nothing else you want from the king of Chandela?" asked Uttam.

He was sharp, she had to give him that. "He's no king, not in my eyes. I want to question him about the killing of the royal family. I found two men who were involved in the assassination attempts and the yatu attack, but they both died before I could interrogate them fully. I believe they were working for him." She gave Uttam a brief account of what had happened in the fort before Daksh appeared.

Uttam gave Daksh an assessing look. "So that is where you went. I guessed as much."

Katyani gazed at Daksh in astonishment. He hadn't told his brother? He'd left the gurukul without telling anyone? No wonder everyone had been so relieved to see him back.

Daksh hung his head. "I'm sorry if I worried you. I was afraid you'd say no."

"It was too much, all at once," said Uttam. "Father dying, the forest burning, your disappearance. At least be forthcoming with me so I know where you are."

"Yes, Brother," said Daksh, sounding contrite.

"As for your plan to attack the fort, I see several problems," said Uttam.

"We'll work out the logistics," said Katyani, eager to contribute and take the heat off Daksh. He'd gone to Ajaigarh for *her*. She didn't want him to be scolded for it. "The wards are broken, and we can scale the walls. We don't need more than twenty yatu to overpower the guards."

"Airya Uttam is talking of *ethical* problems," murmured Varun.

Uttam gave a small smile. "Yes. This is not a course of action my father would have followed."

"That's because he could take on the entire fort himself," Katyani pointed out. "None of us have his power, not even combined."

"True, but he would have ensured that only the perpetrator was punished," said Uttam. "He would not allow injury to anyone else."

"Then we must do the same," said Daksh. Katyani shot him a grateful look.

"How?" asked Uttam. "You are planning to use the yatu. Do I need to remind you they are easily angered and harbor a grudge against Chandela? It has taken us years to persuade them to eat the flesh of animals instead of humans. You cannot control them, and you should not use weapons that you cannot control."

"Shamsher did it," said Katyani. "He used their hatred of Chandela to kill. We, on the other hand, will use their desire to regain their homeland to set boundaries on their behavior. And forgive me, Airya Uttam, but the yatu are not weapons. They are people, of a monstrous kind."

"I agree with you," said Uttam. "They *are* people, and if they participate in your campaign, their safety and behavior are your responsibility."

"You give us your permission?" asked Daksh, his eyes widening.

"If I do not, I suspect you will go ahead without the yatu," said Uttam dryly. "And I would rather not lose my brother so soon after losing my father."

Daksh flushed. Uttam's gaze shifted to Katyani. "How do you plan to protect your forces?"

"Yatu are difficult to injure and much more difficult to kill," said Katyani. "We'll strike at night, take Ajaigarh by surprise."

"If Bhairav set fire to Nandovana, he will be expecting you," said Uttam. "He might even be inviting you. Be careful not to fall into a trap."

"What do you advise?" asked Atreyi.

"Time your attack for the night of the new moon, six days from now," said Uttam.

A frisson of excitement went through Katyani. "For the cover of darkness?"

"Yatu are at their hungriest during the full moon," said Daksh. "The new moon is when they are least likely to view humans as food."

"Everything you do will have consequences for the future of the gurukul," said Uttam, his face grave. "Do not treat this as a battle. Regard it as the capture and interrogation of a suspect."

"Should we bring him back here?" asked Daksh.

"No," said Uttam. "Question him before his court. The truth must emerge in front of his subjects. Take the arrow as evidence." He closed his eyes. "Go now. I must rest before the next ritual."

They bowed and left the lecture hall.

"Airya, please allow me to accompany you," said Varun as soon as they were outside.

Daksh considered. "Fine, you and Airyaa Atreyi may come with us. Everyone else must stay and guard the gurukul and the forest. Summon all the disciples and brief them."

"Yes, Airya." Varun hurried off.

Daksh turned to Atreyi and Katyani. "You both must go to Vilamba tonight. If we want to be in Ajaigarh six nights from now, we have only the next two or three to prepare ourselves."

"What will you be doing?" asked Katyani, a wave of exhaustion washing over her.

"Checking the weapons," said Daksh. "The armory has not been used in a while. I may have to remind the swords what they're for." He gave her a penetrating look. "You need salve for your wounds, and then you should eat and rest."

"I'm fine," she lied.

"You'll be better once I've tended to your wounds," said Atreyi.

"You can take a bath first, if you wish," said Daksh. His lips twitched. "Bathing time rules can be bent in case of emergencies."

"He's right." Atreyi's gaze traveled over Katyani, and she frowned, as if she could sense all her injuries. "Have a dip first, and then come see me."

"What about you, Airya?" said Katyani innocently. "Do you not need a bath too?"

"I can bathe when you are gone," he said, not even blinking, to her disappointment. He was wise to her ways by now.

Katyani's dip in the pool was quick and painful. She winced as the warm, fragrant water washed over her cuts and bruises, and beat a hasty exit. Afterward, Atreyi made her strip in the women's dormitory and applied salve to the burns Chentu had left on her skin.

Later, they went for the evening meal together. It was surreal to sit down to a meal with the other disciples as if nothing were amiss, as if they had not lost the Acharya and did not stand at the brink of armed conflict.

Daksh presided over the meal in the absence of his brother, although he scarcely ate. He caught her eye once and gave a brief smile that warmed her heart. She wished she could tell him to eat more. She wished she could thank him for the medicinal soup he had made for her and beg him never to make it again. Mostly, though, she wished the Acharya was still alive, his dour yet comforting presence anchoring them all, keeping them safe.

She lay down in her hut after the meal, thinking she was far too tense to fall asleep, and the next thing she knew, Atreyi was shaking her awake, telling her it was time to leave.

Daksh and Varun saw them off. "Stay safe," said Daksh. "Don't make any promises we cannot keep."

"Vilamba and I go back a long way," said Atreyi. "We'll be fine."

Daksh nodded, his eyes lingering on Katyani. "I'll expect you back by morning."

She smiled, trying to send a wave of reassurance to him. Of course she'd be back; Atreyi was one of the few people in the world she trusted almost as much as she trusted Daksh.

They set off, Katyani tingling in anticipation. Atreyi asked her to let her start the dialogue with the yatu, and Katyani was happy to let the older woman take the lead. She had no illusions about her own diplomatic skills.

It took them three hours to reach the yatu hideout. Vilamba was waiting for them in the clearing, squatting among the roots of the ancient mango tree. She appeared to be expecting them. She probably had spies stationed at various points in the forest. Once, this would have put Katyani on edge. Now, she viewed the yatudhani as a potential ally—or at least, she wanted to. Atreyi and Katyani laid down their weapons before approaching her.

The scene was far livelier than it had been last time. A huge fire burned in the middle of the clearing, and a yatu was turning a deer on a massive spit. The air was thick with smoke and the smell of meat cooking. A number of yatu were gathered around the fire, speaking to each other in low grunts. Vilamba raised her hand, and they quieted.

"Welcome, Atreyi," she growled. "Long time no see." She cut her eyes to Katyani. "And *you,* I remember. Come, sit by me, and tell me what brings you here."

Atreyi and Katyani approached the yatudhani and knelt before her. Atreyi explained their proposal to Vilamba as succinctly as possible. "If you grant us the presence of twenty warriors," she concluded, "it will be enough for us to take over Ajaigarh Fort. We cannot do it without you."

"You're asking us to risk our lives," said the yatu matriarch. "What's in it for us?"

"Justice," said Katyani, unable to stop herself. "Nandovana is your home, too. Bhairav burned it. He needs to be held to account. As reparation, we will ask him to return the land you lived in for generations."

"Wait here," said Vilamba. "I must talk with my sons." She heaved herself up, creaked to the edge of the clearing, and cupped her hands around her mouth, giving a great holler that reverberated through the forest. It sounded like a war cry, but it was apparently a maternal summons. Yatu poured in from various parts of the forest and stood before her—a hulking troop that would have sent the fear of Yama into the most hardened human warrior.

Katyani and Atreyi sat cross-legged between the spreading roots of the tree while Vilamba talked with the yatu in a series of peremptory grunts. One of them peeled away from the rest and trotted into the trees, heading west. Vilamba lumbered back to them.

"Four of my sons and eight grandsons will accompany you," she said. "The other eight will come from another clan, if they are willing. I have sent one of my nephews as a messenger. My sons are asking if they can eat what they kill. Better not to waste food, yes?"

"No," said Atreyi. "One of our main concerns is that no humans should be injured, let alone killed. Our goal is to capture Bhairav, not to hurt anyone. Your sons must be very careful. They can defend themselves; they can bind the humans who dare attack them, but they must not take any lives."

"You all need to stop thinking of humans as food," put in Katyani. "Any future treaty with Chandela depends upon this. If you wish to get back your land, you must adhere strictly to a vegetarian diet."

"A big sacrifice." Vilamba cracked her knuckles. "Talking of food, please share our repast. We have a juicy deer, waiting to be devoured."

"Thank you," said Atreyi. "But you know the gurukul is vegetarian, in the sense that we do not eat flesh at all. Please go ahead; don't mind us."

By the time Vilamba finished eating, her nephew had returned from his errand to inform them that eight yatu from a neighboring clan were on their way, including one called Papek who spoke some Hindavi and would act as their translator.

Vilamba invited them to spend the remainder of the night in her protection, and Atreyi accepted with such breezy confidence that Katyani was ashamed of her fears. They slept under the mango tree on blankets stuffed with dried grass, lulled by the sound of the waterfall.

At dawn, Katyani woke to Vilamba's surprisingly gentle touch on her arm. Atreyi was already awake, meditating in the lotus pose.

The fire had been put out, the remains of the deer removed. Twenty yatu cradling maces and clubs like hot water bottles slept on the ground some distance away.

"Your army is here," said Vilamba. "Bring our sons back safe and sound."

CHAPTER 23

TWO DAYS LATER THEY WERE ON THEIR WAY, HEADING EAST through Nandovana on the overgrown, leaf-littered path to Ajaigarh. Daksh walked on one side of Katyani, Atreyi on the other. Varun had ridden ahead to rent coaches. Behind them marched the yatu, their thudding footsteps scaring away birds and animals for miles around.

Anxiety knotted her stomach. So much could go wrong. Daksh, Atreyi, or Varun could get injured, or worse. One stray arrow was all it took to kill someone.

The wind changed direction, blowing from behind. Katyani held her breath and counted backward until it changed. The yatu troop, her second big source of worry. Daksh had asked them to take enough provisions for a couple of good meals, and each one carried a sack of cured deer meat. But suppose they lost control at the sight of fresh food and started devouring everyone?

It was hard not to think of them as predators, even though they were now her allies. Shamsher's yatu battalion had mostly perished, but it was not impossible that one of the yatu following her had participated in that massacre.

Daksh slipped a hand into hers and squeezed, as if he had guessed her thoughts. She tried to smile at him. *Stay alive; stay safe,* she thought.

Varun was waiting with three coaches at the edge of the forest. The horses stamped and whinnied nervously at the sight and smell of the yatu, but Daksh quieted them with a few words. Once the yatu were stuffed inside the coaches, the horses calmed down further, and they set off.

They disguised themselves as traders to avoid suspicion and hid their weapons in the undercarriage of the coaches. They avoided the main roads of the towns and halted only at night in an empty field so the yatu could get out, stretch their legs, and eat.

Katyani watched them, perched on the steps of her carriage, a wave of conflicting emotions washing over her. The yatu had always been her enemies; in Malwa, they had still been opponents of a kind, to be negotiated with. But now they were her troops, and she was responsible for their safety and well-being. She wasn't sure how to feel about this progression. If not for Daksh and Atreyi, she couldn't have gone through with it at all.

"Nervous?" asked Daksh, leaning against the carriage next to her.

"Without you, I would have been." Had she said that out loud? She unsheathed her dagger and pretended to inspect its edge to hide her expression. When she looked back at him, he was staring at her, his face unguarded, his eyes soft in the light of the crescent moon. She bent her head, warmth pooling in her stomach.

"My sword is yours," he said, his voice serious.

She bit her lip. *Don't laugh, don't laugh, don't laugh. . . .*

Atreyi strolled up to them, saving her. "We're making good time. We should be there tomorrow night."

Tomorrow night already? Her stomach flipped.

"The night of the new moon," said Daksh with a satisfied smile. "Just as my brother advised."

"Please be careful," said Katyani, her gaze darting between them. "Don't take any unnecessary risks."

"We aren't going there to fight," said Daksh in a reassuring tone. "Only to call a criminal to account."

But anxiety continued to churn her insides. If anything happened to her companions, she'd never forgive herself.

They entered Ajaigarh the next evening. As dusk deepened to night, they arrived at the base of the hill upon which the fort stood. They hid the carriages in a thicket, and Katyani led them in groups of three or four along the goat path up the hillside. Daksh stayed at the top and Atreyi and Varun at the bottom, until all the yatu had been safely transferred to a small clearing two-thirds of the way up the hill. When everyone was gathered around her, she outlined her minimal plan.

"We go over the wall using ropes," she said, keeping her voice low. "We are quiet so no one hears us. If we run into a patrol guard, we bind and gag him. We break into the palace, leaving two yatu to guard the main door. I lead you to Bhairav's suite. We bind anyone who tries to stop us. Once Bhairav is captured, we take him to the main audience hall and summon the court—whoever can be found. Then we question him." It wouldn't be so simple, but they would improvise as they went along. The yatu shifted as Papek translated, their red eyes gleaming in the dark.

"He is likely to have increased the number of guards, especially after our last encounter," said Daksh, frowning. "He will be expecting us."

"But he won't be expecting the yatu," said Katyani.

The yatu could be silent when they wanted. They crept up the hillside, flattening innocent bushes and pushing aside thorny branches, carving a destructive path through the undergrowth that made Katyani wince.

Near the top, she waved them to a halt and went ahead by herself to reconnoiter. She emerged under the starlit sky, the battlements looming above her, and melted back into the trees. As far as she could judge, this was on the opposite side of the fort from its main entrance, which was exactly what she'd wanted.

She retraced her steps to fetch the others. When they were all assembled under the shadow of the fort walls, Daksh asked the yatu to listen for the patrol before throwing the ropes. They could not see the guards on the battlements from this angle and would have to trust the famously acute yatu sense of hearing.

A few nail-biting minutes later, the yatu pointed upward. The patrol was passing. When another full minute had passed, with such excruciating slowness that Katyani could have sworn time stood still, they slung their ropes over the wall, hooked them around the merlons, and began to climb. In five minutes, yatu and humans were over the wall and on the battlements, just in time to encounter the next patrol.

The patrol leader gave a piercing scream, abruptly cut off when Daksh applied pressure to his neck, knocking him out. Katyani wrestled one of the others to the ground, gagging him with his own shirt, adrenaline pumping through her. Daksh used his rope-tying mantra, binding the rest.

"They'll be discovered in minutes." He glanced in the direction the next patrol would come from.

"Follow me." Katyani ran across the battlements and leaped down the nearest set of stairs. Daksh ran beside her in easy strides, Atreyi and Varun on each side of the yatu behind her and Papek at the rear. A fierce surge of pride rolled over her. These were her friends and her troops—her stinky, monstrous, carnivorous troops. No matter her qualms about their nature, they were here because of her, and she would do everything in her power to protect them. The Acharya would have approved of the sentiment.

She led them through orchards and across fields, taking the shortest route to the palace walls. The palace dome glinted in the starlight. The towers were dark but for a lone lamp flickering behind one of the windows.

Behind them, an alarm sounded; the patrol had been discovered.

"Hurry," said Daksh grimly, hauling himself up the wall and extending a hand to Atreyi. Katyani perched on the wall and looked back. Her stomach lurched as she spotted lanterns and torches streaking toward them.

The palace had only one entrance, at the front—another safety feature. They skirted the building, running across open ground. As they rounded the corner to the front of the palace, they came face-to-face with a contingent of guards armed with swords.

Papek issued a guttural order, and the yatu fell on them.

"Don't kill them!" Katyani shouted, but she didn't have to. The yatu plucked the weapons away from the screaming guards and thumped them into submission. One of the yatu uncoiled the ropes they'd brought, grinning at the terrified humans before tying them up thoroughly.

The yatu could deal with the soldiers. Katyani needed to find Bhairav before he escaped the palace. She ran for the steps, Daksh close behind her. The guards at the palace doors clanged the great brass bell that hung near the entrance, nearly deafening her.

She reached the steps, her heart thumping. She recognized a few of the faces at the door. "Amar! Minal!" she yelled. "Get out of my way."

In answer, the men raised their bows and took aim.

As she raced up the steps with Daksh, determined to stop them, a wall of heat blasted her back. She whirled around. Daksh grabbed her arm and dragged her to one side. Arrows rained through the air where they'd been standing. Below them, a yatu who'd made it to the palace steps burned as flames engulfed his body. He screamed in agony: a long, horrible sound that frayed her hard-won self-control. She started toward him, but Daksh caught her hand.

"No. You cannot help him. We must go forward." His eyes blazed with anger.

The yatu fell to the ground, still burning, his flesh turning black. The rest of the yatu drew back, grunting questions at Papek, at Atreyi, at *her*.

She swallowed her nausea. Bhairav had managed to reset the wards—not on the entire fort, but on the palace. She railed against herself for not having sensed it. "Stay back," she shouted. "Guard the perimeter. Let no one enter or exit. Varun, stay with the yatu, and don't let them approach the palace."

The guards at the palace doors nocked fresh arrows on their bows. Katyani let fly an arrow of her own, injuring one of them in his leg. Daksh uttered his rope-tying mantra, using their own tunics to source his magical ropes. The guards rolled on the floor, struggling to break free.

Alarm bells rang throughout the fort. Sounds of fighting came from the palace grounds as the yatu engaged fresh soldiers, pouring in from the gate. Atreyi ran up the steps to join them, and Daksh pushed open the massive wooden doors that led to the entrance hall.

A hail of arrows greeted them, falling from the landing on top of the grand staircase. They flattened sideways against the open doors, but an arrow penetrated the flesh of Katyani's arm. She gasped, then pressed her lips together and plucked it out. Blood trickled down her arm in a thin rivulet.

Daksh's gaze darted to her. "Are you okay?"

"It's nothing," she said, scanning him and Atreyi. "You two?"

"Missed us." Atreyi looked up. "Here comes another volley."

Daksh withdrew his sword and made a single cut in the air. The arrows diverted, as if by an invisible shield. They flew into all corners of the entrance hall, a few finding human targets. Men cried out, and someone shouted at the archers to stop.

"Let's go." Katyani unsheathed her bronze sword and led the way in.

Nearly twenty guards charged them. Steel clashed against steel, and sparks flew as they fell into the sword dance. Katyani parried their blows, trying to avoid hurting them or getting hurt herself. Daksh used his mantra to bind over a dozen of them before he staggered back, panting.

"I need a few minutes to recover my spiritual strength," he said, supporting himself with his sword.

"We'll bind the rest manually." Atreyi kneed one of the guards in his stomach and flipped him over, uncoiling a thin, flexible rope from her pocket to tie his hands.

Katyani grabbed hold of a palace servant cowering in one corner. "Where's Bhairav?" she demanded. "We need to speak with him."

"Those who wish to speak make an appointment," came a voice from above the stairs. "It is thieves and monsters who attack at night."

Bhairav stood at the head of the staircase, surrounded by a dozen guards. He was dressed in battle armor, bow in hand, sword at his belt, and Chentu coiled around his wrist. Torches flickered on the wall behind him, framing his face in fire.

Daksh straightened. "We don't make appointments with those who commit acts of war against us. Tell your guards to lay down their weapons. Surrender to us, and you will not be harmed."

Bhairav laughed, a flat, humorless sound. "Has the death of your father unhinged you? This is my home, and you have invaded it." He cut his eyes to Katyani. "I warned you I didn't want to see you here again."

"Enough." Daksh held up his hand. "You burned our forest, and you will answer for that crime. Come quietly to the audience hall to be questioned."

"How dare you." Bhairav's voice was like a razor. "You attack my home and accuse me of burning yours? I had *nothing* to do with that."

"Then you will not object to answering a few questions," said Daksh. "Put down your weapons. I don't want anyone else to get hurt."

Bhairav raised a fist. The guards around him nocked arrows on their bows.

"Duck!" shouted Atreyi. Arrows rained down on them, and they dove behind the pillars that stood in the entrance hall. A few found their targets in the luckless soldiers who were tied up on the floor.

Daksh nocked an arrow on his bow. "Last chance, Prince."

"I am a *king*," roared Bhairav. "The king of Chandela."

Daksh stepped out and shot the arrow toward Bhairav and his guards. The arrow *multiplied*, each copy striking a weapon aimed at them. With a tremendous crack, the bows carried by the guards broke.

"Drop your weapons and come down," commanded Daksh, his face etched in lines of fatigue. Katyani's heart clenched. He had overextended himself; it would be dangerous for him to use more spiritual power. She caught Atreyi's gaze, and Atreyi gave a small, tight nod.

Bhairav glared at Daksh and tossed his broken bow on the floor. He climbed down the stairs, trailed by his guards. At a word from Daksh, ropes whipped around all the remaining guards save one. Sweat beaded Daksh's forehead, and his hands trembled as he slung the bow on his back. *Stop,* Katyani wanted to scream. *Stop before you hurt yourself.* But there was no way to tell him without alerting Bhairav.

Atreyi moved toward Daksh and laid a warning hand on his arm. "Enough," she said, her voice unyielding as stone. He bowed his head and leaned against the wall, taking deep breaths.

"Fetch the head priest, the dandanayaka, the chief justice, and whoever else is close by," Atreyi told the guard Daksh had left unbound. "Tell them the king awaits trial in the audience room."

The guard looked at Bhairav, his lips quivering.

"Do not look at him," snapped Katyani. "He is a prisoner. Look at me. Do you remember who I am, Vidyut?" She took a step closer to the trembling guard. *"Go."*

"I will accompany him," said Atreyi. She frowned at Daksh. "You will wait here."

"Please take one of the yatu if you leave the palace," said Katyani.

Bhairav's eyes widened. "You've brought the yatu back."

She leveled her sword at his chest. "To the audience hall."

"Would you kill me while I'm defenseless?" he asked.

"I won't kill you," she said. "But I *will* stab you. Move!"

He sneered and turned around. She walked him to the audience hall while Daksh stayed behind, keeping a watch on the bound guards.

Dark shapes leaped on either side as they entered the audience hall.

Shadows. They're only shadows. A torch flickered on either end, providing a little illumination. The hall stretched—dark, empty, unwelcoming. Their footsteps echoed as they walked down the aisle, out of place in the silence. Katyani gazed at the vacant dais, coldness creeping up her spine. The last time she was here, she'd been the one on trial. Her back burned as she remembered Chentu ripping open her flesh and siphoning her power.

She swallowed and pushed the memory aside. She prodded Bhairav's back with the tip of her sword. "Into the prisoner's box."

He turned his head. "You're enjoying this, aren't you?"

Enjoying? No. But there was a bitter satisfaction in it. "I can think of a thousand things I'd rather be doing," she said. "But this is necessary."

"Why did you come back?" he asked when he was inside the box. He sounded genuinely curious. "Why can you not let me go?"

She held her sword steady in both hands, glaring at him. "Why can you not let *me* go? Why set fire to the forest?"

"I did not," he said. "That's just an excuse to take revenge on me."

"I don't need an excuse for that," she spat. "How does it feel standing in the prisoner's box?"

"How do you feel seeing me here?" he countered.

She thought about it. "It's not the same. There're no crowds to witness your humiliation. And I'm not about to beat you to death. Still, it's something."

"I never wanted to beat you to death, Katya," he said. "I wanted you to *forget*. If I'd wanted you to die, you would have died. Just like right now, I can escape if I want to, but I'm interested to see how far you're going to take this charade."

"How would you escape?" she asked, but he only smiled in answer.

Atreyi entered the hall, leading a group of men: Shukla, the royal priest, as cadaverous as ever, his sunken eyes darting from her to Bhairav. The chief justice, clad in an undershirt and lungi, looking equal parts terrified and outraged. The dandanayaka, unrecognizable without his whip and uniform. A court scribe, a messenger, and a few others who could act as assessors and witnesses. The group was followed by Daksh leading the bound soldiers. He looked better, but there were dark circles of exhaustion under his eyes. She would have to ensure he didn't use his powers again tonight.

She understood why he'd brought the soldiers into the hall. He wanted as many people as possible to witness the interrogation of their king, so there could be no doubt afterward of what had happened.

"Welcome to the trial of Bhairav, king of Chandela," said Daksh when everyone had sat down. "He is accused of setting fire to our most holy forest, Nandovana."

"A baseless accusation." Bhairav's lip curled. "This trial is a sham."

"No, but mine was," said Katyani, keeping her voice even.

"As I suspected, you have contrived this whole thing as revenge." He gave a contemptuous smile. "Perhaps you set fire to the forest yourself."

Daksh reached into his quiver, withdrew an arrow, and threw it across the floor toward Bhairav. "Recognize it? This is the arrow that caused the fire. It belongs to you."

"That means *nothing*." Bhairav leaned forward, gripping the box. "Someone else could have taken the arrow from my quiver. Katyani herself used to have access to all my weapons."

"Katyani has not lived here for nearly a year," said Daksh, his face hard. "And only someone who'd learned the mantras from my father could have done this. How many such people exist in Ajaigarh?"

"I don't know," said Bhairav, shrugging. "But you were here with Katyani a week ago, Airya. Who is to say one of you did not steal an arrow from my quiver so you could misuse it and then accuse me?"

"Why would we set fire to our own home?" asked Daksh icily.

Bhairav pointed a finger at Katyani. "She did it. Not me. All I want is to rebuild my life after the death of my family. All I want is a safe home for my sister and my subjects. Now you bring yatu to my door and pretend it is for justice. This whole affair will be a disgrace for the gurukul forever. And all for what? Katyani's revenge?"

"It would be a disgrace if we let it go and pretended it never happened," said Daksh. "Neither Katyani nor I went anywhere near your bow and arrows that day."

"Perhaps she kept an arrow of mine from beforehand. I don't know!" A note of frustration crept into his voice. "All I know is that she harbors hatred and resentment in her heart against me and my sister."

"I have nothing against Revaa, even though she lied during my trial," said Katyani. "Where is she?"

"I am here," came a clear voice. A black-clad, ponytailed figure stepped away from the shadows near the walls.

Katyani's heart somersaulted. Revaa's normally plump, cheerful face looked peaked and tense. Her eyes were red-rimmed, her lips set in a thin line.

"Revaa! What are you doing here?" Anger coursed through Bhairav's voice. "Go back to your room at once."

Revaa crossed the floor and came over to where Katyani stood. "I'd like to tell the court what really happened the night the royal family died, and why I lied about it."

Katyani stared at her, stunned, her thoughts thrown into disarray.

There was a moment's shocked silence, and then Bhairav vaulted out of the prisoner's box. Revaa shrieked and dived behind Katyani. Katyani lunged for Bhairav, but he danced out of her reach. Too late, she realized that he still had his sword. He punched her chest, making her stagger back in pain, and ran down the aisle.

The court attendees shot to their feet. "Stand down," warned Daksh. "Anyone who tries to help him will be punished."

He advanced on Bhairav, his sword out, and uttered the phrase to bind him.

But nothing happened. He'd burned himself out tying up all the guards. Katyani raced down the aisle after Bhairav. Before she could close the gap, he flung a handful of dust on Daksh's face and shouted the words of a spell.

Daksh toppled to the ground. Katyani cried out in alarm, unable to help herself. Bhairav ran past him to the doors.

Katyani stopped, torn between following Bhairav and checking on Daksh.

"Go," ordered Atreyi, bending over Daksh. "I'll take care of him."

"And I'll take care of everyone else," said Revaa, sweeping the court with hard eyes.

Katyani dashed out of the palace, hoping Daksh was all right.

The first light of dawn lit the eastern sky, illuminating a scene of chaos in the carriageway and garden. Groans of pain rent the air. Several soldiers lay trussed on the ground, moaning in agony. Others continued attacking the yatu, using bows and arrows, swords and spears. The yatu growled and tossed them away like paper dolls. Varun stood behind Papek, shouting instructions, his face unrecognizable in its battle fury.

There was nothing she could do here right now. Varun and the yatu had things under control. It was Bhairav who was her objective. She spied him slip out of the unguarded gates and sprinted down the carriageway after him, skirting the melee.

Bhairav ran across the grounds toward the domed entrance of an underground water tank. Katyani's pulse quickened. The secret tunnel to Kalinjar was through one of the tanks. He disappeared through the opening of the reservoir, and she raced up the steps after him.

It was dark and damp inside. Water dripped down the rock-cut walls and the distant roof. In each corner was a pillar, inscribed with Sanskrit shlokas. On the opposite wall was a massive carving of Shiva killing a demon. The tank was far below, lost in the darkness. Ninety-nine uneven, slippery steps wound their treacherous way down to the water level.

Boots slapped on wet stone, and she stiffened. He was going down the steps. She descended carefully, one hand on the slimy wall, the other holding her sword. A green light bobbed at the bottom, along the water's edge. What kind of light was he carrying? What powers did he possess that she still had no clue about? He'd felled Daksh with a single spell. True, Daksh had exhausted his powers, but even so, such a spell would have taken great skill to work on someone like him. Bhairav must have spent years honing his craft in secret. All those times he'd requested access to the forbidden section of the library, ostensibly to read magical history, he must have been teaching himself actual magic. Her insides roiled at his duplicity. How little they'd known him.

She strained her eyes and made out her quarry. "Bhairav! There's no escape. Turn yourself in."

Laughter echoed in the cavern below. "Catch me if you can."

The light disappeared into the wall.

Katyani inched her way down, heart in her mouth. She should have gotten a light. But she'd been so intent on catching up with him, she hadn't given it a thought.

Five steps short of the bottom, she slipped and fell. She landed hard on the clammy stone floor, the wind knocked out of her.

Slowly, she got her breath back and rose to her feet, wincing. No bones broken. Her shoulder only *felt* like it had been dislocated.

She hobbled to the wall where the green light had vanished, taking care not to fall into the dark, still water. The tank was over seven meters deep. She didn't want to take her chances swimming fully clothed with a sword in her hand and a bow on her back. At least her eyes had gotten used to the dim light that filtered through from the entrance far above. She could make out a narrow doorway embedded in the wall. Either Bhairav had been in too much of a hurry to close it, or he *wanted* her to follow him.

She squeezed herself through the slit in the wall. It was too dark to make out much more than the fact that she was in a broad tunnel. The green light bobbed ahead of her, beckoning.

She ran after it, her sandals landing on nameless things that crunched unpleasantly beneath her feet. Overhead, something squealed. She glanced up, and her gut clenched. Ghosts crawled across the ceiling, pale lumps of flesh with glittering red eyestalks that contained a world of madness within them. The eyestalks turned to follow her as she passed. *Katyani,* they whispered, *Katyani.*

No, don't look at them, or you will be in their thrall. She gripped her sword and kept running, ignoring the squelching and crunching beneath her feet, the crawling patches of phosphorescence on the walls. The tunnel was endless, the air dank and stale, but she fixed her gaze on the green light, closing the gap inch by inch.

She sensed the minute breath of a blade and threw herself to the ground. The broad, flat blade of a sword swung above her, narrowly missing her neck. She scrambled to her feet and backed away, heart thudding, her bronze sword held in front of her.

Bhairav detached himself from the wall, his movements fluid, his eyes filled with murder. Steel rang and sparks flew as he struck again, and she blocked his sword with her own.

"Why do you want to kill me?" she shouted, twisting out of reach and parrying his blows.

"Why can you not leave me alone?" he snarled. "I wanted to spare your life, Katya. But you leave me no choice."

He uncoiled Chentu, and her stomach seized. *Not Chentu, no.*

The whip struck her arm, burning her skin. She whirled and danced away, slashing the whip in two with her sword. Chentu gave an inhuman screech of pain. As it was falling through the air, she slashed it again, and yet again.

Bhairav threw down the remains of the whip and brought his blade down on her in an overhead strike. She raised her sword to block it and found empty air. Cold, sharp steel invaded her chest. She froze, stunned, unable to grasp what had happened.

He withdrew his blade, his face intent. It came out dark with blood. *Her* blood.

She slid down the wall, her hand clutching her chest as if she could stem the flow. But it seeped through her fingers, spilling out, taking her willpower and life force with it.

CHAPTER 24

S HE SLUMPED TO THE FLOOR, ON A BED OF FILTH AND BONES AND the empty shells of dead insects. Blood trickled down the dank walls in a steady *drip drip* that sounded unnaturally loud.

No, the blood spilled out of her, the wound a question to which she had no answer.

Teeth gnawed at her sandal. She bit back a scream and kicked, connecting with something solid. The movement sent fresh waves of agony into her chest.

The green light bobbed above her, a diffuse glow with a silvery streak at its heart. A *ghost*? How had Bhairav captured it?

"Does it hurt?" Bhairav bent over her, his face eerie in the green light. "Should I put you out of your misery?"

She summoned her failing strength. "You were my brother," she said, her voice sounding strange and distant to her own ears. "I trusted you."

"Unthinking trust is made to be trampled upon." He examined her with clinical detachment. "You never questioned why my father died and not Ayan's. Why I was not the crown prince, despite being older."

"The crown passes from the king to his eldest child." If she could keep talking, she could delay her end long enough to get out. She didn't want to die in this dark, foul place. The doorway was just half a mile behind her. She could make it out of here. She had to believe that.

"The Lunar dynasty traditionally bestowed the crown on the one who was most worthy of it." His voice hardened. "My father was just a couple of months younger than Jaideep. Shouldn't the succession be based on merit? I did what I did for *justice*."

Tears of rage and grief blurred her eyes. "Ayan was meritorious. He would have made an excellent king."

"So would I. But I knew, from an early age, I would never get the chance." He closed one hand in a fist. "Not unless I took it for myself. The chance so cruelly snatched away from my father."

"Your father died in battle, like a true soldier," she said, her breath coming in short, painful gasps.

Bhairav laughed, a cold, desolate sound that made her skin crawl. "My father died while asleep in the royal tent, *after* the battle, suffocated to death by a pillow. My mother was strangled by her own dupatta in her bedroom."

Katyani's mind reeled. No, that was not possible. She had misheard, or he was mistaken. *"Why?"* The word dragged out against her own will, because she could not, would not believe such a thing.

His face twisted. "After his father died in the war with Paramara, Jaideep saw his way clear to becoming king. The only person who blocked his path was his half brother Karandeep, who was brave and strong and deserving, who would not stand aside quietly while his less accomplished brother took the crown."

Katyani shook her head, even that small movement sending a stabbing pain through her body. "No. Jaideep wouldn't . . . you've been lied to."

He knelt beside her, his eyes burning into hers. Despite everything, she was glad of his nearness. At least he was human—the only other human in this monstrous space. "I wouldn't have believed it either if I hadn't seen it myself. Do you want to know? Do you want to hear what happened? It has poisoned my whole life. It will taint the hours you have left."

"They're . . . already tainted," she whispered. Her chest was a mass of pain, but that was nothing to the pain wracking her insides.

"Then listen. The night my mother was killed, I woke from a nightmare. I slipped out of my room and went to hers. Our rooms were connected by a door, but I didn't want to disturb her, so I stood behind the curtain and peeked inside. Sometimes, just looking at her was enough to calm my fears.

"But that night, I saw something strange. A man was bending over her, as if he were embracing her. Her body jerked, her legs drumming up and down on the bed. A sense of shame came over me. It was that shame that kept me silent until her body stilled, and the man withdrew. I saw his face in the moonlight, tears running down his cheeks. I couldn't understand why my mother's bodyguard was in her chamber, what he had been doing to her, and why he was crying. It was only much later that I understood. And I swore to myself I would never be so helpless again, that I would punish those who had killed my mother, and take the crown that should have been my father's."

"Bodyguard?" Pieces of the puzzle fell into place, making a horrifying picture. "You mean . . . ?" Her voice faltered.

"Tanoj," he said with a smile like a blade. "Our respected teacher, our lifelong protector, our assassin-in-chief. Why are you surprised? Jaideep tasked him with killing my parents. It was an act Tanoj never forgave himself for. But I forgave him. He was but a weapon. All I had to do was make that weapon mine."

"Not . . . only a weapon," she said with difficulty. "He warned the Acharya about the trial. He saved me."

His smile slipped. "Saved you for what? Dying alone in this dark place? I've already done what I set out to do. You can't change it."

"Jaideep killed his brother, so you killed yours?" The truth was a cruel shard pushing into her heart.

"Do you know how I felt every day bowing to the man who murdered my parents?" His voice shook with rage. "The only thing that kept me going was the knowledge I would kill him one day. Him and his wife and his beloved son, and all those faithless dogs in his council who helped him perpetuate the lie that my father died on the battlefield, my mother of grief."

"Ayan loved you," she whispered. Tears slid down her face. After Ayan died, after she lost everything, including her name, she'd thought she'd hit rock bottom. It wasn't possible to feel any worse. The human heart could not bear it. It would break, surely. Shut down, give up, beg for release. She'd been wrong about that. The capacity to feel pain was infinite.

"And you loved him," said Bhairav. "You loved him better than you ever loved me; isn't that true, Katya? Everyone did." An expression of amusement mixed with hatred crossed his face. "I wondered how I would live with myself after his death. But I found that I can live just fine. I sleep well at night. I no longer have nightmares of my mother, her bare legs kicking the bed, her purple tongue hanging out of her slack mouth."

Katyani shivered, coldness creeping into her limbs. *Keep him talking; keep him here.* "How did you become adept at magic?"

His face lost some of its harshness, becoming animated. "I taught myself. The palace library is a treasure no one appreciated, not Hemlata and certainly not Ayan. Oh, the queen tried, but she was a dabbler at best. The most impressive bit of magic she ever did was to bind you. But I—I must have inherited some of the powers of the Chandelas of old. I like to think so. I like to believe I was chosen. That everything I did, I did not for revenge, but because I was meant to be king."

Black spots danced before her eyes. "And Revaa? What does she think?"

He frowned. "I protected her from the truth for too long—my only mistake. It doesn't matter. Chandela needs a king. Without me, it will fall into chaos. Revaa will come around."

She swallowed, trying to stay conscious. "And me? How did I fit into your scheme?"

"You didn't." He tilted his head and regarded her. "To be honest, I've always liked you. Orphans stick together, right? But I knew you'd do your best to protect Jaideep, Hemlata, and Ayan. I tried to have them murdered, but your spies caught wind of my every plan. Tanoj was the one who got rid of them and brought Shamsher into the picture. He gave Shamsher the idea of using the yatu to kill the royal family. Shamsher had no clue Tanoj was working for me. And I had no idea what you meant to Shamsher, no idea Hemlata would transfer your bond to me. I didn't know what to do with you. I still don't. Well, I know what I *should* do. One more stab will finish you off, and it will be a kinder death than what lies in wait once I'm gone."

Don't go, she wanted to say, her heart finally shattering. *Don't leave me alone.*

"But a kind death is not what a warrior should wish for." Bhairav rose and sheathed his sword. "Good-bye, Katya."

He walked away, the ghost light bobbing above him, leaving her in darkness.

Katyani stared at the pale lumps of flesh on the ceiling, their eyestalks reaching toward her, as if to say: *Is it time? Are you finally going to die now?*

She'd had two beloved brothers. She'd had a home. She'd had a life. But it had all been a lie.

Not all of it. Ayan bent over her, his face glowing in the dark like a beacon. *Come on, Katya. Bind your wound. You still have a family to go home to. Did you forget the gurukul? Did you forget Daksh and Revaa?*

She made herself get up, biting her lips to stop from screaming. Her head swam, and she put a hand against the damp, disgusting wall to anchor herself. *You can do it,* she thought. *It's only pain, and pain has a beginning and an end.*

She tore off a long strip of her kameez and wrapped it tightly around her chest, sobbing with agony. Then she tore off another strip and did it again. Hopefully that would slow the flow of blood enough for her to remain conscious.

Fragmented whispers rose around her.

Now you are mine.

Now I will devour you.

Revenge . . .

Pieces of Chentu crawled up to her, hissing like snakes. Her hand scrabbled in desperation for her dagger and found a fragment of Chentu instead. It bit her palm, and she screamed, slapping it against the wall to dislodge it.

Her searching hands finally found her dagger. One of the pieces slithered up her arm and tried to burrow inside the wound the arrow had left. She grasped the end with one hand and hacked it off with the other, slicing a part of her skin with it. Her heart hammered inside her rib cage. She longed for an end to the darkness.

Demented laughter rose around her.

Cut me, and I become even greater. You cannot kill me.

Not with a blade, no. She crawled forward, her breath coming in short, agonizing gasps, searching frantically for her bow. She had numerous wounds, had spilled too much blood—blood that would draw things darker even than the demonic whip. She had very little time. Her fingertips brushed against a gleaming white shank bone, and she snatched her hand away, sensing the spirit it housed. The bone followed, making a knocking sound against the floor.

The walls glowed green and blue, a moving phosphorescence that grew eyes and watched her progress as she crawled on her hands and knees, leaving a dark, wet trail of blood. Behind her, something snuffled and lapped the ground. Terror clogged her throat, threatening to choke her.

Her trembling hands found the bow, and she clutched it, weeping with relief. The quiver was next to it; she reached inside for an arrow, and her gut clenched. It was empty. The arrows must have spilled. She fumbled on the floor with her hands, uncaring of the nasty debris that littered it. All she needed was one arrow. She sobbed when her hands found an unbroken shaft. She nocked it on her bow, drawing back the bowstring until it cut her flesh.

She didn't need a storm this time. She didn't need an explosion of fire. All she needed was a torch. She closed her eyes and pictured a bright, golden flame at the end of her arrow, lighting the passage, chasing away the shadows. When heat licked her fingers, she opened her eyes. Fire crackled at the tip of the arrow.

"Thank you," she whispered, setting down the bow.

A piece of Chentu wrapped itself around her neck and tried to strangle her. She slashed it with her dagger before throwing the pieces on the ground and thrusting the flaming arrow at them. They screamed as they burned, and a horrible smell assaulted her nostrils. She retched and grabbed another piece. One by one, she burned every bit she could find.

The last piece of the whip tangled itself in her hair. She grimaced and clenched it with one hand. She would burn it, even if it meant burning her own hair and scalp. She directed the flame at the fragment, ignoring its screams, ignoring her own pain and the smell of her burning hair.

When nothing but ash was left, three ghostly shapes rose above her head. Tears sprang to her eyes as she recognized the pretas.

They were terribly diminished, skeletal thin, all eyes and bones. But they remembered her. *Katyani,* they whispered in a faint chorus, *you did not forget us. May you find the light you seek.*

They disintegrated, and she wiped her eyes. She wouldn't let that blessing go in vain.

She held aloft the arrow, sweeping the passage with her precious flame. The bone that had followed her lay motionless on the ground, no doubt pretending to be an ordinary bone. The eyes on the wall had vanished with the light. Even the ghosts on the ceiling had retreated.

The wound on her chest was still bleeding despite the strips of cloth she'd wrapped around it. The battle with Chentu had drained her spiritual power. Her body was covered with numerous smaller injuries. The wise thing to do was to retrace her steps to the palace.

But Bhairav had gone in the *opposite* direction. If she didn't go after him now, she might never find him again.

She retrieved a couple more arrows, slung the bow and quiver on her back, and picked up her sword. A black wave of exhaustion rolled over her, and she leaned against the wall until it passed. Her lips were cracked, her throat as dry as dust. If only she had some water.

She began to walk, burning the last remnants of her spiritual power to keep moving. Without it, she would have collapsed by now. The bone followed at a discreet distance, knocking against the ground.

Something shuffled and licked the ground behind her. Despite herself, she stopped. The shuffling stopped too, but the lapping continued. A shiver ran through her. She was being followed by something that was, by the sound of it, drinking her spilled blood.

"What will you give me in return for the blood you're licking off the ground?" she asked, making her voice strong and clear.

Silence.

"You cannot drink if you will not pay, or I will curse you." She had no idea if she could, but it was worth making the threat.

What would be a fair price? came a faint, chilly voice.

She broke into a cold sweat. It had been a guess, nothing more, but she'd been right. Something darker than Chentu had found her. Well, she would bargain for her blood.

"Fetch me clean water in a bowl," she said. "A drink for a drink."

It did not answer, but the shuffling retreated.

She continued to limp forward, trying to ignore the pain searing her chest. But ignoring it didn't make it go away. Like a hungry wolf, it kept pace with her, watching for an opportunity to devour her.

After a while, the passage forked. She took the one on the left because the one on the right was too narrow for Bhairav to pass. *Bhairav, where are you going? What will you do now?* She thought of all the times they'd sparred together, all the times he'd held back, hiding his strength, his speed, his power. All the years he'd spent planning his revenge. How could you live with someone for so long and not know them at all?

The shuffling returned, accompanied by a dragging, clanking sound.

I have brought you water, came the voice.

She turned around, keeping her movements slow and deliberate. In the light of the arrow, she saw the being that had been feeding on her blood. It hunched low to the ground, a small, pitiful sack of a creature, gray-haired and gray-skinned, dressed in rags. In its hands was a small brass bucket, full to the brim.

She resisted the urge to fall on the bucket. "Show yourself."

Slowly, the creature raised its head. She gasped and took a step back.

Red-eyed and wrinkled with bulging veins on its forehead, it was as ugly as sin. But the truly horrifying thing was how its loathsome features resembled her own—the same upturned eyes, pointed chin, and full lips.

Its mouth opened in an ingratiating grin, showing rows of filed, blackened teeth.

"Pishacha," she said, realizing what it was with a sick twist of her gut. The rarest monster of all. "I didn't give you permission to copy my face."

Can't help it, it whined. *I have drunk of you.*

She swallowed. Pishacha had the ability to change face and form, but she didn't know if that depended on who they'd fed on.

I brought water from a well. It pushed the bucket toward her.

"Where is the well?" she asked.

It put its hands on its ears and shook its head. *A bad place. You cannot go there.*

More lies? But she had asked it for clean water, not for the source of the water. It had fulfilled its end of the bargain. She knelt and dragged the bucket over to herself, keeping an arm's-length distance with the pishacha. It leaned forward in anticipation as she bent over the bucket. She sniffed, but the dark liquid was odorless.

It is water, said the pishacha, sounding sulky. Clean *water. No blood, no urine, no feces, no spiders.*

Before it could go on to tell her what else wasn't in the water, she scooped a hand in and sipped. It tasted a bit musty, but it was water all right. She tilted the bucket to her mouth and drank deep, the life-giving liquid sliding down her throat like soma.

When she was done, she pushed the bucket away and got to her feet, feeling stronger. "All right. You can drink the blood I leave on the ground, but you cannot touch me or injure me in any way."

The creature darted forward and licked the blood that had seeped into the ground while she was kneeling. She shuddered and turned away from it. What kind of a non-life did it lead in these tunnels? What did it hope for? Was it capable of dreams? She'd never met a pishacha before. They were creatures of the dark, more so than even vetalas and pretas. They rarely interacted with humans. She had no idea how to get rid of it.

As she walked, her temporary strength ebbed away, and she felt worse than ever. Her head swam; her limbs fought to disobey her. She had trouble remembering why she was there. At last, she stopped and leaned against the wall, uncaring of the many-legged things that scurried away from her feet and hands.

She looked at the pishacha, and her heart lurched.

It was bigger, healthier, much more like her than before. If it stood, it would come up to her shoulders. Its hair and eyes had gotten darker, its skin more brown than gray.

"What are you doing to me?" she managed.

"Drinking the blood you've left on the ground," it answered in a voice eerily like her own. Her stomach roiled to hear it. She tried to swallow her fear and nausea. Why was she weak and dizzy even though she'd had a drink?

It was draining her of spiritual power. That must be it.

"That's not all you're taking from me," she said.

It crouched on the floor, summoning an injured expression. "Have I touched you?"

Not in a way she had noticed. Had the blood loss affected her to the point she could no longer think clearly?

She rubbed her aching head. What had they been talking about? She couldn't remember.

She began walking again, because it was that or freeze and die. The path forked; she hesitated a moment before choosing left at random.

"Not that way," said the pishacha. "He went right."

"How do you know?" she asked.

The pishacha didn't answer. Should she trust it? She couldn't think of a reason it would lie, and she didn't have the energy to question it. She barely had the energy to put one foot forward after another. Why was she doing this? She had no hope of winning a fight against Bhairav in this state.

She turned into the narrow, stifling corridor on the right. Eyeless worms wriggled away at the sound of her footsteps. Spiders as big as her palm scurried up the limestone walls, trying to escape the light of her flame. Several halting steps later, the passage broadened. She heard the sound of water. An underground stream?

The flame burned brightly at the end of the arrow, giving warmth to her shivering limbs. If nothing else, she still had this.

"Put out the light," said the pishacha.

She gripped the arrow and turned around, dreading what she would see.

The pishacha stood upright, barely half a head shorter than her. Its features were nearly identical to hers now. Even its rags had taken on the appearance and texture of her clothes.

She had two options. She could thrust the burning arrow into the face that so uncannily resembled her own. Or she could play along with it.

She would have chosen to fight but for the fact that right now, she could scarcely stay upright. If the pishacha overpowered her, she would die and be eaten and perhaps turn into a pishacha herself.

"Why should I put out the light?" she asked.

"He will see you," it said. "He's not far from here. I can see better in the dark."

She closed her eyes, fatigue, pain, and blood loss sapping her will. She wanted to curl up on the floor and give in. Let the pishacha do what it wished.

But aboveground, Daksh, Atreyi, and the yatu fought for her. Revaa needed her to return alive. And she needed the truth from Revaa; why had the princess lied during Katyani's trial? Had she known the depth of her brother's darkness? The Chandela dynasty hung by a thread. One snap, and it would be gone.

When she opened her eyes, the pishacha had crept closer.

"You've been sucking my spiritual energy," she said.

The pishacha neither confirmed nor denied this.

A frisson of anger went through her. "You've stolen what's not yours. I gave you permission to drink my fallen blood. That's all you asked for, and it's all I granted. You cheated."

"I can help you," it said in the voice that was both hers and not hers. "I can kill him."

"He isn't yours to kill," she said sharply. "He's mine."

"Then I can lead you to him," it said. "Without me, you'll never find him. But you must put out the light and follow me."

And now the face and voice were completely hers. How could she mistrust something that looked and sounded exactly like herself?

She blew out the flame, plunging herself in darkness.

The pishacha brushed past her, grasping her wrist. Its hand felt warm and alive. When it tugged, she followed. With each step, she seemed less herself, more something else—something that could see in the dark. The person before her—it was a person, wasn't it?—appeared tall, straight, and sure of herself.

After a while, the passage opened into a vast cavern with a black, still lake. By the edge of the lake crouched a man, drinking. A small green ghost light hovered next to him.

Alerted by the shuffle of her feet, he spun around, his hand grasping his sword. "Who's there?"

The woman leading her went still, and so did she. The man didn't see them. He put down his sword and bent his face to the water again.

The woman took Katyani's bronze sword and pushed her against the cavern wall, putting a finger to her lips.

That wasn't right. The bronze sword was *hers*. Uttam had given it to her. Katyani grasped the hand that held her sword and said, "No."

The man got up. This time, he spotted them in the shadows. "Katya? You are as persistent as a cockroach. You shouldn't have followed me."

He walked toward them, his ghost light bobbing above, his sword in his hand.

The woman wrested her hand away from Katyani and turned to face him. "You shouldn't have stayed."

"I found another way out of here," he bit out. "But you can't leave me alone, can you?"

The woman slashed his face with Katyani's sword. He barely blocked it in time. They began to fight in earnest, the cavern echoing with the clash of steel.

Fury burned through the fog in Katyani's brain. This was *wrong*. The woman couldn't take her sword like that. She unsheathed her dagger and held it in her palm, waiting.

The woman fought as well as Katyani at her best, whereas the man looked tired. He stumbled and fell, his sword clattering across the floor. As the woman brought her sword down to hack his body, Katyani let fly the dagger. It lodged itself at the base of the woman's neck, jerking her to a halt.

Bhairav—that was his name, how could she have forgotten?—took advantage of his attacker's momentary confusion to roll away and spring to his feet.

Katyani pushed herself away from the wall and ran, stumbling, toward the creature that had stolen her face. She grabbed her dagger and wrenched it out of its neck. Yellowish dust leaked out of the opening, filling the air with noxious fumes. "We're even now," she coughed. "Get lost."

The pishacha bared its teeth. It looked less like her than it had a few minutes ago. "I cannot be killed. I am already dead."

Bhairav grabbed his sword and fell into stance, his eyes narrowed. "What the hell is this?"

"Pishacha," hissed Katyani, glaring at it.

Bhairav thrust his sword into the creature's back. The tip of the blade emerged from its chest and nearly stabbed Katyani. She backed away, pain flaring inside her.

"I will eat flesh today," growled the pishacha, sliding out of the sword with ease. "Do not come between me and my prey." Its body had thickened, its face and voice a sickening blend of hers and Bhairav's. Without warning, it lunged toward him.

"Watch out!" screamed Katyani, and he lurched back, but the pishacha fastened its mouth on his neck. He gripped the monster's head with his hands, trying to wrench it away, his eyes wide with fear.

She grabbed her sword from where it had fallen on the floor and stabbed the creature in the back, twisting the blade until the flesh ripped and yellow dust choked the air. But the pishacha did not budge from Bhairav's neck. Katyani withdrew her blade, exhausted with the effort, blood trickling down her chest.

There was no point trying to stab it or cut it. The only things it appeared to be afraid of were fire and light. But her mind was too scattered, her body too weak to summon fire.

Bhairav screamed and fell. He kicked his legs as the pishacha sucked his blood.

No. She couldn't let him die like this.

She cast her eyes about, desperate for a weapon. The only thing she saw was the ghost light, casting a green glow over the ghastly scene. Maybe the ghost would help if she freed it? She hobbled toward it, biting back her pain, and slashed it with her sword, uttering the words that accompanied preta-expelling rituals.

There was a small squeal and the light vanished, plunging them in darkness.

Great. Now she couldn't see what was happening. She was about to stumble in Bhairav's direction and grapple the pishacha when a soft voice whispered in her ear:

Thank you for freeing me.

She started. "Preta?"

I am an ordinary spirit, lady.

Her heart sank. "Then you cannot help us against that creature."

No. But you can. Pishacha feed on negative energy, on hurt and sadness, anger and suffering. It found you because you were in pain and feeling miserable. If you can conquer your negative emotions, you can conquer the pishacha.

How was she supposed to do that? Her chest felt like it was on fire. Her body was covered with wounds. She had zero spiritual power left.

"Katyani . . ." gasped Bhairav.

She *would* save him, no matter how impossible it seemed. She settled in the lotus pose, forcing stillness on her shaking limbs. "Listen to me, Bhav. We can defeat the pishacha. Will you do as I say?"

"Yes," he said through gritted teeth.

"Empty your mind," she said. "Keep the pishacha away from your face and neck if possible, but think nothing. Close your eyes and count your breaths. The more fearful you are, the easier it is for the pishacha to drain you."

He fell silent. One by one, Katyani picked up each negative emotion, examined it, and put it aside. Yes, she was in terrible pain. But it was only her physical body that suffered, and the body was just a shell. It would die or it would heal, so why should she be distressed by it?

Next, she thought back to her encounter with the pishacha. She'd been angry and afraid, burning the pieces of Chentu. It was the violence of her kill that had drawn the pishacha. Similarly, it was her desire to take revenge on Bhairav that had given the creature a hold over her. Her fear of the pishacha had made it stronger.

But she no longer wanted revenge on Bhairav, and she was no longer afraid of the pishacha. It was a thing of the dark, but the dark had an end. If Bhairav was here, it meant he'd found an opening aboveground not far off. And even if she was wrong about that, wasn't light and dark an aspect of her own mind? Could she not see light even in this hellish place haunted by the bones of the dead? All she had to do was summon Daksh into her mind, the memory of his kiss, or one of his rare smiles, and the darkness was banished. She could recall the brightness of the gulmohar he'd left on her windowsill. And more, so much more: the smell of the earth after the first monsoon rain. The blush of roses in spring. The scent of night-blooming jasmine. There was a world of light out there; she just had to remember it.

"Remember how we used to play hide-and-seek?" she said. "I always won."

He grunted. "I let you win."

She smiled. Why were her cheeks wet? "You found this place, and none of us did, so I guess you won after all."

"I'm going to die here," he said, his voice thin.

"No, you're not. I'm going to get you out. Can you hold your hand out to me?"

"It's still too strong," he whispered.

She crawled toward him. "Keep talking. What was your favorite sweet?"

"You know," he said. "Laddus."

"Yes. I used to steal them from the kitchen for you when we were kids." She put out a tentative hand and touched someone's back. It stiffened. She stroked it, knowing Bhairav would sense her touch, even through the pishacha. "You're my brother, just as much as Ayan was. You know that, don't you?"

"Even after everything I've done?"

"Yes," she said, because it was true. "Let me take you into the light. Give me your hand."

"The pishacha . . ."

"It has no place between us," she said, more sure of herself with every word. "You and I have unfinished business, but it's nobody else's business. Trust me?"

"Yes," he said. "I'm letting go."

A hand grasped hers, and she squeezed it, at the same time elbowing aside the pishacha that was sitting on his chest. It felt light and hollow to the touch, as if she'd starved it with her words. It gave a tired hiss as she pushed it aside, but it did not speak.

She put an arm under Bhairav's head and helped him sit up.

"Where's the opening?" she asked.

"Back to the passage, straight ahead for half a mile," he said between gasps. "Then the passage curves right, and you climb up into a cave."

"Let's go, shall we?" She helped him stand, and together they made their way out of the cavern.

It was difficult walking with Bhairav leaning on her. She kept up a cheerful monologue, talking of the games they'd played as children, the fights they'd had, the punishments they'd endured. It was not just to remind him but also to remind herself who they'd been and what they'd meant to each other. It hadn't been a lie, any of it. No matter what murderous schemes he'd been hatching in his tortured mind, he was also the boy she'd stolen sweets for, the boy she'd sworn to protect along with Ayan and Revaa.

He stumbled several times, and he kept needing breaks, leaning against the wall to get his breath back. She never let him rest for too long; it might become impossible to start again.

At last, the passage curved right, and the path sloped upward. Her eyes sensed light up ahead. "We're almost there."

"Too late for me." His teeth chattered.

"Don't say that." She squeezed his arm. "It's never too late, not for any of us."

But he didn't answer. At the next step, he fell to the ground. She grabbed hold of him, nearly falling herself.

"Don't leave me." His voice was so frail, she could barely make out the words.

"I won't leave you," she said fiercely, tears welling up in her eyes. "I'm taking you out if it's the last thing I do."

She bent over, slipped her arms under his armpits, and dragged him upward. Her chest hurt worse than ever. With every step, blood seeped out of her bandage. Sweat dripped into her eyes; she paused to wipe her face with a sleeve, and her head swam. Was she going to faint?

You can do this, said Ayan from behind her. *You're the strongest person I know.*

"Ayan," she sobbed. "Help me."

He bent beside her and helped her pull Bhairav up, one step at a time. When she turned to look directly at him, there was no one beside her. Still, it gave her the strength to keep going. When light filtered into the passage, she wept with relief. "We're here. Are you listening? Just a little bit more."

Bhairav's head slumped backward; he must have passed out. She bit her lip until it bled. He would be fine once they were outside. They'd *both* be fine. They'd leave all their nightmares behind in these hellish tunnels.

He'd be free of his darkness, and she'd be free of her pain. His crimes might be unforgivable, but she didn't have to forgive him. She just had to save him.

Finally, the passage opened into a small cave filled with daylight. After so long underground, the light dazzled her, and she had to rub her eyes with her hands to make sense of what she was seeing.

The mouth of the cave was barely thirty feet away. Outside was green grass and sunlight. "Come on, Bhav," she begged. "Wake up. See the light?"

But Bhairav did not move.

She paused to get her breath back, to let the ferocious pain in her chest ease a little, and dragged him all the way out of the cave. They emerged onto a small, grassy copse overlooking the Ken River, the sun so bright it hurt her eyes. She collapsed on the ground next to Bhairav, feeling as if she'd been reborn.

"We made it." She put an arm around him, crying. "We're safe."

Bhairav's eyes stared sightlessly into hers, the two whites shining emptily in a blood-drenched face.

She shook him, heart clenching. "Bhav? Don't try to fool me now."

But Bhairav would never try to fool her again.

CHAPTER 25

HOW LONG DID SHE SIT BESIDE HIM, WAITING FOR HIM TO speak, to stir, to wake? It could have been hours or minutes. She rubbed his hand between hers and repeated a mantra for good health, disoriented and confused.

But Bhairav's heart refused to beat; his lungs refused to take another breath. *He's dead,* she thought, unable to believe it. *Dead.*

She closed his eyes with her palm, her tears washing away the blood on his face. She wept not just for him, but for those whom he had killed: the queen who had raised her, the grandfather she'd never known, and above all, the brother who should have been king. She laid her head on his chest and fell into a stupor.

A while later, she was moved, lifted onto a stretcher of some kind, but the pain was too great, and she passed out.

When she woke, she found herself in her old room in the palace, her chest thoroughly bandaged. It was late evening, and a lamp had been lit in one corner. She appeared to be naked beneath a thin sheet, her body covered in pastes and numerous smaller bandages. A smell of honey and neem permeated the air. Her head spun, and knives of pain stabbed her chest. She turned, hoping to see a glass of water, and found Revaa instead.

The princess sat on a chair beside her bed, head lolling back. She was dressed in plain white. Mourning clothes.

Mourning her brother.

Katyani's eyes dimmed. She'd thought she could save Bhairav. But she hadn't. She hadn't saved anyone. She gave a quiet sniff.

Revaa started. "You're awake." She leaned forward and touched

Katyani's forehead. "Your fever broke yesterday, but the vaidya said it would take longer for you to wake up."

"Water," said Katyani through cracked lips.

"Oh, right." Revaa picked up a glass from a tray and helped her sit up. Katyani's chest screamed in protest. She told it to shut up.

She drained the glass and leaned back, exhausted. "I'm sorry about Bhairav."

Revaa wiped the tear that had rolled down Katyani's cheek. "No, *I'm* sorry. I'm sorry I got scared, that I lied during the trial. Bhairav told me he would use the bond to kill you unless I did as he asked. I thought I was saving you, but all I did was condemn you."

So *that's* why she'd lied. It made a horrible sort of sense. Revaa had never been interested in magic and would not have known the limits of what Bhairav could do while he was bonded to her. "What happened after I was taken by the yatu?" asked Katyani. "I told you to remain hidden."

"I did remain hidden!" Revaa's eyes became flinty. "When Bhairav entered, I heard him give orders to remove the bodies, like he'd known this was going to happen. Tanoj found me, and Bhairav flew into a rage, telling me I shouldn't be there, that I could have been killed. Then I knew he'd planned it all."

"I couldn't save him," said Katyani. "There was a pishacha underground. He . . ." She stopped, unable to go on. Her eyes blurred as she remembered his last words: *Don't leave me.* But he'd been the one to leave her.

Revaa squeezed her shoulder. "You can tell me later. We gave him the last rites four days ago, but truly, I lost my brother the day he had Uncle, Auntie, and Ayan killed."

Something hard and knotted inside Katyani loosened. *I still have my sister. But how much did she know?* "Did he tell you why he did it?"

Revaa hung her head, twisting her hands on her lap, seeming to shrink into herself. "He wanted to be king because he was older. He thought it wasn't fair that Ayan was the crown prince." Her breath hitched. "I . . . I didn't realize this was something he wanted so badly he was willing to kill his own family for it."

So Bhairav hadn't told Revaa that Jaideep was responsible for killing their parents. He'd protected her from that devastating knowledge.

Katyani would keep her silence too. Let innocent Revaa believe her brother to be the only villain in this whole affair. It was only half the truth, but perhaps the complete truth would be too much for her. Besides, Katyani had only Bhairav's word for what had happened in the past. Those who could have confirmed it were all dead.

"How long was I unconscious?" she asked. Her chest itched and burned. She wished she could unpeel her bandages and dunk herself in cold water.

"Five days," said Revaa, raising her head. "The vaidya said the wounds on your body will heal, even the one on your chest, which needed multiple stitches both inside and outside. But it will take a long time for you to recover your spiritual strength." She paused, and some of the tension leached away from her face and shoulders. "Your Daksh visits morning and evening to meditate by your bedside. I don't know what he thinks he's doing, because it's not possible to transfer spiritual energy to another person. But no one dares tell him that."

Katyani drew the sheet up to her chin, horror stirring within her. "He's been seeing me in *this* condition?"

"Why are you worried? You're covered in bandages." A small, mischievous grin lit up Revaa's face. "Besides, I always have one of the palace maids stand in a corner while he's here. Can't have you unchaperoned, even if it's your Daksh."

"He's not *my* Daksh," said Katyani, her face heating at what he'd think if he heard Revaa say that. "He's his own person."

"And yet, he won't leave as long as you're ill," said Revaa, her grin widening. "And yet, he risked his life to help you. And yet, when they brought you to the palace on a stretcher, he pushed everyone out of his way, including the vaidya, to take your pulse and assure himself you were alive."

A warm glow suffused her at Revaa's words. He cared about her, just as she cared about him. She remembered the condition she'd left him in, and anxiety seized her. "Is he all right? Was he injured?"

Revaa sprang up from the chair. "I'll let you see for yourself. He gave me strict orders to inform him as soon as you were awake. Me, the crown princess of Chandela!" she added in a tone of mock horror.

Of course, Revaa was the only one left in the direct line to inherit the crown. "Aren't there some distant cousins?" Katyani asked. "Anyone who might give you trouble?"

"They'll try," said Revaa, her expression becoming serious. "Prince Okendra has already sent a letter saying he's 'happy to step in and fill the vacuum.' I can't deal with the hyenas on my own. Will you be my regent until I'm twenty-one?"

Bhairav's words came back to her. *Are you envious? Do you wish I had died too? There would be nothing to stop you being regent.*

Pain squeezed her heart. "I don't want to be regent. I don't *know* how to be regent."

"Well, I don't know anything about being queen." Revaa joined her hands together, her eyes wide. "Please, Katya. We'll learn together."

Katyani exhaled, trying to let go of the past. But the past clung to her like skin to bone. "I'll think about it."

Revaa gave her a brilliant smile, as if she'd already said yes. "I'll get your Daksh." She winked and left the room.

Katyani made sure the sheet was around her shoulders. She just had time to wish her chest would stop hurting and she could comb her hair and brush her teeth before there was a knock on her door. Daksh entered, followed by a palace maid.

He came straight to her bed and halted, without speaking, as if words had deserted him. But his eyes spoke volumes as they lingered on her. He looked unharmed, recovered from whatever spell Bhairav had cast. Her heart lifted, as it always did in his presence.

"How are you?" he asked at last, his mellow voice like balm to her soul.

"Alive," she said, making her tone light, "which is better than the alternative." Her gaze went to the palace maid who had stationed herself against a wall. "Where's Chaya?"

The maid bowed. "My lady, she was dismissed by order of the prince—king—of the *traitor* Bhairav. A message has been sent to her home village, asking her to return."

Relief flooded Katyani. Chaya was unhurt. "Leave us," she ordered. "Close the door behind you." No way she was going to be "chaperoned" while she was awake and conscious. This was a chance to be alone with Daksh, and she wouldn't let anyone take it from her.

The maid hesitated. "But, my lady—"

"Leave," Katyani barked. *"Now."*

The maid scuttled away, no doubt to report to Revaa.

Katyani leaned back, breathing hard. Even this brief interaction had cost her.

Daksh sat on the chair Revaa had vacated, his face full of concern. "You need to get your strength back. I have given the kitchen the recipe for a healing soup made of turmeric, neem leaves, mushrooms, and various healthful herbs. It should be here any minute."

No no, not his soup. "I'm all right." She tried to smile. "Don't worry about me. How about you, do you have injuries?"

"Flesh wounds," he said dismissively. "Nothing worth mentioning."

"And the others?"

"All fine," he said. "Atreyi and Varun have returned to the gurukul. The yatu are back in Nandovana."

But he had stayed with her. Warmth spread throughout her body.

There was a knock on the door. A serving boy entered, carrying a tray with a bowl on it, followed by the same maid Katyani had sent away earlier. A dubious aroma wafted from the bowl to her nostrils.

"Ah, good. Give it to me." Daksh took the tray and balanced it on his knees. He looked up at the two attendants. "You may leave. I don't need help feeding her."

Katyani bit back a grin at their shocked expressions. Daksh was learning fast.

But he seemed to be serious about feeding her. He waited for the door to close, then scooped up a spoonful and blew on it, his face intent. He held it out to her mouth.

"I can feed myself," she protested, both touched and embarrassed. "I'll have it later." In truth, it smelled *very* strange, and she didn't want it at all. She remembered all too well how the previous one had tasted.

"Please indulge me," said Daksh gently. "This is a recipe handed down from my mother. It's extremely effective."

How could she say no after that? She opened her mouth and allowed him to tip the spoon into her mouth. The taste was as dubious as the aroma, but she barely noticed it. She was too busy gazing at him instead: the little frown of concentration as he made sure no drops trickled down her chin, how he blew on the next spoon to cool it down, the way he leaned forward to feed her but was careful not to touch her by mistake.

Had anyone cared like this for her? She couldn't remember. It made her feel all safe and happy inside. And inexplicably sleepy. Here was someone who would keep the shadows away while she slept.

Spoon by spoon, he fed her the entire bowl. When she was done, he dabbed her lips with the tips of his fingers, a smile lighting up his face. "Thank you for indulging me. Now you should sleep."

Oh no, she wasn't letting him go that easily. She'd had the entire bowl of soup; she needed a reward for that. She caught his hand as he made to get up. "Stay with me."

His smile deepened. "Gladly. But the princess will likely send someone to check on us every few minutes."

"Don't care." She snuggled into her pillow, keeping a firm hold on his hand. "Indulge me."

He gave a low laugh and stroked her head with his other hand. A tingle of warmth went through her at his touch. "You scared me," he whispered. "I thought I'd lost you."

"I thought I was lost too, but there was light, and it was inside me," she muttered sleepily. "And the light was you."

She might have babbled some more, but at some point, she drifted off. She woke sometime later, afraid he would be gone, but he was still there, sitting on the chair with his eyes closed. His poor hand was still trapped in hers. She let it go, placing it gently on his lap. He opened his eyes and gave her a look of such tenderness that it was all she could do not to pull him down beside her. She wanted to cup his face in her hands and kiss every inch of it. She wanted to wrap her arms around him and hold him tight against her heart. *Curse these bandages and this weak, wounded flesh!*

"You must be tired," she said, summoning a solicitous tone. "You should lie down too."

His lips twitched. "You told me to stay here."

"This bed is big enough for both of us." She patted the side of her bed, knowing she was pushing her luck but unable to stop herself. "You can lie down right here."

"And risk hurting you?" He shook his head. "Ask me once your wounds heal and those bandages come off." He realized what he had said, and the blood rose up in his face.

"Is that a promise?" she purred, her skin heating at the thought of him in bed with her. "I ask, and you will agree?"

"It depends what you ask for," he retorted. "I should leave now. Revaa peeked in once, and her spies have entered on some pretext or other multiple times. The lamp oil has been replenished twice. I think they mean to burn this room down."

Katyani laughed, then winced as the movement brought a fresh wave of pain to her chest. "My sister has suddenly become overprotective of me."

"You're all she has left," he said somberly. "If she is to be queen, she needs someone she can trust by her side."

"She asked me to be her regent," said Katyani.

An unreadable expression crossed his face. "As I expected. A wise move on her part. Have you agreed?"

Katyani considered. "I think I will. She has led a sheltered life, whereas I've been exposed to every kind of palace intrigue. I know most of the ambassadors and courtiers. It will take a long time to weed out those who are disloyal. She cannot do it alone. Besides, it will be a more interesting job than being a bodyguard. No knowing when someone will try to stab you in the back."

He shook his head in exasperation. "I would have thought you'd had enough of being stabbed to last a lifetime."

The pain in her chest flared in agreement. "Oh, I *have*. I intend to be the one doing the stabbing. Bhairav's web was deep and wide, all the way from here to Kalinjar. I shall enjoy cutting it wide open and watching the little spiders flee for their lives."

A mask of calm fell on his face. "It is your duty. And I have mine. Now that you're better, I should return to the gurukul."

The thought of him leaving brought the shadows back, crowding at her bedside, waiting to pounce. She leaned back and gave a huge sigh.

"I'm in a lot of pain. I feel quite weak. It's that soup of yours. It has sapped my strength completely."

He smiled. "I will stay until you are well. And I will make sure you drink the soup every day. You need all your strength to chase away those spiders. And if you find that Bhairav had an accomplice in the burning of Nandovana, I would be interested to know."

Katyani pursed her lips. "I don't think Bhairav set fire to Nandovana at all."

"What?" His forehead creased. "It was his arrow."

"But he said he didn't do it, and I believe him. Tell me, what possible reason could he have for declaring war against the Acharya?"

Realization dawned on his face. "Someone did it to frame him."

"Exactly. I think it was Tanoj—the only person Bhairav could have shared the Acharya's mantras with."

"Why would Bhairav's lifelong accomplice turn against him?" he asked.

"Balance," she said, gathering her thoughts. This was the last piece of the puzzle. "That's what he said when I asked him why he'd saved me by sending that anonymous message. He hinted he'd done something else too; he said I'd figure it out. He was bound to Bhairav, bound by the vow he'd made to a child whose parents he'd killed. But he cared about things like right and wrong, and he hated what he had become, what Bhairav had become."

Daksh gave a slow exhale. "So he set the forest on fire to force my father's intervention?"

She nodded. "He didn't know the Acharya was gone."

"It sounds like you've solved the last mystery." Daksh gave her an approving nod. "You can be at peace now."

"There's one more thing." She hesitated. She'd debated telling anyone about how she'd sensed Ayan's presence after his death. After all, it could have been her imagination or wishful thinking. But a part of her didn't believe that, and she ended up telling Daksh about each of the four times Ayan had helped her. The telling hurt, forcing her to relive the most difficult moments of her life. Tears slid down her cheeks, and her throat ached.

Daksh took her hand in his own, his touch soothing her. He'd scooted closer as she talked, his face attentive and grave. "What do you want to do about it?" he asked when she was done.

"I'm not sure." She wiped her eyes with the edge of her sheet. "He already got the last rites."

"But you were not present for them," he said. "You didn't get a chance to say good-bye. Maybe that's what you need to do."

She sniffled. "How?"

"Find an item that meant something to both of you. When you are well, I will accompany you to the Ken River, and we will say good-bye together."

His words comforted her, as they always did. When he left, she was plunged into gloom. His presence did not lessen her grief, but it strengthened her. She could put grief aside, she could smile and laugh even through her pain.

But now that he was gone, the pain returned in full force. The awful soup he had made her drink threatened to eject itself from her much-abused body, and she had to summon all her willpower to keep it down. Her thoughts kept going in circles around him. He cared for her; she knew that now, but what did he truly feel? She'd promised the Acharya she would take care of him. But how? If anything, it was Daksh who was taking care of *her*.

The rest of the night was long and difficult, and so were the days that followed, alleviated only by visits from Daksh and Revaa. The princess brought news of the court and asked for her advice, which she willingly gave. This was something she would have done for Ayan, too, had he lived. She would have been his most trusted advisor, and he her king. She wept anew at her loss, at Chandela's loss. What evil men did to satisfy their greed. They forgot they would leave the world empty-handed, just as they had entered it. It was not something she would let Revaa forget, at least.

Daksh gave Revaa sound advice as well, for which Katyani was grateful. He appeared in the audience hall a couple of times, his grave presence, sky-blue robes, and the famous sword giving pause to anyone who was foolish enough to make trouble.

Chaya returned, full of joy at Katyani's reinstatement and anxiety at the state of her health. Once she was assured Katyani would live, she turned her attention to Katyani's appearance. "My lady, what have you done to your hair?" she wailed, lifting knotted clumps of it in her hands.

"Nothing?" said Katyani, which was mostly true. "Wait, some of it burned. Maybe we should chop it all off."

"Never!" A look of grim determination came over Chaya's face. "Now that you have such a handsome and well-groomed admirer, I shall make sure you look presentable. It's *my* reputation at stake."

"What do you mean?" shouted Katyani as Chaya hurried away. Did the entire palace have nothing better to do than gossip? What sort of rumors were they spreading about her and Daksh?

Chaya returned a little later with a variety of combs and oils. Katyani submitted to her attentions, too weak to resist, knowing she should be grateful for the concern.

A week later, the bandage on her chest was replaced, and most of the other ones removed. "Can I leave my room now?" she asked the vaidya as he unspooled a fresh roll of bandage for his assistant to wrap around her.

"As long as you're careful," said the vaidya, smearing a nasty-smelling yellow-green paste on her chest. The pain flared, and she tried not to wince. "You can walk; do not try to run. Especially do not try to fight. If you break your stitches, you can find another vaidya."

She hid her jubilation. "Yes, Airya."

As soon as the vaidya was gone, she got Chaya to help her wash up and dress. Then she hobbled out and asked one of the attendants at the door to fetch Daksh. He arrived, his expression thunderous, ready to scold her, but she forestalled him, explaining the vaidya had said she could leave her room. "I'm going for my first walk," she said. "Coming?"

He fell into step beside her. "Of course."

When they came to the stairs, he offered her his arm. She leaned against it, more for the feel of him than the support, which wasn't unwelcome either. They climbed down, and a sense of unreality gripped her. Any moment, she would hear Hemlata's bell-like laughter, or Ayan and Bhairav ribbing each other, or Jaideep's deep voice describing one of his battles.

"You okay?" murmured Daksh, scanning her.

She smiled at him, returning to herself, grateful for his presence. "I'm fine." Without him, the strangeness of being here without her family would have overwhelmed her.

Palace staff bowed to her as she passed. What a difference it made, having cleared her name! These same people would have thrown her in boiling oil mere weeks ago. She didn't trust any of them, of course. She would have a fine time interviewing them one by one, watching them squirm until they revealed the full extent of their culpability.

Outside, the roses were in full bloom. She inhaled their heady scent in pleasure. One of the things Bhairav had loved most about the month of Chaitra were the roses. A wave of sadness engulfed her as she thought of how he had died. At least she hadn't left him in the dark.

They crossed the garden, the sweet grass springy beneath their feet. She still held on to Daksh's arm, although it was not strictly necessary. They approached the first temple: a stone edifice with carved pillars open on all four sides, a plump statue of Ganesha within. This was where Tanoj had died. Katyani drew a shaky breath and pressed on to the second temple, which was built around an old peepal tree. She let go Daksh's arm and collapsed on the steps outside, exhausted.

Daksh gazed at her in concern. "You have over-strained yourself. You should go back to your room and lie down."

"It's nice here in the sun. I can smell the roses." She peered up at him, shading her eyes. There wouldn't be a better time to ask him how he felt about her. She knew the words she wanted to hear but was unable to bring herself to ask him directly. Suppose he said something like *you're my good friend and that's it*? She'd beat him up and be bedridden for another week. "Daksh, why did you leave gulmohar flowers in my hut when I was ill?"

He started. "What makes you think of them now?"

Katyani poked his leg. "Please don't answer a question with a question. It indicates an unwillingness to answer honestly."

He frowned. "You could not go out, and the gulmohar blooms so briefly. I thought you might like a bit of color in your hut."

"Thank you," said Katyani, sighing. No confessions of love yet. "Second question: Why did you not speak to me for weeks when I returned from the preta-expelling mission with the gurukul women?"

He opened his mouth, but she held up a hand. "Honest answers only."

He took a deep breath. "I have always been honest with you. But possibly not as forthcoming as you are yourself."

"The only thing you mentioned was the incident during your mother's death anniversary," she said, her voice gentle, not wanting to hurt him with the memory. "I asked why you had not spoken of it earlier, but you didn't respond."

Daksh raked a hand through his hair and sat down next to her. "Those two weeks you were away, I thought of you every single day. I couldn't get you out of my mind. I was jealous of everyone you spent time with. It made me angry."

She stared at him, surprise and warmth pooling in her stomach. *Why were you jealous?* she wanted to ask. "Why were you angry?" she asked instead.

"Because it made me unfit for my position at the gurukul," he said. "Besides, I knew you would not stay. I knew your fate would take you elsewhere. I tried hard not to be affected by you. I tried to keep my distance. But ultimately, it was impossible."

Katyani's cheeks heated. "You should have told me how you felt." *You should tell me more clearly what you are feeling right now,* she wanted to scream.

He smiled. "It was not the right time. It wouldn't have changed anything. It might even have hindered you in some way. Now I have answered two questions, can I ask one of my own?"

Her heart skipped a beat. "Ask away."

He looked at her seriously. "Is my soup really that bad?"

She burst out laughing, and pain stabbed her chest. "Ouch." She held herself in, trying to calm down. She might as well forget about getting any confessions from him. "What kind of person are you? You ought not to be making me laugh. Can't you see the condition I'm in?"

"It was an honest question," he said in a reproving tone. "Honest answers only."

"All right, the honest answer is that the taste is very odd, but I don't care, because it's your mother's recipe, and if you think it is beneficial, I will drink it every day." She grinned. "My only condition is that you have to feed me."

A smile lit up his face, and she had a sudden desire to caress his lips with her fingertips. He was so beautiful it hurt. "I have more healthy recipes," he said eagerly. "In fact, I have an entire notebook of them. Many are my own inventions. But I don't know if they'll taste good."

She waved a hand. "Go to the kitchen and demand whatever you need. Tell them you have royal permission. I am willing to be the subject of all your culinary experiments." She would eat anything he cooked if it made him happy.

He took her word for it. That evening, he arrived in her room bearing a pale yellow liquid that was less soup, more stew, with suspicious lumps of an unidentified vegetable floating in it. But he was so excited about his preparation, so filled with anticipation at her reaction, she didn't have the heart to tell him it tasted like a gourd that had passed through a sick cow. In truth, when he fed her anything, she stopped being able to taste the dish itself. His hands had a magic of their own that transformed the most awful medicine into a mercifully bland glop.

Every day after that he supervised the preparation of a new dish for her filled with medicinal herbs, bitter roots, unknown vegetables, and interesting fungi. The day came when her chest bandage came off, and she could no longer pretend to be even a little bit sick. Perhaps his cooking had something to do with her speedy recuperation. He certainly seemed to think so. Her relief at her recovery was tempered by the depressing thought that he would leave soon. He'd only promised to stay until she was well.

At sunrise the next day, he accompanied her to the Ken River, as he had promised. When he saw the scabbards in her hand, he raised his eyes. *"Swords?"*

She caressed the scabbards lovingly. She'd managed to find both her own sword and Ayan's in the armory. "We must have sparred with these a thousand times. They're sister swords, and they'll keep each other company. And I have my own bronze sword now: the triplet to yours and your brother's."

He smiled. "Of course."

This early in the morning, there was no one at the banks of the river. She was glad of this. She unsheathed the swords and laid them on the ground. Daksh sprinkled drops of water on them and began the last rites.

She stood next to him, listening, holding Ayan in her heart. The sun rose into the sky, casting its red-gold light on the blades. She remembered all the times they'd played and sparred together, all the dreams he'd confided in her. Dreams she'd have to help Revaa fulfill in his absence.

Be at peace, Brother, she thought, her eyes stinging. *I love you forever.*

She tipped both the swords into the river. They sank with barely a ripple, vanishing from her sight as Daksh concluded his mantras.

Over the next few days, he helped her say good-bye to Hemlata, Jaideep, Bhairav, and Shamsher as well. When all the little rites were done, she felt wrung out, but also light and free, as if each death had been a rock that she'd finally managed to set down.

The first "official" thing Katyani did was to call on an elderly palace cartographer to draw her a map of the old yatu territory in Chandela. Once Revaa learned of their history, she agreed it was right and just to give them back their land, as long as they could be held to a mutual treaty of do-no-harm. Katyani sent a message to the gurukul, outlining her plan and requesting mediation with the yatu.

The next thing she did was write letters to Nimaya, the Kalachuri royal family, and Aditya. The one to Nimaya was easy; it would pass through multiple hands before reaching the Solanki princess, so she kept it short and sweet, saying she was well and hoped they would keep in touch.

The one to the Kalachuris was easy too: a flowery note canceling Revaa's engagement with the crown prince. They might not like it, but they would understand. Revaa wasn't going anywhere. She was the future queen of Chandela.

The one to Aditya was far more difficult. She wrote and rewrote it multiple times before reducing it to a formal invitation to her coronation as regent. Perhaps he would accept the invitation or send an envoy to the Chandela court. Or he might ignore it altogether. Still, she'd done her duty. She hoped he would do his. She didn't dare hope for more than that.

The ceremony to anoint her as the regent of Chandela was a long, arduous affair held in the main audience hall of the palace, attended by the full court and all of Revaa's distant relatives. Prince Okendra arrived with his entire clan, resplendent in brocade and gold, his hawkish eyes agleam. Katyani had a long, exhausting conversation with him that was like fencing, except with words. He took great pains to assure her of his loyalty and his complete ignorance of how the yatu had entered Kalinjar Fort. She smiled and said nothing. In time, she would find the truth of his words.

She made a point of talking to every cousin, aunt, uncle, and palace official at the gathering. Revaa had forced her to dress up for the occasion in a gorgeous red sari with a gold border. Chaya had piled her hair in a topknot and adorned it with silver jewelry. Katyani had drawn the line at any makeup, but even so, she could scarcely recognize herself in the mirror.

"You look stunning," whispered Revaa while Katyani smiled and bowed to the ambassador of the Chalukyas. They stood at the doorway of the audience hall for the sake of the fresh breeze that swept in from the hall beyond it. "Your Daksh must be awestruck by your beauty."

A frisson ran through her. Did he think her beautiful?

"He's not my Daksh," she said. *But I want him to be.*

She scanned the glittering crowd but didn't spot him anywhere. He'd been present at the beginning of the affair, but perhaps he'd gotten fed up. She didn't blame him.

But having noticed his absence, she couldn't tolerate it. She couldn't stand there with a smile stuck on her face, making small talk with strangers, navigating the political minefields between the ambassadors of various kingdoms, and wondering which palace official was most likely to stick a knife in her back at the first opportunity. She was about to make an excuse to Revaa and go out in search of Daksh when a herald hurried up to the door, stood at attention, and announced, "His Royal Highness, King Aditya of Paramara."

The hall fell quiet. The herald moved smartly aside and bowed low. And then her cousin was standing before her, clad in white-and-gold silk, a silver coronet on his head. She bowed, her heart pounding. "King Aditya, welcome to Ajaigarh."

"You look well . . . *Katyani*." He studied her, a small smile on his face. "Regency suits you. Congratulations."

It was the first time he'd called her by her true name. It had to mean something. "Thank you, King Aditya," she said, blinking back tears.

"Please call me Adi," he said. "We are cousins, after all. I've been looking forward to meeting you again." His gaze strayed to Revaa, who was bouncing on her feet.

"Allow me to introduce you to the crown princess," Katyani began, but Revaa didn't wait for her to finish. She latched on to Aditya's arm, beaming like the sun.

"So *you're* Katya's cousin. I'm glad you could come; I've been dying to meet you. Let me introduce you to everyone." She bore him away into the hall, chattering like a bird, and the excited crowd surged toward them. He threw a slightly confused look back at Katyani, and she gave him an encouraging smile. "We'll talk later," she called. Then she leaned against the doorway and tried not to cry.

I've kept all my promises, Acharya. Only one is left.

She slipped out of the bright, clamorous audience hall and made her way outside.

It was a soft, moonlit night. The guards saluted as she emerged from the palace doorway. She went down the steps and into the lush garden.

The thick, sweet scent of roses past their bloom wafted into her nostrils. By the lily pond stood a tall figure in sky-blue robes, hands behind his back, gazing at the gibbous moon. He looked so perfect, she didn't want to speak and spoil the moment. She glided up to him and stopped a few feet away, her stomach fluttering, hyperaware of the silken touch of the sari on her skin, of the way his robes shivered in the breeze.

"It's a lovely night," she said at last, because she wanted to do more than just look at him.

He turned and smiled at her. "Aren't you supposed to be indoors, Your Highness?"

She made a vomiting noise. "Don't call me that! This is temporary. In a few years, Revaa will be crowned, and I will be free."

"Will you?" He tilted his head, considering. "I think not. This is your home, like the gurukul is mine. And your adopted sister will always need you. Just as my brother will always need me."

Her heart sank. "You've heard from him."

He nodded. "Today. A messenger pigeon arrived from the gurukul. Uttam wants to know when I'm coming back."

She knotted the end of her sari in her fingers. "What did you say?"

"I have not yet sent a reply. I wonder . . ." He paused, as if debating whether to continue.

"You wonder what?"

"If Irfan will propose to you again. And if your answer will change."

What? She stared at him in indignation. "Daksh, for such a clever person, you are sometimes incredibly dense."

He knitted his brows. "Does that mean yes or no?"

She turned away to hide her expression. "Figure it out yourself." After all this time, did he still not know what he meant to her? What *she* meant to him? How could he bring up Irfan at such a moment? She began to walk away, anger and disappointment roiling her stomach.

"Katyani," he called, and she halted, her cheeks burning. "I'm sorry," he said quietly. "I'll be leaving in the morning."

She knew it had to happen and yet, now that he had said it aloud, it hurt her so much she could scarcely breathe. "Of course," she said, gritting her teeth. "Your brother needs you."

"And now that you are well, you no longer need me," he said, a slight question mark in his voice.

Not true, she wanted to scream. *I need you. I will never not need you.*

"Thank you for taking care of me," she said in a flat tone, and it was as if someone else were speaking, because surely she could not utter such formal words to him.

"You look beautiful tonight," he said, sounding wistful. "Well, you always look beautiful to me. But tonight, you look like a queen."

Her heart squeezed. He thought she was beautiful. What did the trappings of a royal title matter? "It's just borrowed clothes and jewelry. I'm no queen."

"But you are a princess," he said. "Even if you were not the regent of Chandela, you would still be a princess of Paramara."

She schooled her expression and turned back to him. "I am no more a princess of Paramara than I was back in the gurukul. Why are you bringing this up now?"

He shook his head. "I don't know. Perhaps because Aditya is here."

"Liar," she snapped, losing her self-control. He was using her titles to justify their separation. "You're reminding me of my place, aren't you?"

"I'm reminding *myself* of my place," he said, raising his eyebrows.

"Which is in the gurukul?" She put her hands on her hips. "Are you sure? Your father once told me you would make your own fate."

"Your Highness?"

A guard stood behind her, his head bowed.

"What?" she barked, irritated at the interruption.

"Crown Princess Revaa requests your presence in the dining hall. Dinner is about to be served, and you must be seated at her right, opposite your cousin, King Aditya."

"I'll be there in a minute," she told him, and he backed away. "Will you join us?" she asked Daksh.

He gave an apologetic smile. "It's my last night here. I'd like to walk in the gardens."

"Suit yourself." She stamped away, head held high. But as soon as she was out of his sight, her shoulders slumped. The conversation had not gone remotely as she'd hoped. Tomorrow, he would leave. The thought tightened her chest. Had she not grieved enough for a lifetime?

She went to the dining hall, trying to breathe deeply. It was a large, high-ceilinged room with a table long enough to seat over two hundred people. Nearly every seat was full, and every lamp was lit. Candles flickered on the table, falling on animated faces. She took her place opposite her cousin, plastering a smile on her face, and devoted the rest of the meal to him and his retinue, spread along the table. Emotions churned within her, and she couldn't stop thinking of Daksh. It was a good thing Revaa talked enough for both of them, and no one noticed anything amiss.

It was hours before everyone left. Aditya agreed to stay in the palace as a guest for a couple of days before returning to Malwa, and it took a while to prepare suitable rooms for him and his staff. At midnight, when she thought she could finally go outside to check if Daksh was still in the garden, Revaa dragged her off to her suite to dissect the evening in detail.

But Katyani wasn't in the mood to gossip about their guests. None of them except Aditya were in the least bit important to her. She interrupted Revaa mid-monologue. "He's leaving tomorrow morning." She didn't have to say who.

Revaa raised her eyebrows in disbelief. "And you're letting him go?"

Katyani scowled, tugging the silver jewelry off her head. "What can I do? He *wants* to go. I tried to talk with him, but he didn't say anything I wanted to hear."

"Sometimes, you have to say the words you want to hear," said Revaa sagely, leaning back on the divan.

Katyani threw a silk cushion at her. "Since when do you know so much about it?"

"I know how you feel about him," said Revaa, catching the cushion, not even smiling. "Why do you care about his words? Are his actions not enough?"

Katyani got up. "I'm going to look for him."

"At this hour?" said Revaa in alarm, but she was already out the door.

She lifted her sari and ran down the steps, into the garden. But she couldn't spot Daksh anywhere. The guards at the palace doorway reported he had gone back inside a while ago.

She went back to her room, slamming the door. It was just as well. He would not like to refuse her, and her request would disturb and embarrass him. She would say good-bye to him tomorrow morning with perfect equanimity.

And what about your gurudakshina to the Acharya, a voice whispered. *You promised to take care of Daksh.*

But how could she decide the difference between taking care of him and satisfying her own selfish desires? Maybe taking care of him meant letting him go.

Or maybe she needed to say the words she wanted to hear.

She fell into a troubled sleep and woke early the next morning in a panic that he would be gone and she wouldn't even have said good-bye.

But when she poked her head out of her window, she saw him standing in the garden, surrounded by a gaggle of children. Relief flooded her.

"Daksh!" she shouted at the top of her lungs. When he looked up, she waved frantically. "I'm coming down. Don't go yet!"

She dashed out without changing her clothes; she was still in last night's red sari. She flew down the stairs and across the entrance hall of the palace.

"Where are you running off to?" cried Revaa, who was standing in the middle of a knot of elderly courtiers, looking put-upon. "Have you eaten breakfast? I need your advice about a question of protocol."

"I'll be back," said Katyani, and she rushed out. Protocol could damn well wait.

Daksh was standing in the same place where she'd spotted him from her window, though the children were gone. He looked fresh and well-rested, his sword at his belt, his bow on his back. Ready to leave. She paused to get her breath back, winded. Although her wounds had healed, her chest still hurt if she ran.

"Why were you running?" asked Daksh, his brows knitting.

"Practice," she said, wheezing. "If I run a little every day, it will get easier."

"Don't overdo it," he cautioned. "Best not to return to the training ground for another few weeks."

She made a noncommittal noise. She intended to get back to training as soon as possible.

He glanced at the palace gates. "I should leave while the day is still young."

"We can give you a carriage," she said, trying to match the evenness of his tone.

"No need." His expression turned wistful. "The speed of a journey is not important. What is important is the direction and destination."

She swallowed. "One of your father's sayings."

"I can't believe he's gone," he said. "All our lives, we knew of the curse, and yet, we never truly believed it could touch him. I guess every-one meets their fate in the end."

"And you? What do you think your fate is?" she managed, willing him to say, *You. My fate lies with you.*

He looked at her out of his deep, dark eyes and did not answer. At last, it was she who looked away, scarcely able to breathe from the maelstrom of emotions that roiled within her. "Let me ask the staff to provision you for the journey."

"No need," he said again. "I have water. I'll get food on the way." He gave her a tender smile. "Stay well, Katyani. You don't need me anymore. This is your freedom. You've earned it."

He bowed to her and turned away. Something squeezed her heart as he began walking down the carriageway to the gate, his robe swirling behind him, the hilt of his sword glinting in the rising sun. One step, two, three, four, and each one an uncrossable chasm, a void that threatened to crush her soul. She wanted to scream at him to come back, but the words stuck in her throat.

He stopped at the iron gate of the palace. The guards bowed to him, and one of them stepped forward to unbolt it.

Turn back, she thought desperately. *At least turn around and look at me.*

As if he heard that thought, he turned his head. There was no smile on his face now—only sadness.

Her feet propelled her forward before her brain could get in the way. She ran down the carriageway and stopped in front of him, panting.

His forehead creased. He placed a hand on her shoulder, his touch anchoring her, as it always did. "What's the matter, Katya?"

It was the name that did it. He'd only ever called her that once before.

"It's not true," she burst out, all her anxiety, her impending sense of loss, bubbling out of her. "It's not true that I don't need you. I have a treaty to negotiate with the yatu, a crown princess to protect, and a court full of snakes that might still be loyal to Bhairav."

The guards at the gate stayed stiff and silent. She knew they were listening avidly, but she didn't care.

Daksh squeezed her shoulder, his eyes warm. "You will be fine. You are the fiercest, most capable person I know. I have complete faith in you."

She ground her teeth in frustration. That was not what she'd meant. Of course she was capable. She needed him for *him.* "Your father told me to take care of you."

"You do not owe either of us anything," he said quietly.

"I didn't finish," she snapped. "He told me to take care of you, but I think what he meant was that I should not let our pride get in the way of our happiness. Do you like me, Daksh? I mean, more than you usually like people? Because I like you a lot. I don't just need you for your skills. I *want* to be with you. You told me Ajaigarh was my home. But my true home lies with you. Wherever you are, that is my home."

His eyes widened. He grasped her hands and trapped them in both of his, a slow smile lighting up his face, giving her the courage to keep talking.

"I know you have your duty, and I have mine," she continued, trying to keep her voice steady. "But that doesn't mean we can't be together, does it? The gurukul is only a few days' travel away. We can spend some time there, and we can spend some time here at the palace, and we can spend some time apart. A few years later, when Revaa is queen, we can go on monster-banishing missions all over Bharat, like your father once did."

Daksh squeezed her hands. "He would like that."

She sniffed. "Until then, we divide our time as best we can. I could bear your absence if I knew it was temporary, that I would see you again soon. But this, your leaving as if you'll never come back? As if we do not mean anything to each other? This I cannot bear."

"Katya . . ." He brushed her cheeks with his fingertips, wiping away the tears. "I'm sorry. I've hurt you."

"You *should* be sorry! How could you bring up Irfan?" she cried. "You are the only person for whom I have ever felt this way."

He took a step toward her, closing the gap between them. "And what way is that?" he whispered, pinning her with the intensity of his gaze.

She took a deep breath, feeling hot and shaky and determined all at once. "I . . . I want you to kiss me again, the way you kissed me in the forest once. I want you to kiss me every—"

But the last word was lost as he finally drew her into his arms and silenced her with his mouth, the kiss an unspoken wish waiting to be made real. She clung to him, her arms around his neck, uncaring of the scandalized glances from the guards. Let them look. Let the entire world look. She'd found the words for her feelings. She'd found her home. And she was never letting him go.

GLOSSARY

Acharya: Spiritual teacher or mentor, leader of a sect, or a highly learned person.

agni: Fire.

ahimsa: Ancient Indian principle of nonviolence to all living things. A key tenet of Hinduism, Buddhism, and Jainism, it is considered the highest moral virtue.

akash: Sky.

Airya/Airyaa: Male/female honorific with Indo-Iranian roots.

asteya: One of the five major self-restraints of virtuous conduct in Hinduism, it means one should not steal, have the intent to steal, cheat others, or receive stolen goods.

Ashwin: The seventh month of the Hindu calendar, overlapping September and October of the Gregorian calendar. It begins on the new moon after the autumn equinox.

Astomi: A legendary people mentioned by the Greek historian Megasthenes in *Indica,* his work on Mauryan India.

Bhagavad Gita: A famous Hindu text, it is a seven-hundred-verse book that is part of the epic Mahabharata. Framed as a dialogue between Prince Arjun and his charioteer Krishna (an avatar of Vishnu) it addresses what it means to be a virtuous person and how to attain liberation.

Bharat or **Bharata:** The legendary King Bharat was an ancestor of the

Pandavas and Kauravas, the main characters in the epic Mahabharata. Today, Bharat is the name for India in several Indian languages.

brahmacharya: One of the five major self-restraints of virtuous conduct in Hinduism, it is often translated as celibacy or chastity. The deeper
meaning is to move beyond the body and toward ultimate reality (Brah-
man). It is the first of the four stages of life, according to ancient Indian
texts, when a student must focus on acquiring knowledge and refrain from
running after temporary sensual pleasures.

brahmachari: One committed to brahmacharya.

Chaitra: The first month of the Hindu calendar, usually corresponding
to March in the Gregorian calendar. The first day of Chaitra is the Hindu
New Year. Chaitra is considered an auspicious month and is associated
with many spring festivals.

daayan: Female paranormal entity, also referred to as dakini in the Puranas. They are fiendish spirits that follow Goddess Kali and are extremely
powerful. Not to be confused with the folkloric chudail, or witch, although
I have borrowed some characteristics of the chudail for my character, nota-
bly the revenge-seeking aspect of her identity.

dandanayaka: This ancient term has been interpreted variously as general, magistrate, and police chief. The post was responsible for maintaining
law and order and appears to have been hereditary. I have used it to denote
the position of chief punishment officer.

daya: The virtue of compassion for all living beings, treating them as one's
own self, with empathy for their suffering and a desire for their good.

dhaba: A roadside restaurant in the Indian subcontinent.

dharma: Hindu cosmic law of what is right and good. It encompasses the
moral duties, laws, and codes of conduct that make up the right way of
living.

dupatta: A long scarf or shawl worn by South Asian women around the
neck, head, and shoulders, often with a salwar kameez. It is a very ancient

garment and can be traced all the way back to the Indus Valley Civilization (3300 BCE to 1300 BCE).

Ganesha: The widely worshiped elephant-headed god, one of the most popular deities in the pantheon of Hindu gods and goddesses. Ganesha is the son of Parvati and Shiva.

guru: The closest word is "teacher," but that does not convey the full meaning. A guru is a figure of reverence, a source of inspiration, and a spiritual guide. They are the one who leads the student from the darkness of ignorance into the light of knowledge.

gurudakshina: The tradition of paying the guru after completion of one's studies. It need not be a monetary payment; it can also be a service performed for the guru.

gurukul: Ancient system of education in South Asia. *Kul* means "home," and thus the word means "home of the guru." The disciples or students would live with the guru, do all the chores, and get educated in spiritual matters, secular subjects, and military arts. The relationship between the guru and disciple was considered sacred and no fees were charged, but gurudakshina was offered at the end.

Hindavi: I asked myself what languages were spoken in medieval northern India and fell into a rabbit hole. Let me sum up around three thousand years of (one branch of) Indian linguistic history for you: Proto-Indo-Aryan → Sanskrit → Prakrits → Apabhraṃśas → Hindustani. Hindavi was one of the terms used for Hindustani/Old Hindi.

jal: Water.

Jyeshtha: The third month of the Hindu calendar, corresponding to May/June in the Gregorian calendar.

kalari or **kalaripayattu:** One of the oldest surviving martial arts of the world, dating back to the third century BCE, it originated in modern-day Kerala. It is a hybrid martial art designed for the battlefield, and training focuses on both weapons and weaponless combat. It draws on traditional medicinal concepts in Hinduism, including healing techniques and knowledge of pressure points in the body.

karma: The sum total of a person's intentions and actions. According to Hindu philosophy, every intent, effort, and action has consequences, not just in the current life, but in future lives as well.

Kali: A Hindu goddess, the most fearsome aspect of Parvati, wife of Shiva. She is worshiped variously as a mother goddess, as a divine protector, and as the ultimate reality.

koel: The Asian koel is a cuckoo with a range of loud, distinctive calls.

Kurukshetra: The site of a bloody war of succession between two groups of cousins, the Pandavas and the Kauravas, in the Indian epic Mahabharata.

Lunar dynasty: In Hindu mythology, the Lunar dynasty, or Chandra-vansh, is descended from the moon deity, Chandra.

Magha: The eleventh month of the Hindu calendar, corresponding to January/February in the Gregorian calendar.

Malwa: A region in west-central India that has been a political unit since ancient times. It was ruled by the Paramara dynasty between the ninth and fourteenth centuries.

mantra: A syllable, word, or a group of words in Sanskrit believed to have spiritual powers. It can be a thought, a prayer, a sacred utterance, a spell, or a weapon. Vedic texts include mantras for ritual and meditation, musical chants, prayers of praise, petitions for godly help, and formulas for healing.

paan: A preparation of betel leaf, areca nut, slaked lime paste, and a variety of ingredients that can include tobacco, candied nuts, seeds, and spices. Very popular in the Indian subcontinent and unfortunately linked to gum damage, tooth decay, and oral cancer.

Pachisi: An ancient Indian game, it is played on a board shaped like a cross. Players' pieces move across the board depending upon a throw of cowrie shells.

panditji: A priest. The "ji" at the end is an honorific.

Pausha: The tenth month of the Hindu calendar, beginning with either the full or the new moon in December.

pranayama: The practice of breath control in yoga, which consists of synchronizing breath with the various poses of a yogic stretch. It is also a breathing practice by itself.

prithvi: Earth.

preta: A type of hungry ghost that undergoes great torment, suffering insatiable hunger or thirst. The soul is stuck in a zone between death and reincarnation as a result of bad karma from having been extremely greedy or deceitful in life. The only way to release them is for their family to engage in a variety of specific funerary rites. In the absence of such rituals, the preta is doomed to suffer forever.

Rigveda: The Rigveda is the oldest known Vedic Sanskrit text. It was most likely composed between 1500 and 1200 BCE in the northwestern part of the Indian subcontinent.

salwar kameez: A traditional South Asian dress consisting of a long tunic with side seams that are open below the waist (kameez or kurta) and a loose-fitting pant held up by a drawstring (salwar). The dress arrived in North India with the Muslims in the thirteenth century, and its use spread gradually. It is a very comfortable dress.

satya: One of the five major self-restraints of virtuous conduct in Hinduism, it means to be truthful in one's thoughts, speech, and actions.

shishya: Student or disciple of the guru.

shloka: This is the poetic form of Sanskrit used in the Mahabharata, the Ramayana, the Puranas, and other Hindu texts. It usually consists of four quarter-verses of eight syllables each.

Shraavana: The fifth month of the Hindu calendar, beginning in late July from the first day of the full moon and ending in the third week of August, the day of the next full moon.

sitar: A plucked stringed instrument that originated in medieval India.

soma: A ritual drink of Vedic India, derived from a now-unknown plant. In the Vedas, drinking soma is supposed to grant immortality.

vaidya: A practitioner of Ayurveda or traditional medicine.

vayu: Wind.

yaksha (m) or **yakshini (f):** Nature spirits that are usually benevolent but are occasionally depicted as mischievous. They are connected with trees, forests, water, fertility, wealth, wilderness, and mountains. They may be considered semi-divine mythological beings.

Yama: The Hindu god of death. He is the son of Surya, the sun god, and the guardian of the Southern direction. He is considered to be the first mortal who died, and thus became the ruler of all those who died after him.

yatu (m) or **yatudhani (f):** Humanoid demons from Indian mythology that feed on human flesh. They are huge and fierce-looking. The more powerful ones have maya, the power of illusion, and some can even fly. I have taken linguistic liberties here; "yatudhani" is actually the female equivalent of "yatudhana." I don't believe the term "yatu" has a female version.

TREES

amaltas: *Cassia fistula* or Indian laburnum, an ornamental tree known for its profusion of yellow flowers.

banyan: *Ficus benghalensis* (or bargad in Hindi) is the national tree of India. It is characterized by aerial prop roots that transform into woody trunks with age. Mature trees can spread laterally via these prop roots to cover a large area. A single tree can become a veritable grove.

gulmohar: *Delonix regia* or flame of the forest, an ornamental tree known for its flamboyant flowers.

kadam: *Neolamarckia cadamba* or burflower tree is mentioned in the Puranas and is associated with Lord Krishna.

mango: *Mangifera indica* is native to the Indian subcontinent and mangoes are the national fruit of India. It's a very beautiful, shapely tree.

neem: *Azadirachta indica* or Indian lilac is widely used in traditional medicine in India.

peepal: *Ficus religiosa* or sacred fig is one of the most important trees of India. It is considered sacred by Hindus, Buddhists, and Jains. It is believed that the Buddha attained enlightenment under a peepal tree.

sal: *Shorea robusta* is an important hardwood species of India. Its leaves are used to make leaf plates even today. It also has medicinal uses.

sheesham: *Dalbergia sissoo* or North Indian rosewood is a significant timber species.

tendu: *Diospyros melanoxylon* or East Indian ebony. The leaves are wrapped around tobacco to make the Indian beedi, a kind of cigarette.

ACKNOWLEDGMENTS

THIS BOOK WOULD NOT EXIST WITHOUT THE HELP OF SEVERAL amazing and talented people. First and foremost, my insightful editor at Wednesday Books, Mara Delgado Sánchez. Thank you, Mara, for your enthusiasm and care for this book, and for making me dig deeper into my world and characters.

Thanks also to the team at Wednesday Books for all your hard work in making this book possible.

My deep gratitude to my agent, Mary C. Moore of Kimberley Cameron & Associates, for believing in my stories and being such a great advocate for my work in all the years we have been together.

My thanks to Keyan Bowes for being the best possible beta reader I could wish for. I am so grateful for your feedback.

Thanks to Ariella Elema for her critiques and tips on sword fighting. And to all the other friends and fellow writers who have been with me on my writing journey: Charlotte, Phoebe, Kari, Katie, and Vanessa—I am so glad to know you.

Much love to my parents, grandmother, and sister for their encouragement of my creative pursuits, and to my children for being my rocks in an unsteady world.

Lastly, thanks to you, dear reader, for picking up this book. I hope you love the characters as much as I did.